Library of
Davidson College

IRELAND

From the Act of Union • 1800
to the Death of Parnell • 1891

*Seventy-seven novels and collections
of shorter stories by twenty-two*
Irish and Anglo-Irish novelists

selected by
PROFESSOR ROBERT LEE WOLFF
Harvard University

A GARLAND SERIES

The Ghost-Hunter
and his Family

Michael Banim

with an introduction by
Robert Lee Wolff

Garland Publishing, Inc., New York & London
1978

For a complete list of the titles in this series,
see the final pages of this volume.

Introduction copyright © 1978 by Robert Lee Wolff

All rights reserved

This facsimile has been made from a copy in
the Yale University Library (In.B225.833).

The volumes in this series are printed on acid-free,
250-year-life paper.

Library of Congress Cataloging in Publication Data

Banim, Michael, 1796–1874.
The ghost-hunter and his family.

(Ireland, from the Act of Union, 1800,
to the death of Parnell, 1891 ; 22)
Reprint of the 1883 ed. published by Smith, Elder,
London, which was issued as v. 1 of The Library of romance.
Includes bibliographical references.
I. Title. II. Series.
PZ3.B2253Gh   1978   [PR4057.B3]   823'.7   78-12230
ISBN 0-8240-3471-6

Printed in the United States of America

The Fiction of "The O'Hara Family"
John Banim (1798–1842)
Michael Banim (1796–1874)
Harriet Martin (1801–1891; see No. 23)

I

John and Michael Banim, writing together as "The O'Hara Family,"[1] with John calling himself Barnes O'Hara and Michael calling himself Abel O'Hara, were the first novelists of Ireland who were wholly of Irish Catholic origin (Lady Morgan's MacOwen grandparents hardly count). The Banims' father, Michael Banim, senior, owned a farm but was also proprietor of a small shop in Kilkenny (Leinster) where he sold powder and shot and fishing tackle. He was the first member of his family to leave the soil. He was eager that his sons should have a good education, but in the end could not afford it for both of them; so Michael, the elder, who had begun to read for the bar, went into the shop.

John attended the famous college at Kilkenny, in the Middle Ages an appendage to the Cathedral of St. Canice, refounded after Cromwell's spoliation, chartered in 1684 by the first Duke of Ormonde, whose family seat was Kilkenny Castle, chartered again by James II in 1689, and moved to its most recent site in 1780. Here Swift, Congreve, Berkeley, and others had been educated; it was sometimes known as "the Eton of Ireland." After two years there, John left to study art at the Royal Dublin Society, boarding in the house of a poor and parsimonious Protestant friend of his father whose domestic economy he found revolting. At eighteen, back at home in Kilkenny, teaching drawing and so launched on his artistic career, he and the illegitimate daughter of a Protestant landowner fell in love. He was rejected by the girl's father, and her death soon afterwards plunged him into deep grief and into a period of dissipation. Traces of these episodes are to be found in his fiction.

In 1820 John Banim left Kilkenny for Dublin, where he became a journalist and assisted his fellow artists to obtain a royal Charter of Incorporation, but soon decided to devote himself fully to writing and completed (1820) a poem he called "Ossian's Paradise." In manuscript it elicited agreeable comments from Sir Walter Scott and was then published as "The Celts' Paradise" (1821). Richard Lalor Sheil (1791–1851), an Irish barrister only a few years older than Banim and already a successful playwright, with his long career as a politician still in the future, became Banim's friend and adviser. He may have collaborated with John on a tragedy, *Damon and Pythias*, which was successfully produced in London (May 1821) with the great Macready as its star and Charles Kemble also in the cast. After writing a pamphlet on George IV's forthcoming visit to Ireland, Banim in 1822 married and moved to London to seek his fortune. His gentle and admiring elder brother, Michael, gave him moral support at every turn. Before John left for London, the brothers planned to collaborate on a series of Irish tales. To the partnership Michael brought far less literary talent and no training as a writer but a more intimate personal acquaintance with Irish peasant customs than John in his life as student, artist, and journalist had ever acquired.

In London, John was engaged by a new journal called

the *Literary Register*, which, however, lasted less than a year, during which Banim first suffered symptoms of the disease that eventually crippled and killed him. At this early stage, before his own career was launched, Banim found himself called upon to advise and help another young Irishman, Gerald Griffin, who was to prove even more talented than he, at the very beginning of his search for fortune in England. He also published anonymously in 1824 a volume of essays entitled *Recollections of the Dead Alive*, satirizing the foibles of the day, including the craze for phrenology, log-rolling book reviewers, and ignorant art critics. There was nothing specifically Irish here. Ireland, however, was to be the subject of the "Tales," whose first series (3 vols., 1825; No. 16 in the Garland series) was now under way; Michael, in Kilkenny, was composing in the rare intervals of leisure from the shop the first story, *Crohoore of the Bill-Hook*, and sending it in brief installments to John, and John was working on the other two, *The Fetches* and *John Doe*.

II

The relatively few modern critics who have commented on "The O'Hara Family's" work have never been quite sure how much credit should be given to Michael Banim for his contributions; and the latest and most authoritative, Professor Flanagan, has quietly denied him any:

Michael was neither a well-educated nor an ambitious writer. The controlling genius was always John's; he wrote most of the important novels and made extensive revisions of Michael's contributions. For this reason it seems sensible to depart from the usual practice of referring to "the Banim brothers."[2]

But this is cavalier procedure indeed. John's surviving letters to Michael indicate that it was Michael who wrote *Crohoore of the Bill-Hook*, though John undoubtedly revised it, as Michael did all of John's work. When John had received the first part, for example, he wrote Michael, "So far as it goes, I pronounce that you have been successful. Here and there, I have marked such particular criticisms as struck me . . ."; and, as the story advanced, "I think I recognise our tithe-proctor, Peery Clancey; the portrait is so accurate I could not mistake the gentleman. Your next door neighbour, Mickle Ryan, is your original, and you have not outstepped nature, or misrepresented facts, in the slightest degree. . . . You tell me you intend to cut off the proctor's ears: slice them close to his head by all means; do not leave a shred; no honest man will say that he does not deserve the cropping."[3] It is of considerable importance to accept Michael's authorship, since *Crohoore* is the first, longest, and best of the novels making up the first series of *Tales*. It astonished its readers in 1825 with its power as it still astonishes us. And if the power was somewhat crude and showed the traces of Michael Banim's inexperience, this is no reason for denying him the credit for its authorship that John Banim himself always gave him.

Crohoore is set in eighteenth-century rural Kilkenny, where the reader finds himself in the household of a prosperous Irish Catholic farmer, employing many farmhands and domestic servants, a household of a kind not to be found in any previous novel of Irish life. A horrible murder and kidnapping, the search for the missing girl, the ambiguous role of the local "whiteboys," the persecution of the peasant population by the tithe-proctors (those local Irish Catholic laymen charged by the established Church of Ireland [Protestant Episcopalian] with the collection of the tithes for the support of its clergy), the prevalence of deep superstition: these are the striking features of *Crohoore*. Still laboring under the penal laws, with fresh memories of the time when (it was said) Protestant troops had pursued Catholic priests like hunted animals, ground down by rackrenting, the peasant "found himself ... compelled to contribute to the support, in splendour and superiority, of that very rival church ... to pay to its ministers the hard-earned pittance he could not afford to his own." Or, as a peasant sings after a "prefatory yell,"

> They must lave off their tithin' an rackin' iv acres,
> Or we'll roast 'em as brown as a loaf at the baker's;
> An we'll nip off their ears, an' we'll lave their heads bare,
> As they do wid the calves in the county Kildare.[4]

Eventually the reader actually sees the whiteboys slice the ears from the head of Peery Clancy, the wretched tithe-proctor. Before the actual operation is performed, the victim is buried up to the neck, and somebody suggests that if an acre of tithe-proctors could be sown in this fashion, it would make a wretched crop indeed. The crop, says another, would be hemp, to make "caravats" (neckties) for any whiteboy who might be caught. Our sympathies for Clancy are hardly aroused, however, because we have also come to know the horrible sufferings of the Delany family, which Clancy has ousted from their shelter because they cannot pay the tithe. Delany finds mere ear-cropping insufficient punishment for Clancy; until forcibly prevented, he is ready with a stone to bash Clancy's brains out. In this world of lawlessness and terror, only the human decencies—friendship, love, loyalty—make life bearable. *Crohoore* abounds in examples of these: between parents and children, between betrothed lovers, between foster-brothers, between masters and servants. It remains a minor masterpiece despite its infelicities of style.

The two other tales in the first series were both largely by John Banim, who sent them to Michael for his criticism. *The Fetches* is set in Kilkenny and its environs in the eighteenth century; its theme is a romance between two young lovers, and the psychological impact upon their minds of the working out of an ancient Irish superstition: the meaning of the apparition or "Fetch" of a living person. The novel is highly romantic, and the scenes along the banks of the Nore amidst John Banim's own favorite youthful haunts are lovingly drawn. But it was in the third story, *John Doe*, later reissued as *Peep O'Day*, that John Banim's talents were most clearly revealed. The splendid opening chapter, however, was by Michael. It describes a "pattern," or rural feast day in honor of a patron saint, including, as it so often did, a general "scrimmage," or skirmish among the men present: fighting for the sake of fighting; John had never attended such a celebration, but Michael had.

Thereafter *John Doe*, set in County Tipperary (Munster) near Clonmel, belonged to John. Ireland in all its strange complexity is introduced to two agreeable young English officers on garrison duty. John Doe himself is the leader of the whiteboys, who call their captain after the imaginary legal personage to emphasize his anonymity, and are themselves locally called "Shanavest" (old waistcoat) or "Caravat" (cravat) depending on their costume. By terrorist methods John Doe hopes to lower rackrents and prevent the payment of tithes. But who is John Doe, and where is he? The English officers, one in particular, have the duty to search him out, a task complicated by the fact that this same officer—a Protestant, of course—has fallen in love with a Catholic girl, daughter of a local landowner who seems to be menaced by the banditti.

Lacking the raw power of *Crohoore*, *John Doe* is better told and faster moving. It includes two memorable priests, one of them a witty and sophisticated and forceful shepherd of his flock, the other a drunkard, making what money he can by performing marriage ceremonies and asking no questions. Both are on excellent terms with the local Church of Ireland clergyman, and all three join forces to try to prevent the population from giving aid and comfort to the whiteboys, who are menacing priests as well as laymen. For the first time in Irish fiction, moreover, the reader is taken to visit an illegal still, and can study the art of preparing potheen. As so often, whiskey plays a major part in the lives of the characters, one of them singing, in Irish,

> Oh, whiskey, the delight and joy of my soul!
> You lay me stretched on the floor,
> You deprive me of sense and knowledge,
> And you fill me with a love of fighting;

> My coat you have often torn from my back;
> By you I lost my silken cravat;
> But all shall be forgotten and forgiven,
> If you meet me after mass next Sunday![5]

This first series of the *Tales* (1825) was well received. Gerald Griffin wrote to his brother that they were "most vigorous and original things; overflowing with the very spirit of poetry, passion and painting," and were "astonishing in nothing so much as in the power of creating an intense interest without stepping out of real life, and in the very easy and natural drama that is carried through them, as well as in the excellent tact ... in seizing on all the points of national character which are capable of effect." He did not mean *The Fetches*, he added, which was merely "a romance ... but ... a splendid one." In the shop windows of London Griffin had seen pictures by first-rate artists showing scenes from the *Tales*, although a mere month before their appearance John Banim had been wholly unknown.[6]

On May 1, 1825, only three weeks after the *Tales* were published, John Banim was already writing to Michael that by Christmas he would have completed a three-volume novel to be called *The Boyne Water*, a historical tale of the decisive battle of 1690 and of the years leading up to it from the accession of James II in 1685. By way of preparation, John not only read the standard works but visited the scene and walked over the terrain himself: the coast of Antrim, Londonderry, Lough Neagh, and the battle site near Drogheda. He intended to visit as well Limerick and its environs so much nearer home, where the last phases of the war took place, and the peace—so generous to the Catholics but never allowed to become effective—was signed; but Michael Banim took over this part of the job for him.

III

Completed on schedule and published early in 1826, *The Boyne Water* (3 vols., 1826; No. 17), as Professor Flanagan remarks, "set a standard which no other Irish historical novel was to meet."[7] It could never have been written without the example of the enormously popular historical fiction by Sir Walter Scott, pouring forth from the presses ever since *Waverley* (1814). When John Banim wrote, *Redgauntlet* (1824) was Scott's most recent novel. Readers of *The Boyne Water* will be struck by the fidelity—almost comic at times—with which Banim follows his model. But, just as each of the best of Scott's novels has a point to make beyond the resolution of its characters' personal problems and of the historical crises within which they are caught up, so *The Boyne Water*, ostensibly a story of 1685–1691, is also a strong plea for religious toleration in Banim's own day, and—specifically—for Catholic Emancipation, in 1826 the major political question in the public's mind.

At the very end of the novel, after the Treaty of Limerick has failed of ratification in 1695 and the penal era is well under way, the novel's Protestant hero in Ireland writes hopefully to his brother-in-law, its Catholic hero in exile on the Continent, that

> The descendants of the men who have sanctioned, and by that means caused the deliberate breach of their own treaty, made in the field, will awake to

vindicate, as far as in them lies, the name of their ancestors. A son, jealous of his father's honor, pays his father's debts ... and Englishmen will yet pay their fathers' debt of faith to Ireland. The Treaty of Limerick will yet be kept.[8]

In 1826, this "prediction" could have but one meaning: the English, one hundred and thirty-four years after the signing of the treaty, were now obliged to honor it by emancipating the Catholics.

The entire novel, indeed, has been leading directly to this conclusion. Robert Evelyn and his sister Esther, of a Protestant landowning family with a house on the Antrim shore of Lough Neagh, encounter Edmund M'Connell and his sister Eva, of a Catholic noble family related to the Earl of Antrim, who live on the Atlantic shore of the Irish Sea near Glenariff. Immediately after the accession of James II in 1685, the two young couples fall in love. Despite their own innate religious toleration, they are caught up in the strife that precipitates and follows the Glorious Revolution of 1688, and are forced to take opposite sides. The fear and hatred between Catholic and Protestant in Ulster have ancient roots, most recently watered by the ghastly Catholic massacres of Protestants in 1641, still vivid in the minds of many of the characters in the novel. The extreme Protestants fear that the new Catholic King will encourage a second round. They are typified by the historical George Walker, militant anti-Papist and soldier-divine, who becomes one of the governors of Londonderry during its protracted siege, and then its bishop. A friend of Evelyn's family, he commands troops at the Battle of the Boyne, and is killed in single combat against a Dominican Friar, O'Haggarty, who is precisely his mirror-image, as bigoted a hater of Protestant heretics as Walker is of Catholics. O'Haggarty also dies in their encounter.

Serving on the side of William III, but without much enthusiasm, Evelyn is enabled by his duties to become personally acquainted with both William and James II; at times he is a privileged prisoner of James's forces, and so comes to know Sarsfield, while at others he serves as aide-de-camp to Schomberg in William's armies. M'Connell, whose family suffers atrocities at the hands of the Protestants, becomes far more committed to James's side than Evelyn to William's, and eventually takes command of a Rapparee band of freebooters helping the Catholic cause. Protestant or Catholic, these figures from the upper classes or from the pages of history books usually have only intermittent life. Banim excels in the drawing of Irish Catholics of lower degree: Moya Laverty, a peasant girl who cherishes a hopeless passion for Robert Evelyn, and several times appears in the nick of time to save his life; Galloping Hogan, the Rapparee leader (a historical person), commander of the force that seizes and occupies and eventually burns down Evelyn's family house on Lough Neagh; Rory na-Chopple, a horse thief who knows the language of horses and can talk them into doing his bidding and who, for all his smiling face, is a ruthless killer who enjoys the sport; and Carolan, the blind harpist with a strong feudal attachment to the M'Connells (based on the celebrated Torlogh Carolan [Ó Cearbhállain], 1670–1738). These persons are as fully realized as Scott's best characters of a similar sort, such as Meg Merrilies, the gypsy woman in *Guy Mannering*. And there are a good many symbolic noble hounds and even an eagle, as so often in the pages of Irish novelists.

In dealing with the leading historic figures, Banim is at pains to show that William is a cold-hearted but fair-minded general, determined not to be stampeded by Protestant extremists and not to be entrapped into persecuting Catholics, while James II he portrays as much misunderstood, even minimizing his cowardice at the Boyne itself. Evelyn and M'Connell go through the long siege of Londonderry with its starvation and misery, and are present at the major battles. Particularly effective is the account of Sarsfield's sortie from Limerick after the first siege and before the second, guided and helped by the Rapparees, through the wild hills of nearby Tipperary to Ballyneaty to blow up an enemy siege train.

IV

Though debilitating illness with intermittent racking pain had been sapping his strength even in these early years, John Banim began at once to write the second series of *Tales by the O'Hara Family* (3 vols., 1826; No. 18). Visited in London by Michael in the summer of 1826, he seemed forty rather than twenty-eight; his hair was white and his step feeble. But by the end of the summer the two novels for the new collection had been completed. To the first and longest, *The Nowlans*, which occupied two of the three volumes of the second series when it appeared later in the year, Michael's explorations of the Tipperary hills near Limerick for *The Boyne Water* made a considerable contribution. It was there that Michael had spent a night in the cabin of a well-to-do farmer with a pretty daughter and a bedridden son, who did not make an appearance and about whom the family was anxious. From this milieu and these fragmentary circumstances John took the inspiration for the opening of *The Nowlans*: he made the sick son a priest and told his remarkable story.

Fully as melodramatic as anything the O'Haras had yet published, *The Nowlans*—set in the Slieve Felim Hills of Western Tipperary (spelled "Llieuve Ieullem" in the story: near Keeper Mountain) not far from the River Shannon and perhaps twelve or fifteen miles from Limerick—tells of a family like the Doolings in *Crohoore*: well-to-do farmers. Daniel Nowlan has married a woman of Protestant origins and vaunted Ascendancy connections but of humble origin, who has become a Catholic. Nowlan's elder brother, Aby, has inherited all their father's considerable wealth. Stupid, profligate, and irresponsible, he is squandering his substance in dissipation, toadying to the least worthy among the neighboring Protestant gentry, and living surrounded by a harem of mistresses and former mistresses and by numbers of his illegitimate children. Drawn from life, this figure is one of the most convincing of all the rich variety of Banim's Irishmen. Aby shows an interest in his nephew John Nowlan, Daniel's son, and—in the hope that John may be made his uncle's heir—John's parents interrupt the boy's training for the priesthood and send him to live with Aby.

In these surroundings, whatever priestly calling he may have had is deeply damaged by his youthful passion for his illegitimate cousin Maggy, who makes passionate love to him. He is not seduced; but although he leaves Aby's, resumes his training, and takes his vows, he is still vulnerable to temptation. He falls in love, as an adult this time, with Letitia Adams, the charming niece of a liberal-minded Protestant local landowner, elopes with her, and marries her. His sister, Peggy, is trapped into marriage with Letitia's brother, Frank, who—quite improbably, it may seem to modern readers—is a deep-dyed villain and a professional robber. The tragic dénouements of these two affairs form the main theme of *The Nowlans*.

This sensational theme of a renegade (and only belatedly repentant) priest made *The Nowlans* a highly original story. Into the unhappiness of John and Letty Nowlan, poverty-stricken, living in Dublin lodgings in the house of a wretchedly underpaid official with middle-class Protestant standards and pride, Banim put some of his own experiences. The setting and the personalities are those of Banim's Dublin student days spent in a suburb called Phibsborough with a family named Wheeler who were acquaintances of his father's. Elsewhere in the novel Banim touches upon those Evangelicals whom Eyre Crowe had put into his story *The Old and the New Light* (No. 15). Here they are mostly English, "sent from a Bible Society in London to investigate the progress of their benevolent efforts among the peasantry of Ireland," but they have a dreadful native Irish collaborator, an ex-priest named Horragan, who cares only for money and rich food and who preaches the new ideas in Irish. The caricature that Banim draws of Horragan is positively Dickensian. It is also rabidly hostile, and is allegedly based on the Reverend Mortimer O'Sullivan (1791–1859).

The Nowlans exhibits a pre-Victorian, Regency frankness in sexual matters, describing John Nowlan's embraces with his cousin Maggy, who later becomes proprietress of a bawdyhouse in Dublin, far more graphically than was usual in 1826. The wicked Frank Adams, who has been one of Maggy's lovers, wants to get rid of Peggy Nowlan by getting her into Maggy's hands, and promises Maggy that "for a season or so, there won't be a nicer article in your shop." One of the novel's most vivid aspects is Letty's inability, as a Protestant, to understand the pangs of conscience that John, as a Catholic priest, feels for having violated his vows and marrying her:

> Letty might suppose they were married; he knew they were not married; he knew they never could be: and though he indulged her illusion, partly in furtherance of his plan to sacrifice every thing to her happiness . . . he stood a renegade, a giver of dreadful scandal, a blasphemer, an outcast, and a marked sheep, she led with him a life of partaken sin and was, in fact, no more than his mistress. Do what he might, he could not prevent that. Immolate himself as he might, he believed he dared never call her his wife; and his blood curdled at the thought.[9]

Equally melodramatic, the other story of the new collection, *Peter of the Castle*, turns upon an entire series of uncertain identities, the truth being revealed only at the end. There is little about the tale that is peculiarly Irish except for the village wedding party and the awe and respect in which the inhabitants hold the local bandit. Banim deliberately declined to identify the exact locale of the story.

Declaring that Ireland's sad history and present misery made it a natural scene for romantic literature and adding that its people moved with astonishing speed from pleasure to despair with "a volatility of heart equal to the French volatility of manner," a reviewer of the new *Tales* hailed them as better not only than the earlier series but than those of Miss Edgeworth, Lady Morgan, or Maturin. Ease of manner, a natural way of telling his story, a straightforward attitude towards horror, and a fine treatment of humorous scenes: these were some of Banim's strengths. Not only was he good at "painting" manners; he excelled "in dealing with the passions in the fulness of their power," more like the old dramatists Webster or Ford than any author of "our time." Obviously a specialist in Gothic romance, the reviewer compared poor Peggy Nowlan's dangers on a trip to Dublin to some of the most famous scenes of suspense in old favorites. But Banim was too gloomy. He was in the same class as Scott "as regards impressiveness," but below him because of "the want of lightness and relief." If he could add these, he would give "Ireland a share in the honours which have been well-nigh monopolized by Scotland." Other critics were even more positive, the *Literary Gazette* declaring that "the author is truly a man of talent and genius," the *Edinburgh Review* that "he is one of the most masterly painters of national character that has yet appeared in Ireland," and the *Literary Chronicle* expressing the "highest opinion of his exalted talents."[10]

V

The year 1827 brought renewed illness to John Banim, who was able to do little new work beyond the revision of the second series of *Tales* for a new edition, with "the too highly coloured scenes of ardent passion . . . altered and amended." Michael, on the other hand, was busy with a full-length three-volume novel, on which he worked at intervals all through 1827. John read most of it that summer, and gave it his approval: he was trying to be altogether impartial, he wrote Michael, but he was sure that Michael "need not apprehend failure." Colburn accepted the novel, the last portion of which was delayed while Michael visited John in England between August and November. He found his brother dreadfully altered for the worse. No doubt John edited Michael's novel, but one cannot regard it as in any substantial measure John's work.[11]

Michael called it *The Croppy* (3 vols., 1828; No. 19), the term used by the extreme Protestants in Ireland, the Orangemen, for Catholics in general, deriving from the cropped haircut adopted by some of the United Irishmen in imitation of the French Revolutionary fashion. It became a generalized term of contempt in Orangemen's mouths as the 1790's wore on and the great uprising of 1798 approached. "Croppies lie down" was a favorite song of Orange military forces. The novel deals with the uprising not in Ulster and Dublin—as does Eyre Evans Crowe's story *The Northerns of 1798*, published the next year in his *Yesterday in Ireland* (No. 15)—but in its chief center in southern Ireland, County Wexford (Leinster) around the towns of Enniscorthy, Wexford, and New Ross. After the mass arrest by the Dublin government of the provincial leaders of the United Irishmen, betrayed into their hands by informers, and the outbreak of insurrection in Counties Kildare, Carlow, and Wicklow, the disorders spread into Wexford, where until recent months prosperity had ruled and the relationships between Protestant landlords and Catholic tenants and middle-class farmers and townsmen had been good. But the undisciplined yeomanry, Orange atrocities, and the deliberately spread rumor that a wholesale massacre of Catholics was imminent touched off an uprising more furious than any other in the south, wholly to the surprise of the inept Dublin government and its military arm.

The bloody disorders in this region, just across the county border from Michael Banim's native Kilkenny, were only thirty years in the past. The fashionable floweriness of his language in describing the beauties of the landscape and the happy lives of the gentry on the banks of the Slaney River, and the stilted highflown conversations he imagined between Eliza Hartley, daughter of a Baronet of highly conciliatory tendencies, and her two suitors only heighten the grimness of the explosion when it finally takes place. Shawn-a-Gow, the blacksmith, whose innocent son is killed before his eyes by the soldiery—but who has been forging pikes for his fellow rebels all along—personifies the determination of the persecuted Catholics. The terrors of the rebellion merge into the complexities of a standard Gothic plot in which Eliza is caught up. Nanny the Knitter, the old woman whose second profession is matchmaking for money, and Rattling Bill Nale, the juggler and manipulator of dice at fairs and military reviews, who betrays both sides for profit, are perhaps the best drawn of Banim's group of Irish characters.

Father Rourke, the militant priest who leads a party of the insurgents and who is hanged at the end on the bridge at Wexford, seems to have been modelled on Father Philip Roche, who suffered the same fate, and not, as has been suggested, on Father John Murphy of

Boulavogue.¹² Eliza's father, Sir Thomas Hartley, a United Irishman in his youth, who is now reluctant to lead the rebels, is under great pressure to take command. He protests against Orange atrocities, is eventually arrested and tried, and (so it seems) summarily executed. He was to some degree surely inspired by Bagenal Harvey, a major figure in the Wexford uprising. Sir Thomas explains himself:

> Never can I cease to wish ardently, and, I hope, purely, for the independence and happiness of my country.... As a Volunteer officer, in the first epoch of Ireland's glory [i.e., 1782–1783], I was an enthusiast. Fifteen years have since sobered down my mind, and yet I see no reason to criticise my more youthful views and feelings. It was the only period, during a lapse of six centuries, that Ireland's sons, pausing in their dissensions, united for her good, and therefore seemed capable of serving her.

But the good old days of the early 1780's have gone. Now Sir Thomas recoils "from the cruel devastations of a civil war." The excesses of the French Revolution have disillusioned him. The "lower orders" of each faith, he is sure, will now massacre all members of the other. "I shrink from the vortex!"¹³

A mass review of the yeomanry, just before the violence starts, is skillfully used to give the reader a survey of the widely varying human beings that make up the government's forces. Some who enlisted are willing to put on a red coat and learn "the theory of a soldier's trade," but shrink from action of any sort. One even steadfastly refuses to load his musket: "Me! ... is it me?

—not I, upon my word and credit; how do I know but I might hurt some one?" Perhaps unfortunately, such pacific amateurs were in a great minority. A wicked young baronet, concealing an earlier marriage, uses the crisis to push his suit with his new sweetheart's family: "a dreadful convulsion is at hand: a bloody extirpation of all Protestants is meditated by the Papists of the country; property, rank, distinction, society—every thing may be swept away: oh! in that coming day of anarchy, amid that hurricane of vulgar and fierce passions, Heaven help the weak and unprotected!"[14]

Characteristic of both sides is the animus displayed by a recruiter for the United Irishmen, who explains to a prospective candidate

> the way we'll scourge them bloody dogs out iv our land, at the same time that we hender them from killin' us; an' he b'lieves every word I say,—no praise to him for the same;—an' I whips out my book, an' makes a man of him, an' gives him the sign; an' he talks to a friend about id, an' makes a man of him too; an' they go and get pikes made, an' hide 'em till the time comes.

As for the explanation of a Protestant United Irishman—

> It is a mistake that every Protestant is an Orangeman, or an enemy to Roman Catholics. . . . the originators of our confederacy were to a man Protestants; its present heads are chiefly Protestants. . . . I am a Protestant, myself. And, indeed, what means our title "United Irishmen," if it does not describe a combination of every sect for our country's good?

this is now hopelessly out of date and meaningless in Wexford at the moment of danger. In Shawn-a-Gow's smithy, the rebel agitator (a desperate villain and liar) reads out the oath that he solemnly declares the Protestants to be taking, "I do solemnly swear, that I will be thrue to the King and Government . . . and that I will exterminate . . . as far as I am able . . . the Catholics of Ireland, and that I will wade ankle deep in Papist blood." And yet, ironically enough, the counteroath which he administers is still the original oath of the United Irishmen that pledged "a brotherhood of affection among Irishmen of every religious persuasion" for "equal, full, and adequate representation of all the people of Ireland,"[15] an oath in the spirit of the American Revolution, which has now altogether lost its true meaning.

Father Rourke, the fighting priest who leads a band of insurrectionists, admits that he does not know whether the story of the Orangemen's oath is true or not; it does not matter, he says, because the Orangemen "act as if it were true—act as if literal extermination of the [Catholic] people was their wish and object." And at one moment, in his ornate and clumsy prose, Michael Banim generalizes from the heart about the Irish character: at the moment when they are most destructive, the Irish peasants are most given to laughter:

> Windows were shattered, and furniture was dashed to pieces and flung out through them into the street; and mingled with the shout of fury came the shout of merriment: the wildest act of destruction, in accordance with the hidden character of the Irish peasant, often producing the heartiest laugh:—hidden we have called that character, and it is so;—its minor

traits, indeed, such as appear, or are put forward, in every-day intercourse, any one may catch; but owing to a long habit of abstraction, or rather banishment from all interchange of social thought or feeling with those ranking above him, the real moral elements that form every kind of character—the springings of the heart, and the mental combinations, no matter how rude, which end in impulse—those secrets of his inner heart, the Irish peasant keeps concealed to the present hour, as well from the oppressors he hates, as from the friends who, if they knew him better, could better serve him.[16]

Said the *Literary Chronicle*, "Delighted as we have been with all the previous productions of these gifted authors, it was reserved for the 'Croppy' alone to impress us with any idea of their full extent of their genius and capabilities. It is impossible to conceive a scene, or actors, better suited to the purpose of such writers, than Ireland and the unquiet spirits of 1798; and equally difficult to imagine in what other quarter they could have received the justice awarded to them in this. The story itself glows with the very essence of romance and excitation."[17]

VI

While Michael Banim was visiting John in England between August and November of 1827, engaged on the final volume of *The Croppy*, reading aloud each night for John's criticism what he had written that day, and "adopting his suggestions as I went on," John also showed him the draft of a new novel of his own:

> I read in MS. at the same time, the rough copy of a tale, which he had put together between whiles and in the lapses between his attacks of pain. This was done without the knowledge of the doctors. He could not submit to the sentence of positive idleness: the tale I allude to was published the year following, under the title of "The Anglo-Irish." It was of a different character from the "O'Hara Tales," and was not announced as proceeding from the same authors.
>
> I cannot say how the "Anglo-Irish" was received —I believe indifferently. The full power of the writer's mind was not brought to bear on it; unhappily, there was a physical inability to strain the brain to its tension at the time it was written.[18]

The absence of the familiar "O'Hara Family" signature on the title page, and the "different character" of the novel, to which Michael Banim refers, did arouse some speculation as to the identity of the author.

Some people thought that the novel was by Lady Morgan's husband, the physician Sir Thomas Morgan, who had written many essays and whom Colburn had pressed in 1826 to try his hand at an Irish novel. Sir Thomas wrote off to his lady, "Colburn wants me to write a political novel. For God's sake make me out a canvas, and I shall try it." Probably he spoke to friends about his project and the rumor spread. So, when *The Anglo-Irish of the Nineteenth Century* (3 vols., 1828; No. 20) appeared anonymously in 1828, some jumped to the conclusion that Morgan had written it.[19] But Michael Banim's statement that he read it in John Banim's own manuscript is in itself decisive.

Despite its lack of the sustained power that characterizes John Banim at his best, *The Anglo-Irish* is by no means to be dismissed as the inferior product of a sick and tired man. Nor was it received "indifferently," as Michael Banim suggests. When it appeared, published anonymously in three volumes by Colburn in 1828, the *Morning Chronicle* said of it, "The incidents of Irish history, and the character, notions, feelings and habits engendered by the unprecedented situation of the people, combine to form a source of interest as fertile and as various as that from which the great Novelist of the North has created his Scotch historical romances," while the *Scotsman* was even more fulsome:

> This novel will be much read. Its great topic—the policy of England towards Ireland—the question, What ought now to be done with the Irish Catholics? is uppermost at present in the public mind, and is momentous if not engrossing; its great staple—the feelings of the English and the Irish towards each other, or rather of the provincializing Anglo-Irish, or Orange, faction, towards their half countrymen—would have been interesting at any time, from its requiring at once a portraiture of manners and an analysis of motives; but it is doubly so now, from the feelings of which it consists, and the manner in which they are dealt with, involving the quiet and prosperity of an empire; and to these attractions we must add likewise the introduction on the canvas of well-known public characters; and, beyond all, and without which the rest would lose all its natural zest, the shrewdness, knowledge of the world, scenic power, and general talents of the author. Who he is we do not pretend to know.[20]

When a modern reader turns to the novel today, he will find much to sustain these opinions, and he will find it all the more puzzling that Professor Flanagan, in the course of discussing John Banim's writings, not only fails to mention *The Anglo-Irish* but even omits it completely from what purports to be his complete list of Banim's works.

What we see in *The Anglo-Irish* is not so much the impact of illness and fatigue—the plot is not much more mechanical or the episodes more improbable than those of the fiction written at the height of Banim's powers—as the impact of Banim's disillusionment with his own past hopes for conciliation and understanding between Englishmen and Irishmen. Whereas previously he had been careful to balance the extreme anti-Catholic and anti-Protestant views of his most violently partisan characters with moderate and conciliatory views put into the mouths of his heroes and heroines—even in the seventeenth century—now, for the first time, he has clearly lost hope and has turned bitter. The loathing mouthed in the 1680's and early 1690's by George Walker and Father O'Haggarty in *The Boyne Water* for all members of the other sect has in *The Anglo-Irish* become the common currency of the small talk of English and Ascendancy gentlefolk on the one hand and of Irish peasants on the other.

Contempt and hatred for the Irish Catholics, mingled with fears of violence and a leaning towards brutal repression, characterize even the casual conversation of the gentry in London and in Dublin. Throughout *The Anglo-Irish*, Banim puts these views into the mouths of his most important characters with such a deadpan seriousness that only a careful reader who has the advantage of knowing Banim's genuine opinions can be absolutely sure he does not mean them seriously. Long pages of the novel, then, are simply slashing and sustained satire, no doubt reporting accurately enough what Banim heard every day in London. As the Clare election of 1828 approached and with it the inevitability of Catholic Emancipation (unsatisfactory as the details of the Bill would be), Banim had so far lost hope that he could no longer suppress his true feelings. Nonetheless, he did not publish them under the familiar "O'Hara Family" pseudonym, long since a transparent disguise for the best-known Irish novelist in England.

The hero of *The Anglo-Irish* is the Honorable Gerald Blount, younger son of Lord Clangore, an Irish peer, who dies at the opening of the novel, when Gerald and his elder brother are still schoolboys. The time (Banim never did properly work out his chronology for this novel) is about 1814. The three guardians of the brothers are "the Minister" (Lord Castlereagh himself), a leading general, also of Irish origin, and a quiet Ascendancy Irish landowner, Mr. Knightly, who actually lives in Ireland. In a long-sustained conference between these guardians and their two wards, the themes of the novel are enunciated. The two grandees batter Mr. Knightly with questions: When *will* the Irish grow any quieter, the "unhappy, misguided creatures. . . . What with Whiteboys and Right-boys, United-men, Shanavests, Caravats, Threshers, Carders, and now, Rockites," it is clear that the Irish "never can be peaceable so long as they remain what they are." They are turbulent, ferocious, they thirst for human life: how can "English gentlemen, or Irish gentlemen of English descent, . . . think of settling in the country?"

There can be no change, the two Englishmen smugly and sadly agree, until "English views, interests, industry—English character, in fact—" replace Irish "views, interests, and indolence." All the people must become "English-Irish." Mr. Knightly seems to assent, and the boys themselves resolve that until there is security in Ireland they can never visit their own large Irish estates, from which, of course, their income is derived. In fact, the guardians agree, with Mr. Knightly demurring so subtly that his ideas are never voiced, that the Irish must be taught another severe military lesson: conquer them thoroughly at last: that is what "our distinguished countryman, now immortalizing himself on the peninsula"—the Duke of Wellington, of course—recommends.[21]

Violently anti-Irish without ever having seen Ireland, young Gerald swears to be "English-Irish." Everything he sees—an incident in which an Irish schoolboy responds with unseemly violence to English bullying at school, a brawl amongst Irish laborers in London, the foul conditions in St. Giles's, a London slum area inhabited chiefly by Irish, the well-deserved teasing he himself receives at the hands of Knightly's daughter, a charming young Irish girl and friend of his sister—contributes to making Gerald as anti-Irish as a self-proclaimed "English-Irishman" can be. At Cambridge, he meets Irish undergraduates—Protestants, of course—but his prejudices are only confirmed: "Cannot these men sit quieter . . . and talk a little less loud, and, in a word, do as others do?" Why don't they stop worrying about their social position? How they "blunder and squabble amongst themselves about the great bone of contention, Catholic Emancipation." And if these Irishmen abroad are so unruly, "what, upon his own soil, must be the genuine Hibernian—papist, politician, and with an O to his name?"[22] When his Irish acquaintances get roaring drunk and play dangerous tricks upon one of their number, Gerald is more convinced than ever. In his young manhood, ready to embark on a political career, he is, we realize, an absentee—like Maria Edgeworth's Glenthorn in *Ennui* (No. 3) or Colambre in *The Absentee* (No. 4), though not so bored as the first or so eagerly well-intentioned as the second—and the purpose of the book is to get him to Ireland so that he may begin to understand things for himself. Meanwhile, many an English reader would perhaps have been content to accept the views of Castlereagh, Wellington, and the rest that what Ireland needed most was more bloodshed.

There is one saving grace: Gerald is already in favor of Catholic Emancipation—for the wrong reasons, it is true: his theory, much in vogue at the time, being that if the Catholics were emancipated, Catholicism would wither away of itself when faced by the natural superiority of Protestantism. Until he goes to Ireland, he is indifferent to the reports of "Captain Rock's" increased activity, of famines, and of his brother's own agent's harshness. "No rents," complains his brother, Clangore, "no lease premiums; no renewal-premiums. In some instances, [the agent] in vain ejects the cotters and small farmers, who will not pay him a shilling; for either the ground remains unlet, or Captain Rock shoots, burns, or drives away, a new tenant."[23] In London, Gerald soon meets "the Secretary," a sardonic portrait of John Wilson Croker, scribbling away during one of his own dinner parties on a savage review of Lady Morgan,[24] and hears the current literary gossip, including a sarcastic remark about the Reverend George Croly—another of the Irish Protestant literary circle that included Maginn and Croker—whose latest novel is predicting the imminent "destruction of Popery, root and branch."[25] At dinner, some blame the sorry state of Ireland upon Sir Walter Raleigh's introduction of the potato.

Others (the Evangelicals) blame the Catholic priests as teachers of evil: "let us say to the people of Ireland, in plain language, 'We wish to change your religious belief, because we know it keeps you poor, ignorant, miserable, and most of all, because it is a blasphemy.'" An open challenge to the priests, mostly as ignorant as their flocks, but some of them deadly enemies trained by the "calculating, evading, cruel" Jesuits, would wipe out their faith in a decade. Irish Catholic children must be sent to schools where they may "hear the words of the book of life." So Gerald is soon induced to subscribe to the Evangelicals' Bible society. In *The Anglo-Irish* it is represented by O'Hanlon, like Horragan in *The Nowlans* a renegade priest who has become "a stout biblical." A visiting Scot says that he does not know Ireland well but all one needs to do is "make her people a moral, and an industrious, and a calculating people." So the chit-chat rambles over all the views and prejudices about Ireland then reigning in society, and Banim gives Croker the last word, when he tells Gerald that it is "All stuff and nonsense.... By virtue of certain old black-letter enactments, these Catholics are, this moment, eligible to political power, without ceasing to be Catholics: but such is the legal ignorance on both sides, that neither Catholic nor Protestant sees or admits the fact."

Castlereagh's trickiness on the issue is lampooned, as he refuses to admit that the English Government (Pitt) had actually once promised political equality to Catholics to get Catholic support for the Act of Union early in 1801. In Parliament, Henry Grattan, "the grey-headed veteran" of the Catholic cause, eloquently puts the Catholics' claims on the highest moral grounds. He is greeted by cheers, and that ends the matter. The basic difficulty, as the intelligent English cynic, Gunning (probably a portrait of a contemporary figure), tells Gerald, is the inveterate and ineradicable anti-Catholic sentiment of the English:

> Englishmen know that they enjoy their present independence; their liberty to read, and think, and speak, without a book-censor, or an inquisitor; to go to church or stay at home of a rainy Sunday; to pass a shovel-hat in the street without being afraid of it,— these, and other comforts, they know they possess, chiefly because Romanists have been and are kept down. And do you think they will set Romanists up again, upon the remotest chance of losing any one of their pleasant privileges?[26]

But all of these exchanges of views are preliminary to Gerald's actual visit to Ireland, which comes about by accident: he is shipwrecked on the coast. Here he falls at once into the hands of the followers of "Captain Rock," from whom he receives good treatment, but promptly escapes. He finds that the stagecoach driver taking him to Dublin has much to tell him about the English: "It's not the best o' you, I'm thinking, ye send over here to us, for samples, to agent us, and steward us, and lawyer us, and then make little of us after making nothing at all of us," says this man, who is in fact a former tenant on the

Clangore estates, evicted by the rackrenting Scotch agent Bignell, against whom a major Rockite plot is brewing.

Says the coachman, Michael Farrell:

> My father took a waste of three hundred acres, or thereaway, from the Irish lord,—he was Irish then,—that owned 'em; and by dint of hard work and careful looking-after, made 'em a good farum at the end o' twenty-five or thirty years. By course, he got 'em at a low rent; but at a short lase too; and he knew that when the lase would drop, he wasn't to expect a new one, on the same terms.

Ready to meet any reasonable demand, he nonetheless found—Lord Clangore now having become an absentee—that the agent now asked "just as much rent ... as we all knew wouldn't lave us a good mouthful o' praties after paying it." So the steward came forward and paid the new rent, because he intended "to split the farum into little takes, and re-let it, to twenty or thirty poor divvles, at another rack-rent."[27] The result for the Farrells was disaster. Michael had joined the Rockites, and Gerald Blount realizes that a desperate appeal from Michael was one of those he had himself received in England and dismissed without paying any attention. His Irish education has begun.

It is continued for a time in Dublin, where he hears a debate between O'Connell and Banim's own friend of earlier days, Richard Lalor Sheil, both mentioned by name and vividly portrayed, as is Sir Harcourt Lees, the Orange clergyman-baronet (also in Crowe's *The Old Light and the New Light*, No. 15), and other notable Dubliners of the period. The hatred and fear of the Irish peasant that he heard in London Gerald now hears again in Dublin: a prominent Dublin Protestant (who is also a dishonest bankrupt) remarks that the Irish "are a half-savage race who hate us, our religion, our superior station, and our English descent, just as the Caffers and Hottentots hate the members and subjects of our paternal Colonial Government at the Cape." They will not take advantage of the kind efforts to help them by establishing schools, to which "they will not send their wild little children, merely because their bigoted priests object to our Bible without note or comment," although this proves how idolatrous and blasphemous their own priests are!

The real trouble, says another Ascendancy gentleman, is the rise of a new class of Irish Catholic professional men and landowners. This has altered the former proper subservience of the lower "caste" and now the Irish Catholics even threaten to take their betters to law. Unbelievable as it seems,

> the son of a fellow whom, thirty or forty years ago, you might have paid with a horsewhipping, or with setting your dogs at his heels, if he presumed to teaze you with a complaint of high rent, or a complaint against your land-steward ... will now threaten to indict you for a common assault at the quarter-sessions, when you only lay your whip across his shoulders. . . .

The remedy? Educate them, convert them, keep them down, make them tidy, set them all to drain the bogs, and especially "thin them," by shipping them off to the colonies, forbidding marriage among them, or, best of all, letting them rebel and killing them off. The climactic toast of this enlightening evening is "The Pope in the pillory, the pillory in hell, pelted with priests by the devil,"[28] which is cheered to the echo. In *The Anglo-Irish* there is precious little left of John Banim's advocacy of conciliation.

The final volume of the novel, filled with further adventures amongst the Rockites, closes with the discomfiture of the agent, Bignell, and with Gerald's decision to settle down and become an Irish landlord. He succeeds to the Earldom and marries the daughter of his tolerant, decent godfather, Mr. Knightly, who has always been deeply sympathetic with the Irish Catholic cause. All this is somewhat stagy and mechanical, reflecting Banim's increasing fatigue as he tried to bring his violent, disillusioned novel to an end. He did so abruptly, promising that Gerald's later fortunes would be the subject of a sequel. He never wrote it, but there was no need for it. John Banim had got off his mind the pent-up furious resentments that were obsessing him.

VII

A temporary remission of his illness and, no doubt, the passage of the Catholic Emancipation Bill (April, 1829) while his next book was in progress somewhat mitigated John Banim's feelings. This book appeared as *The Denounced* (3 vols., 1830; No. 21), under the familiar "O'Hara Family" pseudonym, actually dedicated to the Duke of Wellington, who had been castigated in *The Anglo-Irish*. It consists of two novels, *The Last Baron of Crana*, set in the decades immediately after the Battle Aughrim (1691) and so in some sense a sequel to *The*

Boyne Water, although none of the same characters reappear; and *The Conformists*, set in the later years of George II, between 1750 and 1760. Both stories of the cruel workings of the penal laws, they show signs of John Banim's increasing inability to write full-length novels: prosiness, a certain incoherence, and—in *The Last Baron of Crana*, at least—a degree of mystification about the identity of the characters that sometimes approaches the ludicrous. Moreover, the careful and precise use of local color characteristic of *The Boyne Water* has now vanished, and the setting is left blurred or indefinite: in *The Last Baron of Crana*, largely somewhere in Ulster, apparently not far from Coleraine (Derry) and in a still more vaguely identified region of southern Ireland; in *The Conformists*, possibly the town and neighborhood of Kilkenny itself, although this is never specified.

One thing is clear: in these two novels John Banim was pulling his punches. In his introduction, he tells us why: intending to write of the abuses of penal days, he was nonetheless concerned "how far such allusions might affect, without the will or seeking of the writer, a question *at that time debated*, and it seemed certain, according to the opinions of competent friends, that if no prejudice interfered with the indispensable task, harm could scarce be done." In other words, if Banim treated his subject fairly, his work would not prejudice the passage of the Catholic Emancipation Bill. But, he continues, while the tales were in progress "the question alluded to *became unexpectedly decided*": that is to say, the Bill was passed. Then Banim began to fear that his stories might be criticized as "opening old wounds afresh." So, after the passage of the Bill ("the late great decision"), he "carefully and anxiously reviewed them, remodelled them,—in fact, rewrote them."

It is clear to the modern reader that this process did the novels no good. By curbing his indignation at the operation of the penal laws, Banim further enfeebled his stories. He assures us that the "Lately Made Free" will only rejoice at being emancipated from the shackles that bound their ancestors, whereas those who have disapproved of Emancipation ("the slave's enfranchisement") may at last cease to regret that "the last festering links" of the "old rusty chain of disability" have been broken.[29] But to us he seems to have robbed his own stories of some of the powerful impact they might have had if he had not edited them.

What the modern reader will appreciate and remember in *The Last Baron of Crana* is the warmth of the friendship between ancient enemies, as Miles Pendergast, a Protestant Ulsterman, fulfills the pledge made on the battlefield to his dying opponent Redmond O'Burke, a Catholic of the south, that he will care for O'Burke's only son. The sinister and corrupt working out of the penal laws is shown in the danger to which Burke exposes himself by harboring in his house a small nest of papists, whom he allows to worship in their own faith. The Rapparees appear, of course, this time as righters of Catholic wrongs, Robin Hoods on the Ulster highways, led by the semi-legendary Randall Oge O'Hagan, who is not what he appears to be. There is a fine scene of a bull-baiting, in which the great Irish wolfhound, symbol of ancient Gaelic might, outdoes a vicious English bulldog. And the savage prejudices of Protestant Ulstermen are reenforced from the pulpit by the (historical) Bishop of Meath, Dr. Dopping (1643–1697), a fanatical anti-Catholic.

In *The Conformists*, peace has descended; there is no foreign threat to support the Catholics, and yet the penal laws remain in all their rigor. Moreover, we are dealing now not with last Barons and other grand people but with simple village Catholics of the south, denied the right to worship freely or to educate their children. There is more pathos in the arrest of the admittedly rather slow-witted Daniel D'Arcy for trying to get instruction from a hedge schoolmaster than in all the dangers encountered by the relatively unconvincing grand gentry of *The Last Baron of Crana*.

Dan's father, the once-prosperous farmer Hugh D'Arcy, has been brought to the edge of ruin by the harsh operation of the penal laws that forbade Catholics to hold land by any lease running for more than thirty-five years and that deprived a Catholic at once of any farm that produced an annual profit one-third larger than the amount of annual rent. "The first individual of the established creed who should discover the rate of profit" could immediately seize the land.

> Catholic farmers, seeing themselves deprived of long and advantageous holdings, and even of the profits which they might hope to amass under short tenures, ceased to be agriculturalists, and commenced graziers. [In fact this was possible only for very large landowners, most of them Protestants.] Lands were no longer drained and enclosed; good houses were no longer built on them, or those previously standing repaired; pasturage wasted the fields, which were virtually forbidden to be cultivated; and the real yeomen of Ireland sunk in the scale of social importance, and along with becoming poor, grew indolent and apathetic in pursuits which required little industry and less labour. [The shift to grazing actually took

place because the markets were better for meat and wool than for agriculture. Banim's heart is in the right place but his history and economics are weak here.][30]

Although the Catholic Hugh D'Arcy has been a kind and considerate landlord, his best tenants will not renew their leases, but prefer to emigrate; their successors cannot pay enough rent to keep him going, and themselves often run off. The declassing of the yeomen is vividly portrayed in the decision of young Daniel to drop his efforts at education and cultivate the fields himself. Amidst the grinding injustice of the times, the happy ending of *The Conformists* seems contrived and mechanical.

VIII

These two were John Banim's last sustained works of fiction about Ireland. His next novel, *The Smuggler* (3 vols., 1831), dealt wholly with English scenes, being set in the region near Eastbourne, where he had been living in 1829, and involving him in a disagreeable dispute with his publishers, Colburn having merged with Bentley in a new firm. Banim moved to France in late 1829; his health grew steadily worse. All he could manage was a series of shorter stories, published in the various *Annuals* of the period. These were collections of prose and verse by various authors, sometimes elaborately illustrated and prettily bound for gifts at Christmas. Not until 1838 did a collection of these appear as *The Bit O'Writin'* (3 vols.; No. 24).

Meanwhile Michael wrote *The Ghost-Hunter and his Family* (1833; No. 22), published in the Library of Romance, edited by Leitch Ritchie, a series of cheap one-volume novels designed to break the stranglehold of the expensive two- and three-volume novels on the market. The personages of *The Ghost-Hunter* were modelled directly on John and Michael's maternal grandparents and on their mother's brother and sister. She had often told her sons about her family, and the idea of writing the story was suggested by John in a letter of November 10, 1828. "My dear Michael," he had written, "if health permitted, I could use these people, and bring their real and unimagined qualities into play, with credit to the Irish character, all Papist as it is, sweetly, primitively, and amiably."[31]

Michael also wrote *The Mayor of Wind-Gap* (No. 23), a pleasant and flowery story, published as the first of two novels by "The O'Hara Family" in three volumes in 1835. It is the second novel, however, *Canvassing*, that seizes our interest. Its anonymous author was a newly co-opted "O'Hara," Miss Harriet Martin (1801–1891). She was the second daughter of the second marriage of Richard Martin (1754–1834), M.P. for Galway, the famous "Humanity Dick," portrayed in 1825 as "King" M'Loughlin in Eyre Crowe's short novel *Connemara* (No. 14). Owner of vast estates in Connemara, totalling about one-third of the entire county of Galway in area but sparsely inhabited, and possessor of a splendid and almost inaccessible castle at Ballynahinch, Martin was a famous duellist, a beloved and kind landlord, and a pioneer in the movement for ending cruelty to animals. Saluted in verse by Thomas Moore and Thomas Hood and portrayed in fiction not only by Crowe but as "Uncle

Godfrey" by Charles Lever in his *Charles O'Malley* (1841), the famous and picturesque Dick Martin[32] is most lovingly represented in his own daughter's lively and unjustly neglected novel, *Canvassing*, in which he appears as "Mr. Wilmot," proprietor of Castle Wilmot in Connemara, "good-natured, careless, and extravagant."[33]

In this Galway election he is not himself running for office, but has promised his interest to young Lord Warringdon, an English noble, instructing all Wilmot tenants (the local Catholic forty-shilling freeholders enfranchised in the years before Catholic Emancipation raised the minimum value of a voter's holding to £10.) to vote for Warringdon, whose election manifesto is so written as to suit everyone, "those who cry out for Catholic Emancipation, and those who insist on keeping up the Protestant ascendancy." But there is a contest, and against its background is played out an elaborate and brilliantly written comedy of matchmaking, in which Lady Anne Wilmot procures husbands for both her daughters by supremely clever tactics. Duels are a matter of daily occurrence in what one of the Wilmot girls (the clever one, as Harriet Martin was the clever Martin) calls "this merry, murderous country of ours." There are fine genre scenes among the servants; there is a most sophisticated and handsome Catholic priest, mistaken as a rival for one of the Wilmot girls by Lord Warringdon, who has never met anybody like him; there are the local social-climbing Irish middle classes, anxious to ape English society in every detail; there is a duel between a stupid Englishman and a hot-headed Irishman, who become fast friends immediately afterwards, though both are wounded.

But above all, there is Mr. Wilmot, drawn by his own daughter: "Who is there we'd think of comparing with Mr. Wilmot, in regard to fire-ating; he's the wondher of Ireland, not to talk of the Province [Connaught]." The election, with its drunken disorders and its scandalous irregularities, provides one climax: Pat Conny must be reminded "he was only to be Pat Conny the first time he voted, but Dennis Sleevan the second time, in regard of poor Dennis not being convanient just then, because he was berried last week";[34] and Martin Donovan, whose lease has expired, must be reminded to put a live flea inside the document so he can swear the lease "has life in it." The other climax is provided by Lady Anne's success in securing the husbands for her daughters. Here most nineteenth-century novelists would have stopped.

But in a sort of epilogue, far more awkward in style, and yet imbued with a convincing sincerity, the reader is taken into the households of both the married daughters only a few years after their weddings. Both marriages are disastrous failures. And in the end, even the brilliantly successful Lady Anne admits it would have been better had she done nothing to make the matches but had run the risk that her daughters might remain spinsters. In the clever and witty Maria Wilmot, who puts the dinner table in a roar of laughter and who frightens the men until a man comes along so insensitive that he marries her as it were for a joke, Harriet Martin at thirty-four may have been commenting on her own spinsterhood, destined to last ninety long years: she was too intelligent and too bright, her contemporaries agreed, to attract a suitable husband. But she did write this one admirable forgotten novel, as good in its own way for the early century as in their time would be the best novels written later in the century by her own distant relative Violet Martin ("Martin Ross") (1862–1915) in collaboration with Edith Oenone Somerville (1858–1949).

IX

The Banim brothers' best work was now done. One family tragedy after another, combined with the steady deterioration of his health, reduced John Banim by the mid-1830's virtually to misery. Public appeals and subscriptions provided the money needed to bring him home to Ireland and buy for his last years a small house near Kilkenny on the Dublin road. In 1838, after he had been living there for three years, a collection was published of the shorter fiction written in earlier years. Appearing in three volumes as *The Bit O'Writin' and Other Stories* (No. 24) as by "The O'Hara Family," it included eighteen stories. Most of them are laid in Ireland, and go back to anecdotes or longer tales heard in his youth. They often have the pungent Irish phraseology that marked his best work: a sullen man in a pub is called "as serious as a pig getting a sun-dial by heart." But by far the best is the longest: the title story. Here, without the slightest tone of patronizing, an illiterate Irishman, a former sailor in the British navy, makes his claim on the government for prize money due to him. How he gets it despite the kind efforts of his semiliterate friends, and what he does with it once he has it, form a cheerful Irish comic tale.[35] The collection is our final Banim reprint in this series.

After it was published, John gave Michael some collaboration on the final three-volume "O'Hara" story, *Father Connell* (3 vols., 1842), published in the year of John's death and notable for its affectionate portrait of their own parish priest, Father Richard O'Donnell, who in later years became Dean of Ossory. Yeats admired it. But as a piece of literature the novel now seems too flat and long-winded to deserve republication here. The same is true of Michael Banim's last effort, more than twenty years later still, at a novel of his own, *The Town of the Cascades* (2 vols., 1864), a cautionary tale about the perils of drink. It has always had admirers, but like the various shorter stories that Michael wrote after John died, it should perhaps not be resuscitated.[36]

Into the brief space of a decade or so, between 1825 and 1835, then, the two brothers Banim crammed the nine single novels or collections of novels here reprinted as their best work. Far more of the best stories than is traditionally recognized (despite John's cheerful and grateful acknowledgments) were by Michael, who has seldom received credit. With the striking exception of the angry and disillusioned *Anglo-Irish*, so badly needing revival, all of the Banims' work—whether historical in the manner of Scott or set in their own day and reporting on Irish life—was written, as John declared in a letter putting forth his claims to consideration by the "affluent protectors of literature," with a "uniform political tendency, viz. the formation of a good and affectionate feeling between England and Ireland." And this was true, although—as he himself said later, replying to a generous testimonial from his fellow townsmen of Kilkenny after he returned to Ireland in 1835—his work was inspired "by a devoted love of our country, and by an indignant wish to convince her slanderers, and in some slight degree at least to soften the hearts of her oppressors."[37] This tension, at times scarcely bearable, between natural indignation at the English and the Irish Protestants and a persistent conviction that conciliation held the only hope for the future animated the entire work of "The O'Hara Family," Ireland's first true native voices in fiction.

Robert Lee Wolff

Notes

1. Michael Sadleir, *Nineteenth-Century Fiction* (London: Constable; and Berkeley and Los Angeles: University of California Press, 1951), has an accurate bibliographical description of the first editions of the Banims' works. There is no mention of the Banims in J. Finneran, ed., *Anglo-Irish Literature. A Review of Research* (New York: Modern Language Association of America, 1976). The entry in *The New Cambridge Bibliography of English Literature*, III, 2nd edition (Cambridge: University Press, 1969), lists the Banims' works and the scholarly work about them down to about 1967. There has been nothing since the discussion in Thomas Flanagan, *The Irish Novelists, 1800–1850* (New York: Columbia University Press, 1959), Chapters 11 and 12, which is far from satisfactory. Patrick Joseph Murray, *The Life of John Banim, the Irish Novelist* (London: William Lay, 1857; No. 25) is valuable for the many quotations in extenso from John Banim's letters to Michael Banim and from the correspondence between John Banim and Gerald Griffin. For Harriet Martin, see above and below, text and notes.

2. Flanagan, p. 175. This Flanagan "documents" with a single footnote (p. 175 n. 10) intended to "set forth" the publication history of the Banim novels. It altogether omits two of these, misdates a second, and gives incorrectly the contents of a third.

3. Murray, *Life*, letters of May 2 and July 10, 1824, pp. 125, 139.

4. *Tales* (1825), I, 104, 191.

5. *Tales* (1825), III, 39–40.

6. Murray, *Life*, pp. 154–155.

7. Flanagan, p. 189.

8. *The Boyne Water* (1826), III, 435–436.

9. *Tales, Second Series* (1826), I, 268, 239; II, 53–54.

10. *New Monthly Magazine* XIX (1827), 23–25; other reviews quoted in an advertisement in a publisher's catalogue at the end of Volume I of *The Croppy* (1828).

11. Murray, *Life*, pp. 190, 191–193. Flanagan says only that Michael "collaborated" on the book.

12. Thomas Pakenham, *The Year of Liberty. The Great Irish Rebellion of 1798* (London: Hodder and Stoughton, 1969), p. 267 for Father Roche; pp. 147 ff. for Father Murphy of Boulavogue. Flanagan wrongly says (p. 200) that Rourke in *The Croppy* was patterned upon Murphy.

13. *The Croppy* (1828), I, 272–276.

14. *Ibid.*, I, 161, 253.

15. *Ibid.*, II, 11, 13, 27–30.

16. *Ibid.*, II, 85; III, 7.

17. Advertisement in publisher's catalogue at the end of Volume I of *The Denounced* (1830).

18. Murray, *Life*, pp. 193–194.

19. Lionel Stevenson, *The Wild Irish Girl* (London: Chapman and Hall, 1936), pp. 254–255.

20. Criticisms quoted from publisher's catalogue at the end of Volume III of (John Carne) Anonymous, *Stratton Hill* (London: Colburn, 1829), for the *Morning Chronicle*; for the *Scotsman*, advertisement at the end of Volume I of (Eyre Crowe) Anonymous, *Yesterday in Ireland* (1829).

21. *The Anglo-Irish*, I, 19–27.

22. *Ibid.*, I, 82–83.

23. *Ibid.*, I, 99–100.

24. For Lady Morgan's feud with Croker see my introduction to her novels included in this series.

25. Croly's novel, which Banim (I, 146–147) calls "The Angel of the World," saying that it was dedicated to Canning, was actually called *Salathiel. A Story of the Past, the Present, and the Future* (3 vols.; London: Colburn, 1828), and was dedicated to the Duke of Newcastle. It dealt with the Wandering Jew.

26. *The Anglo-Irish*, I, 156, 161, 237, 205, 169, 191.

27. *Ibid.*, II, 99–100, 101–103.

28. *Ibid.*, II, 262–263, 267, 272.

29. *The Denounced* (1830), I, (v)-viii.

30. *Ibid.*, III, 35, 35–36.

31. Murray, *Life*, pp. 205–206.

32. Shevawn Lynam, *Humanity Dick* (London: Hamish Hamilton, 1975), is a good new biography of Harriet Martin's father. It mentions *Canvassing* only briefly (p. 276). The date of Harriet's death is given as an addendum to the chart in Archer E.S. Martin, *Genealogy of the Martin Family of Ballinahinch Castle in the County of Galway, Ireland* (privately printed; Winnipeg: The Stovel Company, 1891). Murray, *Life*, p. 217, unequivocally attributes *Canvassing* ("admirable story") to Miss Martin, and so did Michael Banim in a preface written in 1865 for a new edi-

tion of the two tales published in one volume by James Duffy. Michael added that he could not explain why the story was published as "by the O'Hara Family." See Sadleir, *Nineteenth-Century Fiction*, I, 25, under No. 147a. It is said by Miss Lynam that Michael Banim and Miss Martin met in Paris.

33. *The Mayor of Wind-Gap and Canvassing* (1835), II, 37.

34. *Ibid.*, III, 35, 18, 175, 179.

35. *The Bit O'Writin' and Other Stories*, II, 281–282, from the story called "Ill Got, Ill Gone." Of the eighteen stories, the earlier appearance of the following eleven in the various Annuals of the time can be traced (in the order of their appearance in the three-volume book edition here reprinted). In Volume II: "The Hall of the Castle" from *The Keepsake*, 1830; "The Half-Brothers" from *The Keepsake*, 1829; "Twice Lost but Saved" from *The Keepsake*, 1831; "The Faithful Servant" from *The Keepsake*, 1830; "The Roman Merchant" from *The Amulet*, 1831. In Volume III: "The Church-Yard Watch" from *Friendship's Offering*, 1832; "The Last of the Storm" from *The Literary Souvenir*, 1830; "The Rival Dreamers" from *The Gem*, 1829; "The Substitute" from *Friendship's Offering*, 1832; "The White Bristol" from *Friendship's Offering*, 1831; "The Publican's Dream" from *Friendship's Offering*, 1829. All of these references except one ("The Half-Brothers") can be found in Andrew Boyle, *An Index to the Annuals, 1820–1850* (all published, Worcester: Andrew Boyle, Ltd., 1967), I, 16.

36. (Banim, John and Michael) The O'Hara Family, *Father Connell* (3 vols.; London: T.C. Newby and T.W. Boone, 1842); Banim, Michael, Survivor of the O'Hara Family, *The Town of the Cascades* (2 vols.; London: Chapman and Hall, 1864).

37. Murray, *Life*, pp. 220 (letter of November 28, 1832) and 254 (letter of September, 1835).

THE

LIBRARY OF ROMANCE.

EDITED

BY LEITCH RITCHIE.

VOL. I.

THE

GHOST-HUNTER AND HIS FAMILY.

BY THE O'HARA FAMILY.

LONDON:
SMITH, ELDER, AND CO., 65, CORNHILL.
1833.

LONDON
BRADBURY AND EVANS, PRINTERS,
BOUVERIE STREET.

THE
GHOST-HUNTER
AND HIS FAMILY.

BY

THE O'HARA FAMILY.

LONDON:
SMITH, ELDER, AND CO., 65, CORNHILL.
1833.

PREFACE.

It is some years since the Editor of this work conceived the idea of publishing a series of original works of fiction, at little more than a fourth part of the usual price. At that time the business of novel-publishing touched upon its zenith. Five hundred pounds were considered by authors to be only a fair average price; and, in some cases, a thousand, and even fifteen hundred pounds, were not grudged by the publishers. The inference is, that the books sold, that the system "worked well;" and, of course, all parties were pleased—even the public, who paid a guinea and a half for three ephemeral volumes, which, if properly filled with letter-press, and entitled a history instead of a romance, might have been bought for less than half the money.

To all reflecting persons, however, there seemed to be something ominous in the very prosperity of such a system. Publications attended by such heavy expenses, and following so rapidly upon one another, could not be conducted in the usual manner. It was not enough to send them afloat upon the stream, and allow them to take their chance of being found by the world after few or after many days. As the moment of the launch approached, the owners became nervous; distrusting, sometimes with and sometimes without cause, the sea-worthiness of their argosie; distrusting the waves on which it was about to float, and the still skies that looked down upon it as calm as fate, they had recourse to every expedient which fear could invent. Steamers were sent out to marshal the way, puff-puff-puffing as they went; oil was cast, in plentiful libations, on the troubled waters, and fair winds bought from every old woman who sold them.

But the rapidity with which such speculations followed each other, was not the cause of all this anxiety, but its consequence: for, otherwise, a very few losses would have wound up the affairs of the concern for ever. In the same way, when an author found favour with the public, the bookseller clung to him, not from gratitude, but from nervous timidity; and when any particular class of novels became popular, it was persevered in *ad nauseam*.

The Editor would willingly indulge himself in tracing the causes of the decline and fall of this system, and of the general paralysis experienced by the bookselling trade, were it not irrelevant to his present purpose. All he has now to do is to exhibit the nature of his own plan, which he has at length matured and succeeded in bringing into operation.

We offer to all authors, great and small, male and female, known and unknown, a patient and speedy hearing.

The price given will be regulated in the first place, by the merit of the work, and in the second place, by the popularity of its writer; and the sum agreed upon will be paid in bank notes immediately on the assignment of the copyright.

Each volume will be fairly brought before the public. No expense will be spared, no cranny of the kingdom unvisited, till its existence is universally known: but here will end the care of the Proprietors. They have, comparatively speaking, no stake in the individual volume, their interest being identified only with the series collectively; and hence they can have no temptation to resort to any underhand means of ensuring a momentary success.

No favouritism will be tolerated, no unjust and impolitic wish implied for the establishment of a literary aristocracy. Each volume will receive fair play, and nothing more. A spirit of honourable emulation will thus be introduced among the contributors; genius will be encouraged and brought forward; and, if the undertaking prove successful, the romantic literature of the country will be advanced in dignity as it is enhanced in value.

One effect of the plan will be to diminish the number of novels; for it is manifest, that no work which is not presumed to be calculated for extensive circulation, will be published at such a price. This will be a benefit even to the booksellers themselves, whatever they may think of it now; for the great majority of existing novels is formed of *unsuccessful* ones. Henceforth the publishers will be more careful in their selection; and, for that reason, successful authors will be less likely to throw away their reputations by writing hastily.

As for the works of fiction which circulate only among the lower classes of the libraries, they must improve in quality, or the manufactory will be ruined.

The novel-publishers in this country, it is well known, have been long divided into two classes—the Cheap and the Dear; and of these two, the latter have in general had the advantage in the quality of their productions, while those of the former have answered better, in the aggregate, as mercantile speculations. The inference is, that worthless novels are bought freely by a large class of the public, simply because they are cheap; and the fact, although sufficiently startling to literary pride, will not appear surprising, if we only remember that novels, so far as their sale is concerned, must be viewed in the same light as other luxuries of commerce, which habit has converted into necessaries. These works, however, as well as the former class, will now experience the effects of competition in the market, in more ways than one; for it is *our* ambition to do away with *all* distinctions of price, by producing A SERIES OF NOVELS AND ROMANCES, GREATLY CHEAPER THAN THE CHEAPEST, AND FULLY AS GOOD AS THE BEST THAT HAVE PRECEDED THEM.

The length of the works published in the

Library of Romance, will depend upon circumstances. In general they will be complete in one volume, containing as much letter-press as three volumes of the cheap novels, or two of the dear ones. On this subject, however, the Editor will lay down no positive rules. Sometimes they may extend to two volumes, and sometimes a good deal less may suffice to fill a volume than the quantity specified. All will depend upon the nature of the work.

We now repeat, from the prospectus (which may be had gratis at the publishers'), a list of the several objects which come within the scope of the undertaking.

I.—Original Novels and Romances, by eminent living English authors.

II.—Original Novels and Romances, by unknown or little known authors, when they appear to the editor to be worthy of such fellowship.

III.—Translations from foreign languages of newly published works, or works that have never before appeared in an English dress.

IV.—Novels and Romances adapted from foreign languages, to suit the taste and manners of English readers.

V.—Reprints or adaptations of American works, either newly published, or little known in this country.

With regard to the Editor's own contributions, which of course are not meant to be alluded to in the preceding remarks, all that can be said of them is, that if they are not fortunate enough to meet with the indulgence of the public, they shall be at once discontinued.

THE GHOST-HUNTER

AND HIS FAMILY.

ADVERTISEMENT.

THE following sheets have not had the advantage of being corrected by the Author in their progress through the press; and the indulgence of the Irish reader, therefore, must be solicited for any sins of orthography they may exhibit.

The story, as the Editor is given to understand, is fact, and the characters, more especially those of the ghost-hunter and his family, sketched from life. This, however, is of little importance, if the work be found as true to nature—and to Irish nature—as he believes it will.

ADVERTISEMENT.

The following sheets have not had the advantage of being corrected by the Author in their progress through the press; and the indulgence of the Irish reader, therefore, must be solicited for any sins of orthography they may exhibit.

The story, as the Editor is given to understand, is fact, and the characters, more especially those of the ghost-hunter and his family, sketched from life. This, however, is of little importance, if the work be found as true to nature—and to Irish nature—as he believes it will.

THE GHOST-HUNTER

AND HIS FAMILY.

CHAPTER I.

About fifty years ago, Randal Brady lived in a suburb lane of a considerable city in the south-west of Ireland, and, compared with the lowly domiciles around him, his was a house which boasted superior advantages. His "aharluch glohn agus thinagh, vohn brightal'tha," * became the focus of attraction for those who relished an evening spent in innocent chat; and, during the cold nights, his latch was often raised by many whose own homes afforded them but little warmth. Under his roof, indeed, a poor neighbour's face never proved unwelcome; nay, the poorer the visitor, the more cordial was his reception; so that "the warmest corner" was not given, as the world generally bestows its favours, but rather was allotted to him who most needed its aid in counteracting the shiverings of poverty.

---

* "*Aharluch glohn agus thinagh, vohn brightal'tha,*" is an Irish phrase, bearing this translation—" a tidy hearth and a pleasant bright fire,"—which, in its full meaning, always supposes the accompaniment of a cheerful group, enjoying, in a winter's night, the comforts of the merry blaze.

Let us be permitted to describe the interior of the good Randal's house. Although thatched, it was tolerably large, affording two sleeping chambers on the first floor, and two on an upper story, which, however, were gained by the humble agency of a step-ladder: but the greater portion of the lower floor was occupied by *the* apartment which served—like the cobbler's stall—"for parlour, and kitchen, and all." According to general usage, the chimney of this widely-envied room occupied almost the whole extent of the gable farthest from the door. Beneath it was a large grate for the winter's fire, embraced by capacious hobs; and, as a mark of economy, there was also a stove, or smaller fire-place, only occasionally used in summer. Goldsmith's notices of his country are generally conveyed in a sneer. He says, that,

> "In some Irish houses, where things are so-so,
> *One* gammon of bacon hangs up for a show."

Now, if a contrary display may be taken as denoting circumstances above the taunt of "so-soishness," Randal Brady was an independent man; for not only gammons, and hams, and flitches, made a goodly appearance above and in the chimney, but there were also among them sundry sides of beef and salted legs of mutton — the which we can recommend to our inexperienced English readers as materials for a very capital dish at a solid, sensible dinner. As to the furniture of the apartment, excepting its unusual state of tidiness, it was pretty much like that of other "comfortable" houses in Ireland, at the time we treat of. The "dresser" was well adorned with shining pewter; the seats were by no means of uniform size or character there were four or five sycamore chairs, as white as old mortar and assiduity could make them; there was one arm-chair of black oak; and there were many stools and straw " bosses,"*—the latter great favourites of certain old women, who, in their wandering incursions into Randal's house in an evening, pretended to choose them as the lowly resting-points of conscious poverty, which, at the same time, afforded a closer affinity to the fire than stool, chair, or arm-chair itself. The floor was compounded of mortar, and of something else, which we forget, kept in good repair, and always well swept; the walls were evenly plastered and constantly whitewashed—characteristics of some rarity; but a few articles, disposed by way of decoration around, hinted at peculiar traits of the mind and accomplishments of the master of the house. On brackets, suspended by the walls, stood plaster casts of various figures, somewhat rude, it is admitted, yet, having been moulded by Randal Brady, " his own self," highly admired by his neighbours for their execution, if, indeed, they were not considered as master-pieces of art. The top of the dresser boasted similar ornaments; but the grand result of the good man's united talents as sculptor, mechanist, and philosopher, remains to be honourably noticed. Merely with his penknife he had shaped out two little men, to a perfection of form and feature which surprised all observers; and he had given to each a pair of coal-black eyes, using a heated knitting-needle as his tool, and from between their joined hands protruded a notched piece of wood, vividly representing a saw, and to each point of the saw was affixed a potatoe of calculated weight; and thus—the legs

---

* Low seats made of twisted straw ropes.

and feet of the figures being secured to the shelf of the dresser by wires—the little sawyers, once set a-going, bent forward and regained their upright positions, incessantly, to the wonder and delight of every visitor. His honest neighbours were, indeed, convinced that Randal Brady had discovered the perpetual motion; and, simple as was his work, perhaps he came as near to the puzzling desideratum as any dreamer we remember to have heard of.

Whether in festivity or devotion, Randal was very particular in observing the customary pranks, or rites, of each season of the year. On Shrove-Tuesday night, the ring was hidden in the peculiarly made "Irish pancake;" and it would irk us to refrain from noticing, in this place, a little occurrence which happened on a particular Shrovetide, inasmuch as it marks a feature of the character of Mrs. Brady, the "vanithee," or good-woman of the mansion.

Besides the family, one or two young people had stepped in, on this occasion. Mrs. Brady had exerted herself to the utmost of her housewifely skill in preparing the batter for the cakes; and when it was agreed that the first of them should be tried, she went into a remote corner, and mysteriously dropped her wedding ring into the measured bowl-full which was to form it. The magic cake was fried, having been turned with a most skilful toss in the air, by Randal Brady; and then it was fairly divided, so that each person should have an equal portion, and of course, an equal chance of obtaining the ring. It is scarcely necessary to explain that he or she to whom the prize might fall, was thereby to be doubly benefited. By simply putting it under his or her pillow that night, a matrimonial partner was sure to be dreamt of; and, moreover, the reality of the vision would certainly, beyond doubt, become one flesh with the happy dreamer before the next Shrovetide.

While the wondrous cake was dividing, Randal Brady proposed that his Betty and himself should try their fortunes as well as the younger members of the group, and Mrs. Brady assented, in thoughtless glee. Each individual received a portion; each held up the half-transparent piece of cake before the candle—Mrs. Brady obtained the ring. The boys and girls hid their disappointment under an affectation of great enjoyment of the unmeaning freak of chance; remarking that the good woman had a husband already, and that, even were she single, fifty-five was rather an advanced age at which to go a-wooing. Mrs. Brady herself, however, became suddenly grave. An expression of great trouble and anxiety overspread her face. She looked at her husband who was smiling at the moment, but she thought his smile a sad one as he said—

" And are you goin' to bury me, at last, vanithee?" His tone was jocular, yet it touched the chord which was thrilling in the good-woman's heart; she cast her bit of the pancake into the fire, and, but for the activity of her daughter Rose, her wedding-ring must have been melted down; then in the almost childish energy of her nature, she fell on her knees before her husband, looking up at him with clasped hands and weeping abundantly; and in the utter simplicity of her honest soul and uncalculating mind, thus addressed him:—

My humble prayer this night is, that the sod may cover my head, long before the grave opens for you, Randal Brady;—" and here she took his hands in hers, and vehemently continued, " and if 'twas the will of Heaven that I was left to mourn over you, Randal, in the could church-yard, don't you b'lieve an angel, if he stood fornent you, sayin' 'id, that mortial man cauld ever make me forget you! No, Randal! If lord, or earl, or juke—if the king himself brought his goulden crown, and his goulden sceptar, and *laid* them at the thrashold o' the dour, and said,—' Betty Brady, it's you I'll make my queen———' my answer to him would be—and you know it would, Randal—Randal, *ma graw!* 'Go your ways, honest man, Betty Brady will have no call to you!'"

The self-fancied object of a monarch's devotions in a possible contingency, notwithstanding her reliance on her virtuous affection for her husband, continued so strongly to urge her terror of the prognostic of the pancake and the ring, that she was not restored to self-possession, until her smiling spouse undertook, with assumed seriousness, to prove that by refraining from putting the ring under her pillow that night, all evil consequences would be avoided: and Mrs. Brady at last became convinced and comforted.

Lent follows Shrovetide; and Lent was one of the seasons of strict religious observance under Randal Brady's roof. During its continuance, all festive amusements were banished from his fireside. But Easter Sunday brought its feast, and, without any feeling of impropriety, its dance also. Upon that auspicious day, as well, indeed, as upon all great festivals, Randal clothed himself in his marriage-suit of pearl-coloured broad-cloth, and put on his three-cocked hat: and his dinner was the best his circumstances could afford. One of his sons played passably well on the violin; and, after dinner, he would approach his wife with smiling formality, and lead her out to move a minuet, the tips of his fingers, through respectful gallantry, barely touching the tips of hers, and his cocked hat under his arm; and she would make her distant curtsey to his every bow—the whole gone through, (on his part, at least, though not on that of his spouse,) for the purpose of exciting the merriment of their children; for a minuet was beginning to be out of vogue, and the gravity and formality of that piece of old nonsense were duly appreciated by the improved tastes of the younger part of the assembly. A country dance succeeded, performed by the whole family, and any visitors present.

The "coal bogue," or feast of eggs, was not forgotten on Easter Monday. The Christmas holidays were spent in true holiday style in his house: and on Twelfth-night he did not fail to provide a sufficient number of loaves, one of which he himself, and, in turn, each member of his family, threw against the door of the dwelling: an Irish couplet, always used on such occasions, being repeated at every bang:

"In God's name, we banish hunger from this house
To-night, and every night until this night twelvemonths."

Without the house, as well as within, there were persons interested in the close of the ceremony; ancient beggars, in fact, who, leaning upon their staffs, calculated the quantity of food to which it was to entitle them. Every thump they set down for a loaf; and, as surely as the last was heard, the door opened, and the arithmetic of the expectants proved to be correct.

CHAPTER II.

It was the eve of All Saints. The usages of the night were duly observed by Randal Brady, and they marked his creed and character.

In the middle of his sitting apartment stood a small table, covered with a snow-white cloth; and upon it were two lighted candles, and a large amber-headed rosary with silver decades, and a massive silver cross attached to it. Close by the table knelt the father of the family. A prayer-book was in his hand, from which he read the office for the dead; and his wife and children knelt around him, and joined in the responses. It is not our duty at present to argue, whether or not it be a sinful practice to pray for the immortal repose of those who precede us to the grave. We have only to note occurrences.

As Randal Brady knelt by the table, his body bending forward in the earnestness of devotion, and the light of the candles falling full upon his face, his appearance was truly patriarchal. His large hazel eyes, yet unfilmed by age, although he reckoned sixty-four years, were occasionally turned upward, in awe or fervour; or, as the name of parent, child, or other kindred, occurred in his orisons, occasionally moistened with tears, which, sometimes overflowing the lids, stole along the slight furrows in his yet ruddy cheek. The expression of his mouth well accorded with the tone of solemn supplication in which he preferred his prayer. His forehead was traversed by wrinkles, but none tending to the eye-brow, and all free of acerbity. His head was bald almost to the neck behind, and the scanty white hairs — retaining even in age their youthful curl — which fell over his ears, at either side, completed the venerable contour of his head.

His wife knelt next to him. Her dimpled cheek, when she wedded in her nineteenth year, had been faintly tinged with the rose — that delicate tint was now faded; but in the flashing of her dark eye, as it glanced towards heaven, and in her attitude of entreaty, as she raised her arms and hands above her head while joining in the responses, might yet be detected an abundance of her youthful fervidness of character.

Retired into the shade of the apartment, knelt the elder daughter of the old couple, a young woman in her twenty-fourth year, whose expression of devotion differed widely from that of her mother. Her hands met mildly before her bosom, her person bent gently forward, her head meekly and reverently drooped, or was occasionally elevated, with a quiet motion. All this distinctly marked an infelt and unostentatious piety.

Her sister, on the contrary, a pale girl of sixteen, kneeling almost on her mother's heels, was boisterous in her prayers; she indeed "worried heaven" with them. She smote her breast often and vehemently, and her responses were delivered in an unvaried wailing accent, without character or individual expression.

A lad of nineteen knelt at one side of the table, acting, directly, as the respondent to the litany. Throughout his whole look and manner there ran a startling expression of impetuosity. His petitions for mercy to the dead, were bursts of intense feeling.

Another youth, two years younger, manifested, even at his prayers, the cautious self-esteem of his character. He knelt as closely to the fire as it was possible to do with any regard to what he knew to be his father's ideas of propriety during a time of devotion, and he repeated what was expected of him as if he were saying a task.

There was yet another young man present, who, although no member of the family, prayed as piously as any of them; and had Rose Brady, the elder daughter, turned her eye towards him as he knelt, directly in her view, she might have noted that William Duncan was unconsciously copying her fashion of devotion with great power of imitation.

Agreeably to the customary formula, prayers were first offered up " for the repose of the souls of the faithful departed," without naming any one. Then followed petitions for kindred, friends, or neighbours; and then for all benefactors. After this, the old man paused a moment, as if deciding upon some other name which might have a right to his prayers and those of his family, and all were silent with him. He resumed, in the following words :—

" And we humbly beseech the throne of mercy, through the merits of our Lord and Saviour, and by the intercession of his blessed mother and the saints in glory, that He will grant eternal repose to the soul of our deceased neighbour, Dennis Whelan!—let us pray—"

Randal here repeated aloud the first words of that

co 2/4/82

CLASS NO.	AUTHOR Banim,			L.C. CARD NUMBER 78-12230
ACC. NO. 4610	TITLE GHOST-HUNTER AND HIS FAMILY			CARD SETS ORD. D. L.C.
LIST PRICE $11.50	PLACE	PUBLISHER Garland	YEAR 1978	L.J.
DEALER Garland	VOLS.	SERIES Garland (1833)	EDITION	W.I.
NO. OF COPIES 1	RECOMMENDED BY Holland	DATE ORDERED 12/29/81	COST 828 B 2171g S.B.N.	OTHER
ORDER NO. B 11468	FUND CHARGED Eng	DATE RECEIVED 1-27-82		

LIBRARY OF DAVIDSON COLLEGE
DAVIDSON, NC 28036

prayer of prayers which was given as a model for christian supplication by the meek lips of Him who knew the nature of man as well as the attributes of man's Maker, and who therefore must be received by all Christian people as unerring and sublime authority regarding the tone in which human prayer should be uttered, so as to prove acceptable to Heaven. Randal sunk his voice after pronouncing aloud, as we have said, the first words, and then proceeded in silence. When he had ended the prayer, and judged that the others had done so too, he again said aloud—

" Mercy and salvation to him !—

" May he rest in peace !"

To each of these ejaculations his eldest son responded with stunning abruptness and peculiar meaning, while his eyes glared fitfully; and when the " amen" escaped his lips, his teeth were set hard, and seemed to grind together. Such strange and wayward extravagance of manner was not unusual with him on other occasions; but it seemed that the name of Dennis Whelan, and the fact of praying for the repose of his departed spirit, had some mysterious effect on the ever vibrating nerves of Morris Brady.

The long evenings of winter were always spent cheerfully, and often merrily, under Randal's roof; but the observances which, on this night, had engaged him, his family, and visitor, left an impression of deep sobriety on the minds of all, and with looks, action, and demeanour expressing what they felt, the group arose from their knees. The old man slowly turned down the book on the table, at the page where he had left off reading, and took his accustomed place, in his old black arm-chair, before the fire. The candles remained burning, as was usual on each All-souls' night, because it was expected that any persons who might enter the house before the hour of repose, should kneel down at the table and pray for the dead. Morris Brady provided himself with a slate and pencil, and went on with the solution of a problem in Euclid, for, wild as was his head in many respects, it was a mathematical one during its quieter and more abstracted moments. The younger lad placed himself to his perfect satisfaction near the blazing fire. Mrs. Brady and Rose sat beside a little shining oak table, and took up their needle-work; the younger girl followed, with her knitting; and William Duncan, the visitor of the evening, and indeed of every evening lately, drew as near as possible to the female group.

CHAPTER III.

"Randal *aroon*," said the vanithee, breaking the silence after a while, "as for this poor Dinny Whelan"—again Morris Brady started, and glared strangely around him—"may he rest in pace, poor man! Well, it was only this day I larned that the poor little wife an' the poor little daughther Dinnis left behind him, didn't close an eye, by nights, until last night of all, ever since the day the good neighbours carried him to the grave."

"He left them without a friend but God, and God is good," observed Randal Brady, bowing his head reverently.

"Tisn't that, father," said young Morris very abruptly.

"No, indeed, Randal, avourneen; tho' what you say is the blessed thruth, and good for all your family to hear. Morris is right in sayin' that I meant something else, when I spoke o' Biddy Whelan and her poor little girl not sleepin' o' nights."

"Well, Betty, and what did you mean?"

"Very willingly I'll tell you, Randal"—and as the good woman had only been coquetting to have the question put, she now assumed all the importance of a story-teller setting forward on her tale, with a peculiar smack of her lips, which told her relish of the occupation.

"I put a few little things into my apron, Randal, for I knew the poor widow was in want of a neighbour's help"—Randal pressed the hand which had for some time rested on his knee, and Betty smiled her gratification at his approval—"an' I set me down to chat awhile: for there's nothing makes a little gift more pleasant to a poor body than to be very friendly and cordial when you're a bestowin' id, and there's nothin' lightens a heavy heart betther than to tell its sorrows. An' so, the little wife an' daughther tould me what I'm goin' to tell you, Randal. Dinnis Whelan, rest to his sowl, was found dead at his loom, as you know, when the daughter went to call him to his supper, an' the piece o' linen he left in it, afther him, wanted ten yards, or thereaway, to be finished; an', so you see, *a-chorra*, the very night afther he was carried to his last home, the mother an' the daughther, sleepin' in the next room, were awoke from their rest by the noise o' the loom goin' on, fast at work; the threadles risin' up an' down, an' the shuttle dartin' from side to side. Bud there was a great differ, Randal, between the noise of the loom that night, and when Dinnis Whelan used to be at work at it; the rattle it made was frightful; every stamp on the threadles shook the house, an' every time the beam was pulled, it was like the hammerin' of a great sledge on the ould walls. An' so the loom went on, night afther night, until the very last night of all, as I tould you, when the ghost was laid; but how that good turn was done for 'em, they wouldn't inform me."

"Will you tell us what *you* think of this story,

father?" asked Rose Brady, pausing in her work, and looking with quiet reliance at the old man.

"I know what you mean, Rose, my child," he answered; "but my mind is not made up as to whether or no apparitions of the dead now appear on earth. Not to say any thing of the spirits tould about in the holy writins, I've heard, from creditable people, such stories of ghosts, that I would be a forward man to gainsay them downright. Nothing of the kind ever came in my own way. But, about poor Dennis Whelan's spirit,—my notion is, that if it were the will of God his sowl came to wandher among us, it wouldn't be for the sake of fumbling in the loom, over an unfinished piece of linen."

"Did the ghost weave any more of the linen that the live man left behind him, mother?" again questioned Rose. Morris Brady uttered a scoffing sound, and continued to work, seemingly in a passion, at his geometrical problem.

"That's a good, sensible question, *ma calleen*," observed Randal—" can you make answer to it, vanithee?"

"Why, then, no I can't, *a-chorra*, because it never came into my head to question the good people about it, an' they never tould me. But there might be a rason, Randal, why Dinnis Whelan's sperit would be sent back to work in the loom."

"And what rason will you give, Betty?"

"I'll tell you what come to my knowledge, an' I'll lave you to judge for yoursef and for us all, Randal. I know 'that a word to the wise is a peck of advice.' And I wouldn't open my lips to say what I'm goin' to say, if Dinny Whelan was in the land o' the livin'; for, when we're talkin' of our neighbours, we ought to guard the tongue: 'the least said, the soonest mended;' and, ' a silent tongue can't shame its owner.' We shouldn't vilify nor backbite, for ' there's few can throw the first stone.' But Dinnis is now gone where our tongues can't blacken him, an' so I may tell my story."

Thus did the vanithee, as usual, endeavour indirectly to impress on her husband that she was always alive to the good lessons she had heard him preach in his family, as well to herself as to their children; and then she proceeded, again sadly encumbering her narrative with self-evident and accepted moralizing, to say nothing of her exhaustless proverbs.

" Well, *aroon*, what would you have of id, only this:—Dinnis was given to a very sinful practice, God forgive him; there's no one can gainsay that ' an idle head is the duoul's workshop,' Lord save us!—or that ' industhry meets its due reward.' Bud it's thrue, also, that ' there is a time to brew, and a time to bake;' and this never came into the mind o' Dinnis Whelan, even in the way of all others that it ought to come; for he used to work of a Sunday, Randal, *a-chorra*, and he wouldn't go to the house of God: an' not to keep holy the sabbath-day is a grievous sin against the commandments." She paused for praise, as if she had invented a new doctrine.

" Indeed and it is, Betty, *a-cuishla*," assented her husband.

"Well: now give ear to me, Randal. Dinnis Whelan was sthruck dead of a Sunday night: and he was at work all that blessed and holy day. The bell rung out for seven o'clock mass; and it rung out for eight o'clock mass, an' he heard it the second time; and it rung out for nine o'clock mass, an' he heard it the third time; and it rung out for twelve o'clock mass, an' he heard it the fourth time; but his shuttle only went the faster: an' the ould wife came to the dour to him, sayin'—' Dinny, the last bell is ringin,' —go to the house o' God, on his own day, an' in his own blessed name:' but Dinnis only cursed and swore at her, and frightened her away; an' that same evenin' we all know what came to pass. Well, *a-vourneen,* tell me this: mightn't it be for a punishment on his poor sowl that he was sent to rattle in the loom, where he lost mass, and where he lost his life, together!"

"Pugh! there was no ghost there at all," suddenly asserted Randal Brady's elder son. He spoke with startling energy, and every eye was fixed on him. "—Tho' I wish there had been," he added, setting his teeth, clenching his hands, and rolling his disturbed eyes.

"Morris, that's a bluff sayin'," observed his father; are you positive of its thruth?"

"As sure as I have a head on my body, Sir," Morris replied, impetuously.

"And how did you make so sure about the matther, my boy? you may have been mistaken, Morris."

"I'm not mistaken, Sir, cravin' your pardon; I did make sure of id."

"Tell me how, my good boy."

"I sat at the loom myself, all night, watching for him."

"And he did not come to you?"

"I could neither see him, nor hear him at his work: not a mouse stirred in the dark."

"Oh Morris, Morris! were you crazed in your wits?" asked his mother.

"No, mother, I had my senses the same as ever."

"There was no great sign of sense in that action, child: what would you do—the Lord purtect us!—

if the sperit of ould Dinnis Whelan came upon you in arnest?"

"I'd question him," replied Morris, standing suddenly erect, knitting his brows, and glancing forward, as if preparing himself on the spot for an interview with the disembodied likeness of the crabbed old weaver,—" I'd question him, 'till he'd make known to me the throuble that was on his sperit; an' then I'd give id rest an' pace, if mortal man could do such a thing for him."

"But, you poor mad fool of a boy," continued Mrs. Brady, " supposin' that ould Dinnis was sittin' in the loom, before you, wid his ould red night-cap on his head, an' his ould jock fastened wid a nail undher his chin, an' *croonawnin'* his ould song of Death an' the Lady, and that he started up to pummel you well, for disturbin' him in work—what would you do then, you poor crature?"

"I'd throttle him!" cried the extravagant Morris, thrusting out his arms, and holding nothing at all very tight by the nape of its neck, as it were—" that is," he added, " if it was possible that a sperit, without bones or flesh, cauld rise an arum against a livin' man, so as to hurt him; but, tho' I b'lieve in ghosts, as firmly as I b'lieve in the gospel, what foolish people say on that head I don't put my faith in at all; how could it be? what's in a sperit, without his knuckles for thumping at you, any more than there is in a blast o' wind?—only I'd like to find out the thruth; I'd like to put one of 'em to it."

"By my good deed," said the lad at the fire, " I always thought it was a snugger thing to be in my warm bed, of a could night, than to be comin' home to it, shivering, afther watchin' sperits in the church-yard."

"What does Daniel mane, Morris?" asked his

father; "did you ever spend your nights in the church-yard?"

"I'd give the right eye out o' my head to have discourse wid a sperit," was the answer.

"And you often left your bed at night, and left your father's house, to look afther such things, Morris?"

The lad now perceived the aim of his father's questions; he discovered, in the seriousness of his tone, and in the mild severity (if we may so express ourselves) of his regards, that his father was displeased with him. He had forgotten himself when making the former avowals; but he now recollected that he had always taken precautions to conceal his ghost-hunting sorties, in the consciousness of doing wrong. He hung his head, and remained silent.

"Spake the thruth to your father, a cuishla-machree," exhorted his mother, fondly; "'open confession is good for the sowl,' and you know I often tould you that 'one lie brings many.'"

It was to his eldest sister that Morris looked for direction. Rose glanced encouragingly at him, and her open smile he at once interpreted into a recommendation to speak truly and courageously. He was about to acknowledge his fault, when the latch of the door was quickly raised, and the entrance of an occasional and strange visitor, interrupted for the present the confidential family explanation.

A little old woman suddenly made her appearance. Although much advanced in years—for her body bent forward, and she supported herself on a staff, with a crook at its top—still her limbs bore her actively, and it was not with a creeping pace she advanced towards the circle at the hearth. Her neck protruded from her chest, causing her head to be much in advance of her body, and she glanced up at those she addressed from the corners of her eyes. Her face was much wrinkled, and of the colour of hardened putty; her nose sharp; her lips puckered; and, altogether, her aspect bore an expression of the most venomous acidity. A short crimson mantle, much faded, fell over her shoulders, fastened under her chin by a hook and eye; her garments beneath were neither untidy nor ragged; and her head was furnished with a large uncouth straw hat, doubled down over her ears, so as to assume a bonnet shape; from the constant wearing of which, as well as from its being a very unusual article of dress among the lower classes around her, she had received the name of "Hesther Bonnetty."

"Out o' my place there!—out o' my place!" were her first words, when, without turning to shut the door after her, she had hobbled to the hearth: "out o' my place, I say!" and she held her crutch over young Daniel's head.

"Oh, by all manes, Hesther," he answered, most unwillingly leaving his warm corner; "shew me the one dare sit between you and the fire, any day or night in the year."

"I'd cut your crown if you thryed for id, you brat," observed Hesther, as she placed her "boss" on the spot from which she had ejected Daniel, who, taking his three-legged stool with him, as a garden-snail drags his shell wherever he goes, was obliged to resettle himself in a climate some degrees less genial than that in which he had lately luxuriated.

"Hee, hee!" squeaked Hesther, when she had seated herself, "the ould father of evil ought to take his own; and if my curse can sink you, Joe Wilson, to where you ought to be this night, my curse I give."

"Don't have them wicked words in your mouth, Hesther," said Mrs. Brady, in a tone between reprehension and pity, for Hesther was reputed to be somewhat light-headed.

"Let the ould duoul take his own, I say to you again," repeated Hesther, with increased venom.

"Considher the night that's in it," continued Mrs. Brady.

"Considher the night that's in it? Is that what you tell me to do? hee, hee! what counsel you give me, Betty Brady!" Hesther cried, scoffingly; "an' don't I well know what night this is? isn't it All-sowls' night? and don't the bad sperits of them that done evil, come upon the earth this night?—Aye; this is the night that sends them over-an'-hither, *threena-halah*,* up an' down. My deadly curse upon this night, I say. There's no rest nor pace for me this night. The throubled sperits cross my road, and stare at me wid their glassy eyes out o' their grave-livery! May All-sowls' night never come again! or over an' over I say may the duoul hould his own, an' not let them loose on me! See! see, now! the very moment I'm spakin'!—he is between me and the fire—och, Joey, an' if its fire you want, fire burn you!" and she glared as if she beheld some frightful object at her knee.

"What do you mane at all, Hesther?" questioned Morris Brady.

"What's that to you? or to any one but my own sef? only, I tell you, Morris Brady, that I can see them when no other body can; 'twas a curse was put upon me, no matther for what reason: and, I tell you, the evil sperits quit their graves this unlucky All-sowl's night; an' wherever I go they're wid me."

"What were you spakin' about Joe Wilson?" continued Morris.

---

* Helter-skelter.

" What was I spakin' about him? Do you know the place he was murthered at, in the *bosheen?* 'tis asy to mark it to-night, there's such a fine moon shinin' out for 'em all. Well, 'twas along the bosheen I came to see ye, an' by course I passed the spot. No rain came since Joey was found sthretched there, to wash the marks from the ground; an' there's a red cross, made wid his blood, on a broad stone in the wall."

" Well, Hesther?" questioned Morris, fully absorbed.

" Well? for what do you cry your ' well, well,' at me? I met Joe Wilson's ghost on that spot; yes, there we met with one another; and he followed me when I passed him, givin' him my heavy curse; an' he crossed the thrashold o' this house, afther me! an' now he's between me and the fire, as I tould ye afore; I see him—I feel him."

There were different movements throughout the family at this announcement. Mrs. Brady crossed herself, and drew near to her husband. Randal only looked compasionately at his wretched visitor. Rose consulted her father's face, and adopted his feelings. Her sister and her younger brother clung in terror to each other. William Duncan looked from Rose to her father, and tried, in his turn, to copy them. But Morris jumped up, and darted a step forward towards the spot pointed out as occupied by the ghost of the renowned Joe Wilson.

" Hie you away! hie you away!" muttered Hesther, as if addressing the apparition; " we'll meet to-night again, if that will satisfy you—only lave me at pace now. Hie you away! aye, there he's goin' at last— an' there he's gone; an' may the duoul pin him up where he ought to be! *Och ma-vrone!*" she continued, sending her keen glance round the circle, and grinning hideously, " good luck an' good fortune to the hand that broke Joe Wilson's skull! an' may the same fate fall on every one of the same crew, that come here to push aside the good ould stock o' the land! May all of his sort be sent away from us, seed, breed, and generation, kith an' kin! a black an' burnin' curse fall on them, I pray!"

" Hesther, there must be no more cursin' at my hearth-stone, such a night as this," said the man of the house, mildly, but determinedly.

" I'll curse them as long as there's a tongue behind my teeth, Randal Brady."

" Are you certain sure you met Joe Wilson's ghost in the bosheen?" asked Morris, after returning from the door, at which, holding it half open in his hand, he had been standing, and gazing wistfully and fiercely through moonshine and shadow, after the invisible departure of the apparition, in consequence of Hesther's half exorcism and half compromise.

Hesther gave him a smart tap of her crutch, as she cried—" Hah! did you feel that, you great *gawk*? didn't I tell you I met him face to face? and wasn't once enough? I saw him as sure as you found the crook of my stick on your shouldher that moment; or as sure as the moon was shinin' to show him to me; aye, an' I'll see him again to-night, afore my eyes close; and I tould that too, once this evening; I will —if ould Nick doesn't clutch him—an' that he may is ever an' always my prayer."

Mrs. Brady was shocked at the continued profanity of her visitor, and addressed her in a serious strain.

" Hesther Mc Farlane, remember the words I say to you—' it's a long lane has no turnin';' your own time for goin' out o' this wicked world isn't far away;

an' it may happen that some people you'll lave afther you will remember your wicked fashion o' cursin' the dead, and that there will be few or none to say, God be merciful to your oun self; 'civility begets civility,' Hesther; be civil to the departed, and then (we don't answer for Mrs. Brady's corollaries) the like civility will be your portion from the livin', when the grave is closed over you. So, lave off sayin' curses, Hesther, an' think o' the Christian duty o' this night; and get up, an' go at once to the table, and kneel down at it, and offer up your prayers for the faithful departed. 'Tis betther to do that, than to be quarrelhin' wid the dead."

Hesther rose and hurried to the table. When she stood opposite to it—

"It would be an hour's work," she said, "for me to kneel down, and rise up again; an' so I'll say my prayers stannin';" she put both her hands on her stick, rested her protruding chin on them, and went on with her devotions.

"Let all o' ye join with me—young an' auld as ye are. I pray this night, from the bottom o' my heart, that the poor wandherin' ghosts that have the fashion o' crossin' my path, an' grinnin' at me, an' sitting by my side—an' all other poor wandherin' ghosts; I pray from the bottom of my heart, that my heavy curse may 'light on em' now, an' at the judgment day—amen."

"Oh, tattheration to you, woman!" burst forth Mrs. Brady, enraged to the highest pitch that her good advice had been so shamefully disregarded; but before she could finish her sentence of reproach, Hesther was beyond the door, and all heard her spiteful laugh, as she hurried away.

It was some time before the horror excited by

the irreverence of the wicked old woman, subsided in Randal Brady's family circle. When all were again tranquil, he called his son Morris to him:

"Morris, when that poor deranged crature came in, I wàs questioning you whether you were in the habit of risin' from your bed, in the middle of the night, and quitting your father's roof, to go rambling about, without his license or knowledge?"

"I'm longin' from my heart to meet a ghost, an' spake to it, father."

"Then you have left the house, at night?"

"I have, Sir."

"Often, Morris? tell me the thruth."

"A good many times, father."

"Ah, then Randal," said Mrs. Brady, "see, he does tell you the thruth, plump an' plain; an' sure he desarves praise for that."

Randal understood the mother's anxiety to extenuate her son's fault. He took no notice, however, but addressed the lad:

"Morris, my son, pay attention to the words o' my mouth. First of all, 'tis very foolish of you to let your head be runnin' on such wild things. 'Tis a most exthravagant desire of yours; and exthravagance in anything is bad and blameable. I make some excuse for your green years, on account of the past; but I bid you to guide yourself betther, for the future. I said to-night that I would'nt take upon me to deny that spirits sometimes are visible to the eyes o' livin' men; but, mind me well, Morris, I *do* take upon me to say that, in ninety-nine cases out of every hundred, people's own foolish fears shape very simple things into terrible apparitions. I'll give you a proof, that happened to myself once, when at work in the counthry. I was comin' home late at night, an' I met a stout, able man, an' three full-grown women, running against me, quite out of breath, and I questioned them, an' they tould me if I had a regard for my safety I would turn back, as they had just seen a frightful sperit."

"And didn't you never mind what they said, father, about turnin' back? didn't you go sthraight on, and stand before it?" questioned Morris, not able to suppress his excitement even while undergoing his father's expostulations, for errors brought on by that very failing.

"Yes, Morris, I did go on an' stand before it."

"And you commanded it to answer you, in the name o' God."

"Listen, Morris, and you shall hear. Interrupting me is not the best way to let me tell my story to the end. I went on my road, an' the man followed me at a distance; an' I went up to the apparition that made him so much afeared, an' it was nothing but an ould white horse, with his fore legs up against the fence, looking in at a meadow he could not reach, because his hind legs were tied together to prevent him. And I called to the man, and he called to the women, and they all came back, and were convinced of the thruth, instid of running home, out o' breath, with a story to frighten a whole parish."

Morris gave a deep, hard sigh, as he remarked, "It was a pity, father, you had no satisfaction or reward for your courage."

"You mistake, again, Morris. I had the satisfaction and the reward of setting four people right in a matther that might have weakened their minds, and, through them, hundreds of others, if they had remained in their foolish mistake. But listen to me again, Morris.

"What I am afther saying to you only consarns the silly part of your conduct; and I wish I had nothing but foolishness to blame you for. But you left your bed, and you left your house, at an unseasonable hour, without your father knowing it. Many a one has come to disthruction by doing that, Morris. A spirit isn't the most dangerous thing that walks by night. The doers of evil deeds, the dhrunkard, the profligate, the robber, and the murtherer, go out in the night-time. They know that their actions will not bear to be looked on, and they go out to do their wickedness when the honest part of the world is takin' the useful rest that God made the night for. Morris, no good man can be a night-walker; and I now forbid you, upon the pain of incurrin' the sin of disobedience to your father, to lave my roof, again, at an improper hour. I forbid you to take the boult from my dour; I forbid you to stale out o' my house, through the darkness, upon any account whatever. And now my good boy, God bless you; God bless you all."

Rising from his arm-chair, Randal Brady made the sign of the cross over the bent heads of his whole family, and then retired to his sleeping apartment. While the others were following his example, William Duncan approached Rose, and leaned over the back of her chair.

"I am going to lave you to-morrow, Rose," he said. She looked up into his face; and an upward look from a pair of loving eyes is very effective.

"Indeed, William? On your business?"

"Yes, *ma-chree*. There's a good piece of land waitin' for me to survey it, twenty long miles from you, Rose; and I won't work with as light a heart as I used to do at home, for I won't see you in the evening, when my day's labour is over. Your smile won't meet me; your little hand won't be held out to give me a welcome."

"And there's one in this house will miss *you*, too, William. How long must you stay away?"

"Rose, don't you know I love you too dearly to let more than a week go over my head, without seein' you? I will come home every Sathurday night, plase God, hopin' for a happy Sunday."

"And, in good deed, if 'tis in Rose's power to make the Sunday happy to you, happy you will be, William."

"If 'tis in your power, you say? oh, my own Rose." William here took a seat close by hers, and held her hand, and stole an arm round "his own Rose;" nor did the young girl show any disapproval of his movements: "you well know, my own, own colleen, that when you look at me as you do now, I'd be happy if every other cratur in the wide world, except my poor mother, turned against me. Rose, tell me one thing;" she looked assentingly and attentively— "do you, do you love me dearly? very dearly?"

Rose smiled with a quiet humour at the question which resulted from her lover's earnestness. Immediately, however, she became grave, and there was a slight reproach in her tone as she replied, resting her arm on his shoulder—"William, if I was a quarrelsome girl, I'd say something to you for asking me that."

"Quarrel with me, Rose, if you like; you'll have it all to yourself; I'll give no battle."

"Aye, by my word, and some people would, and with reason, William. But I will answer to you once for all. God forbid that, if I did not love you dearly, I cauld sit by your side as I am sitting. I'll tell you my full thoughts. If a young girl has anything to be ashamed of, when she gives her love to a young man, she ought never to say the word, even tho' she tould the thruth in sayin' it. You an' I knelt down to my father's grey hairs, William Duncan, and he put my hand in yours, and he prayed for a blessin' from heaven upon both of us; and he tould me that I made a choice that gave gladness to his heart; and my poor mother kissed me when she said, crying, ' God bless you, child;' so, there is nothing wrong in telling you that I *do* love you dearly."

" Aye, but very, very dearly, Rose?"

" Now, shame on you, William; there was only one 'very' on your tongue, at first; but little matther about that; if I put in the two words, I firmly b'lieve it would be nothing but the blessed thruth: are you satisfied now?"

William Duncan did not answer—in words, at least; and if he did in any other way, we pride ourselves on being above saying a syllable about it. Let every generous reader be content with understanding that there was between the two young people, a permitted love, single and honest in its nature and quality; and, after this, we defy malice to direct one shaft against Rose Brady for her tolerance of her lover's actions, whatever they might have been.

In a short time, some murmurings of two voices were heard, and that little occurrence we are at liberty to allude to, though indeed not to dwell upon. It is proverbial that such sounds have little interest for any witnesses, or even over-hearers, of two persons placed in the situation of William and his mistress. Content therefore, with having shown in the beginning of our story, the terms on which William Duncan and " his own, own colleen" stood, we shall conclude the chapter by stating that the youthful conference was interrupted suddenly and not pleasingly. Rose's young sister opened her bed-room door, to say, crossly, that the night was wearing, and that she was sleepy, and couldn't rest while people were talking and amusing themselves in the room next to her; upon which Rose bade adieu to William, outside the threshold of the door, and stood in the moonshine, looking after him till the sound of his footstep was lost in the silence of the night. Then she stept into the house, and while placing the heavy wooden bolt across the door, sighed heavily, though not sorrowfully: and then she entered her little sleeping nook; knelt down and prayed a considerable time, taking into account the coldness of the weather; and slept soundly and healthfully until morning dawned.

CHAPTER IV.

Randal Brady had been endowed naturally with an intellect much above his equals in life; nay, much above the generality of his superiors. It is probable that, had his education and lot permitted it, he would have become a distinguished member of " the republic of letters." But having received only so much early instruction as falls to the share of those who, in after life, are to earn their bread by the sweat of their brow, he could cultivate but by snatches, and to a limited extent, the original powers of his mind. His acquirements, however, such as they were, and such as had been only attainable after the hours of daily labour, rendered him a very eminent character in his humble circle.

Randal Brady was a man of science. He had fixed a dial in his little garden. People of less knowledge would have regulated the gnomon during the sun's meridian; but this critical point was adjusted by him at noon of night, under the guidance of the polar star. Randal might be truly called a respectable astronomer. His nomenclature of the heavenly bodies was not, indeed, exactly such, though perhaps as useful to him, as that adopted by other star-gazers. For instance, he distinguished the constellation *Ursa Major*, by the more homely epithet of " The Plough," as he traced some similarity of shape between the sign, and the implement of industry so called. He could calculate the epacts, and tell the day of the month on which Ash Wednesday would fall, without consulting the almanack: and he could use, and explain the use of, the dominical letter in the calendar. He was rich enough to have purchased a watch, had he thought proper; but he chose to use a ring-dial of his own manufacture, the degrees being described thereon with a sharpened nail; and on a sunny day, when asked the hour, he would pull this forth, hold it up to catch the solar ray, and, with not a little of the peculiar ostentation of a *savant*, oracularly announce the time to the gaping inquirer.

Randal became a true believer in the Newtonian system, and profoundly argued the matter against the evidence of his neighbours' senses: for some there were among them, men of high pretensions too, who would not be convinced that the earth kept for ever going topsy-turvy. At " The Mortality Club," a certain clever carpenter generally had the room with him, notwithstanding Randal's erudite explanation of his incomprehensible doctrines. This philosopher would insist, for instance, that in case the world whirled round about in the manner stated by Randal and " ould Newton," the rooks of a duly specified rookery would often find themselves out in their reckoning of time and place. For, suppose that the earth turned one way in her orbit, while the rooks flew another way, when quitting their nests in the morning, to go a thieving and plundering for the day, it was a clear case that the rookery must be some thousands of miles away from them, by the time they thought of returning home in the evening.

"By the liquor in my hand, honest neighbour," said the carpenter, " if what you're sayin' was the thruth, this hearth-stone would be in Ballycowndhawn to-morrow mornin', an' I'd be there wid it, if I sat hard by it; a thing I won't do, but sleep in my own honest bed—me and my ould woman together."

Added to all his attainments, Randal Brady was a man of sound sense, of equable temper, of great firmness, joined with great placidity of character, and a good practical Christian, without the slighest approach to cant or acerbity. We have ourselves seen him seated at the head of his family, dealing forth pious exhortations, with deserved praise or deserved reprehension, and so are enabled to form an estimate of his character. Upon the whole, it is not surprising that such a man was reverentially beloved by his wife and children, and highly esteemed and respected by his neighbours.

His wife, the good Betty, had been a sad enthusiast in her nineteenth year. Randal was then a handsome man, and young, too, although her senior; with a countenance mild, smiling, and intellectual. Betty Reynolds even admitted that she loved him " to folly," and although she was of another religion, and connected with some of the most influential shopkeeping families in the town, she abandoned both advantages for his sake, changing her creed with her condition—for Randal could not be wrong in any thing; and, conformably with her character, she became as fervid in the practice of her new religion, as she was in her affection for her husband. Although loving a hearty laugh, Mrs. Brady would not, during Lent, venture on a more decided mark of merriment than a smile; and on Good Friday she would bare her feet, loosen her fine head of hair, and let it fall over her shoulders; and in this outward manifestation of woe she would go from chapel to chapel, praying and mourning.

Mrs. Brady's husband had once been severely burnt. She travelled forty miles on the occasion to procure an ointment for his wounds; and it had the desired effect, and Randal's leg healed up quickly. Thenceforward she kept by her a stock of this unction; and, when its fame became known, she frequently dressed, with her own hands, the burnt limbs of ten persons in the course of a day. The consequence was that she acquired a reputation for skill in the treatment of almost all other ailments, internal as well as external, and Mrs. Brady did not gainsay the honours tendered her—to which, in fact, time and experience seemed fairly to entitle her. There is and was a certain disease very prevalent in Ireland. Rabelais, noticing its existence in another day and country, styles it "*faute d'argent;*" and this affliction is the radix of another—or rather both are concomitants— namely, emptiness of stomach; in curing whereof Mrs. Brady was pre-eminent. The *materia medica* were drawn from her stock of provisions, administered in the shape of savoury broths or soups. Such nostrums could do but little mischief, in any case, while in the removal of the ailment above noticed, (no matter under what name presented to her, such as " heart-burnin'," or " wather-plash in the stomich," and so forth,) they were quite effectual; and many who came to consult her in a weak and languid state, left her house re-nerved and refreshed, lauding her medical knowledge, and blessing her bounty.

The elder daughter of the old couple could not be called beautiful, for her nose was neither Roman nor Grecian; nay, as we wish to speak candidly in all cases, we must confess that it was rather broad at the base, and perhaps about the sixteenth of an inch too wide. But then her lips were cherry-red, and beautifully formed; her forehead was as smooth as polished ivory; her cheeks were round and peachy, and, in colour, " like to the Catherine pear, the side that's next the sun:" her chin was full, marbly, and a little dimpled; and as for teeth, Rose might be excused for unnecessarily displaying them, had she had the vanity to do so. The eye is the gem of the countenance; and Rose could boast two dark hazel ones, beaming with good nature, or with affection, full of sense and intellect, and sometimes shooting forth a sly humour. She was not tall, but her figure was nicely moulded. Richardson, while enumerating the perfections of his Clarissa, (poor, poor Clarissa!) relates that her attire always bore the gloss of newness. We claim the same praise for our humble little heroine, and we add that whatever she wore, seemed of the exact colour, kind, and pattern, which became her best.

She was as cheerfully industrious as a bee in the garden. Almost from her childhood she had been accustomed to earn something for herself, and by assiduity and prudence in her occupations, she was enabled not only to contribute to the comforts of the family, but to " put money in her purse:" and that purse, a capacious one of gold-flowered silk, lay in a deep corner of the chest in her bedroom, and into it guinea after guinea found their way, until Rose had laid up her own dower.

Randal Brady discovered, at an early age, a similarity of mind between Rose and himself, and did not neglect to cultivate it. While yet a child, he would take her by the hand, early on the summer's mornings, and they would stroll out together to ad-mire and inquire into the history of nature : we mean, of course, as much of it as he could trace, chiefly for her amusement. He would pass a knitting-needle through an apple, to point out, by candle light, the phases of the moon, or the alternations of day and night. To her father's precepts she owed her method of reflection and mental precision ; her deep sense of religion ; and, in a great degree, her habit of personal neatness, and her taste for personal decoration: for, when she was a growing girl, it was his hand that contrived a certain machine of chamois leather, within which to encase her nearly jet-black hair at night, to prepare it for falling over her neck in glossy curls next morning. In a word, the intercourse between the father and daughter was of the most endearing kind ; and the natural affection of consanguinity became delightfully enhanced by the mutual interchange of ideas, tastes, feeling, and judgment.

Although, as we have said, Rose was no beauty, yet could she boast of a greater number of serious admirers than many who surpassed her in personal attractions. Not long before the opening of our tale, she had to regret the abandoning of his home by a respectable young man to whose addresses she would not listen, and who sought to dissipate in absence the passion she could not encourage. Another of her suitors, having ascertained her partiality for birds, taught a starling to pronounce, in the most feeling manner—" Rose, James Ryan loves you;" and then presented her with the little go-between.

A third admirer sought to make way in her heart by a different sort of bribery. On Sunday mornings, when she returned to breakfast from early mass, she would find her cup and saucer decked out with the gayest and most fragrant flowers ; and hanging against the door of her sleeping apartment, she would detect paper-bags crammed with fruit—the ripest, the rarest, the most seductive. Rose selfishly enjoyed the perfumes of her nosegay during her morning meal, and appropriated the peaches, the plumbs, the cherries, the pears, and even the apples—although, fortunately for her, there was attached to their acceptance no forfeit, as in the case of poor mother Eve! In truth, she received these nice things, literally, as offerings at the shrine of her manifold attractions, and ate them up, too, almost all, on that comfortable understanding. But the unfortunate donor was nothing the better of his gifts. He did not suit her; and she did not fall in love with him for the sake of his temptations.

The foregoing instances we select from many, to prove that, even in personal merit, Rose Brady, humble as was her lot in life, should not be called unworthy of being our heroine. There was yet another lover besides, of a rank far above that of the modest little girl it was his pleasure to woo; but with regard to him we shall be silent for the present. The nature of his pretensions, and their consequences, will appear in the sequel of our history.

From all that sought Rose's favours, William Duncan bore away the prize. Rose had good sense, as well as genial affections, and she fully comprehended that mere good looks were not the only quality requisite in a husband, for which reason many a suburban Adonis was passed by. But she had also determined in her mind—and the most sage and reflective heads will admit she was right—that, provided a lover suited her tastes and judgment in other respects, there was no absolute necessity for his being ill-favoured, if Providence should otherwise have ordered it. And, on this principle, when her reason and her heart approved of William Duncan, she did not reject him because he happened to be, what he could not help, a handsome young fellow. He had indeed brilliant cheeks, curling locks of light brown, a laughing eye, a merry smile, a manly carriage and address, and, withal, a well-turned leg. Of late years, this latter recommendation is scarcely necessary in a man; but, at the time we treat of, the unnameables reaching only to the knee, and there tightly buckled, and the stocking fitting close to the nether member, gave to the possessor of a handsome leg a manifest advantage over his spindle-shanked or heavy-ankled compeers.

As to the more solid qualities which determined Rose's preference, William Duncan was clever and assiduous in his business as a land-surveyor, and promised to get on prosperously in the world. He was a good son to his aged mother; a good brother to a fatherless sister, whom he had portioned respectably; and a moral and religious person in the strictest sense of the words. Moreover, the manly ardency of his address enabled him—while the starling's first tutor, and the offerer of fruits and flowers, were tardily hinting at their purposes—to act like a bold general, and carry the fortress by assault.

William possessed a vein of arch humour (considerably dulled, however, since he became a lover.) He could tell merry tales; he played on the flute; and he taught Rose's starling to imitate from it some of the softest Irish airs, to the traitor's own great delight, for he would flutter his wings with joy at the approach of his music-master. It was a rare, talented bird, as well as a false one. While William played for him, the little shining amateur would turn up his ear to catch the tune; and, in William's absence, he would, at Rose's request, imitate what he had heard so faithfully, as to beget in her mind vivid recollections of his instructor. Thus was the faithless wretch doubly perjured. Not only he did not plead for him who had educated him, nourished him, housed him, and finally sent him forth an accredited diplomatist for that very purpose, but he really advanced the interests of a rival, to the eternal prejudice of his old patron, tutor, and benefactor.

Morris Brady, Randal's eldest son, was the least handsome of the family. There was, however, nothing disagreeable or repulsive in his countenance; although his manner and expression bespoke a singular character, in which the reader may already have concluded that great impetuosity and daring formed the principal features. When suddenly addressed, his head jerked round, and his eyes glanced quickly and wildly; and, in moods of strong excitement, which were frequent with poor Morris, all his actions were the results of headlong impulse. His enunciation was rapid, but not continuous; and he spoke in bursts of assertion, his mind as it were flashing its convictions.

Excepting a knowledge of languages, his father had given him a very good education. He delighted to plunge into the depths of mathematical calculations, and no problem was too abstruse for his mental powers. Indeed, difficulties under any shape, whether intellectual or bodily, seemed to be but incentives to almost audacious exertion. Once, in his boyhood, when bird-nesting, he was on the bough of a high tree which broke under his weight, and came down tumbling, to the terror of his companions. Morris, however, did not passively submit; in his descent he grasped another branch, instantly re-mounted the tree higher than before; and there—merely because he would defy, and overcome the danger—swung himself to and fro, crying out, shouting, yelling, and grinding his teeth like a maniac. All his associates had a kind of fear and awe of him in his fits of extravagance; and, no matter at what odds in point of years or strength, Morris never lost a battle in pugilistic warfare. Indeed, his wild, demon-like face and manner, and the vehement discharges of abuse with which he accompanied every thump, often stood him in more stead in winning a victory, than his knuckles or the force of his arm.

Morris's imagination absolutely gloated on the marvellous. He was quite sincere when, to our knowledge, he assured his father, " he would give the right eye out of his head to spake to a sperit." In truth, the passion of his soul, and the ambition of his life was to meet, face to face, one of those fearful sights from which others shrink. It was part of the theory relating to visionary beings, that there were some mortal eyes to which they could never become visible, while to others they revealed themselves in all their terrors and mysteries: and Morris, persevering as he had been in his researches after fairies, ghosts, and other supernatural things, at last began to fear that his want of success was attributable, according to the doctrine mentioned, to a want of the faculty of perceiving them. But this growing conviction, though it sorely irked him, did not as yet induce the ghost-hunter to give up his wild and strange pursuit. Even a few nights before we introduced him to the reader, he was standing, erect and determined, beneath the withered yews in the church-yard, his eye glaring on the undulated graves, and his ear listening to every sigh of the wind through the long, luxuriant grass which covered or surrounded them; and the very night previously he had, as we have heard himself admit, stolen into the widow Whelan's house, to question old Dennis concerning his nightly operations at the loom. These attempts, however, were only renewed failures; although, as shall soon appear, he was shortly to be gratified in his heart's longing, to his heart's content, and to his own cost, into the bargain.

With the two remaining personages of Randal Brady's family we have but little concern; but as we profess, truly and really, to attempt sketching a group from the life, we may as well put them on the canvass in the back ground.

The one was a handsome lad of seventeen, principally remarkable for a cunning selfishness of character. From the precepts and example of his father he was, indeed, well-conducted; but all his views tended to his personal gratification; and his self-love allowed him to chuckle over his own escape from the many difficulties and perils to which his elder brother's ardent nature daily exposed him.

The other was a girl, a year younger than this uninteresting youth. She inherited much of her mother's enthusiasm; and this had taken an overstrained turn to religion, as we have had occasion partly to witness. She would be a young saint. She made the discharge of her spiritual duties a matter of much ostentation; but we are bound to admit that there was no hypocrisy in her young heart, and that her thoughts and her life were pure and taintless. The calls to prayer were frequent, and occupied a considerable portion of the day; they did not, however, bring her principles to bear on certain constitutional failings. She was a little envious of her sister's superior riches and attire; not duly taking into account that Rose owed those advantages to her own steady industry. And Nancy Brady had, moreover, no inconsiderable spice of a trait described by Burns as belonging to the " unco guid:" she would wail the lot, and blame the errors, and publish them, to boot, of those for whose conversion she prayed, and whom, she felt confident, lacked her own perfection of goodness, and "state of grace." But let little Nancy pass: we repeat that we shall have very little to say to her or of her; and we may add that, except as Rose's sister, we don't care much about her.

CHAPTER V.

THE wicked old woman called Hesther Bonnetty, positively asserted to Morris Brady that she had encountered in the *bosheen*, or narrow way, near his father's house, the ghost of a certain Joe Wilson; and if the declarations of others were to be credited, she was not the only person to whom the apparition had become visible.

Luke Branigan, a manufacturer of very hard felt hats, with which he travelled to different fairs, was the possessor of a small dusky, bay horse, with foxed ears; the most cunning animal, perhaps, of his species. From his colour, his shrewdness, and the artificial cut inflicted on his ears, Luke imagined that he bore many points of resemblance to the hero of fabulists, Reynard: and accordingly bestowed on him the appellation given to his supposed prototype, in a celebrated Irish hunting song, namely " Maddherra Rhua," or " the Red Jade." Luke Branigan was provided with a well-hooped iron chest, in which he put his hats; and, placing this in his little horse's cart, and setting his back against it, he had scarcely any necessity to use rein or halter in guiding Maddherra Rhua; nothing more being necessary than to show the animal the high road to any given place where a fair was held, and this done, he made his way by the result of his own observations. His master seriously boasted that he knew the days of the month on which the different fairs of the country were appointed, as well as the almanack-maker; but, however this might be, the good man was famed for placing extraordinary reliance on his little foxy-coloured steed.

Luke Branigan was very fond of sleep. When at home he plodded directly from his bed to his plank in the morning, and as directly from his plank to his bed at night; and, during the day, every moment he could snatch, without his wife's knowledge, from his occupation, was spent in his favourite indulgence. He was blind of an eye; which gave occasion to a rival felt-hatter to remark, that " if·Luke Branigan had two eyes to sleep with, he'd sleep day an' night, to his dyin' hour."

Trusting to the well-proved steady sagacity of Maddherra Rhua, Luke Branigan generally slumbered away the journey to a fair, even in the teeth of his honest anxiety to dispose of his hats to good advantage: and hence it is but reasonable to conclude that, when the cares and bustle of the day were over, and after allowing himself some sleepy refreshments at the place where he had effected his sales, he should have a good sound nap along the road homeward, in the night-time. And, indeed, well he might, and no blame to him: little Maddherra Rhua never failed to convey him safe to his own door, whether the moon shone out to light his way, or the darkness of a stormy night obscured it. He proceeded by the very shortest route, too, for well he knew every turn by which a dozen paces could be subtracted from a journey.

A few nights after the opening of our tale, Luke,

as usual, was sleeping away, the road homeward; and Maddherra Rhua had entered the formidable *bosheen* where Joe Wilson had been murdered, and which was now generally known as the scene also of his ghostly visits to this world. It was a shortcut to Luke Branigan's house in the suburb, and therefore the little horse had chosen it. Habit had rendered his master tolerably alive to any unusual movement on his part; and Luke half awoke as Maddherra Rhua stopped suddenly. His one eye opened wider when, before he could exert himself sufficiently to ascertain the cause, his steed gave way to explosions of furious snorting. He looked round him. Maddherra Rhua snorted louder and louder. " God bless the baste, an' myself, likewise," muttered Luke; for, with feelings of the most helpless terror, he found they were exactly opposite the broad stone in the wall, marked with the red cross.

" Back again, Maddherra, aroon—back again, for the love o' the virgin!" he cautiously whispered, but Maddherra stood stock still, and snorted again as if he would burst his nostrils.

" It would be a good deed to thry an' get down, if it's the will o' God I'm able, an' lade him back by the halther," continued Luke, in soliloquy; when, ere he had time to ascertain his capability to follow his own advice, the ghost glided noiselessly by him; fully within the vision of his best eye—nay, almost sufficiently near to touch his person. An instant's pause the apparition made, to fix one withering look on the unfortunate Luke Branigan: it was beyond question the face of Joe Wilson. Luke had known him well.

The cause of Maddherra Rhua's mortal terror passed on; and the little horse, regaining his presence of mind, sped homeward at a brisk pace, without word or guidance from his poor master. He stopped at the door, and neighed, or rather giggled, as was his custom, to announce their arrival. Mrs. Branigan answered him by speedily appearing, and great was the good woman's alarm, on finding her husband lying senseless in his cart; at first she thought he was only asleep, a thing to which she was used; but when her tongue, and a few good slaps on his shoulder, failed to awaken him, as on former occasions, the real state of the case occurred to her. This adventure Luke related upon his coming back to his senses, fully accounting for his swoon by an appeal to the well-known fact that the most courageous man will faint, either at the moment of encountering a ghost, or immediately on gaining a human habitation, after the apparition has passed away.

Being a very dreamy man, as well as a sleepy one, there might have been something imaginative in Luke's story; but the fact of the ghost's appearance was put beyond question by the testimony of Darby Doughny, the smith.

He had been to Kate Motley's—a well-known name in his time, and remembered to this day by some old topers of the last century. There, over many pots of the good dame's *shebeen*, Darby had

"Relaxed his ponderous strength—."

But Kate's *shebeen*, if it produced mental relaxation, was too generous and stout a beverage to weaken the body; so at least did Darby Doughny think, as he issued from her house, late at night, accompanied by his very incompatible and yet much-esteemed friend, little Shorsheen Demphy, the tailor. He knit his brows, scowled around him, puffed forth much heated vapour from his swollen cheeks, and swore to the passive son of the needle that there was nothing on earth he wished so much to hear that moment, as even a whisper of disparagement against the sickly Shorsheen, or his trade. Shorsheen gratefully acknowledged the implied promise of protection, and on this friendly footing they reached the entrance to the far-famed *bosheen*. Here the tailor represented to his companion the impropriety of risking an encounter with the terrors of the narrow way; but the smith bellowed loud at the well-meant remonstrance. He would not go round about, like a dog, for all the ghosts that ever walked. Shorsheen was urgent; and although he loudly proclaimed his dependence on the powers of Darby's arm against any human force, still he positively refused to commit himself even to *its* safeguard, when a wicked ghost was in the path before them.

Darby Doughny had, but the moment before, threatened violent battery against any human creature who should dare to speak slightingly of his companion; but he now pushed the shivering tailor from him; told him that he was not even the fortieth part of a man; and blustered on alone. Shorsheen immediately took to his heels, and was speedily at home, next door to his neighbour the smith. The latter had not arrived; and after some time elapsed, Mrs. Doughny questioned the tailor at her threshold, concerning her husband's absence; and he was just about to recount to her the fool-hardiness of his friend, and the peril he had incurred by acting against his counsel, when Darby, pale and trembling, staggered past them, into the house, and fell on his own floor, with a sound such as his anvil might have made, had it met with a similar adventure.

Darby Doughny had encountered the ghost; his courage had forsaken him at his need; Kate Motley's *shebeen* had evaporated in cold perspiration; and when he unclosed his eyes a perfectly sober, and a wiser man, he admitted, even to his diminutive old friend Shorsheen, that, "never again would he be the fool to tempt a bad sperit."

These are but two well-authenticated instances of the appearance of Joe Wilson's ghost, out of many, by the recital of which Paddy Naddy, the barber, contrived to smooth the crumpled visages of the sufferers writhing under his blunt razor. For Paddy made it a regular part of his business to provide himself with all the true tales of wonder going: and though he was the worst operator, in his way, all over the town and suburbs, yet was his shop much frequented for the sake of his gossip.

We will not say that Paddy Naddy might not have embellished his narratives, (therein, indeed, lies the excellence of all of us good story-tellers;) and Paddy was just shrewd enough to know that the more powerfully he engaged the attention of his victims, the less sensible would they be of the torture inflicted on their faces.

In truth, the fearful pranks of Joe Wilson's ghost became the engrossing topic of conversation throughout the whole neighbourhood, as well at Randal Brady's fireside, during the November nights, as at every other around him. Although Morris had not yet submitted his downy chin to Paddy Naddy's inflictions, he constantly frequented his shop for the latest anecdotes of the troubled spirit, and he heard them repeated, or added to, under his father's roof every evening.

The effect of all this upon the extravagant temperament of the lad may be supposed. His imagination constantly dwelt on the bold achievement reserved for him, at the idea of which the bravest of all other men trembled. Yes—he felt that he could dare an encounter, front to front, with the unearthly being, whose deathy-pale face and " cold gleaming eyes" had felled to the earth the stalwart and brave Darby Doughny, as if he had been a weakling girl. True, his mind pictured the communication between human and supernatural beings as most awful, solemn, and even terrific; yet his nature took a wild and revelling delight in the indulgence, by anticipation, of such sensations.

Randal Brady kept his eye on his wayward boy; and the deep, taciturn gloom into which he saw him sink, or again the eager glance of his dark eye, as he listened to the half-whispered stories of the dreaded apparition, did not escape the notice of the watchful and anxious old man. He took an opportunity of calling Morris, a second time, to his side, and reminding him of the paternal command that, on no account whatever, he should absent himself from his home at an unseasonable hour of the night.

" You know, Morris," the father concluded, in his calm but resolute tone of voice, " that when I lay my commands on one of my childhren, 'tis for rason good in my own mind, and to my own conscience, in the sight of heaven; and you know, too, that my commands must be the same as the law to all my childhren, while their father's house is their home; remember that well, Morris, and God bless you."

CHAPTER VI.

RANDAL BRADY had broken in upon Morris's reveries, at a moment when he was ideally engaged in confronting the renowned apparition. In the vivid picture of this interview called up by his wild fancy, the former injunctions of his parent were forgotten; and under the hurried excitation of his feelings he had impetuously resolved to face the ghost, in reality, that very night, at twelve o'clock. His father's renewed admonition dispelled his dreams, and again presented a formidable barrier to their indulgence. Long habits of obedience compelled him to promise to himself that he would not now, for the first time, rebel against paternal authority.

But his acquiescence with the old man's commands was not a cheerful one, as had hitherto been the case with Morris. His highly-wrought sensations subsided into moody discontent. He did not remonstrate; but, as he retired to his apartment for the night, impatience and dissatisfaction darkened his brow. He knelt down to his prayers, but merely muttered them over, while his chin rested on the palms of his hands, and his intensely-expressive eyes gazed on vacancy.

"By my faix, Morris," remarked his brother, from

his bed, speaking in his usual quiet, canny manner, "it's you that's pious and good to-night; you're a long hour at it."

Morris jumped up, and began to undress, as if his attire were scorching him. He bounded into his own bed, lay on his back, and staring straight upward, relapsed into his former gloomy mood.

"Upon my word an' my deed, Morris," continued his brother, "I'm thinkin' you'd give your Sunday coat to be hand-and-glove wid the ghost this blessed night, instid o' bein' snug and warum where you are."

"Hould your pace," answered Morris, turning sharply round; "hould your pace, an' go to sleep; I'm not given for talkin'."

"I'll folly your notion, my boy: it's the purtiest thing in the night-time;" and he shortly kept his promise, leaving Morris to his reveries.

All became still within and without the house; but Morris did not sleep. The candle, which he had neglected to extinguish, was nearly expiring, occasionally sending up glares of light, and then sinking into dimness. At length, gradually, and to himself imperceptibly, his eyes began to close—slumber was just stealing over his faculties. Suddenly he bounced up in his bed, and stared around him, asking, "who calls me by my name?"

The candle gave its last strong flicker upward; and, in the—to his eye—lurid, supernatural light which it threw over the apartment, he did indeed see a pallid face looking at him through the little window at the foot of his bed! He winked his eyes, and then glared them wide open. "'Tis there still!" he cried, jumping out on the floor. The candle finally sunk in the socket, leaving him in darkness. He groped to the window, flung it open but saw nothing without, save the white gleamings of the moon, here and there contrasted with some shadows, wherever any object interrupted the sickly light. "I'll be afther you," he muttered, groping about for his clothes. He was half dressed, when he heard his brother's voice, asking him what he was doing. His father's repeated commands rushed to his recollection, and he was shortly in bed again. Now, however, he did not relapse into sleep. The morning dawn found him watching the window; but there was no return of the real or fancied vision.

We all know that the desire of attaining an object is, proverbially, strong in proportion to the difficulties in our way. Morris's thirst for hunting down Joe Wilson's ghost increased from hour to hour. For many nights he slept but little, still on the watch; his pulses throbbed at the least sound: but night after night passed away, and he received no second visit.

His desire heated to passion, of which the effects were visible in the almost trembling abruptness of his manner and utterance, and in his haggard looks, and the redness of his wild yet fine eyes. He began to level the obstacles which lay between him and the gratification of his yearnings. Exclusively of the peculiar relish he had for the feat he burned to undertake, an encounter with the poor troubled spirit was, he argued, a good action in itself; and this he shewed in the following clear manner.

It was part of the universally received creed appertaining to ghostly appearances, that their wanderings among us arise from something connected with their previous sojourn on earth—from the leaving undone, for instance, some action, upon the due performance of which depended their repose and happiness in eternity; and that they haunt their former dwelling-places in the flesh, until some daring mortal questions them, obtains from their lips instructions what to do— because no ghost can perform his own work on earth without human agency — and then faithfully goes through what is necessary to secure their rest in another world, and their final departure from this.

Taking the matter in this point of view, it appeared plain to our young casuist that, in braving all the horrors of an interview with a supernatural being, he would with some risk to himself, be only undertaking a work of considerable Christian charity. Since he felt courageous enough for the task, he ought to attempt it; indeed, it seemed as if he were called to it; and his father's arbitrary objection was not reasonable, inasmuch as it interdicted an action so praiseworthy. What were the assumed grounds for issuing the mandate? That going out at night might lead to evil company, and evil acts. But Morris felt quite confident that he would associate with no improper persons, nor commit any crime. Vice had no temptations for him; so, at least, he contrived to convince himself: and, moreover, he was positive that were his father as well assured of his virtuous resolutions as he was, the prohibition against giving rest to Joe Wilson's troubled soul would never have been spoken.

We will not follow the wayward Morris in his arguments against his sense of duty. Enough that they convinced him, or that he allowed himself to think they did.

Finally, the tenth night after the opening of our story, his brain whirling with uncontrollable desire, and fiercely banishing, in a fit of frenzied resolve, the better promptings of his nature, he hurried on his clothes without, as he thought, awaking his brother;

cautiously unlocked and unbarred the door of the house, and bounded over the threshold. He would not pause; onward he hastened.

The nearest path to the place he sought lay through the neighbouring church-yard, to gain which he had to cross a garden slightly enclosed, and an open field. As he approached the stile leading into the burial-ground, a large dun-coloured dog, which seemed to have been couched upon its steps, started up, and its red eyes glared into his. For an instant he paused terror-stricken; he had heard of evil spirits assuming, among other strange ones, such an appearance. But he soon sprang forward. The dog jumped into the church-yard, Morris vaulted over the stile, and stood sternly in the path, looking around him: but around him were only the tomb-stones, and the head-stones, and the little grassy mounds which covered the dead, —things to which he was by this time quite accustomed. The dog had vanished.

He paused awhile in the shade of his old friends the yew-trees, which were motionless, and black in the night, like gigantic plumes above a huge hearse. Holding his head daringly high, he sent a scrutinizing glance into every familiar nook and corner of the dreary place, but not a living or a moving thing was visible.

This, after the disappearance of the dog, must be considered as only a passing repetition of many former challenges to the ghosts of the whole mass of mouldering or mouldered mortality in the church-yard. Being on the spot, it was but right to give them, all and each, a renewed chance of availing themselves of his services. He soon held on, in his pursuit of the individual ghost which had lured him forth on the present occasion.

Bounding over the graves, and, now and then, boyishly vaulting over the head-stones, he stood on the stile that gave entrance to the burial ground, at the side opposite to that by which he had approached it. The next instant he was in Joe Wilson's bosheen.

This little green lane, lately become so celebrated, led, with many a curve, from one extremity of the suburbs to another. It was altogether lonely. Its breadth might be about four paces. Here and there it was overshadowed by trees; and bounded, at either hand, by hedges of sufficient growth to cast a gloom over it, even in day-light.

When Morris Brady jumped into this deep and solitary lane, he found that he was still at some distance from the middle, where Joe Wilson's murdered body had been found. The moon was on the wane; but, as the night had more than gained its noon, she stood high in the heavens. The sky was frosty-clear; and the cold light struck fully down upon the narrow way, shining brightly on the centre, and distinctly showing the broad stone and its indents; while, at either side, under the shadow of the overhanging hedges, although they were now nearly leafless, nothing could be perfectly distinguished.

A piece of wall, inserted into the mass of earth on which the hedges grew, to prop it up in that particular place, marked the spot where murder had lately been done; and on a broad stone in the wall, was, as we already know, a terrible memorial of the event. Nor had old Hesther Bonnetty exaggerated, when she avowed that the middle of the road, opposite to the wall, was yet uncleansed of blood. The dull-red stains were even till now distinctly visible in the line of brilliant moonshine, which, as we have said, ran along the centre of the bosheen.

As Morris Brady approached the well-known place, he did not fail to recognise the fatal tokens; and, notwithstanding the continued boldness of his advance, and all his previous audacity, he felt dread and awe stealing over his heart at the sight. Scarcely slackening his pace, however, he stood on the very spot—on the marks themselves. He did not, at once, turn his regards towards the wall. Yet a kind of stir without the accompaniment of noise, caught his side vision. He jumped fully round, and confronted the appearance; and there, bending over the remarkable stone, and too visible to leave a doubt of its presence—although, owing to the deep shade of the hedge above, somewhat indistinctly shaped forth—stood a human figure.

Morris's skin crept, in spite of him, as if in horror at the cold current now running beneath it. He took off his hat, crossed his forehead, and repeated aloud the names of the Trinity. The figure slowly raised its drooping head, and Morris saw the features of Joe Wilson—pallid, indeed, and strangely changed—yet still the man's well-known features: and again did the ghost-seer wince under the cold, unwinking, passionless, mindless, lifeless stare that was fixed upon him.

Suddenly his courage returned, or, rather, a daring determination re-nerved him, and in a wild and startling tone he exclaimed—

"In the most Holy Name, this night, I, Morris Brady, command you to tell me who and what you are."

There was a moment's dread pause; in which Morris heard the hollow beating of his own heart. A deep, but low voice replied to him, "The spirit of the man murthered on the spot where you stand."

" In the same name, once more, tell me what it is that puts throuble on you;" and now Morris's own voice sunk low.

" None dared to ask before ; and the dead must be silent till they are questioned."

" I know it—can I give rest to you ? "

" You can—if you have the heart to do it."

" I have the heart," answered Morris, his impetuosity returning ; " and what's not sinful I'll do, if living Christian has the power."

" Listen, then ; " and Morris conceived that the figure rose to more than mortal height ; " Listen—to-morrow night, as the clock sounds twelve, meet me in John's abbey church-yard, at the head of my own grave; on that spot meet me, or, Morris Brady, rue your challenge !"

As the last strangely-cadenced words died away, the figure, which had previously began to move, was no longer visible.

CHAPTER VII.

For a moment Morris stirred not. A great confusion of mind, though even yet unmixed with fear chained him to the spot. Suddenly he recovered himself, however, and bounded after the apparition, which had disappeared round a turning of the bosheen, a few paces from the wall. Clear of the turning, Morris's eye could follow a considerable portion of the length of the lane; but he saw no object in motion.

He became faint, and leaned against the fence of the bosheen for support, and it was some time before he could assume sufficient bodily strength to return home. He succeeded at length, however, in gaining his bed without discovery, but sleep was farther than ever from his eyes. "To-morrow night, in John's abbey church-yard," rang in his ears; he seemed to hear the words repeated in the silence of his hushed soul.

Although, during the next day, his conscience did not fail to upbraid him with his disobedience to his father; although he feared to encounter his father's ook, and fancied that the old man's mild eye was glancing severe reproach at him; still Morris would not recede from the self-sought adventure. A gloomy spell—a fate—seemed, to his own mind, to bind him to go on. Nor did he forget the last words: " on that spot meet me, or, Morris Brady, rue your challenge!" He had proceeded too far to return back: " returning were as dangerous as go o'er; "—and more so, Morris argued, inasmuch as to obey a ghost's commands had less of peril in it, than to brave its displeasure by disobeying them; particularly since the ghost-hunter had sought the interview, proposed the questions, and offered the services himself.

As the night drew on, his excitement attained a fearful height. Yet, when the silence of repose seemed to have fallen on every living thing, Morris felt urged to his fate by an impulse which he could not control; and, sometime before the last hour of night, he stood at the head of Joe Wilson's grave, beside the ruins of the old abbey.

The weather had changed during the day. It was a gloomy November night. The rain flew over the blackened sky; the wind came in gusts, heralding its approach by hollow moanings, which grew louder and louder as it advanced, until at last it swept hissing, and whistling, and roaring, through the mouldering, but beautiful arches of the ruin, beside which our adventurer paused. The seared leaves of the alders, and the other chance-sown trees that increased the gloom of the unroofed space within, rustled against each other as the gusts swept by; then their branches waved and rattled, casting the leaves in crispy showers to the ground: and then those which remained trembled as the blustering visitation passed away. The rushing river was not far off, and the noise of its waters filled up the pauses of the blast.

The moon, which had shone out so vividly the preceding night, as if to assist in luring Morris to his doom, now refused him a beam to cheer the darkness around, and, morally speaking, within him: for it was not surprising that a night like this, approaching its dread noon, should, in such a place, have a sympathetic effect on his distempered imagination. He stood, awaiting the striking of the hour of midnight, his head drawn back, his dark brows knitted together, his eyes flashing through the gloom in the interior of the old building, and his ear catching every sound in anticipation of the appearance of the being he had come to meet.

At length, the sonorous town-clock slowly began to toll twelve. Each vibration met an answering throb in Morris's bosom. He counted the last stroke, as it swung along the returning gust; and, an instant after started back, raising his hands before him in an attitude of intense and solemn wonder. It could not be the echoes of the ruin which returned that last clang so distinctly; no, it was the bell fixed in a mouldering steeple of the abbey, which never tolled save to welcome the dead to their homes within its precincts—Morris felt that the sound was produced by no mortal hand.

It had scarce died away, half suffocated by the wind, when he heard his name uttered within, in the same deep tones which had replied to his questions in the bosheen, on the previous night.

"I am here," he answered, in a voice scarcely less thrilling than that to which he responded.

"Enter the abbey," continued the unseen-one. Morris, collecting his firmness, bent his body to pass through a low, arched door-way, half choked up with rubbish and weeds. Standing to his full height, in the interior of the building, he scowled around him, and jerked his head from side to side, as was his fashion, when much excited. In those parts of the ruinous space around, which were not sunk in utter blackness, he could perceive nothing of the apparition of Joe Wilson.

"Your bidding is done," resumed Morris, after a pause; "I am standin' in the middle of the place."

"Stand at the head of the Prior's tomb," still commanded his invisible companion.

Morris endeavoured to ascertain the spot whence the voice came, but the careering gust seemed to bear it round and round the building.

He knew the Prior's tomb well. In his early boyhood, it had been one of the rallying points of his sports. Often had he and his companions contended for its possession, carrying on a small warfare, as if for a fortress; and often did their youthful shout ring above the ashes of the forgotten dignitary. Nay, often had the identical Joe Wilson, whose ghost now summoned Morris to a conference at the Prior's tomb, been one of the thoughtless rioters; and he was always the last who remained with Morris, when the evening row was over, seated on the crumbling and weed-hampered old monument, until the shades of night began to creep over the ruin; and here they would perseveringly excite each other's supernatural predilections—not fears—by the recital of the most approved and authentic tales of horror.

It was an oblong monument, raised against one of the walls of the old building: its sides were elaborately, if not elegantly, sculptured with figures of the Apostles; and upon its upper slab, the marble effigy of an ecclesiastic in his robes lay at full length as large as life, one arm extended at his side, the other crossing his breast, and holding a crucifix.

Notwithstanding the profound darkness of the corner in which it stood, Morris found no difficulty in occupying, at its head, the position named to him.

"Are you here with me to hold to your pledge?" resumed the voice.

"I am here with you to give you rest an' quiet if I can."

"The mortal man who questions the dead ought to hold a fearless heart; or woe be to him."

"My heart is sthrong," said the courageous though eccentric lad; yet he uttered the words with some effort; for the voice which spoke now seemed fearfully menacing.

"The secrets of the dead must be kept as close as the grave keeps their rotting bones; or treble woe on the betrayer's head."

"I'll guard the silent tongue."

"He who meets the dead, and challenges the dead, must obey the dead, or tenfold woe be to him."

"Morris Brady *will* obey the dead."

"Swear on oath! swear it to the dead!"

Morris hesitated.

"Swear!—or rue this night!—Swear!" It seemed to the young man as if mingling with the gust, the tones were re-echoed, in shrieks, through every corner of the ruin.

"I will swear to you!" he, in his turn, screamed forth, as he stamped his foot on the rubbish on which he stood.

"Lay your hand upon the Prior's head."

Morris grasped the figure; but instead of touching, at the point where he expected to find it, the marble head of the effigy, his fingers passed over the front of a skull; he felt the eye-holes, and the nasal orifice, and that for the mouth. He recoiled an instant, but sufficiently recovered himself to replace his hand on the disagreeable object.

" Swear by the soul of him who has been murthered! Swear by your own soul! Swear by the darkness of the night! and swear by every spirit that hearkens to the oath—to be silent—and to obey the dead!"

" I swear ! " and Morris again spoke in a shout, and as if some will other than his own had moved his tongue.

" Follow me, now," continued the voice ; and, as it ceased, the figure of the bosheen glided through the low arch-way into the burial ground without.

Morris sprang after it. The apparition passed into an adjacent street of the town, by a turn-stile at the boundary of the church-yard, and, with noiseless step, hurried on.

CHAPTER VIII.

Mr. Barnaby Roundhead was a " protestant settler" in the good city in which, with its environs, the scene of our tale is laid. The explanation of this term, " protestant settler," involves the necessity for a page or two of local history.

It is known that James the Second, like the wisehead he always proved himself to be, re-modelled the corporate charters of almost all the cities throughout Ireland; in consequence of which catholicism for some time wore the mitre with a higher head, and the mayor of our city was seen at mass in his official costume. But James could not win the battle of the Boyne, and so away he went to Saint Germains, and away, also, went the political existence of the religion he had tried (in our modest opinion) to scandalize, by unnaturally connecting it with political power and pompous display. That no evil chance may ever confer on it the favours he failed in perpetuating to it, is our honest and hearty prayer.

But to our purpose. Catholic dignitaries of every kind participated, of course, in the fate of the ecclesiastical ones. James had scarcely left the kingdom, whose blind fidelity to him he knew so little how to value, when our good mass-going mayor, and his brother aldermen, with all their underlings, were compelled to retire from office, leaving their places to be filled by a nobler race; and then was poor James's charter laid aside, and that of his namesake, James the First, revived in all its glory.

This charter had been cunningly devised for the utter and speedy extirpation of popery. Amongst other clauses, with this view, it provided that, after a short time of residence, all " protestant settlers" should be entitled to the freedom of the city, no matter whence they came, or who or what they where. The result was, that good and true men dropped in, year after year, from England, Scotland, and the province of Ulster, many of them not arriving in a very dashing style; which is to say, that their habiliments were not, perhaps, exactly new, nor their one pair of shoes much the better of the wear and tear of a long journey. No matter: though no prophets in their own country, they possessed, in their creed, a good patent of gentility among the popish natives of our city, now gnashing their teeth in secret, under the overwhelming degradations of the penal statutes of William and of Anne.

Persons of the older stock could not be expected to regard those new-comers with a very favourable eye. In truth, though compelled to bow before their superiors in public, they indulged against them, in private, a very respectable portion of loathing and abhorrence. Ridicule, always so formidable a weapon in true Hibernian hands, afforded partial vent to their smothered ire; and, in conversation with some of the descendants of these malcontents, we have ourselves been entertained by a ridiculous kind of nomenclature of the "settlers;" although, had the speakers traced back their own names to their roots, they might have found matter for a similar description of commentary upon them also.

But, according to our bitter critics, you could find, among the new arrivals, Whacks, Straps, Sharps, and Blunts; and Nailors and Tailors, and Weavers and Carpenters, none of whom followed the occupations described by their names; and Whiteheads with black hair, and Blackpoles with red hair; and Tom's son, and Dick's son, and Jack's son — names which sounded as if the fathers of those to whom they appertained, had stood in such a relative situation towards their offspring, as not to think them worthy of a paternal appellation at full length, "or as if they had never been baptized in a christian manner, but had a name thrown at them as you would throw it at a dog:" and then there was Whittle, and Spittle, and Nosey, and Posey—and these, and similarly euphonous titles, the satirists would tag into lampoons; while for further game to hunt down, they had Deers, Harts, Hares, Rabbits, and Woodcocks.

Amongst the rest, at the time of our tale, flourished Mr. Barnaby Roundhead—and he was "a settler." Whence he had come, like Lara's page, he never told. That he could not be English, however, his accent proclaimed. At his first arrival in our city he was pennyless, nor did he profess any distinct calling. He supported himself, as well as he could, by doing anything he was asked to do, and of which his limited intelligence was capable, by his predecessors in the privileged town, who had already reaped the advantage of their legal superiority.

By degrees, however, he got on. He was a grave

little man, wearing a passionless, harmless face, and of devout demeaour at church; which qualities recommended him to the situation of clerk, as soon as the office became vacant. A certain wealthy grocer, of his own fortunate creed, and who had once been as humble in circumstances as himself, fixed a favourable eye on Barnaby; tried him as an errand-boy; found him trust-worthy and industrious, precise and discreet; initiated him into the mysteries of serving at the counter; and finally adopted him as his confidant, and—himself waxing as fat as he was rich, and therefore somewhat inclined to repose from labour—Barnaby became chief manager of the business of this monied man.

The grocer died suddenly, and without offspring; not having long enjoyed the dignified leisure he had proposed to himself. Barnaby Roundhead married his widow; gave up his clerkship at church, the salary of which, together with that allowed to him by his late master, he had almost entirely saved; and was now the head and owner of a profitable concern, and daily adding to its capital. Indeed, by mere and sheer economy, nay, penury, rather than by any cleverness as a merchant, he became eventually possessed of great wealth, and, without knowing how to write his name, grew into an alderman, under the beneficent charter of James the First, of unpedantic, and happy memory.

Mrs. Roundhead's first husband had been a portly, ostentatious man, whose sway was absolute at his own fireside. The good woman, grievously enslaved during his lifetime, selected Barnaby for a second trial, because, from her observation of his character, she knew him to be the very antipodes of the man she had tried before him. Passive, creeping, and subservient in all his actions and demeanour, it was quite plain, she argued, that he would be to her the same noiseless, pains-taking drudge he had been to her deceased tyrant; and that with him for a yoke-fellow, she should live in peace, plenty, and independence, during the remainder of her life.

But the bride soon found that of two husbands of totally different dispositions and manners, each may arrive at the same point of plaguing his spouse, though by very distinct approaches. During his master's lifetime, Barnaby Roundhead had been frequently applied to by his then mistress for certain pecuniary aid for her privy purse. He had not failed to gratify her reasonable demands; nor would it be a sin against charity to hint, that he might occasionally have done a little for himself in the same way. After his marriage he recollected all this; nay, we strongly suspect that he thought the matter over, at the very moment the connubial knot was tied. At all events, no sooner was he legally installed lord and master of his old mistress, and of all unto her appertaining and belonging, than he took good measures not only to protect himself against a repetition of her secret depredations, but to bring back into the firm of the house whatever amount of her savings might now prove to be in existence.

From his bridal couch, at break of day, up rose Barnaby Roundhead. Having noiselessly attired himself, he stole his wife's keys, rummaged her drawers from top to bottom, and from bottom to top; crept like a ferret into every hole and corner of the habitation; and before the good dame awoke from her dream of future indolence and independence, had secured whatever coin she possessed, and every other valuable he could lay hands on, and locked them up in a little closet, previously prepared for the purpose, with bolts and bars of treble strength.

Mrs. Roundhead was terrified at these symptoms; and still more so at the sight of the miserable meal which Barnaby had provided for their morning repast. This, however, was only the beginning of her troubles. When she first approached the till, after her marriage, her little husband ran squeaking to her, pushed her back, dancing on his heels, pretending to tear his hair, and whimpering, as soon as she began to expostulate with him. In fact, though not without great difficulty, he got her out of the shop, and never allowed her to re-enter it.

From morning to night he watched with ceaseless assiduity, lest human eye should glance upon his day's earnings; and when the time came to lock up, and bar and bolt his shop for the day, and when he had locked, barred, and bolted it, Barnaby hastened, with the utmost trepidation, to secure the last scrapings in his innermost den. His wife, naturally a timid woman, found that opposition to his proceedings was quite useless. He did not, indeed, bluster and look big, and shake the house with his stentorian mandates, like her former good man: but then, if at all thwarted in his measures, he whimpered, and scratched behind his ears, and tramped with his feet, and kept that up, until, for bare peace-sake, she was obliged to give way. Mrs. Roundhead, by her feminine bending to the storm, had escaped unhurt during her first marriage; nay, had weathered it, with her own small cargo of money, safe and sound; but here was a little being whom she had raised to share her whole wealth, only, it appeared, that he might hold it all to himself, and growl over it with the tenacity of a cat clutching her prey. Penny by penny he doled out to her the pittance absolutely necessary to sustain nature ; but any indulgence beyond that was altogether out of the question.

After a reasonable time spent in lamentations over her unimproved fate, she began to look around her for the best means of enduring it. Mrs. Roundhead recollected her sensible proceedings, with Barnaby's help, against her first despot; and now she thought she would try something of the same kind on Barnaby's self, without any assistant save her woman's wit, and a tolerably clever blacksmith. She knew that he was no accomptant : that as he could not write, and had as yet no shopman, he kept no figured minutes whatever of his money; and that, so limited, so imbecile was his order of mind, he could not even count his guineas, beyond the number of ten or twelve, and then keep the amount in his head. She knew, in fact, that he adjusted this matter by measuring his gold and silver, by the half-pint, the noggin, or the pint; so that it would not be difficult to purloin, if the affair were managed cautiously, a guinea or two at a time,—provided access to the treasure could be gained. A master-key soon effected this preparatory point; and Mrs. Roundhead began, little by little, to appropriate some of her own money, and hoard in her turn.

These details will hereafter be found useful in conducting our true history to an end.

A year after this marriage, the good dame presented Barnaby with a daughter. At first this circumstance by no means expanded the griping heart of the father;

but, as the baby grew up, and as her young beauties and innocent smiles beamed upon him, there was, in her single regard, some relaxation of his miserable nature. Upon more than one occasion, after having twisted and turned between his fingers a new halfpenny, he was known to bestow it on little Patty; and her influence over him increased so surprisingly as she advanced in years, that at length he would enrich her with a shilling in the week, an act of liberality amply sufficient, in his esteem, to demonstrate the strength of his affection. Barnaby did, in truth, love the little Patty; that is, he gave her all the love he could spare from his money; and, though it went grievously against the grain, he bestowed upon her as good an education as her native city could afford, as well in what were considered accomplishments as in sterling acquirements.

Two years before the commencement of our tale, Mrs. Roundhead left her little Barnaby a widower. The expenses of the funeral touched him to the quick, and he gained credit for a sorrow after the dead, which was bestowed on his departed guineas. At the present period of our story, we would describe Barnaby Roundhead as a dwindled, wrinkled, care-worn little being; his eyes far sunk in his head, and half puckered up with the wrinkles known by the name of " crow'sfeet ;" his jaws hollow; his mouth pursed into a very trifling orifice ; and his nose enlarged in proportion to the decrease of his other features so much, that, with a slight stretch of fancy to eke out the reality, his face might be said to terminate in a beak. His unvaried attire bespoke extreme misery. A little sharply pointed three-cocked hat, shining, not with the gloss of newness, but of constant handling, sat on a whitish full bottomed wig, worn and ragged. He wore an outside Kersey coat, found in the wardrobe of the former lord of the tenement,—" a world too wide" for the withered little body it now encased; and this was fastened close under his chin, and descended to his heels. His shoes might vie with the famed pantofles of Mustapha; and he could boast three pairs of pied hose, to keep which together had been the constant care of his deceased spouse, whose neglect of them would have produced a woful fit of whining, tramping, and pulling at his ears. The superintendence of these articles of his dress was now in the hands of his daughter Patty, who successfully managed to keep one, at least, of the things he wore, clean and in good order.

His daughter was now in her eighteenth year—a timid, fluttering creature, all heart, and that heart soft and milky, and thrilling to every call upon its sensibilities. Her frame was aërial—resembling the female shape spiritualized; and in each gentle, willowy, graceful motion, there was something so touchingly feminine and helpless, that she seemed to claim support from every one who beheld her. The meek expression of her countenance supported eloquently this appeal for sympathy and protection, and savage indeed must have been the nature which could breathe roughly on such a flower. Her blue eye glanced tenderly and apprehensively; her pale cheek was dimpled; her lips were vermillion red, dewy, glistening, and always parted, and in tremulous motion; her light brown hair, of a gossamer delicacy, fell in shining ringlets on her shoulders; the blue veins were pencilled, minutely but distinctly, on her neck and temples; and the slightest emotion brought the blood in such a torrent to her cheeks, that it seemed ready to burst, like the juice from a grape, through the delicate transparency of her skin.

In this place we have but one word more to add of Patty. She was the loving and beloved friend of Rose Brady.

CHAPTER IX.

Some people may think the former chapter a digression from the main business of our story. We assure them, however, they are mistaken; and we add, that it is absolutely necessary to submit yet another chapter—a very short one, though—of new matter, before we can take up the broken thread of our narrative.

Fifty years ago, the city in which Barnaby and his fair and gentle daughter resided, was, amongst other remarkable things, distinguished as the theatre of action of a knot of young bloods, who avowedly associated together for the enactment of all the daring and desperate pranks which ingenuity could devise, and wickedness execute. They were, generally speaking, the descendants of the "settlers," who had arrived at wealth and local rank and place under favour of the city charter and of the popish penal laws, before mentioned. Of course, near connexions of theirs, or else near and dear friends of such, filled all the posts of civic and legal authority: hence, their wild and fearful practices met with little check; indeed, while the idle and disorderly of inferior grade—or creed—might, perhaps, have been punished readily enough, the young daredevils of whom we speak ran their course almost with impunity.

In candour, we must however say, that many of their acts gave their elderly relations great concern, and that private cautions and admonitions were abundantly bestowed upon them. But these young bloods only laughed at the greybeards, and their demon-like pranks went on; until at length the band became so formidable, that no peaceable citizen dared appear abroad, at their hour of nightly rule, when, full of wine and of every kind of lusty wickedness, they were prepared to go to any lengths dictated by fancy, or unbridled passion.

A cross-grained old man, who, perhaps, for that especial qualification, had been employed to collect the toll at " the custom-gap," was one night thrown over the bridge into the river, through the clear waters of which his body became visible next morning; and it was confidently whispered about, that some of the worthies of the " hell-fire club," as they rejoicingly stiled themselves, had been the murderers. No vigorous investigation was legally instituted; and this confirmed the rumour.

The prime leader—the arch-fiend of this knot of daring offenders—was the same Joe Wilson, whose ghost now haunted the *bosheen*, and in company with which, or at least close in his train, we have seen Morris Brady leave the ruins of John's abbey.

Joe Wilson had been nephew to Mrs. Roundhead— her brother's only son. The mortal terror of our city was he, before his sudden departure out of it. At all hours of the night, his drunken yell was heard through the streets, and at the sound, masters of houses arose to ascertain that doors and windows were well secured, and virtuous little maidens crossed themselves, and trembled in their beds. Away and along he scampered, like an incarnate devil, his awful bludgeon levelling every one who opposed him. As a duellist, in the day-light, he went beyond all panegyric; for although he broke the heads of persons of vulgar degree with a suitably vulgar weapon, yet any offence to his dignity perpetrated by " a gentleman"—which title he was pleased to apply to himself also—produced a challenge, and, before the opening of our story, he had most honourably put to death four of his fellow-creatures: for deadly was Joe Wilson's aim.

He was a very handsome young scoundrel; and on this account alone—if we except the overpowering impudence of his address—his conquests among the fair sex, of every rank, had been as numerous as his triumphs over his own. Never was he known to turn from his object, when once started in pursuit of it, no matter what obstacles presented themselves.

His father had left him wealthy; but Joe Wilson was as careless of money as he was of everything else, and it melted away from him. We believe that since his glorious time, there has not been such a thing as a gaming-table in any country-town in Ireland; but one of those pests of society did exist in our poor city, at the period of which we are speaking. In truth, the comforts of the gentle youths of the " hell-fire club " would have been imperfect without that appendage. And, as it soon became generally known that our Joey had dashed through his patrimony like a man, and yet, that his expenditure was as lavish as ever, some, if not many, there were, who suspected him to be in a fair way of honestly earning the title of black-legs.

Joe had arrived at the highest pinnacle of wicked

eminence, when his body was found, stiff and cold, in the bosheen ; and if the outrages previously committed by him on others had been passed over, so also, we are bound in candour to own, was the injury inflicted on himself, at the hands of some rival or rivals in the art of knocking people on the head. No trouble was taken to discover his murderers, who had so mutilated his features, that it was by the colour of his hair, his dress, his linen, and the contents of his pockets alone, that his body could be identified.

In truth, his friends and relations scarcely regretted being thus rid of him. Many of the latter he had laid under contribution, since the loss of his own property ; and they had expected a repetition of his blackmail, and dreaded to refuse it, because they dreaded him.

Portions of a woman's dress were found near his body : and it was generally supposed that he had justly forfeited his turbulent life in the act of insulting one of the other sex, whose protector was able and willing to guard his charge, and revenge her wrong, even to a dreadful excess, into the bargain.

Finally, it could not be said that Joe Wilson's death was much lamented even by his own companions, to whom he had lately become formidable ; and (although the communicators forgot that, out of a certain place, to which in their hearts they doomed him, " there is no redemption,") it was little matter of wonder in the shop of Paddy Naddy, the bad barber, that the ghost of such a wicked fellow should be wandering and unquiet, and still bent on mischief.

And so ends our chapter—a very short one, as we promised it should be.

CHAPTER X.

AND so again we are now free; that is, as far as we can at present see our way before us—to go on in a more straight-forward manner with our history.

The blast which roared and blustered round Morris Brady's head, and that of the ghost of Joe Wilson, amid the ruins of John's Abbey, was making a great uproar, at the very same moment of the night, in the chimney and at the window-shutters of the sleeping-chamber of Rose Brady's little friend, the daughter and only child of Alderman Barnaby Roundhead, grocer, and late clerk of St. Mary's.

Upon a pallet, at the foot of Patty's bed, reposed Ailleen Morrisay, her occasional lady-woman, and maid of all work to her father: and Ailleen's heavy breathing, occasionally changing into a more sonorous sound, told plainly that the god of sleep had bound her to her pallet with the strongest fetters he could select from his store.

As for the gentle Patty, one of her fair arms was thrown over her head; the other, devoid of covering, lay upon the outside of the bed, its little hand convulsively grasping the counterpane; her voice murmured most melancholy music, and tears stole from under her long-lashes, and ran down her pale cheeks.

Suddenly she changed her position, and ceased her murmurings. Her arms were extended forward; then they dropt down, as if struck with paralysis; and, uttering a faint scream, Patty started up, sitting in her bed fully awake, and looking fearfully around her.

"God protect me!" she softly ejaculated, pressing together the palms of her little hands, and resting her head upon them—"And was it only a dream? oh, what a dreadful one! Yet, terrific as he looked, and although I wept and shuddered to gaze upon him, I wish—I wish I had not awoke to my real suffering! Oh, I wish I could fall asleep, and never, never waken—not even for the judgment-day. No, no—not for that! Oh, that the grave were my only bed, and—Father of mercies, forgive me for the thought—that there were no sense or recollection in it or beyond it!"

The tears flowed plentifully, as she raised her head, and pressed her hands against her fluttering bosom.

She started. A slight noise had reached her ear. After a pause of great alarm, she sank down heavily on her bed, and drew the covering upward, as if for concealment. She held her breath and listened. "'Tis there again," she whispered, so faintly, and with such sickly fear, that her spirit seemed dissolved within her.

A fierce blast swept across the house-top, eddied down the chimney, and, with the aid of the quantity of soot it drove before it, succeeded in extinguishing the candle which lay on the hearthstone.

" Good heaven guard me!" muttered the unhappy girl: darkness, in the depth of night, brought tenfold agonies to her usually waking eye, and shattered nerves, and breaking heart. She called to Ailleen; but Ailleen's unaltered breathing gave no sign of intelligence. " Oh, if *I* could sleep so soundly!" moaned the poor Patty.

The noise occurred again, and again she called to Ailleen, in her loudest tone; in one, indeed, rendered almost frantic by terror. But Ailleen heard her not.

Trembling in every joint, and her teeth chattering, she half arose from her bed, but once more sank down, as her apprehensive ear caught the sounds which had twice before broken the silence of the night. Not until after many efforts could she again venture to sit up; but her great fear of the darkness and the loneliness became unendurable; and she at last succeeded in gaining the floor, and groping and creeping to the pallet of her attendant.

"Ailleen, Ailleen!" she whispered, grasping the shoulder of the somniferous girl: and Ailleen, remotely conscious of being touched, muttered through her sleep—" Lave! lave, now, Jim!—lave, I tell you!"

" 'Tis I, Ailleen—'tis I! oh, waken, waken!" petitioned the shivering Patty.

" *Minawyay*, Jim!—take off, you bould rogue! take off, I bid you!" again raved the drowsy Ailleen, as she half-felt a second appeal at her shoulder.

" Ailleen, good girl, waken for heaven's sake!" was softly breathed at her very ear.

" Och, an' why not, misthrause, it's comin'!" was answered in a voice which startled our timid Patty; and the stout-built Ailleen bounced from one side of her pallet to the other, and fumbled with her hands, as if searching for something—" Ullaloo !" she continued, in a lower key," " where on the livin' earth, did it walk to ?—an' it's a wondher what does the poor young misthrause want wid you, for one smoothin'-iron? You'd be looking sthraight in a body's face, if we did'nt want you. It's comin', misthrause!"—as if bawling from the kitchen up to the parlour—" it's takin' its time, bud it's comin'!"

Ailleen roared so loudly, that the sound of her own voice almost wholly broke the spell of deep sleep which was upon her; and—" God mark my sowl wid grace, what's that, will anybody tell me?" she cried in great trepidation, feeling herself pushed again:—" An' where am I, an' no candle lighted—an' what's come acrass me at all?"

" It is I, Ailleen—it is I,"—answered her mistress.

" Arra, aye; is id the misthrause you are, Miss Patty?"

" Yes, Ailleen, yes—and I have had such a terrible dream!" she stooped her lips to the girl's ear, and continued in the lowest whisper—" I dreamed that the ghost stood over me in his blood, and stretched out his arms, and wanted to snatch me to him"—and she leaned her forehead on the solidly round shoulder of Ailleen, and the naturally compassionate creature felt her mistress's warm tears flowing abundantly over it.

" The ghost, misthrause! the ghost *a-chorra!* ugha—ugha"—Ailleen shuddered to her very marrow. " Och, an' where's the wondher for a shiverin' o' could to be comin' all over you *musha!* If such a misfortinate thing found its way into my own head, instid o' the mighty pleasant dhrames that was botherin' the brains out o' me, you'd find it asy enough to take the sleep off o' my four bones!—bud, misthrause dear, don't be lamentin' yourself so bitther—don't *a-cuishla-ma-chree* – don't *a-lanna !* " With the tenderest commiseration, she wound her brawny arms round the weeping Patty; " don't be frettin yourself to a natomy, I tell you, my own darlint misthrause; an' sit down wid me now, an' I'll say a hanful o' nice prayers that'll do for us both, an' has the vartue o' banishin' anything wicked;" and Ailleen began her fervid orisons.

" Listen! listen, Ailleen! was there not a noise in the lobby?" interrupted Patty.

" Oh-a! oh-a! misthrause. I'd give you a guinea in ould goold, an' don't say that!" and Ailleen unceremoniously clung to her mistress, and, indifferent to the companionship, her mistress clung to her, as if there were certain safety in participated danger; and thus they remained for some moments, the galloping pulsations of their hearts keeping exact time, as they pressed against each other.

" All is silent, now,"— whispered Patty, at last raising her head.

"'An' lade us not into timptation'—no, there's not a mouse stirrin' now, misthrause dear—' bud deliver us from evil, amin!'" answered Ailleen.

Again they listened intently; the continued silence somewhat re-assured them.

" Wid the blessin' o' heaven, an' may be the wind is to be blamed for id, misthrause darlint," observed Ailleen.

" Oh, I hope so, Ailleen—but in this darkness I cannot live! the candle has been put out by the blast down the chimney; and will you, my good girl, light it again at the red turf in the kitchen grate?"

"Aye, indeed; an' so I *would* give it, for he— any way at all but to the ghost," strangely replied Ailleen, after starting, and then indulging in a solemn pause.

"Give what, Ailleen?"

"The life that's in my body, misthrause *a-chorra!* an' why not, on your arrand: bud heaven above only knows if mortial eye 'ud ever see the size of a bee's knee o' me, if the ghost found me night walkin' out o' my vartuous bed, this hour o' the night; don't, now, misthrause honey, don't ax me to thramp down to the kitchen."

"The terror will kill me, then, before morning dawns. I cannot outlive this night!"

"Never give ear to a word o' that, *a-lanna;* wait, an' you'll see that we'll both bounce up at daylight, safe an' sound, an' as merry as any two rogues o' sparrows that ever hopped."

"Oh, Ailleen! the darkness is horrible to me!"

"Well, poor crature, I b'lieve you're bad enough; an' there's only one thing for id, afther all; myself would'nt know your little finger to have an ache in id, if Ailleen could cure id; so I'll go, misthrause, I'll go an' light the candle for you; an' I hope the Lord 'ill have marcy on my poor, sinful sowl, whatever comes o' the rest o' me."

And Ailleen arose, heroically wrapt some covering round her, and groped towards the hearthstone for the candle; not, however, without having many of the iciest pangs of mortal fear.

"I have it, misthrause; and I'am goin'; and the heavens be your safeguard till I come back to you, if it's a thing I ever lay livin' eyes on you, again; so luck an' grace be round you, an' about you."

"Stop, Ailleen," cried Patty, suddenly starting up; "I am too selfish, my good girl, to send you alone, to face danger which I ought to share with you at least; besides, I could not stay here alone in the darkness, so we will go together."

"No, misthrause dear, stay where you are; just rowl yourself into a *grawnage*,* my darlint, an' hide your head undher the clothes, an' if there's no more than half a leg left hangin' from my poor body, I'll be back to you agin, like any race-horse."

Patty was determined.

"*Haen-hanna* † then, *a-cuishla*; come then, an' *chrossa-christha* be our guard this night;" she made the sign of the cross first on her own forehead, and then on that of her mistress; "we'll venthure, now, *a-lanna*."

Arm in arm, they left the chamber, clinging together, and starting and gasping at every step. They descended without injury to the kitchen.

"You often heard, misthrause," joked Ailleen, when, after she had succeeded in lighting her candle by blowing hard, on her hands and knees, at the sod of red turf left in the kitchen grate, they were now ascending to the hall of the house—"You often heard what them rogues o' boys says on the head o' keepin' up a bould heart—'faint heart,' says they, 'never won fair lady,'—an', faix, to spake plain thruth, it's bould enough they are, in regard o' that same sayin'; an' so, misthrause, the worst is now past an' gone, an' we'll soon be snug in our nests agin; an'—Och! marcy to my misfortunate sowl! what's that?"

This break in her discourse was caused by feeling

---

* Hedgehog. † Be it so.

her mistress suddenly press her arm. Looking into Patty's face, she saw her staring with terrified eyes up the staircase which they were about to ascend from the hall. Ailleen glanced fearfully in the same direction.

"Did you not hear a soft tread above?" questioned Patty, in a whisper so low, that Ailleen's "devouring ear" could scarcely catch it.

No, aroon, no,"—this answer was querulously pronounced—" we'll make our way, in the name o' God, this night."

They ascended the stairs, Patty shivering, and almost stupified. The door of their apartment was within a step of them.

"Didn't I tell you right, misthrause dear? Here we are again."

They turned into their asylum, but recoiled as soon as they had done so; for, at the further end of the room, somewhat obscured in the shadow, stood a tall figure, stooping over Patty's couch, its features invisible from the bent position of the head. They did not, could not utter a cry—a sound, so complete was their paralysis of terror; their breath was suspended; while their distended eyes remained fixed on their unexpected visitor. The figure raised its head, and the two girls distinctly recognised the features of Joe Wilson; not blood-stained, as Patty's recent dream had pictured, but clayey pale, and mournful as the grave.

Poor Patty gazed on the apparition, as if, without an act of the will, her nature sought the certainty, the unquestionable presence of the object she beheld: then uttering a low, heart-breaking wail, she fell senseless upon the ground.

Ailleen had been spell-bound from the first glance; transformed to stone she indeed seemed to be, although her robust nerves would not allow her to faint, or be deprived of all power of observation. The apparition moved towards her; she dropped on her knees, hoarsely shrieking, and, with shut eyes, held her face flat to the floor, with precisely the same feelings with which a coward would lay his head on the block, sure of the coming blow. But no hurt nor harm did Ailleen receive; and after a sufficiently long pause, she ventured to look up, and around her. The apparition of Joe Wilson had passed out of the chamber.

As if by a sudden impulse of frenzy, she now jumped upright, put the candle on a table, shut the door with a bang, locked and bolted it; dragged chairs and a heavy trunk, and placed them against it; and then snatched up her prostrate mistress, and bore her to her own pallet; and, finally, with an explosive sob, Ailleen sank down by her side exhausted.

She was aroused from her state of stupor by such a tumult of sounds as nearly deprived her of reason: and now was Ailleen's position and expression the *beau-ideal* of agonized terror. She sat up, her knees crippled into her chest, the knuckles of both her hands locked into each other, and, being thus joined, pressed against her chin; her eyes rolling, without the power of vision; her whole frame palsied; and the cold dew oozing from every pore.

There was a tramping of feet along the lobby without; there were loud voices in fierce contention; there were the jostling and dragging of a deadly struggle. Ailleen decided in her own mind that all the churchyards of the city and its vicinity had yielded up their dead, and that legions of ghosts shook the house with the horrid din. Notwithstanding her conviction to this effect—if the most confused and shattered conception could be so called—she soon, however, became aware that the voice of her living master, Barnaby Roundhead, mingled with the uproar; and presently she recognised that of a person more dear to her; namely, Jem, her fellow-servant, upon whom her dreams had been running, when her mistress succeeded in awakening her from her sufficiently profound sleep.

Joe Wilson's ghost, then, with many of its friends, was maltreating her master, and, more particularly, ill-using her lover. She had not previously uttered the slightest sound; now she drew in her breath, in a long preparatory manner, and sent it forth again unwilled, in a shriek so tremendous and enduring, that, if really directed against the dead, even them it might have appalled, and sent scampering back to their lawful tenements. When she had finished, horror at the consequences, to herself, of this almost unconscious manifestation of sympathy for the sufferers, took possession of Ailleen's breast. She bounced up from beside the still insensible Patty, and, because it was a little farther from the door, darted into the bed of the latter with the celerity of a chased rabbit into his burrow, and there buried herself, head and all, in the covering—her mistress being momentarily forgotten in her desire to save herself from something scarcely short of annihilation.

Lying as still as the shaking of her body permitted, Ailleen's ears were yet wide open; and, after a manner, she continued to follow up her observations.

The voices and the struggling increased in loudness, then became more faint, and then died away; a clapping of doors followed, to which silence a second time succeeded.

A faint and most melancholy moan from her own pallet reached her, although with difficulty, through the dense mass of blankets, sheets, and counterpanes, under which Ailleen lay ensconced. Recollection, and with it, dread remorse, now assailed her heart. She groaned loudly in answer, and, regaining her mistress's side, ejaculated—"Och hone! the heavens crown me wid holy forgiveness this black night—an' that it ever will or can, is what I'm wondherin' at!—Oh, the poor, poor misthrause!"

"Ailleen! is it gone?"

"Whist, whist, *a-lanna ma-chree*—spake so asy, that it 'll go hard wid me to hear you"

"Is it gone, I say? Oh, I could not again look upon it, and live one instant! Tell me, Ailleen; are its stony eyes now fixed on us! whisper in my ear, and tell me!"

Ailleen, again, contagiously horrified, readily brought to mind, that, notwithstanding her locking, bolting, and otherwise fortifying the door, the ghost either might have re-entered with the greatest ease through the key-hole, or perhaps not have passed out at all, though she thought it had; and thus she replied to her mistress, again hiding her head:

"Afther your words, misthrause, I wouldn't look if you ped me."

"Just one glance, Ailleen—only one, if you would not have me die, this instant, at your side."

"In the holy name of all that's good, I'll go by the misthrause's bidden," at length consented Ailleen.

She again uncovered her head; first gave a fitful glance, and quickly withdrew her eyes, to provide against danger: then allowed herself a wider range of vision; a second time recoiled, gained a little courage, and finally succeeded in gazing round the whole apartment. And oh! then came the blessed relief of a lengthened inspiration, half sigh, half moan.

"It does watch you?" faintly asked Patty.

"Daddy-honey! an' where is it?"

"You do not see it, then?"

"No, *a-cuishla*—but do you?"

Gradually they became convinced that they were alone in their chamber, and their paroxysm of terror began to subside.

"Ailleen, I feel my heart sicker and fainter than ever; the death stroke has in reality come at last."

"Howld yourself up, my poor sowl, an' don't say that sorrowful word to Ailleen."

"The look of the dead *has* called me; oh, I feel it, I feel it!"

"If my prayers, mornin', noon, an' night, can save you to me, misthrause, you'll live to become an ould, shaky, grey-head, widout a tooth to crunch a crust in id. Bud, sure the ghost behaved himself dacent an' purty to us, poor cratures that we are—not all the same as wid the poor ould masther an' my poor Jim—the Lord be marciful to the both!"

"What do you say of my father, Ailleen?"

"Ah, then, sure enough, now that I think of it, the faint was over you, an' you never hard them divvle's doins—God, an' others, too, forgive me, for callin' 'em by so bad a name this night!"—Fear of the consequences of her profanity chastened Ailleen's tongue.

"I am ill, and not able to bear suspense, Ailleen; tell me, at once, what has happened to my father!"

"The heavens pity id, poor soul! the heavens pity id! When I come to my siven sinses, *a-lanna*, there was the terribliest, oh! the terribliest noise, just beyond the threshold o' the door, that ever my eyes opened on; the ghost had the poor masther by the nape o' the neck, an' another o' them had my poor Jim by the scruff o' the head; an' they were knockin' 'em agin the wall, my *lanna;* an' they were screechin', my *graw;* an' every screech ran thro' the poor heart that's inside o' my body, like so many sharp soords, 'till it's tore into babby rags, every born inch of id; an' thin I hard the ghosts draggin' the poor masther, an' poor Jim, down the stairs, an' haulin' of 'em out thro' the sthreet dour; an' I hard 'em roarin' in the sthreet, beggin' for marcy, 'till you'd feel pity for 'em if you were a pavin' stone, let alone a tindher-hearted Christhen; an' then I hard their lamentations, goin' away thro' the farmament, till the both went beyant my power o' hearin'."

"Hush—is not that my father's voice through the house this moment?" asked Patty.

"Oh, glory be on high! they're sthreelin' thro' the house, once agin!—Oh, Jim, Jim—the heavens lend you a helpin' hand, this heavy an' sorrowful night!"

They both struggled with the audible beating of their hearts, and listened eagerly. The voice of Barnaby Roundhead was indeed heard, raised to a piercing cry of anguish, and, according to his usual practice, when vexed, he danced about on his heels, and clapped his hands: all of which sounds the two bewildered listeners interpreted into the most horrible supernatural tumult. He drew near to Patty's chamber, keeping up his wailing and its accompaniments, and now calling out her name; this somewhat re-assured her; he stopped at the door, and knocked loudly, still invoking her; she and Ailleen put questions to him, of which the purport was to ascertain if he was alone, and no ghost at his heels; and having received satisfactory answers, Ailleen, blessing heaven at every step, got out of bed, removed her barricade, unbolted and unlocked the door; and Barnaby Roundhead, quite alone indeed, danced into the apartment.

CHAPTER XI.

THE miserable little old man seemed scarcely to know where he was, although he had so loudly called for admission into his daughter's chamber. Without a sign of recognition, he continued to tramp up and down the middle of the room, and to clap his hands, and whimper and wail, and scream out, as he said, "Woe to me this night! oh, sorrowful is this night! penny by penny I saved it! penny by penny I scraped for it! and 'tis gone, gone, gone from me!"

"Father, dear father, what troubles you?" asked Patty.

"A rifled and plundered ould man! a beggar in my ould age! Oh! oh! oh!" And he raised his voice, and increased his antics, to a piteous excess.

"Father, wo'nt you tell me what is the matter?"

He hurried over to her bed-side; he sat upon a chair; he contracted every wrinkle to a double expression of woe; his fingers crippled, and his head and hands shook with a palsy of grief and wrath, as he squeaked forth: "May a curse wither the arm that rifled me! Eight naggins o' the goold — four pints o' the silver! —all, all taken from me!"

A loud knocking at the street-door interrupted his querulous fury. Seeming to have expected the summons, he started up, snatched the candle he had brought in with him, and in feeble speed hurried out of the room, and along the lobby, and down stairs, screaming to the person he concluded was at the hall-door—

"Force him to yield up my goold! my goold an' my silver likewise! force him to yield it up, or take his life for it!"

For elucidation of much of the last chapter, as well as of the knocking now heard at the door, we must turn back a little.

Upon an errand, suggested to his master by himself, James Brown, or as Ailleen affectionately called him, Jim, the house servant, and, to a very limited degree, the shopman of Mr. Barnaby Roundhead, had, about half an hour previous to the knocking, sallied out into the streets of the town, bare-headed and bare-footed, and otherwise but imperfectly attired, so hastily had he been summoned from his bed that night, and so urgently occupied ever since. His diligent pace was now a run and now a trot, as he passed through the sleeping city: and not many minutes had elapsed before he stopped before a mean-looking house, situated in a narrow lane, branching directly from the main street.

Here he knocked and knocked so vigorously, that the neighbourhood echoed to his thumping. After a while, the door was suddenly pulled open; a great woolly head made its appearance, and a voice as gruff and as fierce as that of a mastiff on his nightly post, bayed forth—

"By the lord of Skerrin and all his dogs, I'll

slaughther you! Who are you, an' what do you want, routin' me out o' my second sleep in this fashion?"

" Oh, Misther Withers! our house is robbed, right an' left, an' my masther sent me for you, to lay hould on one o' the robbers!"

Something like a short scoffing bellow was given in reply; and then the head disappeared, and the door was banged too with violence.

James Brown waited some time, to ascertain if he was to receive any further satisfaction. All remained silent within, and it seemed that the person he wanted had regained his bed, to try and pick up the odds and ends of his second nap. The trusty and anxious James knocked again.

The door must have been unbolted stealthily, for it was dashed wide open of a sudden, and the head, with its body and all, rushed out, half attired, and Misther Withers seized the offender by the throat, flourishing an old rusty sword about his ears.

" Now, you rogue's kidney that won't tell me your name—now I'll do for you!"

" Stop, stop, Misther Withers! sure the night isn't so pitch dark but you might know I'm Jim Brown, belonging to Misther Barney Roundhead: an' I tell you we're plundered, horse an' foot, an' have one o' the thieves in a thrap, for you to lay hands on him."

" Hee, hee!" barked Jack Withers, in a more amiable tone, " an' so they got at little ould Barney's shiners at last?"

" There's a power o' money gone, Misther Withers, a power o' money."

" Merry be the thief, say I; ould Nick might dance

in a body's pocket for Barney: never saw a *keenogue**
of his for grand-jury summons, or any other bit o'
paper; did they carry off the whole lot?"

" There's no knowin' yet, Misther Withers."

" How many wor in id?"

" We don't know that, either: we saw bud one, an'
we have him locked up for you."

" You're sure he can't give leg-bail? there's never
a cross to be got by that."

" If he doesn't make his way thro' the key-hole,
there's no chance of it, Misther Withers."

" Stump away, then; stump away."

He again re-entered his house, and soon came out,
fully and officially attired as mayor's sergeant of the
city. A great, heavy, three-cocked hat surmounted
a night-cap which he had drawn over his woolly head;
a blue, loose, frock-coat, daubed here and there with
broad yellow tape, and ornamented with huge yellow
buttons, covered his portly person, its large round cape
hanging between his shoulders; and this was obliquely
traversed by one white leathern belt, from which appended his scabbardless old rusty sword, that trailed
on the ground; while in his left hand he held a rusty
pistol, and with his right shouldered a goodly ouken
cudgel.

As they hurried along, Jack Withers questioned
James Brown regarding the robbery. James's answers
we condense.

It was utterly surprising how the robber or robbers
had got into the house. Every door and window had
been bolted and barred at the usual hour by Barnaby
Roundhead's own hand, who put all the keys into his

---

* Half a farthing.

own pocket; and then James's master had, as was his invariable custom, accompanied James into his bedroom; left with him a very short scrap of candle, locked him up, also, as well as the house, and so retired. And James Brown remained out of bed only while he was saying his prayers; and having been very tired, from a hard day's work, (for, Heaven knew, he was kept close at it,) quickly fell asleep; and he could not tell what hour of the night it was when his master stood over him in the bed, a candle in his hand, shaking him violently, and then ran about the room, and whined dolorously, calling on him to arise, as there were robbers in the house.

James Brown accompanied the shivering little man towards the spot indicated by the noise; which was heard within a certain room that had been the state apartment of the former lord of the mansion, the windows of which had been built up by the present possessor. They pushed at the door, but it was locked. Barnaby, however, had his bundle of keys with him; he applied the proper one, and the door opened; and a young man appeared in the centre of the apartment. He had raised a board of the flooring, and, holding a candle over the place, was looking down into the chasm. Barnaby and Jim both recognised him: it was our ghost-hunter—Morris Brady.

He offered but slight resistance to his captors; until, in passing Patty Roundhead's door, they attempted to search his person; and this he furiously and successfully opposed. They dragged him on to the room chosen, in consequence of its great security, as his temporary prison. Here, also, Barnaby had got the windows solidly built up, and had supplied the door with a strong lock, and an iron cross-bar; because here he was in the habit of stowing his odds and ends, no matter how valueless.

In this den, although Barnaby clung to Morris like a weasel, and James Brown exerted all his strength, the prisoner still baffled their renewed attempts to search him. They gave up the contest, locked him in, and then, at his own suggestion, James Brown hurried off to seek the aid of Jack Withers, the mayor's serjeant.

This account of the night's adventures was finished as Jim and his companion gained Barnaby Roundhead's door. They knocked loudly, as we have seen, and, keeping up his incessant wail, Barnaby descended to let them in. Bar, and bolt, and chain, and lock, he had carefully secured, after James Brown's departure in search of Withers; and now, with a trembling hand, he removed, one by one, those impediments to the entrance of his visitors. When they had got in, he again made sure the main entrance to his fortress, before he would address the bailiff, his voice being heard only in its continuous wretched whine, accompanied, while at-work at the door, by the rising and falling of his little spindle legs.

At last he turned to his new ally, seized him by the arm, cringed before him, and looked most supplicatingly into the gruff and stern countenance of Jack Withers.

"You are a strong man—and you are a man of the law—a man in power:—you will force back the booty from the robber and plunderer, and return it again to its right owner?"

"Hugh—hugh! That will all happen as the thing may turn out to be;" and Jack Withers pursed his lips, bent his brows, looked judicially doubtful from under the sharp peak of his three-cooked hat, and went on:

"I say, there's overhaulin' a fellow the one way, an' overhaulin' a fellow the other way; there's a sarch upon caption, if a man pays a man; there's a sarch, by right, when a buffer hops into the stone cage; an' there's a sarch by rason of a warrant o' sarch, that comes on the score of an affadavy before myself, an' his worship the mayor o' the city, when we're in the office, at office hours, in the day-time."

Either Barnaby did not understand the jargon and its object, or he affected not to do so. He pulled the bailiff close to him, and his voice became wofully fretful, as he urged, "tie him by the hands for me, and tie him by the legs, and force my threasure from him, and the prayers of an ould man you and yours shall have for ever."

"Pheu! a barrel-bag full o' your ould prayers wouldn't pass for a man's spittle. The caption fees! Pheu! the caption fees!" and he stretched out his hand.

"I—will—give—you—money;" promised Barnaby; "yes, indeed I will; here is money for your services." Barnaby writhed as he slowly drew forth the proffered bribe; he hesitated and sighed, ere he bestowed it; and when the shilling at last lay on the broad palm of the bailiff, he looked at it almost with tears in his eyes.

"Cromwell's curse purshue your beggarly heart!" thundered forth Withers; "what did you put down this for? There's the double of id goes to bail a mud-lark. Here!" to James Brown,—"here, you starved hound! buy yourself brandy-snappers with it."

But ere Jim could pick up the coin indignantly hurled at him, Barnaby, with an activity surprising for his age, had secured the rejected shilling.

"Open the dour!" bellowed the bailiff; "open your dour, an' let me out o' your miser's den!"

"I will bestow a large reward—I will enrich you with a—good—sum—of—money;" exclaimed Barnaby.

"Lay down a yallow balloon, then," said Withers, again extending his "itching palm."

"A whole guinea!" cried Barnaby, aghast; "'tis not in the house afther the plundher, unless you find it in the robber's pockets for me;" and he sat at the foot of the stairs, near which they stood, wrung his hands, and wailed more miserably than ever.

Withers affected to grow violent in his requests to be let out: he lowered his demand, however; and Barnaby eventually parted with half a guinea in gold, as if it had been so much of his heart's blood.

The reality of the bravery which is ostentatiously exhibited one may be allowed to doubt. Certainly, little Barney Roundhead showed no personal fear, now that the question was the recovery of his money. He held the light, and led the way up stairs. Jack Withers, relinquishing his gigantic cudgel to James Brown, flourished his rusty sword, and slashed the walls with it, as he followed, bellowing forth threats against "the rogue's kidney;" while Jim crept cautiously after.

They reached the door of the temporary prison. With shaking hands, Barnaby turned the key in the lock; yet, when the door was opened, the excited little creature ran fearlessly in, while the bailiff stood at the door, roaring out:

"Stand before me, and deliver yourself, the King's

prisoner, or I'll chop you into sparables! Come out here, till I sarch you!"

A scream escaped Barnaby, within—"He is not here! he is gone, gone, gone! and my goold and silver is lost to me for ever!"

Withers ceased his bellowing. He entered the room cautiously, as also did James Brown. Barnaby was whirling round and round, like a dancing dervise, and holding up the candle to every object of old lumber; but the prisoner was not visible. He had really escaped, although there was no entrance to the chamber except the door, and although Barney had found that bolted and locked, as he had left it.

CHAPTER XII.

It yet wanted about two hours of day-break, when the family of Randal Brady were aroused from deep sleep by a loud thumping at the door of the house. Surprise, though not alarm, was created by this unusual occurrence; and when the knocking was heard a second time, Randal Brady stood inside the door, demanding of those without the nature of their business.

Great was the good man's astonishment, when he heard admittance peremptorily demanded by the well-known bull-dog voice of Jack Withers; and he was in the act of striking a light, the better to enable him to obey the clamorous requisition, when the door was rudely flung against the wall, and Withers strode in, Barnaby Roundhead shuffling at his skirts, and James Brown moving cautiously after. The suddenness of the burst startled Randal Brady, and for a moment he overlooked the important fact that if the bolt had been across his door on the inside, as was invariably the case during the hours of sleep, such an abrupt entrance could not have been effected.

"What's the rason o' comin' to my paceable house

in this boistherous way, at such an hour, Masther Roundhead?" he asked, in his quiet way, coolly eyeing his visitors.

"Bang the door there, an' shoot the boult across it, Jim Brown," ordered Jack Withers. Jim obeyed.

"An' now bring the robber by the neck, fornent us, or, by the piper! I'll lay caption on every sowl in the house—goose, gandher, goslins, an' all."

"Upon your life, and upon the safety of your sowl, give—give me back my money, Randal Brady," pleaded Barnaby.

Randal Brady gazed at them.

"It is not very asy for me to understand ye, all at once," he said: "but you, Jack Withers, talk to me of a robber; and you, Masther Roundhead, talk to me of givin' you up your money; and all that is strange enough. Howsoever," he continued, smiling placidly, "if a robbery is done, you mistake the house—there is little doubt of that. Look at me, and recollect me. I don't say it by way of foolish boast; but there are few that know me would lift my latch to hunt a thief."

"Gallows-end to you!"—began the bailiff, in his invariably ruffian-like manner.

"Be civil, Jack Withers," interrupted Randal Brady; "I'm inclined to dale civilly by you, no matther whether you desarve it or no; do the same by me in my own house, or I may make you remember whose house it is."

"Civility begets civility; don't forget that, my good man," said Mrs. Brady, who, having hastily attired herself, was now at her husband's elbow, assisting him to put on his coat.

"Cromwell's curse to you both! there isn't

kith or kin o' you could tache dacency or civility to me."

"Well, what is your business here?" demanded Randal Brady, in a tone of steady authority.

"Bring the robber fornent me, I say again; till I lay my lucky hands on him—an' that's my business."

"I spoke plain to you before on that head. We have the name of being honest people here, thank God; and this house is no place for hiding robbers."

"Hah—the ould palaver, once again—I never knew one o' your sort that couldn't hould a parley; a smooth tongue is a thief's picklock; lave my way there, and I'd bet the King's picture on goold that I'll soon be rubbin' down his shouldher-blade."

"*My* piece o' goold is in your purse, arn' it? force my coins from him, and I will give you more money," exhorted Barnaby, at the ruffian's skirts.

"Phaugh—you're hindherin me, I till you; lave— let go!" and he shook off his little appendage.

"Who are you in search of, man?" questioned Randal Brady, confronting him.

"Aye, what do ye want at all, good people?" seconded his good woman; "there's no wrong thrumpery undher this roof, I bid ye; 'who goes to the sheep's house for wool comes home shorn;' remember that."

"Thundher and turf! an' what purty sheep's faces ye both have, axin' the question; I'll let ye into the sacret, maybe, when I lay the five fingers on the garçoon that grabbed this cratur's goold an' silver."

"And what is your rason for thinkin' that he is undher my roof?"

"By this blessed stick in my hand, Job was a

madman to me! Where would I come to search for the fox but in his earth?"

"Let me have the name of the person you are in search of," continued Randal Brady, slightly and only vaguely troubled by the bailiff's last insinuations.

"There's more of id, again! By the oath o' man, I'm asthray if it's bamboozling me you are, or whether you are in arnest: why, it's a cock o' your own breed I'm coorsin'; do you undherstand me now?"

"A son of mine, honest man?"

"Yes; a son o' yours, honest man."

Randal Brady's smile was not only devoid of apprehension, but it expressed a cool certainty of the assertion which accompanied it.

"Why man, no son o' mine and o' this good woman," laying his hand on his wife's shoulder, "would covet a *thrawneen* * belongin' to another."

"I wondher at you, man!" broke forth Mrs. Brady with her sex's readiness and volubility, at the same time copying, as well as she could, from her husband, an attitude of natural dignity, and allowing her dark eye to flash with angry pride: "I wondher at you from my very heart! Tell me, how comes it into your foolish head at all, to dhrame that a boy of ours would answer to the name o' thief or robber? Minawyah! shame be upon you! To stand before the mother's face, an' say that scandal of one of her childhren! Shame to you, a thousand, thousand times! There isn't a child that ever drew my milk, that wouldn't rather die—aye, give up the ghost an' die, stretched starvin' upon the could pavin' stones o' the street, that couldn't hear him or pity him, before he'd

---

* Paltry Weed.

rise his hand to take a neighbour's crumb unlawfully,"
—tears stopped her rapid utterance: they were not,
however, tears of grief, but those of maternal pride,
love, and wrath: and there was about the simple and
virtuous woman such a genuine air of truth, that even
the habitually rude bailiff half doubted the certainty
of his information, while he could not help feeling a
momentary respect for the father and mother he saw
before him.

"An' you—you!" continued Mrs. Brady, bending
on little Barnaby a look of piercing indignation—
"you, Barney Roundhead, that had some o' my own
blood in the veins o' your wife; my wondher at you
is great above all things! Is it come to your turn,
Barney, to limp over my threshold, an' call my son—
rogue? Is id because a thatching of sthraw covers
my house, that I'd rear up children to bring shame on
my honest husband? Barny, none of Randal Brady's
name would touch your dirty goold: your dirty goold,
that you gave up rest and pace for, God an' man, to
scrape together!"

"Betty Brady!" screamed the little man, with
sudden energy, "I will spake into your ear privately;"
and with as much celerity as his shrivelled frame was
capable of exerting, he shuffled to a distance from the
others.

Mrs. Brady looked after him commiseratingly; he
stood anxiously beckoning to her. She moved to him
with a lofty air. The little man caught her gown and
pulled it. In compliance with the invitation, she
bent her head to him.

"Yes, I don't forget it—I never did: my wife
Polly was blood cousin to you, Betty Brady."

"Well, *aroon?* an' what good or harm was that to
me or mine?"

"An' you yourself are my own cousin, by marriage with Polly."

"Aye, an' so I am; but not by my own choosin', I'd have you to know. I never put the cousin on you, Barney. 'Twas 'welcome thrumphery for want of company,' my good man." While Mrs. Brady was under high excitement during her speeches to Withers and Barnaby, she had forgotten her proverbs; now she was sufficiently cool, and on the watch to recur to them.

"You would'nt do injury on a harmless body that was your poor cousin Polly's own chosen husband?"

"*Gho vich a dhui uth*,* poor crature of a man! what put that foolery into your simple head this blessed mornin'?"

"I am sure you would not, cousin Betty; if it were for nothing but for the sake o' my poor child Patty, that loves your child Rose so well."

"What *cuggerin*'† is that on your weasel-snout, Masther Barney Roundhead?" questioned the watchful Withers.

"Oh, that man!" resumed Barnaby, addressing Mrs. Brady in the closest possible whisper—"he is a large man, and a sthrong man, and a man of little honesty, and sinfully fond of gain." Barney twitched and fumbled in coming agony, at Mrs. Brady's skirts: "And if he lays hold upon my money, he will exact goold as his fee! Listen, listen! I will go privily with you to your son, and you will beseech him to restore the coins, and there will be no looker on"— here he tried still more to diminish his whisper— "there were four naggins o' the goold, and there

---

* Now, God bless you.   † Close confidence.

were four pints o' the silver—good measure to the brim; and if the same measure is rendered back to me, I will hold my pace for your sake, cousin Betty; an' no harm shall fall on the lad; an' I will call him a good lad, an' I will declare to others that he is an honest lad."

Mrs. Brady broke loose from her cringing and petitioning detainer.

"Why, then, my heavy hathred be upon you, you kiln-dried little bit of a mortal! Was it to tell me, once again, that a son o' mine would put shame on his mother, you beckoned me over to you, wid your little ould crooked fingers? Tattheration to you, you thing o' little value —an' that's what I ever and always thought you! Och, there's thruth in the ould sayin', ' convince a fool against his will, he's of the same opinion still!' *Minawyah*, from this to the day of judgment! I tould you often, you crature, an' I have the same word for you now, that you made your money your God, an' that you b'lieve that all the vartue in the world lies in id; but let me make known to you, what all the people knows before, that my childhren were arly taught that ' a good name is betther than riches;' they did'nt spake plain, when they could say the ten commandments—an' in them they learnt, ' thou shalt not covet thy neighbour's goods.'"

Mrs. Brady was guilty of this piece of sound abuse of the widower of her deceased cousin Polly, in her loudest pitch of voice; of course, the bailiff heard every word of it, and the natural energy of the speaker again so affected him, callous-hearted as he was, that he recurred to his doubts of the accuracy of the information he had received.

"Where are you, Jim Brown?" he cried out.

"I am here to the fore," mildly answered the person summoned, advancing out of the shaded corner of the apartment.

"Will you take your book oath it was one Morris Brady you seen in the house?"

"I could take my oath of it, with a safe conscience. Did'nt I hould the light to his face? Had'nt I him in my hands? An' don't I know him this many a day; aye, well enough to spake to him?"

Mrs. Brady uttered a scoffing and most angry ejaculation.

"As heaven is above us, I found him robbing me—plundering my little earnings from me!" whined Barnaby, wringing his hands, and otherwise setting himself in puny motion, as usual.

Randal Brady began to have some sickening misgivings. He had cast his eye towards the ladder ascending to Morris's sleeping apartment, in hopes of his appearance, but no Morris came down; although, as Randal argued, he must have heard the noise below, and, consistently with his fiery nature, ought in that case to have stood at his father's side. Mrs. Brady's faith in her son's integrity was, however, too strong to permit a doubt to enter her mind. She addressed her husband, her smile full of confidence as she spoke.

"Well, Randal, *aroon*, did you ever come across such a self-willed set o' people? but 'wilful folk must run their tether's length;' call the poor boy to them, *a-cuishla-ma-chree*, an' then, maybe, they'd see their foolish error.

"You are right, Betty." He turned round and addressed Rose, who stood a little distance behind him, silent and observant: " Rose, light another candle, and give it to me."

Rose quickly obeyed. As she handed the light to her father, they looked into each other's eyes. The same serious apprehension glanced from mind to mind.

With a suppressed sigh, Randal Brady heavily ascended the ladder. He walked across to Morris's bed. It had been slept in. He became a little re-assured. He felt it. It was cold. He turned rapidly and eagerly to that of his younger son. It also was untenanted; but he soon caught the lad's figure, as if hiding in the shadow at the far end of the apartment.

" Daniel, come here to me;" and Daniel stealthily approached on his toes. " Where is your brother Morris, my boy ? "

" I don't know, in honest truth I don't, Sir,"— only eager to exculpate himself from any possible accusation.

" What! is not Morris in the house?"

" I—I b'lieve not: father — but don't blame me; I wasn't awake when he stole out; that is, this night; and he wouldn't be stopped by me if I was."

The old man staggered backward.

" Here, child, take the candle from me or it will fall," he said, faintly. Daniel obeyed, and he saw his father totter to his bed and sit on it, while his arms fell lifelessly at his side, and big drops of perspiration rolled from his forehead over his deadly pale face.

When Randal again spoke, his voice was scarcely audible:

" And so, against all the advice I gave him, and all the commands I laid upon him, your brother left his bed last night, and quitted his father's house, Daniel?"

"I didn't see him, as I tould you, Sir, last night of all, getting up to go out, by rason I was asleep; but—"

"Last night of all? what do you mane? did he go out other nights of late?"

"He did, father, the very night afore last."

"He did? God pity me! He did, Daniel? and you never gave me warning?"

"I thought Morris might thump me, Sir, if I tould on him."

"You thought your brother might thump you, Daniel, for warning his father of his disobedience? and he went out the very night before last? and other nights of late? Oh, Morris, Morris!" cried the choking and now weeping father, "may you never suffer, here or hereafter, for the shame and the sorrow you have brought on your mother and on me!"

"What plottin' are ye at above there," roared Jack Withers, at the foot of the ladder.

Randal Brady trembled at the sound of the rude voice which, until this moment of anguished conviction, had not troubled his equanimity.

"Shew me the face o' the rogue's bird, or I'll make a caption o' the whole breed, I tell ye once again."

The old man, after crossing his forehead, and looking upward for an instant with clasped hands, arose from the bed, slowly and unsteadily passed over the floor, and descended the ladder to encounter, as he might, the insolence which he could not now reprove; and to listen, patiently, to terms of reproach only bestowed upon the worthless and the bad, with the self-degrading consciousness that he could not disclaim their application.

"Hollo! so you staggered upon id? you forgot your arrand, you ould thief-rearer?" roared the wretch Withers, when he saw him descend alone, and marked his agitation; "clear the way here, an' let one Jack Withers thry his coaxin' ways wid the *bouchaleen*."

"Patience, patience," said Randal Brady mildly, putting his hand against the bailiff as he rudely dragged him from the ladder he was descending.

"Patience? blurr-an-ages! is that your word? by the lord of Skerrin an' all his dogs! if poor ould Job was the mayor's serjeant at the present moment, he'd curse an' blow like a born throoper! Patience in throth! By the book, it's myself is the moral o' patience! lave my way, I say!" and snatching the candle he hastened up the ladder, blustering as he went. With the eager tenacity of a leech, little Barnaby clung to the steps and followed; nor did the dutiful James Brown remain below.

"What manin' is that on your face now, Randal Brady?" asked the good woman of the house, taking her husband's hands in hers, while her countenance fell under the contagious gloom of his.

Rose, stepping forward, glanced the same query,— and, having been mutely answered, clasped her hands together, and her figure bent in the earnestness of her affliction. "Betty," answered Randal Brady, not able to suppress his tears, "Betty, *mavourneen*, go cry over your son; and, Rose, *machree*, go cry over your brother. He is not above, and he left the house, thiefishly, last night, and the night before,"—his voice failed him. "I will only say, thanks be given to God this morning, we are punished for our sins of pride in thinking ourselves sometimes, maybe, betther than other people."

Rose shrank back appalled. But the poor mother only clasped tighter the hands she held, and looked with an indescribable expression of supplication into her husband's eyes, as she said—" Randal, them intherlopers may take an oath for id;—bud, surely, a-roon, *you* don't mane to tell me that Morris Brady would turn robber? You wouldn't call your son by such a name, to the face o' the mother that bore him?"

" I pity you, my poor Betty, I pity you," was all he answered.

" Tho' you're his father, Randal Brady, I couldn't b'lieve it from your mouth. It couldn't happen. I wouldn't give id credit, if 'twas a saint that spoke id. Didn't I nurse him at my breast? Didn't he grow from child to boy undher his father's and his mother's eye—an' wasn't God's holy name the first word in his mouth—aye, before he could call his father by his name? An' didn't I know my boy? Didn't I know my own poor Morris, that was an' is as much above a low action, not to talk of a thievin' one, as the thruest gentleman in the land? I did know him, Randal, an' I do; an' they are liars that tell you he would cast shame on his mother—oh, Randal, Randal, you don't take my word for it!" she continued, in an altered voice, when she saw the big tears rolling through the furrows in her husband's cheeks: " You don't, Randal; an' you are doin' what I never observed you doin' before in your life, an' what nothin' bud your son's disgraceful acts could make sich a man as you do—you are cryin', Randal, *a-vourneen!* cryin' like a child, over his downfall! Oh, God pity you, Morris —pity an' forgive you, for bringin' the tears into your father's eyes!"

Her dependence on her own opinion of Morris wholly gave way; and bursting herself into a wild agony of weeping, she sank upon the floor, and hid her face on her hands and knees.

Randal Brady took a chair in silence. Rose stole to its back, her elbow resting on it, and her outspread palm across her eyes. The lad Daniel had crept down the ladder, and into a corner; and the younger girl sat weeping and shivering in the shade of another. And thus they remained, while the bailiff and his companions tramped over their head, tossing about every thing in their way.

"Randal," sobbed the good woman, "you and I never knew sorrow before, since the blessed an' happy day we met."

"No; never an hour of what could be called sorrow, Betty; and, even now, if it was the will of heaven to send us the sorrow without the shame—if that boy was in his grave, we could bear up better against it, I believe: but, even so, welcome be the will of God."

"Oh, Randal, Randal, where is the poor sinner hidin' his miserable head!"

"You remind me of what I have to do, Betty," said Randal Brady, in a low, cautious voice; "I must search him out, an' hide him, an' screen him from ——" he could not utter *what;* the half-formed words became painful lumps in his throat.

"Father dear," whispered Rose softly, close at his ear;—he turned his head to look her; there was a tremulous approach to a smile in her watery eyes, and on her quivering lip, and an expression of mild conviction in her voice and manner, which made the blood rush warmly to the old man's heart, as she continued—

"I go with my mother's opinion. I do not believe that Morris is what they call him."

"No, Rose? And why do you think him innocent, my own good child?"

"For the same rasons that make my mother think so; and because I know him, heart and mind, as well, if not better than she does. My poor Morris could not be a robber, father. He was, and he is, too brave a boy, too proud a boy, too high-spirited a boy, too loving a boy. Besides, and worth all that and more, he was, and he is a good Christian, and could not disgrace himself or you, or fly in the face of his God."

She pressed her gentle hands together, and they were tears of affection for her favourite brother which now fell from her eyes.

"Is that all, *my lanna?* is that all you can say for him? So his father thought, too, Rose my darling."

"And so I still think, Sir; and, with your lave, I have more to say. Morris went out to hunt the ghost in the *bosheen:* and, whatever has happened, some one—some livin' man—imitating the ghost, led him on without his knowing what he did."

"My own *colleen-dhass!* your father's own pride an' threasure you are!" Randal took her hand, drew her to him round the chair, and held her in his arms: "and you were always his pride and comfort! The good and great God, the Father of fathers, pour down blessings on you, my child!" He now laid one hand on her head; Rose bent a knee;—"For all that you have been, and for all that you are to me and to your mother, and to poor Morris, and to us all, I pray that prayer for you; and, for the words of comfort you just now dhropt on my heart, I particularly pray it; for, in them words, Rose, there is thought and wisdom, and, with divine help, they may lade us out of this great day of throuble."

"Thank you from the heart, father dear, for your love, an' your praise, an' your good prayer," answered Rose, kissing the old man's cheek as she regained a standing position at his side; "Yes, father; wid the sthrong help you spoke of, we may yet find out the thruth o' the story, and give back his honest name to Morris."

"You are right, a cuishla *gal ma-chree.*"

Here the searchers clamorously interrupted a scene and feelings with which they could have had so little sympathy, but which even their unsuitable presence in the good and virtuous house could not prevent.

"'Ill quest him out, if a nut-shell covered him," roared Jack Withers; and he was about to enter the sleeping chamber of the old couple, when Mrs. Brady suddenly sprang up from the floor, and stood at the door of it, confronting him.

"What is your business in this room, I'd be glad to know? Is the most sacret place in the house of honest people to be ransacked by every *shooler?* *

"Take yourself out o' that, you faggot," and the bailiff pushed her.

"Not a step: you shall never put your foot over this threshold, my hectherin' don; you come here to belie my boy; an' you're on a fool's arrand, if you think yourself welcome undher my roof wid sich a story."

"Give way, give way, you thief's mother!"

"No, man! go wid your slandhers elsewhere,"

---

* A wandering worthless person.

continued the inconsequential Mrs. Brady; "into Randal Brady's an' my bed-room the likes o' you shall not come."

Again the bailiff pushed her, but he could not effectually remove her from her position. Randal Brady rose to take her out of the struggle; but, ere he reached the spot, Withers raised his cudgel, and struck the poor woman to the ground. The blood flowed profusely from her temple as she lay insensible.

Rose screamed in horror, and ran to her mother. All the natural self-possession and placidity of Randal's character forsook him. With the vigour and quickness of youth, he snatched down from the wall one of his own basket-hilted cudgels, and fell upon the cowardly assaulter of his wife. Withers shifted his pistol from his left hand to his right; Randal struck it upwards, and it went off harmlessly; and, an instant after, the blustering agent of the law lay senseless at his feet.

During the short contest, Jim Brown had opened the door and ran off. Randal trailed his bulky antagonist to the threshold, and cast him out. He was yet high in wrath, when the cringing figure of the little Barnaby caught his eye in a remote corner.

"Quit my house, and quit it instantly!" he cried to him.

"Give up my goold—my goold an' my silver, Randal Brady!"

"Begone at once, I say!"

"No, never will I begone without my goold and my silver! Never!"

Randal seized the little being. The miser fastened his long meagre fingers in his collar, still squeaking forth cries for his " goold an' his silver;" and it required the full exercise of Randal Brady's strength to loosen the tenacious gripe of the pigmy creature. At last, however, he did succeed in shaking him off, outside the door, which he then barred; and finally he was at leisure to pay attention to his wife.

Rose, sitting on the floor, held her mother's head on her lap, after having bound it. The two other children were weeping over her. Randal took his wife in his arms, and bore her into their bed-room. She recovered from her insensibility. He washed her temples, and found that the wound was only superficial. He knew he was skilful enough to act as surgeon; and the day broke when he had finished his dressings and bathings. He half-reclined on the bed, holding his wife's hand. The other members of the family sat apart in the chamber. All were silent. It seemed to have been individually, though tacitly agreed upon by all, that the only subject on which they could speak was too painful for discussion.

Again the door of the house was violently assailed. His children looked with alarm into Randal's face. Exhausted as was the mother, she rose upon her elbow.

"Hurry, Randal!" she cried, faintly; "hurry to the dour! 'tis the poor sinful boy! we must hide him safely, Randal—he is our child."

The old man walked steadily and coolly to the door, and unbarred and opened it. Two other mayor's bailiffs, accompanied by a guard of soldiers, confronted him, and entered the house. The bailiffs laid their hands upon him, and called him their prisoner in the king's name. He had assaulted the mayor's sergeant in the legal discharge of his duty; and moreover stood suspected of having been a party to the robbery committed by his son.

"Ye may loosen your hands from me," he said; "I will go with ye quietly and paceably. I only request you to let me say a word to my family, before we lave the house."

The bailiffs were not such brawling ruffians as their superior, Jack Withers. They respected the old man's subdued grief; and following him only to the door of his wife's apartment, allowed him to pass in.

He approached the bed. Twice had she endeavoured to rise, but her strength failed her. Her husband addressed her:

"My poor Betty, you see I am a prisoner, and I must quit you and the childhren, but only for a time, it is to be hoped. Yet however things come to pass, we are Christian people, and we should be ungrateful sinners if it happened that, in the first throuble that has come upon us, we did not bow down the head and say, 'welcome be the will o' God.' Betty, listen to me :- you were always a good, a loving, and an obedient wife to me, and I now lay a husband's commands on you, that you will not attempt to rise from your bed till you are well able to do it."

He turned to the rest of his family: "Childhren, come here to me. The misfortune that falls on us this morning, comes of the sin of disobedience. If your poor brother had listened to his father's counsel, he would not now be a skulking outcast—he would not now be called robber. Be dutiful to your poor mother, while I am away. Daniel and Nancy, I desire ye to stay within the house, mornin' and evenin,' till ye hear my words again. Rose, my whole dependance, afther heaven, is on you. You must be the mother and the father of this family for a while. Take good care of the mother, Rose. You will come to me with my food. Daniel and Nancy, what your sisther advises you to do, you are to do. Hand me down my prayer-book, Rose; and when you bring my breakfast, by-and-by, bring with it the holy Douay bible, and some other book or two. Betty, *ma-chree*, God be with you. I will pray for your good health, every mornin' an' every evenin', and the Lord may hear me, though I pray from a prison. God bless ye, childhren, and may his grace be with ye. God protect you all."

There was nothing clamorous in the grief of those he addressed, and he now scarcely shed a tear himself. His wife clung to him; his children caught his hands, or embraced his knees. They knelt before him. He laid his hands separately on their heads, as he gave them his parting benediction. He kissed them; he kissed his wife; and then putting on his hat, and not seeking to pull it over his brows, he walked amid the bailiffs and the soldiers, through the streets of his native town, and was lodged in the common jail.

The stoic preaches indifference to human calamity, but his dogmas result from human pride, and they are naught but the ostentatious parade of human reason. Were the world's eye turned away from him, when tried by the test of real affliction, his practice would be widely different from his theory.

Randal Brady, though a good, homely philosopher, was no stoic. He felt his visitation, and did not act a lie by assuming indifference to it. But he also felt the efficacy of that doctrine, which alone can assuage the sufferer's pang. He knelt down in his prison, and said aloud, " 'Thy will be done on earth, as it is in heaven;" he bowed his grey head in Christian resignation, and he arose strengthened with the Christian's comfort. Oh! blind or inverted must be the reasoning, which would tell a mortal sufferer that his paradise is on this earth.

We disclaim religious cant; but we could not faithfully illustrate the character of one of our most esteemed personages, did we neglect to notice how he bore up against the first real misfortune he had ever encountered.

CHAPTER XIII.

RANDAL BRADY caught eagerly at the hint thrown out by his daughter, as to the charge made against Morris. Reflection added to the probability of her surmise; and he came to the almost certain conclusion, that some villain had personated the ghost of the entombed Joe Wilson, with the view of committing theft in that disguise; and that his son Morris, under the wild conviction of an intercourse with a supernatural being, had been made the tool of the impostor, without having willed a crime.

This view of poor Morris's conduct gave him great consolation. He hoped he might be able, in alliance with Rose, and after speaking with the ghost-hunter, to clear up the mystery; and he longed for his personal freedom, chiefly on that account.

We turn to Rose at home. When duties to be performed imperiously require attention, notwithstanding a preoccupation of the mind by calamity, even the constrained effort to discharge them confers a mental benefit and relief, as the forced and artificial action of the lungs restores the vital spark to a seemingly lifeless body when rescued from the water. And Rose Brady had duties to go through, and duties that could not be postponed. Scarcely, therefore, had her father crossed the threshold, when she did all she could to dry her tears, and arrange her ideas and her little plans; and, hour after hour, her endeavours were more and more successful; till at last, observing her orderly activity, and even the expression of her features, few would think what a load of grief was on her heart.

Rose bathed her face; assisted by little Nancy, put the whole house to rights; lighted her fire; prepared her father's meal, and took it to him. Upon her return, she was her sick mother's nurse; her brother and sister looked to her as their guide; and her words spoke hope and comfort, and induced, in the minds of those around her, patience and fortitude throughout the whole day. It was not until Rose was alone at night, that her tears streamed afresh for the sufferings of her parents, and for the fate of her beloved brother Morris.

What had become of the wayward lad? where was he hiding himself? Perhaps he had fled from his native place, nay, his country, for ever. Rose's heart fell at that surmise. The idea of a separation between her and Morris was, in itself, sufficiently afflicting; but the reflection that his own true confession to her of the details of his unlucky adventure—would be indispensable to expose the imposition practised upon him, re-establish his fair name, and restore him to his family and his friends, excessively grieved and agitated her, when a thought of his self-expatriation suggested itself.

The civil powers were on the alert to apprehend Morris. At Rose's instance, friendly neighbours and relations also exerted themselves to discover what had become of him; but days passed away, and the united efforts of friends and foes proved fruitless. Morris Brady was not heard of.

It was the fourth day subsequent to the robbery in Barnaby Roundhead's house, and Rose had just come back from the jail, whither, as usual, she had gone with her father's breakfast. Her mother's fever was now passing away; the old woman therefore required less constant attendance; and Rose retired into her own little room, to cogitate and reason with herself in private.

Hitherto, in daily hopes of her father's return to his family, she had delayed adopting any distinct plan for finding out the impostor of the *bosheen*, in Morris's absence. Randal Brady, were he at liberty, would undertake, she well knew, the difficult investigation himself. But now that there appeared no speedy prospect of his release from prison, Rose sat herself down to decide whether she should not engage in the necessary task in her own person. She soon came to the conclusion that it was her duty to do so: and were good and promising measures once arranged, she further felt that she had nerve enough to act upon them. In case of success, how well would she be rewarded for any trouble or danger she might encounter! and how delightful was the anticipation that, through her exertions, her father and brother might be restored to their home, and freed from the stigma which lay upon them!

The only question now seemed to be, what were the best steps to begin with, for the accomplishment of her purpose? And Rose's mind actively set to work on this point.

Her reveries were interrupted by the rising of the latch of the door of her room. She turned, and saw the round, full, rosy face of Ailleen Morrisay laughing in at her; and presently the whole short dumpling figure of the girl entered the little apartment.

The true Christian name and surname of the visitor, as we have repeatedly recorded, were Ailleen Morrisay; but she answered with equal good-humour to another title bestowed upon her, and by which she was best known—namely, Ailleen Lahon, or Broad Ellen. The honorary epithet did justice to her personal formation, of which, indeed, the horizontal line was sadly out of proportion with the perpendicular one. But this little troubled Ailleen Lahon; and she got over it, generally, by asserting that, "she'd make a brave, tall, fine crature, if she was bat out;"— that is to say, if she were hammered on an anvil, so as to stretch her, as a smith stretches a lump of iron. There was not under the sun a better-tempered poor girl, nor a more affectionate and disinterested one, than our Ailleen. Mrs. Brady, upon a merrier day, remarked that "there was thruth in the ould sayin', laugh and be fat,' in regard of Ailleen Lahon;" and Mrs. Brady was right; for, in proportion to her risible habits was Ailleen's person addicted to the rather common-place mode of matter spoken of; fat, indeed, she might be called, even to the tension, nay, almost to the bursting of her fair skin.

Ailleen had a particular gait of going along the streets of her native town. Her step was short, substantial, and quick; counting, perhaps, four to a second. She waddled, and with good reason; for there existed an absolute necessity for relieving one leg of the burthen it bore, by poising the body to one side, ere she could securely lift up the other. She puffed as she made her way; she carried her head with the chin pointing almost to the zenith, in order to give her lungs as much freedom as possible; and, also with the same view, her mouth remained wide open. And as the ostrich uses his pinions to aid his speed, and keep him steady across the desert, Ailleen industriously worked her bent arms, backward and forward, as she threaded the mazes of the city, hot, puffing, and exhaling like a steam-boat. Such was the person who now broke in on Rose Brady's severe cogitation.

"God save you to-day, Miss Rosy," she said, dropping into a chair opposite the looking-glass, and observing herself with great complacency.

"God save you, Ailleen, and how are you?" answered Rose, in a mild accent, the sadness of which Ailleen did not perceive.

"*Mostha*, I'm most beautiful well, my darlint; ah, then, who duv you think I met, comin' sthraight agin me, along the sthreet?"

"Indeed, I can't tell, Ailleen."

"An' who should id be, *a-lanna*, bud ould Aldherman Lodge, wid his big critch, an' his little critch, helpin' the crature to walk? an'—'hollo, come here to me, purty girl,' he says to myself; 'faix, an' aye, I will, wid all my heart,' says I to him, back again; I wish, purty crature,' says he a second time to me—I wish'—(only think o' the poor ould mortial, Miss Rosy!) I wish I was as fit to be married as you are;' 'then,' says I, 'by my throth an' you're not, ould gintleman; an' I can tell you what's more—you never will;' an' worn't that a downright thruth for me,

Miss Rosy? but I see you're not mindin' what I say to you, *a-cuishla*."

"Go on, Ailleen," replied Rose, in an absent manner; in fact, since Ailleen mentioned the name of Alderman Lodge, she had been mentally occupied in appropriating him to her plans for discovering the mock ghost of the *bosheen.*

"I will, Miss Rosy; 'well, an' when *are* you goin' to do id, wid the priest's help, my darlint?' says Alderman Lodge to myself; 'soon and sudd'n, plaise God,' says I. 'To-day night, if I could help myself.' 'Sure it's not goin' to lave me you are, my jewel?' says he, when he seen me for comin' my way, a little fasther than he could keep up with. 'Indeed and it is,' says I, makin' answer. 'God speed you then, *ma colleen dhass*,' says he. 'A bright good mornin',' says I, 'an' I hope you'll get to the end o' the sthreet by night-fall.'

"Wid that word away I goes, Miss Rosy, *a-lanna;* bud I wasn't twice the length of my apron-string from him, when another body gives the love-lock a little pull from behind."

Ailleen touched one of the bunches of hair which hung on her neck, to point out distinctly what she was pleased to call "love-lock;"—

"An' who do you think was afther me now, *a-graw?*"

Rose did not reply to the egotistical question of her visitor. Ailleen's high spirits distressed her. But, to poor Ailleen, an excursion along the streets was an event of great glory and excitement. Her occupations at home were numerous, and her opportunities for seeing and being seen were few; so that when she once got out, Ailleen enjoyed herself in her very heart. She had a good-humoured word for every one she met, and every one she met delighted to accost her. Often before, she had entertained Rose and her mistress with an account of her perambulatory adventures; and, in the glee of the present moment she could have gone on to the end of the chapter, had not Rose, when she pressed her former question, stopped her by saying, with tears trembling in her eyes—

"I'm not in a humour for joking, my good Ailleen, as I used to be."

"Ah, thin, an' sure you're not, my darlint; *musha*, see how everything went clean out o' my head! In throth, *a-lanna*, I'm hearty sorry for your throuble, or else an inch of Ailleen Lahon is not sittin' on this chair afore you."

There was no affectation in this sudden sympathy on the part of Ailleen. According as circumstances acted upon her, her head and heart were addicted to the most rapid changes from mirth to melancholy, and from melancholy to mirth. She had left her house that morning deeply and sincerely grieved for the sufferings of her gentle young mistress; old Alderman Lodge fell in her way, and had Ailleen's bosom been big with its own sorrows, she must have enjoyed, nevertheless, her encounter with him, and their smart exchange of dialogue, to say nothing of her untold anecdote of "the love-lock:" and now that Rose called back her wandering wit, sincere tears stood in poor Ailleen's own eyes as she addressed her:

"It went to my heart, *a-vourneen*, to hear tell o' your grief; I'd be glad how happy you'd be; an' it would put throuble on me if a dog o' your's came by mischief."

"I know that, my good Ailleen, and I am thankful to you for it."

"An' sure we have our own sorrowful times of id at home, Miss Rosy, my darlint; the poor misthrause—" Ailleen burst out crying—"the poor misthrause is dyin', I'm sore afeard; throth, you'd feel pity for her, if you had a heart o' the hardest marvle in your body, so you would. Oh, Miss Rosy! ever since the misfortinate night we seen the ghost—"

"The ghost, Ailleen? what ghost?" interrupted Rose, much interested.

"You didn't hear tell of it, *a-lanna!*" in great wonder that an event so astounding, and particularly so since it had occurred to herself and her mistress, should so long have remained unknown to a single human creature.

"I now hear it, for the first time, from your lips, Ailleen.'

The voluble girl recounted for Rose the appearance of the ghost of Joe Wilson to her and Patty, in her master's house, adding a few terrific particulars, just to heighten the interest, and to demonstrate that "it was no wondher her poor wakely sowl of a misthrause" should be brought to the grave by the visitation; adding, that if she herself had not been blessed with the lives of ten cats, she never could have survived the pummelling she got, and of which the marks were still visible on her person; "an' all for doin' nothing' against the unloocky sperit, only keepin' the darlint misthrause from his ugly claws"—Ailleen, by her own account, having resolved from the outset that the apparition should not get one, if it did not succeed in abducting both.

Rose ascertained from Ailleen that this happened the night of the robbery, and then paused thoughtfully, and with a cheered heart. The villain who was masquerading it as Wilson's ghost, was in Barnaby Roundhead's house when her brother had been said to have committed a disgraceful crime. That was confirmation of her first judgment; and, at the same time, Rose thought she began to see her way in investigating the mystery, by the glimmer of the unexpected information thus received.

Upon farther reflection, one thing seemed unsatisfactory to Rose's mind. Ailleen, when closely questioned, insisted that, to the eyes of her mistress and herself, the features of the ghost were identically those of the dead and buried Joe Wilson, whom both had known, long and well; and Rose began to think it impossible that any man could so closely resemble another, as to give an impression of the identity of that other so vividly, as appeared to have been effected in the present case.

The idea of a real supernatural appearance began therefore to grow upon Rose. She recollected that in her brother's entrance into old Barnaby's house, and in his departure from it, there had been something very extraordinary: something which human agency could not account for. And if, indeed, he had been led on by an apparition, the aim or purpose of such a being could not be to commit a robbery; and, unless influenced by the commands of a superhuman director, Barnaby's gold or silver Morris would never have touched: so that the little old miser's charge might, in this instance at least, fall to the ground.

A second time Rose's calculations wavered. Did Ailleen exaggerate in speaking so confidently, for her mistress as well as for herself, of the features of the apparition ? Patty Roundhead could solve the query. On the whole, there was exciting matter of investigation opened to Rose Brady : and when at length Ailleen declared that the real object of her visit was to bear a message from her mistress, requesting to see Rose, our heroine cheerfully and promptly obeyed the summons.

CHAPTER XIV.

But exclusively of her own personal motives, Rose, although plunged in the deepest domestic troubles, would have gladly gone to see her dear young friend. Most sincerely did she love Patty, and there were other reasons why she should try to forget for an hour her own sorrows, to administer to those of the drooping girl.

Rose had solemnly promised Mrs. Roundhead, a few moments before the death of the latter, to do her utmost to be a sister and a mother to her child; and she undertook the trust the more readily that her heart urged her to the acceptance of it. For a number of years she had been the close confident of Mrs. Roundhead, who looked up to her for advice and consolation in many a family emergency. Of Rose's goodness, prudence, and honour, the poor woman had the highest opinion; as one proof of which, she intrusted her, before her own departure from this world, with a purse of gold of a thousand guineas, the result of the private savings before alluded to; and this purse was meant for Patty, whenever the girl should be inclined to change her maidenly condition: for, from Mrs. Roundhead's observations, she much doubted whether Barnaby would part with his beloved gold, even to secure an eligible establishment for his only child. Rose vowed inviolable secrecy as to this deposit; and observing her promise even with regard to her own family, she buried it deep in a spot which no one could ever suspect to contain so weighty a treasure. This circumstance will be found to have been worthy of notice.

From earliest childhood, Patty's tender nature clung for support to her half-cousin. As she grew up, and even after gaining the full years of girl-hood, she was a secluded being. Her father dreaded the expense likely to result from allowing her to visit gay people, or to be visited by them. The frequent calls of the modestly, though always neatly-clad Rose Brady, gave him, however, little uneasiness; and often and joyfully would Rose come on an evening to cheer poor Patty with her playfulness; for, although we have not been able, from her situation in our history, to put forward this feature of her character, blithe and playful as a bird in spring was little Rose Brady. In truth, the half-cousins loved each other well and truly.

"Oh, my dear Rose! how I have longed to see you!" cried Patty, on the present occasion, hastening to embrace her friend with all the eagerness her feeble state of body would permit.

"My poor Patty!" and Rose hastened to her, and threw her supporting arms round the almost fainting girl; "tell me, why do I find you so wakely? It is enough, in good thruth it is—and as much as I can bear—to have misery in my own little home, where we used to be so happy; but to find you dhroopin' away before my eyes, will break my heart at once.

You must not give up this way; have courage, my own poor Patty, and the Lord will be your friend, and make you better in health, and give more comfort to your young days."

"It was a selfish thought of me, Rose, to afflict your kind, kind heart, when I knew you had griefs of your own pressing on you; but there is no one—no, not one, so true and tender to me as Rose Brady; I cannot lay my head on any bosom so soft as yours, and no one soothes me as you do; no one speaks so gently to me as you do; and no one will make allowances for my weak, weak nature as you do, and—as you *will*," added Patty, tremulously, and in some confusion;— "and don't blame me, then, dearest Rose."

"Indeed and I will blame you."

Patty started, and looked up. Rose continued, pressing her gently to her breast—" but, my *graw bawn*,* not for that; not for what you were saying; not on my own account. No, in thruth, Patty: in the worst sorrow I could be in—and I'm nigh hand in that at present—you must never have a grief untould to Rose. But I *do* blame you for bein' cast down, as I now see you at my side. Patty, whatever ails you, in mind or in body, 'tis a sinful thing not to have a full reliance on God's goodness. He is all-sufficient: an' I know it from myself, what we often think to be an evil, is the best thing in the end. Indeed now, Patty, you must bear up, if it was only for your own poor Rose's sake; you know I love you well and dearly; and you ought to love me as well and as dearly in return"—a soft embrace was Patty's only answer—" well, well, I know you do; and for my sake then, rouse yourself, and be well."

---

* White Darling.

Rose, I could show you a black spot opposite to my heart," sobbed Patty; "and I feel that heart is breaking."

"Now, now, for shame, Patty! I will not let you be talkin' in that fashion. Your little heart is not breakin'; it has no cause to be breakin'."

"Oh Rose, Rose dear"! interrupted Patty, as if she would contradict her friend's assertion, although she spoke no farther words.

"Indeed, and no it hasn't, I bid you; and it will be as well as ever, if you promise me not to fret it; yes, in throth, Patty *vourneen*, you will be happy yet with Divine help, if it is not your own fault."

"If it is not my own fault, you say? Oh, and I do believe you, Rose! and oh, Rose, I feel—I am sure —there is but one thing can ever make me happy!"

"And what is that? can Rose help you on the road to it?"

"No; but do all she can, Rose can't stop me long on the road to it. 'Tis the grave I mean—a quiet grave."

"Once over again, Patty, I tell you I will not listen to such words from your lips."

"But how can I help speaking them? The death stroke is on me. The eyes of the dead have called me out of this life, and I am answering to the summons. But, as you say, Rose, I have to blame myself. Had I taken your sisterly warning; had I put the fatal love from me in time, before it fed my poor heart's blood, I should not now be as I am; the dead could have no claim on me."

"Patty," said Rose impressively, "I have a serious question to ask of you."

The girl quickly raised her heard from Rose's

shoulder, trembled, and looked into her friend's face with an expression of alarm which Rose could not understand, because she knew of no grounds for it, in any subject they could possibly talk over together. She made no remark, however, but put her question.

"Are you positively certain, and will you say it is impossible you could be deceived in asserting, (and now think well before you answer me,) that the face of Joe Wilson appeared to you the night of the robbery?"

"Oh, Rose!"—with an expression of great relief, Patty allowed her head again to rest on its chosen pillow. "Oh, I am as certain of it as I am of having my arms round your neck this moment. I looked full, and I looked long, before I fell, struck down before it, into that pale, wretched face! Others might, but I could not be deceived, my own Rose! and you know the reason; you know his features were too well (ah, yes, too well, too well!) stamped here,"—she pressed Rose's hand against her heart,—" for any semblance of them, to take their own place. Yes, Rose, yes. Living, I loved him; dead, I love him; and he has asked me to join him in the grave, and to the grave I hasten. But why did you ask that question?"

"Your father says he has been robbed; and robbed by my brother Morris, who was found in this house. Morris left his own home that evil night, to go hunt Joe Wilson's ghost in the *bosheen;* and I was thinking that some one, disguised as Joe Wilson, personated his apparition to lead my poor Morris into mischief for his own game."

"No, no, Rose: that is a false supposition. I saw *his* features in this very room, on that very night, as sure as ever I saw them before, and as sure as the last sight of them has numbered my unhappy days; death-like they were—but still—his."

"And an awful thing it was to look on them, Patty, dear, that I grant you. But you must fight up, bravely, against the shock, *ma-vourneen;* pray to God to help you; your own Rose will pray for you mornin' and night; and you must conquer. And, listen to me now, my dear little soul; what I am goin' to say, I have often said to you before; an' I wouldn't rake it up to you again, only I know that, oftentimes, the best cure for a disase gives most pain; an' one can't help it. He never, never was worthy of my Patty's tendher heart and innocent mind; in thruth he was not. You never could have been a happy woman with him; God allows all for the best; an', may be, he was taken out o' this life to hindher him from corruptin' your white an' spotless nature, and to save you from a bad, bad man."

"That is the only word I never could, and never can, believe from your lips, dear :" this was said by poor Patty without anger; indeed, that passion had no place in her moral composition. "A little wild he was; and the scandalous world told stories of him, and you gave the world credit; but had you known him the half as well as poor I knew him, you would change your opinion. Oh! he was mild, he was gentle, he was loving!"

"Well, well; I don't want to distress you, Patty, *a-chorra,* but you will do one thing for Rose; promise her you will thry to be better; and when she is happier her own self, no earthly thing in her power will she leave undone, to help to make her Patty happy too; and we'll talk of him another time; and it may turn out that you will change my opinion of him:

but be well, Patty, be well; do, an' may the heavens bless you!"

"Rose," replied the poor girl, with a weak smile, that glimmered over her worn and faded cheek, like November's watery and chance sunbeam, over the dismantled landscape; "Rose, I do not want to be well, and may God forbid I should be!"

"And may God pardon you that prayer, Patty; for 'tis flying in His holy face to say it!" chided Rose, rather severely.

"Don't be cross with me, my only friend, and we so near parting for ever. Oh, Rose, Rose!" here she hid her face in Rose's bosom, and her strange agitation again occurred; "I could tell you something— and, before I die, I will—but not now—not now—'tis impossible!" They interchanged gentle tears and a soft downy embrace: after a pause, Patty resumed:

"There is another thing I want to say to you; and it was chiefly to say it, that I sent Ailleen Morrisay to ask you to come to me: for I should not disturb you in your sorrows and in your duties, merely to make you cry about myself, Rose. Well, God knows how soon we may part: now do not look at me so sorrowfully, but listen. You have a thousand guineas given to you by my mother—listen, I tell you, Rose—do indulge me. The dead have no need of gold; and it is yours, my own dearest Rose;—pray, pray let me make an end, for you do not as yet understand me. Your brother Morris—I touch on a delicate subject, I know,—but, from all I hear, your brother has not done credit to his sister"———

"Patty *a-chorra*," interrupted Rose, "you told me just now, that you would not b'lieve certain words out of my lips about a certain person; I say the same to you now, on the head o' your words about my poor Morris; an' I tell you, he has done nothing to discredit his sister, himself, or his father's grey hairs; an' that, undher God, the same will be made plain to the world."

"I hope and pray you may be in the right, Rose, as you always and ever are, although appearances are so much against him. But give ear to me. My father will not appear against young Morris Brady, if his beloved gold be returned to him; he has told me so often; give him the gold you possess; it is more, even by his own account, than he has lost; it cannot be better bestowed than in making my Rose and her family happy again; and do not deny me my request, dear, dear friend; do not, if you would wish to give me some comfort on my death-bed."

Rose looked at her half-cousin tenderly, tearfully, and admiringly. She kissed her pale and hot lips, and it was some time before she could speak. At length, however, she answered:

"This is only what I could expect from my own good and loving Patty, But, *a-lanna*, listen to me now in your turn, and let me say my own sayin'. An' first about yourself, Patty dear. With the blissin' o' heaven, the mournful thoughts you have in your head will come to nothing: an' you are in no state to be dhramin' o' giving away your good purse-full o' goold to any body, or upon any account whatever. Twenty times over I tould you that, an' I tell it to you again; an' if you give me cause to repate it another time, you will vex me, Patty—a thing I know well you wouldn't like to do.

"And now about Morris. Morris Brady is my brother, an' I know him well; an' tho' people say it, an' tho', for the present, his sister cannot, with any hope to be heard, stand up for him an' his good name, yet I declare to you, as I declared to you before, that, in my heart an' soul, I am as certain he never touched your father's money, as that we are sitting here together this blessed day. And I'm not done, Patty; hearken to me to the end, as I hearkened to you.

"Even if I was quite sure that your goold would bring my father an' my poor wandherin brother home again, safe an' sound to our little cabin, I would not put a penny of it to that use: an' don't mistake me, Patty, my rason is this. If I did take you at your word—and a kind and a sisterly one it is—then the world, or suppose your father only, would think them guilty of an action they never dhreamt of. No, no, Patty; your goold, and ten thousand times as much along with it, could not buy us the happiness we want at our humble fireside, and that you would like to see us enjoying there. It would not buy us the happiness that a good name gives. It would fix a bad name, that we don't deserve, on us. No, *ma-vourneen*, I rely on the good and just God to send them home to their family, without a spot on them. No; I will still keep your own for you, Patty, and may Providence long spare you to enjoy it, and reward you well for your good intentions."

There was much more of tender confidence between the girls before they parted.

CHAPTER XV.

On the night of the day of her visit to Patty, Rose Brady sat alone at the fire; her brother Daniel and her sister had retired to their beds, and her mother slept. Rose's mind was fully engrossed by the importance of the objects she had in view—namely, the liberation of her father, and the vindication of Morris from the heavy charge made against him. Again and again she debated how she could best set to work, alone and unassisted. Without any lowering doubts of herself, Rose began to wish for some friendly and confidential advice and assistance.

There was one who, were he at hand, she was certain of commanding. But she knew that William Duncan had gone twenty miles from home the morning after their last interview. A rapid step approached the door, and some one knocked smartly at it—some one? did Rose, in her mind, say " some one? " No, indeed; she knew well whose foot it was, and in a few seconds the heavy bar was removed from the door, and the object of her thoughts bounded over the threshold. He took the hand of welcome which was extended to him; he took—we may tell this time—more than that; in fact, he embraced his betrothed mistress more earnestly than he had ever before done; and with a peculiar expression, too, of cherishing her, of solacing her, and of condoling with her, which did honour to his manly and disinterested love.

" You look terribly heated and fatigued, dear William," said Rose, as they sat down together at the fire.

" Twenty long miles since five o'clock, Rose; and the worst of the journey to me was, that every mile seemed ten."

" Twenty miles since five o'clock! you do not mean a-foot?"

" But I do, though; my horse was laid up: I couldn't get another at hand; and I wouldn't stay away from you one moment."

" Why, you must have run the whole way, poor boy!—an' so, William,——"

" An' so, Rose, I am here to stand by you, my own Rose, against the wide world! and, if livin' crature can do it, to bring your poor father an' our poor brother home to you again, an' soon."

" 'Tis like you, William dear."

" Oh, Rose, when I heard this evening for the first time, that misfortune was undher your roof the last five days, I thought my senses would fail me! ' Rose will say I am careless of her sorrow,' was my first thought; and my foot never rested since, till I stood an' knocked at your dour."

" I wouldn't have opened the dour at your knock, William, this time o' the night, an' I sittin' alone, if I had that opinion of you."

" Well, an' somehow, I guessed as much; for, along the road, afther the first dhread went off, I rasoned with myself, and I said, 'supposin' I was in her case, would Rose grow cold or careless to me?'"

"An' what answer did you make yourself, William?"

"No, I said, Rose would not neglect me only for being in misfortune."

"And, indeed, you answered well for me. But, my poor boy, you are weary, an' you are hungry an' thirsty; we must look afther a bit an' a sup for you; an' you won't think the worse o' your little supper, because Rose's hand sets it down before you."

There was something done in consequence of this little speech; and then Rose stood up and busied herself at her self-imposed task.

Her stock of provisions was not very extensive. She had, however, a large bowl full of eggs; and, at the very top of the heap were three, in particular, marked with a cross in ink, to denote that they had been laid that day; and these, previous to the entrance of William Duncan, Rose had destined for her father's breakfast next morning. Now she took them out of the bowl and put them on the table; a little qualm of conscience smote her: was she about to prefer another person's comfort to that of her father? Filial affection guided her hand to the matchless three, and one of them was restored to the bowl: but love lifted up her arm, and the two others were dressed for her visitor.

Nay, the triumphant little deity was not satisfied with this sacrifice; he actually made Rose half skim the bowl of milk which had been set to provide cream for Randal Brady's breakfast; and the spoil of the larceny was given to William Duncan.

Whether by accident or design, Rose was further able to set before her hungry lover bread manufactured by her own hand, and, as she well knew, exactly to his taste in certain particulars; and "Kirkeen" butter, and plain butter, she also placed at his disposal. In tea Rose was an epicure; and to crown William's repast, she produced some of so rare a quality, that it perfumed the apartment; and all her skill was exerted to draw it, and to brew it to the highest pitch of perfection. From a little corner cupboard she fetched cold meat; and when all her materials were ready, Rose spread a nice white cloth over her little round work table; arranged them on it; drew the table near to the fire where William sat, and finally took a seat opposite to him, occupying herself in supplying him, hot and hot, with potatoes roasted to a certain luxurious crispness, by careful and judicious turning on the fire.

William Duncan watched all Rose's motions with a constant eye, from the beginning to the ending of her hospitable proceedings in his favour: and her eye often encountered his, and smile for smile was interchanged between them. Indeed, taking into account the state of his stomach, as well as the increased value which, all lovers admit, a mistress gains during a short separation from her adorer, we question if William Duncan ever thought Rose so handsome and engaging as on the present occasion. Can it be much wondered, indeed, that with such tempting viands before him, and a fast of some seven hours, and a walk in frosty weather of four, to edge his honest appetite, and Rose's good-tempered smile to cheer him on, if he made a manful supper?

When he had done, he took his entertainer by the hand; and, without hesitation, she assumed her privileged place at his side.

"As your foot came to the door, William, I was thinking of you."

"And how did your thoughts run on me, Rose *ma-cuishla ma-chree?*"

"I was thinking that, if you were here, you would advise me what is best to be done for the poor father and brother."

"As to that, *ma colleen*, there is more good sense in your little finger, than is to be found in me from top to toe, except when my own business that I was brought up to is the matther in hand. But two heads are betther than one, at any rate; so, let us sit so close that a shaving could not fit between your's and mine, and by that means we'll surely hit on what's the best to be done."

"Tho' I'd wish to give you word for word when you're in spirits, my dear William, you won't blame me if I find it hard to be merry to-night."

"'Tis *I* am to blame, Rose; 'tis I am to blame; I ought to have recollected myself, and kept a joke for another time: only you will make some excuse for me, when you call to mind how very happy I am to have you sitting by my side once again."

"No indeed, William, you are not to blame at all: I only grieve that I can't find heart to make you as happy as you deserve."

"Listen, Rose; I swear to you by—"

"Don't swear, William; no oaths;" and smiling softly, she put her little hand across his mouth. The lips must have been marble which could have refused to press in turn against the palm which pressed them. Of course William could not speak till Rose permitted him; this she soon did, however, and he resumed:

"Well, Rose, I won't swear; and I believe you

know that it is no fashion o' mine to give way to that foolish as well as bad habit; but, without swearing, I'll tell you the thruth, an' the thruth only. There is more happiness for William Duncan when *you* talk to him in this confiding way, than if all the rest o' the wide world were layin' riches at his feet."

" And, without the smallest oath coming from your lips to make your saying sure, I tell you I believe you."

There was much more endearing and egotistical conversation between the lovers, which, in mercy to all readers not in love, we skip, in order to take up the discourse at a time more useful to us; though, even now, we cannot help it if Rose and William will occasionally digress from business, to talk about themselves.

" And you did not b'lieve what they said of Morris, when you heard it, William?"

" Tut, tut, Rose, I b'lieved no such thing. I know what Morris is, from a boy—from a child up to this day: I know that if the notion came into his wild noddle, he'd jump headforemost into the river, afther a sthraw, at the time o' the highest flood that ever tore along its banks; but I know, too, that he'd no more stoop to lift up another man's substance, than he'd raise a hand against his father's grey hairs. Oh no, no, Rose, I gave no ear to the story I heard. But they did not tell me exactly how the foolish charge came to be made; for, in thruth, I didn't wait to put many questions, when it got into my head that you might want my help."

" I cannot tell you, my dear William, what a cheering thing it is for me to hear, out o' your lips, that

L

good opinion of the brother I love. It is when the world frowns we know the value of a thrue heart."

" 'Tis no fashion o' mine, Rose, to go about, sounding my own good name; but I don't boast when I tell you that my heart *is* thrue and loyal; an' if it wasn't, William Duncan would not own it for an hour—if he could help it."

Rose pressed his hand, and—(but hush.)

William then asked Rose to put him in full possession of the whole matter. She did so; and after the narration, communicated to him her impression that Morris had been induced to enter Barnaby Roundhead's house, under the influence of a supposed supernatural leader. For, notwithstanding Patty's earnest assertions on the subject, Rose had come round to her first opinion of a mock ghost; she calculated that the two girls had been terrified beyond the power of making sure observations; particularly as their minds had, immediately before, been pre-occupied by thoughts of the vision.

"And I had come to the resolution, William, before you entered the house, of ascertaining the thruth of the business."

"And how, Rose dear?"

"The only way to proceed is to discover who put on the likeness of Joe Wilson's spirit. If this man is found out, we may learn from him what has become of Morris; and from Morris's own story measures may be taken to show to the world that he is wronged."

"Very right, Rose: and what did you intend to do, in order to catch the sham ghost?"

"I was thinkin' of goin' out myself, to meet the apparition on his nightly walk in the bosheen yonder."

"You, Rose! how you frighten me!"

"I know I am only a weak girl, William, and I know there would be danger in my path; aye, great danger; but then, a father's and a brother's happiness and good fame are very precious things to the daughter and the sister; and I would be in a good and a holy cause; and God would be with me, and defend me."

"Don't spake one word more about it, Rose; 'twas your good angel sent me here, trotting along the road, to save you. 'Tis now half-past eleven," he continued, looking at his watch; "and by all I heard before I went into the counthry, this misther ghost, or whatever else it may turn out to be, walks along the *bosheen* every night at twelve?"

"So I have heard, William."

"This very night then, *I* will cross his path: and if there is flesh and bones under his bad skin, he'll account to me, or I'll know why he refuses."

"William, I will go with you: you may be hasty and run headlong into danger. I will stand by you, and my word will warn you."

"No, no, Rose; no such thing: don't blame me for being so blunt; but this is a man's work, an' a woman would spile it. Have no fear about me. Alone I go. And I'll just take this little shillelagh for company," reaching down that which had felled the bellowing and brutal ox, Jack Withers. "No other help I ask; and if Ould Nick himself comes there, I'll have him by the horns, or he must account to me."

"Dear William, let me accompany you."

"See here, Rose. Your own father taught me how to use this sapling, and he says I can now give himself a lesson on it; and if it doen't work well in its ould masther's cause,—*nau bocklish.* * Rose, without a

---

* Never mind.

bit of gasconading, there never yet stood before me a man that could daunt me; and if it is the case, as you say, that a mortal crature plays those pranks on the good neighbours, I'll give him permission to cock his pistol, if he has one, and before his finger comes to the trigger I'll have him at my feet."

There was, without flourish, a manly confidence in his own prowess, which did not lose its value in his mistress's eyes.

"I have not the least doubt of your courage, William; my only fear is that it may take you too far; that, for the sake of laying your family cudgel upon the injurer of the family it belongs to, you will not be cool enough to think and to parley. You know, William, your business is to make a discovery, not to break bones."

"I see, Rose, I see now; and I promise you—I give you my hand and word, that if the impostor goes down on his knees, and openly confesses every iota of his roguery, and answers every question I may put to him, without humming or hawing, I will lodge him in jail without cracking his crown; but, Rose, if I find him sulky, and not inclined to talk, or if I detect one little lie on his tongue—in that case, Rose, I make you no promise of any kind. But now, Rose, you must make a promise to me. I guess what's passin' in your mind. You're thinkin' of stealing out afther me. I can hear of no such thing; and you must declare on your sacred word, that you will stay in the house till I come back to you."

"William, I don't like to make that promise, because ——"

"I won't listen to your because, *ma-chree;* the promise I must have; come, come, the time is slipping away; I ought to be in the bosheen some minutes ago."

" Well, William, if I must I must; and so I do promise you."

" On your sacred word, you will not follow me this night, but stay here for me ?"

" On that pledge, I say I will not follow you this night, and here I will wait till you come back."

" My own darling girl you are ! I'm off then. God be with you, dearest Rose."

" The heavens bless you and shield you, William." A short embrace which, however, made up in honest ardour for its want of duration, was given and taken, and he darted over the threshold. Rose looked after him until his form mingled with the darkness of the night; she lingered until his footstep failed to sound on her ear, and then she re-entered the house and sat down, thoughtfully and anxiously wishing better luck to the new ghost-hunter than had befallen a former one.

CHAPTER XVI.

It will be recollected that, on the night when our tale began, a certain little wicked old creature, Hesther M'Farlane, or Hesther Bonnetty, her more usual appellation, made her appearance at Randal Brady's fireside; and also, and what is of more importance, that, from her foul lips, Morris Brady first derived the exciting intelligence of the visibility of Joe Wilson's ghost in the *bosheen*.

We are now compelled to have much more to say to old Hesther Bonnetty.

She was a native of the town in which the occurrences we detail took place. Her parents were reckoned " comfortable in their times." Their house was of long standing in their popular line of business; and they had the reputation of being the brewers of the very best *shebeen*.

At all hours, from eight in the morning to· ten at night, a huge pot simmered on their kitchen fire; and he or she who consumed to the measure of one quart of their *shebeen* was, as a matter of course, entitled to a slice of the beef contained in the cauldron, together with the round of a loaf—payment being expected for the liquors only. Those generous times are past and gone. The thirsty man must now be contented with a very thin potation indeed, compared with the almost glutinous beverage imbibed by his happier forefathers; and he must pay for it, into the bargain, treble the price demanded of them for an article ten times, aye, it has been sworn to us, twenty times better. As for the cut of beef and the round of the good home-made loaf, the sellers of liquors now-a-days can hardly find such fare for their own tables.

Hesther had been a beauty; and "Hetty of the Red Cow," the sign, for three generations in her family, of her parents' house of entertainment, was in her youth quite as celebrated as their ale. But Hesther was as vain, and arrogant, and ill-tempered as she was beautiful. To her numerous admirers she behaved very scornfully; but, though she dealt harshly enough by them, the true gall and venom of her nature seemed reserved for any unhappy girls who dared dispute with her the palm of female sovereignty, even in the case of a single one of her rejected lovers; so that however her young neighbours of her own sex might display and insist upon their charms in her absence, none durst venture on a flirting manœuvre, nay, hold up their heads before her. They dreaded the deadly spite of her tongue, put forth in the shape of the most cutting satire and ridicule, or perhaps venting itself in a blighting calumny.

In her pride of prime, we may hence conclude that Hesther had but few feminine acquaintances; she certainly had not one friend. And when this haughty and scurrilous daughter of Eve, notwithstanding all her previous scorn of the male sex, became guilty of an irrecoverable and unhidable false step, it cannot be wondered at if the outcry against her was general and violent. In vain did Hesther endeavour to brave the consequences of her error; in vain did she sally forth into the streets, determined to let the world see how exceedingly little she thought about it. Insult, derision, or contempt met her at every step, and she returned home crest-fallen; the natural gall of her heart made ten times more bitter.

In a short time Hesther left the place of her birth, taking with her all the ready money possessed, after lives of great industry, by her parents. The sister beauties of her town, at least all those of her own humble rank, looked cheerful and greatly relieved after her departure. But her father and mother drooped. The world went wrong with them. They lost their business; they closed their doors; the kitchen-cauldron lay, bottom uppermost, in a corner. "The ould Red Cow" was blown down by a storm; and the poor couple died in wretchedness, after having severally bequeathed a curse to the unnatural cause of their ruin.

Between forty and fifty years after this event, Hesther re-appeared, at first unknown and unrecognised, in her native city. Indeed, it was impossible for any one with whom she impudently claimed acquaintance, to discover in the sallow, wrinkled, and spiteful physiognomy of the old woman before them, the slightest residue of the charms which had once distinguished "Hetty of the Red Cow."

But although she failed by every other means to make herself known, she still possessed, in unimpaired, if not augmented force, her tongue—for age, we believe, seldom injures in a woman the powers of that little member; and Hesther could at least inspire fear and wonder by her knowledge of the details of long-gone scandal, which the hearers, for nearly half a century, had hoped lay buried in the grave with its author.

In the first instance, after her unwelcome return, Hesther took up her quarters among the poorest of her species; but even to them the incessant virulence of her speech rendered her unendurable. Door after door became shut against her; until at last, muttering curses against every human being, she was compelled to choose her abode in a place where, with the exception of rats, bats, and screech-owls, she was the sole inhabitant.

One of the principal streets of the town ran straight to a bridge, which crossed a good broad stream. Along the little quay branching from the bridge, at one hand Hesther hobbled her way to the rear of a ruinous old mansion, of which the front faced the street mentioned, and which was nearly the last next to the river. It had long been untenanted; its out-offices were in complete ruins; the hall which they had surrounded lay in heaps of rubbish; and over this rubbish the outcast old woman would scramble to her home—a cellar, namely, of the deserted house, which she gained through a narrow arch-way, and a flight of stone steps. This den was arched over head, and divided into two apartments; and in that next to the entrance Hesther dwelt. In one corner was a ricketty bedstead; and when she slept, she was protected against the damp only by a piece of straw matting hung against the wall at the head of her miserable couch. There was some clumsy contrivance for a fire-place in another corner; and a three-legged stool, and a straw boss, completed the catalogue of her furniture. Into the second apartment, accessible by an open door-way in the solid party wall, Hesther never entered, though she often directed her voice into it from her bed at night, praying for heavy curses on the gambolling or scratching rats, whose occupations, or whose vagaries therein, would not let her sleep. Sufficient light crept down the stone steps, from the arched door above, to let her see what she was about in the day time; but the unexplored portion of her residence was perfectly dark.

There were many remarks passed by shrewd observers, when it was known that old Hesther Bonnetty had taken up her abode in this deserted place. Vague rumours had for some time been afloat, that she held intercourse with others than her own shunned and shunning fellow creatures; and these arose chiefly from her own manner of speaking; for she would threaten any who roused her wrath with ruin and perdition, and assert her power to effect her threat; and as it was pretty well known that earthly power she had none, the plausible conclusion was that she confidently depended on agency of an unearthly description.

What might have been the exact extent of people's suppositions on this subject, has not come within our knowledge. Exclusively, however, of the fact of her having chosen so lonely a place of residence, it was plain that old Hesther could not, with her own hands, have drilled a hole through the top of her den, to let the smoke out; nor have so thoroughly repaired the dilapidated door, through the head of the stone steps, as to be able to bolt and bar it against all intruders. Without any extraordinary stretch of understanding, it might, indeed, have occurred to the commentators, that, if Hesther could boast of supernatural assistants, they might as well have supplied her with a comfortable and respectable domicile off-hand; or, at any rate have given her an entirely new door, instead of patching up, no matter how strongly, her old one; but speculations of this kind are not generally famed for consistency.

Witch or not, fairy woman or not, ghost-seer or not, Hesther had lived in this suspicious place for about two years before our acquaintance with her. Over her outward rampart of rubbish she daily clambered, and out into the streets she daily issued, to levy contributions for her miserable existence. Not, indeed, that she sought to arouse, in her favour, the charity of good Christians; no such thing; she extorted what she demanded by the terror of her tongue; and the bribe for quietness was bestowed, as some savage nations sacrifice to their divinity, not to engage his good offices, but to wile him from his wicked intentions towards them.

We should not have felt ourselves authorized to be thus particular in our notice of Hesther and her den, did we not find it necessary to pay her a visit upon our lawful business, namely, the furtherance of our tale, with which, unhappily, the old sinner has more to do, than, had we our free choice, we should have consented to.

On the same night, and nearly at the same hour that Rose Brady and William Duncan conferred together, as has been faithfully reported in the last chapter, concerning Morris Brady's fate, Morris himself was sitting *tête-à-tête* with Hesther Bonnetty in her dwelling.

The old woman was placed on her boss in front of the decaying fire, and Morris Brady was seated further back in the shade of the apartment, on the only other seat it afforded—the three-legged stool. Their single taper—and that shed but a niggardly ray—was the pith of a rush greased, which Hesther had fastened in the slit of a piece of wood, driven into the wall, at one side. Morris seemed deeply absorbed in his reflections; and Hesther was keenly observing him from the corner of her snake-like eyes.

"This is the night he was to give his summons," he said suddenly, rather to himself than to his unamiable companion : "to-night we were to meet again. "Oh! I would give the world's wealth to be out of this toad-hole!"

"An' a curse blister you! who sent for you to come into id?—did I invite you to cumber my flure? did I?" turning fiercely, and fixing her piercing eyes upon him.

"An', if you don't like to have me here, neither was it by choice I came."

"Don't I know that widout you're tellin'?— *hannuch thu, murroch thu*—if lock, or boult, or bar could have kept you on the outside, you had never darkened my dour; bud the evil sperit stood over me, an' tould me of your comin'; an' well he knew I was in his power, and daren't say him no."

"Was Joe Wilson's ghost an evil sperit?" questioned Morris solemnly.

"*Och-hone-ee-oh!* it's well your tongue gets loose

at last. Four nights and five days you're skulkin' in my place, throwin' a shadow on my flure, and doin' no good bud atin' an' sleepin', and ten words at a time never come from you till now. But listen. There isn't that man or woman above the ground can tell you about sperits the same as I can."

"Then give answer to my question."

"If it's plain I will; if it's not plain, curse on the word you'll hear out o' my mouth. Say id again."

Morris made no answer. Hesther most angrily commanded him to repeat his former question.

"You heard it before plain enough; an' I'm in no humour to spake the same thing twice, to plaise your whim."

Hesther looked almost incredulity at the audacious reply offered to her dignity. Then her rage exploded in a fierce burst of abuse, until, for peace sake, Morris re-stated his question.

"I asked you, and I ask you, was Joe Wilson's ghost an evil sperit?"

"Before I tell you my mind, you must tell me yours. Let me hear from your mouth all your doins the night you met the ghost in the ould abbey, an' swore an oath to him at the head of the prior's tomb, wid your hand on a skull."

Morris started, and then asked, "How did *you* come to know that?"

"Hee, hee-e!" Hesther's laugh was a lengthened squeak. "I heard o' the like afore, maybe, an' that was a token to me; go on wid your story; what did you do, and where did you go, when you left the berrin-ground?"

"The sperit walked before me through the sthreets o' the town, and I followed him."

" But though you saw him movin', your ear caught no footsteps?"

" No; an' I remarked it at the time."

" Hee-ee!—there's no sound from a sperit's thread."

Morris continued: " We went into the heart o' the town, an' I found it hard enough to keep the ghost in sight without racin' afther him. For a little time I lost him, an' thought the air took him from my view. But passing Mr. Roundhead's house, I saw him standin' at the door. He beckoned to me again with his arum. The dure opened before him without his touching it, and I walked afther him into the house. There was a light round the sperit as he went up the stairs, but how it came I could not see nor undherstand."

" 'Twas a sulky red light, like the light from our fire here."

" It was exactly," assented Morris, much interested. " Can you explain it to me?"

" *Och-hone-a-ree!* an' I have good right, so I have, to know all about id. But put no questions till a finish is made of your story. Go on wid id."

" I went up the stairs in the sperit's thrack. Before I came to the lobby I saw him at a door. It opened wide for him' as the hall door had done. He turned and looked at me to follow, and I went into the room in his steps. There was a tall candle burnin' on the floor. While I was whonderin' at it, the sperit left my sight; and though he had gone in before me, I now saw him standin' outside the door-way.

" ' Count four boords from the window towards yourself,' his voice said.

" I did his biddin.

" ' Rise it up,' he commanded me again."

"What did you find undher the boord?" interrupted Hesther, eagerly.

"There were only some ould garments and some papers undher it," answered Morris.

"Are you sure there was no money?"

"I saw no money. The sperit's voice came to me a third time, when I had raised the boord:

"'Take up the paper tied with the black ribbon, and sealed with the black seal, and put it carefully in your bosom,' it said.

"I saw the paper on the top o' the rest, an' I did take it up, and put it into my bosom. There came a noise through the house. The sperit addhressed me once again.

"'They will saize on you, and you will be locked up a prisoner; make no struggle against them; your business here is ended, and I will free you if they put a thousand locks and bars upon you: make no sthruggle I say, unless they offer to sarch you, and then resist with your life, for the paper you have they must not touch nor see: they are near you now; stoop over the hole again, and look into it, and don't fear to meet them.'"

"An' you were saized on?" asked Hesther.

"I was. A little while after the sperit passed from before my eyes at the door, Mr. Barney Roundhead and his boy came upon me. They took me to another room, and locked and boulted me in. It was pitch dark. I couldn't see a stime, no more than if I was in the grave."

"An' the sperit was as good as his word?"

"Yes. All was soon quiet outside. The dour opened of its own accord; light came into the room; the sperit stood abroad on the lobby; he beckoned me;

I followed him; he led me harmless out of the house; every lock, and bar, and boult, and chain, gave way before him. I thraced his steps to this place. I could not see him when I came in, but I heard his low hollow tones close by me:

"'Mind your oath. Keep the paper safe till you see the dead again. And for five nights dare not to put your foot over the threshold of this safe retrate; on the fifth night from this I will summon you to do more work for me.'"

"You are positive sure you took nothing from the house but the paper?" again questioned the old woman.

"I am positive sure that I took nothing else whatever."

"Is that paper now upon you?"

"It is, as safe as when I found it."

"Take it out o' your bosom an' show id to me."

"It shall not quit me."

"Let me look on id in your own hands."

Morris drew forth the paper. It was exactly such as he had described it. Hesther eyed it askance.

"What writing is that on the outside of id?"

Morris read from the packet—

"The last will and testament, duly witnessed, of Joseph Wilson."

"An' now you want to be tould, was id an evil sperit that led you through the night?"

"Yes, that I want to know, if you can thruly tell me."

Hesther turned fully round to him, placed her hands on the crook of her crutch, and her peaked chin on them, and fixing her piercing eyes on his fine, wild ones, continued:

"You unlooky spawn of a boy! it *was* an evil sperit. There are none bud the tormented sowls that walk the arth on the *duoul's* arrand have power over me."

"How did they get that power over you?"

Morris was at last in his glory; he had met and discoursed with a ghost, and done him some good service; and now he was in a fair way of receiving capital lessons in all that relates to the economy, manners, habits, and somewhat puzzling motives of action of the dim and shadowy world of apparitions.

"How did they get that power over me? hee-ee-e! I'll tell you then; and, mind now, my words are to be a comfort to you."

The expression of the hag's face was hideously malignant.

"Hearken to me well wid both your ears. Aye, listen to me, young Masther Morris Brady, an' take good note o' what I'll say,; 'twill be a pleasant story to you.

"Hee-ee-e! I was livin' by the sey-side in the north counthry, only you'll never know where—never know where, if the knowledge was to save your sowl. An' my house was a house for thravellers to stop at. An' of a blowin', stormy night, there was a man sleepin' in id, a way-farin' man; they said he had money; but I'll not plaise you wid givin' you the knowledge of that either; no, never will you larn o' me whether he had or no. Well, sure that man never woke from his sleep; an' it's no matther to you how he came by his death; bud I'll let you into this mooch o' the news; there was another man taken up for killin' the thraveller, but he had no more hand in id than you had, that wasn't in the land o' the livin' at the time; hee-ee-e!

"Well, again. The ghost o' the hanged fellow haunted my house, an' there was no rest or pace for him. He vexed me, an' I said I'd meet him; an' 'tis by what happened to myself wid that ghost, that I guessed you took an oath on the ould skull in the ould abbey; for I did the same thing by min' in a church-yard in the north, an' I swore to do every thing he'd bid me.

"Bud, when he tauld me o' the thing he wanted me most to do, I kep' off from doin' it, like an *aunshuck** as I was; to tell you the blessed thruth, Masther Morris, I didn't half like the business."

"What did the spirit command you to do? questioned Morris, as she paused, grinning gleeishly at him.

"To get my own lawful husband hanged on the gallows-three, *ma bouchal*."

"Why? for what cause or reason?"

"Whisper—for takin' away the life o' the thravellin' man that slept so sound in our house, the night I spoke to you of."

"Oh, surely you didn't keep your oath in that?"

"I tould you afore, I didn't half like the work. The husband I had at that time was as comely an' as pleasant a young blade as a woman's eye ever looked upon; an' I didn't quite agree, off hand, to turn him over to the *nebbeah*;† howsomever, I was runnin' on it in my mind, *a-vich*."

"What!" interrupted Morris, indignantly, and with his usual rapidity.

---

* Simpleton.   † Jack Ketch.

"Becase," continued Hesther, not now allowing herself to be disturbed, "I heard before what comes o' breakin' an oath to the dead; an' more betoken, there was as well-lookin' an' as hearty a boy as my husband ever was in his best day, comin' round me at that same time. But, while I was dilly-dally on the matther, the ould *duoul* dhrauned the husband on me, an' then I couldn't do what I was the fool to lave undone.

"An' now listen as I tould you to do. From that day to this the sperit haunts me; an' because I broke the oath to the dead, every evil sowl that comes to the good Christhens on the divel's arrand has power over me; an' for that same rason, I daren't refuse shelther to your unloocky head when an evil sperit tould me to give id to you: an' for that same rason again, here you are to be a plague an' a curse to me."

"Because you broke an oath to the dead, every bad sperit has power over you?" asked Morris, reflectively and solemnly.

"Yes, every imp o' darkness that torments this arth to do evil. I knew it would plaise you—hee-ee-e! An' mind me again. I have more comfort in store for you. Because I broke an oath to the dead, ruin and desthruction came upon me, root an' branch, kith, kin, an' relation; all were taken from me; till here I sit, an ould broken-down wandherer, without one livin' sowl to give me a kind look or a kind word, an' all because I broke the oath to the dead; an' isn't that pleasant for you to hear, *ma bouchal?* hee-ee-e!"

"May the Lord protect and guide me!" ejaculated Morris fervently.

"Aye, pray, pray, before it is too late. But harkee me, harkee me. There was a mortal sin, twice repated, on your sowl, or the sperit wouldn't have the power to put that oath; an' I'll tell you what the sin was. Against your ould father's commands you quitted his house two nights runnin'. Isn't that the thruth, Masther Morris Brady?"

Morris stared at the malevolent old creature, who squeaked in glee at the terror she saw she had excited; and "five nights," he said sorrowfully, "I have not been at home, and Heaven knows what may have come upon all there. Father, I can never stand before your face."

"I don't think he'll ever let you darken his door again—hee-ee-e."

"I'll quit this dungeon and fall on my knees before him;" and, at the impulse of the moment, he was rushing to the door.

"*Och-hone-a-ree!* do, brave boy, an' my blessin'— that brings a curse where it falls—go wid you. Do, break your oath to the dead, an' I'll have company among my good fellow-cratures."

Morris turned and scowled at her, and his mind fled back from its purpose.

"What do you stop for now? Why don't you give me a riddance o' your sight? Why don't you quit the dungeon an' the toad-hole?" continued Hesther.

"Stop your tongue from tormentin' the heart within my body, you evil ould *culloch*," answered Morris furiously.

"Foul blisthers to your tongue; do you dare call me by such a name, stannin' on my own floor?" and her eyes flashing venomously, she started up, ran to the young man, and raising her crutch, continued:

"Get over my thrashold! lave my place! and may every damned imp purshue you to your own! quit, and let me shut my door upon you."

"Keep from me, you witch of Endor; don't touch me, I warn you."

The lad looked dangerously at her. She paused. For an instant she had unguardedly given way to her spiteful though impotent rage; now she checked herself, and retreated to her *boss*.

There was silence between the belligerents for a short time; but only for a short time could Hesther tolerate it. First, while poking with her crutch the embers of the decaying fire, she began to mutter indistinctly; by degrees her words became clearer, and her voice grew louder and louder, until at length it regained its usual pitch of screaming discord.

The theme turned out to be a tirade against the family of her unwilling guest, maternal and parental. One of the Bradys, she asserted, had been hanged at Gallows-hill, for an underhand connexion with a famous gang of freebooters; and as for those from whom Morris was descended, on the mother's side, Hesther reproached him with the odium of having "a black protestan' dhrop" in his veins, and insisted that one of his mother's ancestors had been town-crier, and therefore was Morris entitled, according to Hesther's vocabulary, to the epithet of "a bawler's breed." But all this geneological dissertation was lost on Morris, who, in utter contempt and carelessness of his miserable associate, had deeply plunged into his own reflections.

As people of ardent temperament will do, he burst into soliloquy.

"Oh Rose, Rose! if I could speak with you, you'd guide me on the right way."

Hesther turned her needle-like glances on him.

"Aye, aye, Rose is the posey of your garden; she'll always have my good word, if I hadn't a second to throw at a fellow-creature. Rose never yet shut her door on ould Hesther; no, nor the mother she come from, to tell the thruth; but, Rose, you're my likin' above the whole lot."

"I never was in throuble yet, that my sisther Rose did not bring me out of id,' continued Morris, still as if to himself.

"An' if there's one alive to take you out o' your present hobble, Rose is still the little body to do id," observed Hesther, in marvellous acquiescence and benevolence for her.

"Oh that I could spake with her, only for one minute!" Morris passionately and affectionately exclaimed.

"Hearken to me, Morris Brady," resumed Hesther, quite astonishing the lad with her approach to blandness of tone; "there's no great ill-will in me, afther all, to one o' your name; an' it's well the *shoolin* ghost that brought you here knows that. *Garçoon*, you're in the power of what's to be feared, an' a virgin woman, that turns from the thought o' sin, bids defiance to ould Nick himself, an' there's no time to lose; Rose must meet you here to-night, and that a few minutes before the hour that the sperit will call you again."

"How can I get her to come to me?"

"Send her a word in writin', an' I'll take id to her, an' let me manage the rest."

"There's nothing to write with, or to write on, in this place."

"Wait a bit; don't disparage my house over agin; wait a bit."

The old woman rose up, issued through the door and up the stone steps, and Morris heard her poking and clattering among the rubbish at the rear of her premises. She returned with a fragment of a slate and a rusty nail.

"I know well, *garçoon*, that Rosey, my purty posey, won't quit her father's house on my word, to thraverse the sthreets o' the town at this time o' night; and so here, write down your message on this, an' by the critch that keeps me from fallin' on my face, Rose will be wid you, and soon."

Thrown off his guard by his own impetuous wish to see his beloved sister, although there were grounds of suspicion for a cooler head, in the unusual condescension and earnestness of old Hesther Bonnetty, Morris wrote on the scrap of slate the following requisition:—

"Dear sister Rose,

"For the love of God in Heaven, this night come and speak with me. I believe I have done what is wrong—I depend on you above all the world to bring me right, and to tell me what I am to do. Oh, dear Rose, will the poor father ever give me his blessing again? Rose, come to me; I am in Hesther's vault; she will bring you to me; do not refuse.

"Your loving brother,

"MORRIS BRADY."

"Read the writin' for me," demanded Hesther.

Her request was complied with.

"That 'll do, that 'll do. Sit down now an' wait for me; I'll soon be here, an' Rose by my side."

The hag hurried out, and left Morris to the rats, and his own solitary reflections.

CHAPTER XVII.

Rose Brady continued seated before her decaying fire, anxiously awaiting her lover's return from his encounter with the ghost of the *bosheen*.

A hasty step came up to the door. It was not like his, and yet she thought it could be that of no other person. She arose and listened. The foot paused outside, and the latch was gently raised. Rose, however, had taken the precaution of barring the door.

"Is it you, William?" she asked, doubtingly.

"It is; open, open," was whispered.

Rose softly undid the heavy bar, lest she might awaken her mother, or her brother or sister; she as cautiously opened the door, but drew back in great amazement and some alarm, when, instead of the person she expected to see, the forbidding countenance and the hag-like person of Hesther Bonnetty met her eye.

The old woman quickly hobbled into the house, closing the door after her, and beckoned Rose to the fire.

"Hesther, what is your business here this time o' the night?"

"Come here; come over to me, Rose; I'm here on

your unloocky brother's arrand, an' that's my business, if you want to be tould."

"On my brother's errand! *Do* you know any thing of poor Morris?"

"I do; I know all about him; aye, an' betther than any one else."

Rose half shuddered: it was the first time she had seen anything like a smile on the venomous and puckered features of old Hesther: and that which she now contemplated gave no assurance, Rose felt, of good will.

"Oh! what have you to tell me of Morris? where is he? what has become of him?

"He's hidin' undher my neighbourly roof, ever since the night he quitted his father's, *ma-colleen-dhass,*" answered Hesther, trying to perfect her smile into something very friendly and alluring, while she nodded at Rose.

"Undher one roof with you! My God! what sent him there? what is he doing there?"

"*Hannuch thu, murrach thu,* didn't I tell you? Hidin' himself, hidin' himself; an' blessin' God to have a friend when the purshuit was hot an' hard afther him."

"He went to you for shelter, and of his own will? do you tell me that?"

"My heavy curse stick to the *gawk?* do you think I sent for him? did I want such a *sthockooch** to darken my flure? He come, I bid you, of his own free will, to crave a hidin' hole, for charity; charity from Hesther! hee—ee—e! from Hesther that has nothin' to give, but what she gets from them that

---

* Uninvited guest.

wishes her sthretched at the bottom o' the sey! But there's one house that was always ready to resave me, an' where I never got the look o' hathred or dislike; an' I opened my dour to the son o' that house in the hour of his throuble."

All this was terrible information for Rose Brady. For it occurred to her with the force of conviction, that unless Morris knew himself to be guilty of crime, he would not screen his head in an asylum such as the wretched Hesther could afford him, or stoop, for five days and nights, to such companionship as hers. The anchor on which Rose had rested seemed torn away from her.

"And my unfortunate brother went to *you* to hide," she said, in a low, unsteady voice, sinking upon a chair.

"From Jack Withers an' his crew o' kidnappers; an' he found that the ould woman that has every body's ill word didn't command him over her thrashold; no, nor didn't put money in the heel of her hand, by bringing the hound on the hare in her net."

"Hesther, you know what they say Morris is guilty of; tell me, do they make a thrue charge on him? Is he a disgrace to his father's age?

"He crossed my palm when he crossed my thrashold; an' more money was to the fore, to make sure o' me; an' more again, for the atin' an' the dhrinkin' o' the best."

This lying assertion on the part of the wicked old wretch, went farther than anything else she had advanced to confirm Rose in her worst fears. She might have doubted the crone's disinterestedness, but Rose could easily understand that she would afford protection for gain, and Morris could have come by his money only in one way.

"He desarves a coach an' four horses, for shewin' ould Barney's goold the daylight—hee-ee."

"Miserable Morris! oh, what is to become of you!" wailed poor Rose in agony.

"It's well sorry he is, an' more shame for him, on the head o' what he done; and he was for quittin' his snug hidin' hole to-night, an' scamperin' sthraight a-head, he didn't know where, like a sthrange dog wid an ould kettle at his tail."

"Oh, no, no, no! he must not do that! You must persuade him, Hesther, to rest with you until I consult my father."

"*Och hone-a-ree!* Hesther might as well think o' knocking a horn off o' the moon with her critch. He's a sthrong-headed garçoon, an' he'll have his own way. The father of him couldn't keep young Morris Brady in his bed, when he once thought o' quittin' it in the dead hour o' the night. You must come to him, Rosey-posey, he'll be said an' led by you."

"Me?—yes, Hesther, yes! I will go to him early to-morrow morning."

"Jack Withers or else the ould *duoul* will have Morris afore to-morrow comes. He'll lave my roof to-night. What put in your pate that my ould bones could hould him? an' if he venture a leg over my dour-stone, you'll bid him good by, on a long journey, at the gallows foot."

"I cannot go to-night, Hesther, the hour is too unseasonable—and"—

"A blisther on your tongue! what does Hesther care? Stay where you are by all manes, an' let him thry his fortun'. A good riddance of him Hesther will have."

"Heaven direct me for the best!" prayed Rose: we follow up her thoughts:

" Surely, William Duncan cannot blame me for breaking my word to him to stay in the house, when he knows the cause. But I had better await his return, and he will bear me company. Oh, Morris, Morris, God forgive you, and pity me, and all of us, who suffer in the heart along with you!"

" By the critch, I am proud you're stayin' at home, Rose Brady. 'Twas against my grain I came to see you; an' now I'll have a free house afore the mornin'."

" Morris sent you to ask me to come to him, then?" demanded Rose.

" Yes—an' like an auld *ounshuck*, I said aye to his biddin'. But 'tis pleased I am you're taking your own way, like himself; he's a born eye-sore to me, I tell you; for his sisther's sake I wouldn't dhrive him through my dour; but you can't lay his fortun' to me if the goat takes his jump of his notion: so *bannocth lath*."*

" Hesther, do not go for a little while."

" Hesther will go—aye, will she ; what Hesther said she'd do, she done it; there's no blame upon her; an' it's time for her to seek her home, and rest her ould bones, what she hasn't done these four nights. Here take this from my hand; it went from my head that I had id; here's some botheration scratched down on a slate, that Morris Brady tould me to give you."

Rose approached the light and read her brother's request to visit him.

" My poor Morris! heaven help you this night! Hesther, I *will* go with you; only wait a short time; a friend will soon be here to take care of me through the town."

---

* Good Night.

"What's that your sayin'? There's one to come wid us? An' who is that one?"

"You know him well, Hesther; he is a thrue friend to our family; it is William Duncan; and he will not keep us waiting long."

"May a burnin' curse be your portion! Duv you think I'd open my dour to him, or to any one like him? I'd see the whole bad breed o' the Bradys sthrung up in a row, afore my roof should cover him. If Morris Brady doesn't quit my place two minutes afther I get home, I'll make him rue id. Jack Withers is nigh at hand."

"Oh, Hesther, could you think o' that!"

"You'll see; let me go my ways, or I'll hit you wid the critch!"

"Well, Hesther, patience, and I will go with you this instant."

While the old hypocrite continued to mutter threats of departing alone, and of informing Jack Withers where Morris might be found, Rose quickly attired herself in her blue cloth mantle, and galash, or hood; and pulling the running-string of the latter, so as to nearly close it over her face, she followed the scolding beldame. The door of the house was left only latched.

Perhaps had Hesther paid a visit to any of our fair readers after the perusal of the last chapter, she would not have been with any of them so successful as she was with Rose Brady, in inducing reliance upon her story and her guidance. But it may be necessary to state that, up to this period of their acquaintance, Rose had had no reason to regard the hag as an evil doer. Hesther was known to the whole family, indeed, solely as an object of commiseration and charity; and the supposition that her mind was occasionally, if not always crazed, added to their interest in her regard. Rose did not, therefore, harbour any suspicions of wrong intended against her. She felt that her brother's safety was in her hands; she knew he was incapable of guiding himself; she loved him well and tenderly; his supposed guilt could not weaken the force of her affection; the necessity for seeing him was extreme; and she decided that she ought at once to accede to the prayer of his written petition, of which the authenticity was evident to her at a glance.

Throughout the whole parley with Hesther, the thought of breaking her promise to her lover was what most caused Rose to hesitate. But she argued from her heart, that William Duncan had intended the engagement to be binding only so far as he was himself concerned; and she felt no doubt of his forgiveness, when her motives should be made known to him.

Before leaving the house, Rose had proposed to Hesther to rouse up her young brother Daniel and get him to escort them; but for good reasons—or rather for bad ones—this was successfully resisted by the ancient sinner. Few persons were ignorant of the features of the ruinous and lonely place, in which Hesther Bonnetty had assumed an independent and domineering residence. Rose felt, therefore, no apprehension as she followed her guide over her outworks of rubbish, to the low arched door which gave entrance to her cellar, for, previous to her departure from her own home, Rose's mind had been prepared for some such scene.

"Come! down wid you—down wid you! there's no time for pickin' steps," screamed Hesther, as she paused a moment, looking down the stone stairs into the almost perfect darkness of the vault. Rose did not, however, hesitate long. She entered the apartment.

The single rushlight had burned out. The place was feebly illumined by the red embers of the fire alone. In a remote corner from them, on the three-legged stool, sat a man, drooping his head over his folded arms.

"My poor Morris!" sobbed Rose, falling on his neck.

Clinging and ardent was the embrace which instantly responded to her gentle, though most affectionate one. Never before, Rose thought, had a brother so caressed a sister, but she excused Morris's violence, in consideration of the convulsive state of his present feelings, as well as of the general vehemence of his nature. She was forced to sit on his knees, and when Rose resisted a little, burning lips pressed against hers; with a great effort she sprang up, gazed into the face now no longer hidden from her, and, scanty as was the light in which for an instant she intensely scanned it, Rose saw that it was not Morris's, but that of another whom it froze her blood to look upon.

She uttered a shuddering moan, shrinking down, and wringing her fingers through one another. She looked round for Hesther; the old traitress had left the den. She ran up the stone steps to the door; it had been locked on the outside. She was—she *was* alone with a fearful companion.

CHAPTER XVIII.

About half an hour had elapsed since Rose's entrance into Hesther Bonnetty's den of wickedness. During that period of time, her voice might have been heard, occasionally in accents of indignant or of weeping expostulation, occasionally in those of abject and despairing entreaty. But finally her screams rose high, and loud, and long, and shriek followed shriek without intermission.

"Almighty Father have mercy on me!" she prayed in a woman's bitterest agonies, when a woman is good and heart-pure.

The door was shivered to atoms from without; she sprang up to it, frantic, wild, and still shrieking fearfully: William Duncan, foaming like a lion in his deadliest rage, and flourishing Randal Brady's favourite cudgel, received her in his arms.

"William, William! He who protects the feeblest of his children, when they love him and keep his holy word—He sent you to my prayer." She flung herself round his neck, sobbing convulsively and hysterically.

Some precious moments were lost in mutual embraces. At length her champion said, " Free me

Rose—sit down on these steps—free me instantly; only half my work is done."

But Rose, in her scarcely abated passion of terror, only more tenaciously clung to him, as she cried, " Oh no, no, William ; you must not go down into that place : danger, death is before you."

Not go down !"—he laughed scornfully and wrathfully—" danger before me ! I will go down, Rose, if a dozen pistols were ready pointed at my head. I will go down, not to draw back an inch, till I am satisfied and you are revenged."

" No, no, you must not think of it."

" Tut, Rose, you spake folly now—mere childishness." He disengaged himself, and hurried into the vault. Light was necessary. He tore open Hesther's miserable pallet, and threw some of the straw it contained on the embers of the fire. This gave a good glow, by help of which William Duncan saw Rose following him, while she moaned and wailed incessantly : but the blaze enabled him to discover no other person in the miserable apartment. In vain did he search every nook and corner. He saw the open space leading into Hesther's spare chamber. Appropriating more of her straw, which he held lighted in his hand, William entered the thrice-dark vault. It was quite empty, not even containing any object which could conceal a human being. William stood a moment amazed and confounded.

" Escaped ? escaped ?" muttered Rose, in equal if not greater consternation.

" Yes : and how ? " asked her lover.

" The masther he serves only knows," she answered.

" Who was he ?" continued William Duncan.

" Come with me out of this bad and frightful place,"

pleaded Rose; " we must not, ought not to stay here one instant."

" That is no answer to my question."

" Don't ask me to answer you here; oh, not here," she whispered in his ear.

" Rose, I have to tell you I am not to be fooled. Do you know the man that made you cry out? Who is he? What is his name? By all that's good I must and will know; he must stand before me and answer for it."

" Come home with me, William; oh, take me to my home! I beg it of you, I beseech it of you. Grant me my prayer! you will; oh, I know you will."

" Rose," resumed her lover, laying his hand on her shoulder, and searchingly regarding her—" Rose, I forgot myself on one point; you promised to stay in the house for me, till I should come back to you from the *bosheen;* why did you break that promise? why did you quit your home, at the dead o' the night, to come to this den? What man did you meet here? Do you want to hide him, or anything relating to him and you, from William Duncan? Look up into my eyes, Rose, and tell me that."

" No, no, dearest William. I do not want to hide him from you, I want to screen *you* from *him.*"

" Screen *me* from *him!*" scoffed her lover; " and why so, Rose?"

" Another time I will tell you."

" Now—now, upon this spot, tell me; or, Rose, if you refuse, I *will* set it down that you *are* keeping him from my arm; that—my God! I cannot bring myself to say it."

" No matter, I cannot tell you now, William; think

what you like; let the consequences be what they may to me, I cannot."

Mr. William Duncan began to enact some of the sensible pranks of a lover getting jealous. He snatched away his hand from Rose's shoulder, as he would have done had it lain on the top of a red-hot stone; he stamped upon the floor very much after the fashion of little old Barnaby Roundhead, only with greater energy and effect; and finally he bounded up the stone steps in magnificent wrath, leaving his trembling mistress to follow, and to clamber over the rubbish abroad, as well as she could.

Rose did follow him, in an agony of terror, which seemed to lend wings to her speed. Though William, too, walked on at his best pace, she soon closed upon him, and clung to his arm. He did not, for some minutes, seem to notice his companion; at length, he condescended to stop suddenly, to look into her face, and almost to bellow forth—

" Rose, will you, or will you not, tell me the name of the man that you left your father's house, in the teeth of a solemn promise to me, to meet in that accursed place?"

"William, William," replied Rose, in accents scarce audible, "I implore you to spare me! I feel, in good thruth I do, at my heart's core, what thought of me you are letting come into your mind; but have pity on me, William! even though you suspect me to be an unworthy creature, I must—I must guard the silent tongue."

Without reply he hurried on again more rapidly than before. Poor Rose was compelled almost to run, in order to continue her hold of his arm. After a considerable time, during which neither uttered a word, her angry lover again stopped short, again regarded her, and again spoke:

"Rose Brady, I am one who never knew what double dalin' is; I hate it; I can't bear it in any one I love; it isn't honest; an' there can be nothing friendly or open-hearted where it is. Remember, Rose, remember the understanding that you and I are on. I plighted you my throth honestly and heartily, and the blessin' o' my whole life is in your hands. Tell me, then, tell me fairly, have I not a right, a positive right, to put the question? Rose Brady, what brought you where I found you, and whom did you steal there to meet?"

"You have the right, William, justly and honestly; I do not deny that."

"And—my God!—if I have the right, justly and honestly, ought not you to give me a just and honest answer?"

"I ought, William; but for the present I dare not."

"Nonsense—folly, Rose; nothing else but folly is in your words. Dare not!—if 'tis for me you have any fear, I tell you it would be kinder of you, Rose, to pull the trigger of a loaded pistol at my head, than to let me go away from you with my present burnin' thoughts. If 'tis for yourself you have a fear, depend on me, Rose—depend on William Duncan, your plighted husband—to shield you from all danger, wrong, or villany; he is able to stand for you against the world, and as willing as he is able, if—if you yourself do not put him from your side."

Rose leaned her forehead on the arm to which she clung, but made no answer. After a short pause,

William Duncan's voice changed from its stern hastiness into accents of deep solemnity.

"Rose, when you tell me that you dare not answer me, do you mean that you are ashamed to spake the thruth to me? Did you lave your father's house, at the dead hour o' the night, with that ould hell-hound Hesther, to give a meeting to some one that—I can't say it!—by my eternal chance, I can't say it!"

The words, indeed, stuck in his throat, and he shook from head to foot.

"Lord have mercy on me!" ejaculated Rose, without raising her head.

"And is this to happen, Rose—is this to happen, afther all the store of blessed happiness I thought I saw before me? Oh, my God! are we to go away from one another? Am I to part from you with a blight upon my heart? And while I mourn over your loss, Rose, am I to shed salt tears over your fair name also?"

Again the young man's voice failed him; but it was now interrupted by sobs, and a low wailing.

Rose at length raised her head, and lifted up her lustrous eyes to his face. She had herself been weeping plentifully, but her tears were now dried; her cheeks and lips were pale, and it was something more intense than grief which had blanched them.

"William, dear, it is terrible to hear you crying; very terrible; to listen to you a moment longer would kill me; and altho' I may sorely rue the part I take, and altho' you may sorely rue it, as well as I,—I will satisfy you."

They now stood in the environs of the town, near to Rose's home, beside a large and high square stone castle, which had once formed part of the fortifications on the city wall; but the wall, in this place, having been long demolished, the whole structure was at present in ruins, protruding considerably beyond the line of the suburban street. The moonlight shone full upon the lovers; but, in the direction opposite to the planet's position in the heavens, the castle flung a dense shadow; and peering into this shadow, just as she was about to commence her explanation, Rose started, and fixed her eye on something which seemed greatly to trouble it. Her lover, having his back to the old ruin, confronting Rose, could see nothing; but she certainly recognised a figure, which stood for a moment in the shadow, and then melted away out of it.

"William," she said, in a tremulous whisper, and in a tamed and terrified manner; "to one thing you have said I can plainly make answer—your eyes will never dhrop a tear over Rose Brady's good name. It is very thrue, she might, only a little while ago, have been forcibly and barbarously made unworthy of you; but a merciful and good God, working thro' you, saved her from that. And I intended to tell you more—to tell you all, your piteous tears did so make me shiver; but now that I recollect myself again—I cannot—indeed, indeed, dearest William, I cannot!"

"Keep your secret, then!" he shouted out; "keep it for him that it most concerns—not for me. Rose Brady, a good night for ever!"

He left her standing alone. Looking in anguish and fear around her, she fled after him, again seized his arm, and cried, "for the sake of your own mother, if not for my sake, do not leave me alone in the sthreet!"

Whatever may have been his feelings, he allowed her to lead him towards her father's house, It was not, as we have said, far off; and, walking very rapidly, they soon gained its door.

"Now, William, you will come in with poor Rose?"

"By the moon and stars above me! never; unless you promise that, inside the threshold, you will satisfy my mind."

Again Rose glanced around in terror. The same figure, still unseen by William Duncan, which had disturbed the shadow of the old castle, glided silently round the corner of the house. She knew her words were listened to; she knew that, even under her father's roof, and with shut doors and windows, she could not be sure of evading the ears which were stretched to catch what she would say; and her teeth chattered as she for the last time refused her lover's request.

William Duncan turned on his heel, and rushed from the door. She looked after him, in some dread that the figure which haunted her might follow him to do him harm. But as she glanced after her rapidly disappearing lover, the object of her mortal fear and detestation re-appeared, and stood still, at some distance, in the direction opposite to that taken by him: and from this Rose became assured that a close watch upon her, rather than any vengeance upon William Duncan, was the point in view.

With her eyes bent towards those which she knew were fixed on her, and with a recurrence of almost all her agonized fears for herself, she groped behind her for the knotted string of the latch of the door, pulled it, darted into the house, shut the door instantly; barred, locked, and otherwise secured it; saw that all the windows were fast, and then, shaking in every limb, fell on her knees in the middle of the floor, and lifted up her hands and eyes in prayer.

CHAPTER XIX.

THE morning sun had for some time been beaming into Rose's little bed-chamber, before she was conscious that it shone upon her. It found her sitting on her low work-stool by her bed side, her head resting on the bed. Rose had dreaded to undress and lie down after ending her devotions in the outer apartment.

As she now raised her head and gazed on the morning beams, which were quivering around her, the young woman's face was pale, and over-cast with a care-worn expression, most unusual to it. She called back the occurrences of the past night; and, after some reflection, prayer was her resource again.

Her aspirations were ardent; and the close of her extemporaneous address to heaven will illustrate the state of her feelings :

"It is on you alone, oh my God, who have already so miraculously preserved me and supported me—it is on you alone, alone, I rely for assistance, and for direction on my way! In you alone I put my hope and my trust, for my family and myself, at the opening of this day! Guide me, and prompt me in the things

I have to do, if it be your holy will; and give me strength and courage, oh Lord;"

When she had ended, Rose set about arranging her disordered dress, and otherwise attending to her toilet: and then she tried to bend her mind to her unavoidable duties. But it might have been visible to the least interested observer, that a great, great weight lay upon her heart. During the whole of that morning she would frequently pause in her occupations: her bosom would heave; her eye would become troubled, taking an expression of anxiety, still not free of terror; a shuddering breath would escape her parted lips; then her own low moan would startle her from her reverie, and she would heavily proceed in whatever business lay unfinished before her.

Yet did Rose succeed in observing her numerous domestic obligations. She ministered assiduously at her mother's bed-side; anticipating the poor woman's wishes, and soothing her grief and alarm for her son's fate, and her husband's imprisonment: and she prepared breakfast for her younger brother and her sister, with as much exactness as if her mind were perfectly at ease, and her spirits as buoyant as ever.

Daniel descended to breakfast before his sister little Nancy. Rose was glad to sit alone with him for a short time. While revolving the occurrences of the previous night, she had judged that Daniel, according to his character, had cautiously listened to the conversation between her and Hesther Bonnetty, before she issued forth, on the treacherous invitation of the hag, to visit Morris; and she concluded that it was by his instructions William Duncan knew where to follow and to find her, upon his return to the house from the *bosheen*.

One glance of her eye at Daniel, as he sat down to breakfast, was sufficient to confirm her in her suspicions. He shook his head cunningly, and looked with a knowing smile towards her.

She at once endeavoured to ascertain the extent of what he knew. Daniel began by being mysterious; but by degrees she discovered that, in the first place, he had peeped down from his "loft," and had seen her and William Duncan sitting very close together, and gathered, pretty accurately, the substance of their conference: that afterwards he had been aware of Hesther Bonnetty's entrance into the house, and of a long conversation between her and Rose; although, owing to the almost whispering tones which both used, the nature of the topic between them he had failed to ascertain. But he saw his sister and the vicious old woman go out together; and he it was, indeed, who had set William Duncan upon Rose's track.

Having obtained from Daniel all the information he could impart, Rose betrayed great anxiety to bind him to silence. She besought him earnestly to keep strictly to himself all he had seen and heard. This was, in a slight degree, injudicious, so far as regarded Rose's pocket. Daniel perceived her eagerness, and tried to turn it to good account; insisting that, "By the dad, it was only a right thing to go an' tell his father of the night's doins."

Rose showed farther and greater alarm at this hint; and, knowing the person she had to deal with, began to drive a bargain with Daniel; and Daniel higgled, and "priced," until, as wages for his secrecy, and for his promises to that effect, he succeeded in, pledging Rose to purchase for him, within a given and certain time, a new suit of Sunday clothes, and a new "carline" hat.

Rose then abandoned the subject, convinced that she had gained her point; for, exclusively of the sordid temptation to stand by his bargain, she knew that, however uninteresting was the lad in many respects, still he possessed, in common with every member of her father's family, an implicit regard for truth, and for a promise once given.

Rose sat at the table while her brother and sister took their breakfast, but she shared scarcely a mouthful with them. Her father's morning meal was tidily prepared for him, and she was about to convey it to his prison, when Hesther Bonnetty hobbled over the threshold.

An involuntary exclamation of loathing and horror burst from Rose, and she drew back and stared at the old fiend in fearful astonishment. The crone glanced eagerly around. Nancy Brady, having finished her breakfast, had left the room to rehearse some of her prayers or penances. Daniel sat idly at the fire. Hesther hurried over to him, seized him by the collar, and addressed him in an under tone.

" Make answer to me in the thruth, you *gawk !* "

" Lord save us, Hesther, what's come over you now ? "

" None o' that palaver for me. I'll crack your crown if a lie comes out o' your mouth ! Did you see Rose an' me together last night ? "

Daniel admitted his offence.

" Did you overhear our words ? answer that to me, an' answer thruly, I bid you again ! "

" No; ye spoke too low."

" Is that the thruth, is id ? "

" By the dad, it is the downright thruth."

" Here, swear it on the book to me—give me your

book oath that you say what's thrue." She snatched a prayer-book from the shelf of the dresser, and offered it to the boy. Daniel looked terrified at the idea of taking an oath. He had been taught that to do so, except in cases of imminent necessity, was a great sin. He glanced at Rose.

"Hesther M'Farlane," said Rose, in a voice the most distant and solemn, "none in this house would dare profane the Most Holy Name on so slight a rason, an' at your biddin': my brother Daniel shall take no oath for you."

"Did he hear the discourse? unravel me that, Miss *Maddherra*, * an' make answer at your peril; aye, at your peril!"

"He did not hear what was said."

"Will *you* stand by that word, an' at your own peril, I tell you again?"

"As I live, I spake the thruth, an' he will keep secret the little he knows from——" Rose hesitated and shuddered.

"From your ould daddy?"

"Yes—from my father."

"Are you sarten sure? an' will you stand by that too?"

"I am; I have his solemn promise, and I know he will keep it."

"On your head be the woe, an' on all your heads, if he don't. Mind me, and undherstand me."

"I do undherstand you," answered Rose, again drawing back, and again shuddering.

"You were on your way to the jail?"

"I am going there with my father's breakfast."

---

* Jade.

"For rasons, an' for good rasons, you can't, an' you musn't go there. Gape at me — do, as if there were more heads than one on me; but I tell you you can't, an' you guess my manin'; your tongue might be gaddin'; there's no dependin' on your likes; I'll take the old man his victuals."

"You—you?" stammered Rose, in surprise not unmixed with alarm.

"Didn't my speech come plain to your ear? give it to me; I'll stuff him for you; an' mind what I tell you, you young gawk," turning to Daniel; "if a word comes out o' your lips o' what you saw last night, by the cross o' the critch, I'll make you rue id to your dying day."

She snatched from Rose's hand the little basket of provisions. Rose did not gainsay her; she shook her crutch at the gaping lad, and hurried out of the house.

Daniel put several ingenious questions to his sister, but she declined to answer them. With a countenance still heavier than before, she continued her household occupations; then having paid a visit to her mother, she retired into her own little room, and was soon plunged in a profound reverie.

As on a former day, she was interrupted by the unceremonious entrance of the puffing, the blowing, the pursy, the whirligig-pated Ailleen Lahon.

"Och, then, the sorrow's in me, if I ben't glad to see how bravely you look, my darlent Miss Rosy: oh, then, *minawyah* you, for one Jerry Fennelly!"— and she clasped her head between her hands, ran over to the glass, and there kept on turning her face from side to side, and smiling comfortably at the reflection of her own facetious features. She then proceeded to unpin the wings of her cap, while looking in her own eyes, she continued:

"Why then, my darlint, I'm here to tell you that there's people an' people in id;—musha, botheration to you, Jerry! you're the downrightest *rooluch** of a boy!—no, in thruth, you don't care the value o' this pin who's lookin' at you; but you'll go on wid a body fornent the face of the wide world!—but—

> ' Let us alone before the people,
> And *neceum pothe*† behint the steeple.'

"No, that's not your fashion, Jerry; never's in me, bud you'd pull a body about, if the priest was within the length o' my apron-sthring o' you! An' just look at the figure o' my poor cap afther you, that I was clear-starchin' till my hands ached! But it's little you care; aye, an' look at my new neckáter, more betoken! what a life we lade wid 'em for boys! It's a long day till I stand to discourse you again, Jerry."

It is quite impossible to say how far Ailleen's tongue might have run on in this strain, had not the melancholy tone of Rose's voice checked her jocular mood. Rose asked how her Patty was that day.

"Why, then, in good thruth, my darlint," with a heavy and sincere sigh, "not much to brag of the poor crature;" and Ailleen sat down with her yet disarranged cap between her hands, her street-romping with Jerry Fennelly quite forgotten.

"I'm afraid, *a-lanna*, that it's not the poor misthrause's lot to ate a peck o' salt in this ugly world; she breaks my heart every moment, tellin' me that the dead came to call her to the could grave, an' that

---

* Rake.   † Give me a kiss.

she'll go by his biddin'; my grief, *asthore*, that I have it to tell, but she's wearin' away to a 'natomy. Och, the sight o' that gaddin' ghost was an unloocky sight for my poor misthrause!"

"Indeed, Ailleen, it was a sore visitation for others, as well as for poor Patty. Ailleen, you have heard that my brother Morris was found in your masther's house that night; has it been discovered how he got in?"

"Och, my darlint, an' sure it's we had the ould work on the head o' that, since you were beyand there; an', with the heaven's help, I'll thry an' reharse id for you."

Ailleen detailed to Rose how the "divartin' ould Aldherman Lodge," as she styled him, and who at present filled the office of chief magistrate of the city, came to Mr. Barnaby Roundhead's house to inspect the premises, and to ascertain, if possible, how entrance had been effected. But, according to Ailleen, all his scrutiny proved useless; nor lock, nor bolt, nor bar, had been injured; nor in window, door, roof, or wall, had anything like a breach, or a hole, been made. From this his worship concluded that the intruder must have been in league with some inmate of the house, and he had examined Ailleen, "her own self," on the point; and, during the despatch of business, had called her "a rosy rogue; not manin' a rogue in earnest, only a rogue the way that boys an' girls does be goin' on wid their roguery;" and, likewise, he had informed her, "more nor forty times, that she was the moral* of a purty creature." But as regarded the real point at issue, Ailleen was acquitted, to the worship-

---

* Model.

ful mayor's satisfaction, of all suspicion of aiding or abetting in the case of felony before him; for, according to her mistress's testimony, Ailleen had not left her sight on the night of the robbery, either before or after it took place.

The only other person liable to suspicion was James Brown; and his master testified in his behalf, that, with his own hands, he had locked James Brown into his room early on that memorable night; had taken the key of the door with him to his own chamber; had also locked it and himself in, preparatory to retiring to bed; and when awakened and alarmed by a noise in the house, had found the key where he had left it; and on proceeding to James Brown's door, had seen that it was secure, and James fast asleep.

James Brown, therefore, could not have admitted the burglar; nor could he have assisted in his mysterious escape from the house, inasmuch as he was absent himself, in search of the mayor's sergeant, when Morris Brady disappeared.

The visit of the ghost of Joe Wilson to Patty and Ailleen was mentioned to his acute worship. And on this point the " divartin' ould aldherman" did not deliver any direct opinion; but it was evident to him that the supernatural wanderer, if really ascertained to have been in the house at the time of the robbery, must have glided into it for the honest purpose of arousing Mr. Roundhead, and putting him on his guard; because Mr. Roundhead had distinctly heard a voice without his chamber door, telling him to arise and protect his property.

But, in fact, nothing could be made of the puzzling business, although Alderman Lodge spent a whole day in probing it and poking at it. However, before taking leave of little Barnaby, he pledged himself to return to it the next day, and the next, and never cease till he had fully cleared up the mystery.

Rose inquired if his worship had kept his promise, and was now successful?

Ailleen replied in the negative, and took it upon herself to account for his *not* having kept his promise. What she was about to say, Rose must consider and treat as a great secret.

Widow Sheehan, the mayor's landlady and housekeeper, had informed Ailleen, that on the night of the day of the investigation at Mr. Roundhead's house, his worship himself had been favoured with a visit from the ghost of Joe Wilson!

At this unexpected disclosure, Rose looked greatly interested.

Yes, Ailleen continued, her " darlint Miss Rosey" might be quite sure of the fact. The alderman had retired for the night, and widow Sheehan was passing his door, " as soft as anything," when she heard a voice within addressing him. Who this could be she naturally paused to ascertain. The door suddenly opened; she heard the words, " make no farther inquiry into the affair," and the apparition stalked forth. Loudly screamed the widow, and down went the widow " all of a lump;" and when she recovered her senses, she found the magistrate supporting her; and he warned her to be as silent as the grave regarding what she had seen, and particularly what she had heard.

This information was matter of most serious importance to Rose. Her manner showed that it was so. She sat silent some time, her eye brightening, and her bosom occasionally heaving with long-drawn, relieving sighs. In truth, our heroine began to feel almost sure, that by prudence and perseverance, she might, with divine help, extricate her family and herself from their present trouble.

As on a former occasion, however, doubts of the truth of Ailleen's story presented themselves to her mind. She made the girl repeat the anecdote of the ghost's last visit: Ailleen did so, and was tolerably consistent with her previous version of it; adding renewed injunctions of secrecy to Rose; for the widow Sheehan had told it to no other human creature but herself, warning her " on her life," not to allow it to go further; and she, Ailleen, had veritably mentioned it to no living thing but Rose, " barrin' her gossip."

Rose put on her cloak to go and see her drooping cousin: the appearance of Ailleen Lahon being always accompanied by an invitation from Patty.

CHAPTER XX.

Although free from the feverish flutter in which Rose had last found her, Patty was greatly altered for the worse. The marks of rapid decay were upon her. Her eye was sparkling bright, her cheek sunken, and her once red and dewy lips pale and clammy.

Rose felt shocked at soul to look upon her. The young girls silently embraced; then they gazed at each other; Rose slowly shook her head; and her moist eyes were full of tender reproach.

Patty read their meaning. A sigh of exhaustion broke from her very heart; and her head, as usual, relyingly drooped on her friend's bosom.

"I can't help giving you blame, Patty," Rose softly whispered: " afther all my words to you, an' what's worse, in the face of what you know 'tis right to do, you are fretting away your health, day by day, hour by hour."

" Rose, I know well I am dying, and what is the use of struggling against the will and the doom of Heaven? Indeed, Rose, I sent for you to-day to bid you farewell;" sobs checked her, and Rose's own bosom heaved with struggling sorrow.

When Patty re-addressed her, it was in accents of melancholy seriousness, insisting upon the certainty of her coming death. Rose thus answered her:—

"Patty, you and I know each other a long time: an' you can say for me that my tongue was never given to spake evil words against my neighbours."

"Indeed, Rose, I can and do say for you, that the most faulty were always made less so by your tongue, and that when all the world blamed, you found some charitable excuse for error."

"Well then, Patty, my own *graw bawn*—but, come now, come, let your head rest where it is; that heart of mine you hear beatin' so close undher your cheek, is full of love to you, my *lanna*; and it would not let me say one little word to hurt you in reality; and you will believe me, that what I *am* going to say isn't told to pain you, but to cure you, and to make you well entirely, if I can do it."

Patty bore down her cheek against its soft pillow, and the gentle pressure of her arms, also, told her confidence in her friend's affection.

"I know very well, Patty, that when a young girl loves, she ought to love dearly; for the rason that the more the heart is fixed on the man that is to be her husband, the less will she feel the crosses of the world, which all husbands and wives are doomed to feel in this uncertain life together: do not begin to cry so, my dear Patty, or I can't go on; and my conscience tells me, that my duty would not be done by you if I was to hide what I have to say."

"I will listen to you, Rose," she replied, in tones of the deepest misery. Much alarmed, Rose gently raised the young creature's head to look into her face. Patty's eyes were closed, as if they shunned the scrutiny, and an expression of despair spread over her features.

"Patty, open your eyes, and look up at me." She slowly unclosed her lids, and her eyes told the same story of a broken heart that her features had done. A slight spasm passed through her frame. She spoke, and her voice was not now weak and wailing, but solemnly impressive.

"Let me hear all you have to say, Rose—and—perhaps—when you have done—I may find something to tell you, in return."

"My words are too afflicting to you."

"No, no; do not mistake; it was a sad, sad thought of my own which they avowed, and which overcame me. No, Rose; go on; your little voice is soothing in my ear:" she laid her head on its former resting-place.

"Well, then, Patty, I will go on: I was saying that a young girl may love, and love dearly; but it is only when God himself blesses her choice; and oh Patty *a-lanna*, what a terrible thing it is for soul as well as body, in the next world as well as in this, for a young girl to place her love upon a bad man!"

"I understand you, Rose; but I abide by what I said before on that subject."

"Patty, what *I* say, I know—I *know* to be the blessed thruth. Never was *he* fit for your love; never, *a-lanna*, never! While he was trying, like the enemy of mankind, to rob you of your pure heart—now stay quiet, my *graw*, and let me finish; heaven knows it is an affliction to myself to talk to you in this way, an' I wouldn't do so, only for one purpose—but while he was gaining your young, fresh love, Patty, he was after ruining many other innocent creatures, and, at the very time, plotting on others again, or else sinning with them; oh yes, Patty! many a good and virtuous girl has he dragged into shame, and then left to the world's scorn! And, Patty, upon my good thruth, and upon my sacred word, he had great crimes of a different kind to answer for; he was a gamester, my *lanna;* he was a robber; and—terrible to say, he was a shedder of his fellow-creature's blood!"

Patty started up, clasping her hands, and looking with an eye of terror and consternation at her cousin.

" Rose, Rose! can this be?"

" It's the thruth: I could prove it to you; it is not upon hearsay I come to spake it to you; I know that I spake the thruth."

" Then may Heaven help me! for oh, I stand in need of its help!"

" And God *will* give you help, blessed be his holy name! He never turns his face from those who put trust in him. Don't be so cast down, my own *graw.* It was not to grieve you that I made up my mind to tell you this. No; but I'll let you know what I expect from you, now that it is told. I expect that if that bad young man were standin' before you, alive and well—"

" Oh, that he were!" sobbed Patty.

" If he were, Patty, I expect—I hope—now that you know what he was, that you will tell me you would turn from him; that you would not go on loving such a one as he was. Yes, Patty; *that* I expect from you; for, altho' you are a darling of my bosom, I'd sooner see the grave-sod over you than see you that man's wife."

" Rose—" she hesitated and shivered.

" You want to tell me something, my poor *graw;*

tell it, whatever it is, to your own Rose, who never hides anything from you."

"Rose, there is a reason why I should love that man, living or dead, if he was as black as crime could make him. Oh, in his grave, I do still dearly, dearly love him!"

"Now, now," said Rose, rather reproachfully "do not say that, Patty; it would make me very sorry for you; indeed, indeed, it would make my heart bleed."

"Rose, Rose," answered Patty, winding her arms round her cousin's neck, while she looked beseechingly into her face, "if you abandon me—if you give me up—there will not be one—no, not one! not one! to smooth my short journey to the last home! not one to close my eyes! not one to weep for me—in pity, at least—when I am dead and gone!"

"What are you thinking of, Patty? Rose Brady could never forsake you."

"Do you say never, never?"

"I do, my *graw*—never, never."

"Nothing could change you to me?"

"Nothing: not even the commands of my own father and mother."

"But there is one thing—Rose, I am going to try your love for me."

"Try it, and do not fear it."

"You cannot guess what I mean?"

"No, indeed; I have not the least notion of it: tell it to me at once."

"I will —oh! I cannot! it is killing me, and yet I cannot! But let it kill me; and then it will be buried with me, and none will ever know it. Rose, perhaps when I am closing my eyes, never to open them again on the light of this world; when my spirit is on the wing out of this life; when I am gasping my last in your arms—then, perhaps, I will whisper it to you: because, then, I could not feel the loss of your love; in my grave I should not know that you loathed and despised your miserable cousin."

"Patty, if I were your mother, I would lay my commands on you to open your breast, and give me your confidence."

"Nothing can turn a good mother against her child; will you stand by me as a good mother would?"

"Again and again, Patty, I ask you will you put confidence in me? No mother ever loved her child, and no sister ever loved her sister, better than I love you."

"Then, Rose, listen; put your ear closer to my lips—I must not hear my own words while I whisper them."

The trembling and most unhappy girl glued her lips to her cousin's ear, and in four words—four words scarcely syllabled, breathed her withering secret.

Rose uttered a cry of horror; sprang to the middle of the room; flung herself on her knees; spread her hands over her face; bent her forehead to the floor, and there lay prostrate, seemingly delivered up to agony.

Patty's arms dropped at her sides; she fell back in her chair helplessly; her eyes closed, her head hung forward on her chest; she seemed dead—dead under the last stroke of despair.

Both girls remained for some time motionless and silent. Patty at length moaned out, "I knew it would be so—she *has* abandoned me!"

She heard Rose move. In shivering anticipation

she slowly and feebly raised her head, and half unclosed her eyes. Rose was now on her knees; her streaming eyes solemnly turned upward. With the slow gravity of deep devotion, Patty saw her close her palms before her forehead, and, after a moment, separate them, and stretch her arms towards heaven; but the words of her prayer came only in inaudible whispers from her lips. As she ended her supplication to God, Rose Brady bowed down her head again almost to the floor, and remained some time in that position. She then deliberately stood up; wiped with her handkerchief the tears from her eyes and cheeks; and the long look which, finally, she cast on the poor Patty, had in it more of sorrow than of anger.

Patty gazed on her with pitiful supplication. Her frame trembled to an excess almost sufficient to expel her shattered spirit from its nearly exhausted tenement. The arms which had hung at her sides, so long and so hopelessly, she timidly extended; drew them back with a start, as if she had received a check to her advances; then, meekly, humbly, and most sorrowfully, folded her hands over her bosom; and a heart of stone it must have been, which could have withstood the beseeching though mute misery of her look.

Rose Brady's heart was not a heart of stone; she extended her arms also; she hastened over to her cousin; she again took her protecting place at the young creature's side; and, with a convulsive sob, Patty once more laid her worn cheek on Rose's bosom.

"Oh, blessed be heaven for this!" she murmured; "you do not then, Rose, cast me from you! You pity me, and you forgive me, and you have prayed to God to forgive and to pity me, with your pure lips and your pure maiden heart? and, when I am leaving you, Rose, you will give me your embrace, and your kiss, and—your blessing?"

"My own poor, poor child," answered Rose, "do not think I will say, now or ever, one single sentence to add sorrow to your sorrow. This—this only I will say, my *cuishla;* if you had pierced my heart with a sharp dagger, it would not have given me such terrible pain, as did the four little words you have whispered in my ear. Oh, my poor *graw bawn!* I could cry over you till my heart's blood came with the tears!"

Mutually embracing, they wept plentifully together. Rose resumed:

"When your poor mother was dying, there was nobody with her but you and I: do you remember, Patty?"

The girl assented.

"You were kneeling down by her bed-side, and she held your hand; and I was sitting at her head, supporting her. Her dying eyes turned to me, and the look they gave is present to me this moment. 'Rose,' she said, 'you must be a mother and a sister to my poor child; promise me, in the face of heaven, that you will.' 'I do promise you,' I made answer, 'I do promise before the face of heaven, that, to the hour of my death, I will be a mother and a sister to your child.' 'Here is her hand,' the departing woman said; 'take care of her:' and so she put your hand into my hand, and died." Patty's increasing tears told how she felt this recapitulation.

"It is not to bring you new grief that I spake of this," continued Rose Brady; "but now that I know your secret, the time is come that I must keep the promise I made to your dying mother in the face of heaven. In good thruth, Patty, the great love I have for you, ever since I helped you to dhress your doll until the present hour, would send me barefooted over the world, to bring you home happiness; but, afther all that, I b'lieve there is nothing short of my awful promise, that ought to make me run the hazard of doin' what I have already made up my mind to do for you."

"Rose, tell me the meaning of your words—will you not?" asked Patty, in breathless interest.

"I can't do that now, my *lanna;* but I have to act towards you, at present, as your mother would act, if she was alive on this earth, and I hope that will be my justification to man and God, for goin' in the road of danger; don't ask me any more questions, *a-cuishla;* a mother, and a mother's love you now want in your affliction; and a mother I'll be to you, and a mother's love I'll give to you. Patty, I must save you from yourself, and I must save you from a bad world. If I fail in what is before me, you will not on that account be worse off than you are now, my poor *cuishla;* if God gives me success, I won't say you'll be quite happy, but you'll be—I can't tell you more till another time. And now, good by; for what's to be done is to be done quickly; heaven bless you; an' only thry to bear up, Patty, an' all may go well, an' we two may be pleasant, aye, and merry together, some future day: to-morrow, if I am alive, I will see you again; an', maybe, with divine help an' a blessing, bring you some good news; kiss my lips, Patty, and good by."

"May God be with you and guard you, my own good, good Rose."

"Aye, in thruth, Patty, His hand, alone, can help us. Often has my father tould me that he is a proud and a foolish man who puts reliance on his own courage, or on his own strength, when grief visits him, or when the enemy tempts him to do wrong. At first, Patty, what you whispered was so frightful to my heart, that I could think of nothing but it; but my father's words came into my mind, like an inward voice from heaven; and, afther my prayer for you, I petitioned for light an' strength on my own account, and then I could think; an' now I am sthrong to do my duty by you. Patty, *a-lanna*, raise you own heart to your God, and He will hear you, and to you He will give sthrength also. May His holy blessing now be with you. To-morrow I will be here again."

They kissed each other a second, a third time, and Rose went on her way.

CHAPTER XXI.

Her galash pulled to its greatest tightness to screen her face, and her mantle held under her chin, Rose proceeded along the streets demurely, and yet with the pace of one whose errand requires despatch.

She turned into a baker's shop. Behind the counter was a smooth-cheeked, buxom dame, occupied in knitting, except when she attended to a customer; and seated in a well-cushioned arm-chair, in brisk chat with her, was a man about sixty, of burly person, large, puffy features, and amorous black eyes. His dress was of the best material; his wig of three buckles; his three-cocked hat was still worn in the rakish fashion adopted in his youth; and his limbs were wrapped in flannel, and rested on a soft footstool, doing penance for their master's life of jollity. And this personage was Ailleen Lahon's "divartin' ould aldherman Lodge," mayor of our good city, as the white wand standing against his shoulder fully denoted.

Being a bachelor, he despised the cares of an establishment of his own, and therefore occupied apartments in the respectable house of the widow Sheehan, or " widow *na Sedhogue* " that is, widow of the cake.

The scandalous world whispered other reasons for his selection of a landlady; but perhaps it was solely on account of his gay character, that the winsome dame suffered in the estimation of her neighbours.

Upon entering the shop, Rose Brady walked straight to his worship; she let go the running string of her galash, and it fell back on her shoulders. The alderman instantly recognised an old acquaintance; indeed he was on easy speaking terms with every pretty girl under his civic jurisdiction.

"Hub-bub, bousy! Rosey, my posey, is that you?" jocularly demanded his worship, at the same time unconsciously trying to stand up; "oh! ah! the curse o' Scotland on the first fellow that invented the gout! many a purty crature puts her tongue in her cheek at me of late; there was a day I'd run down the swiftest doe of the herd; but I might as well be in the stocks at present, as have you before me, Rosey; there's no such thing as getting at your cherry lips: tell me, did you ever make a present of a little kiss in your whole life?"

"Is that a fair question, your worship?"

"No it isn't then, now that I think of it; but upon my good conscience, I'm informed you have never yet parted with a single one; however, I intend to punish all churlish girls of your sort, that would starve the world,"—his worship seized his rod, and held it up with great glee,—"I'll send out the bellman this very day, and proclamation shall be made by 'special orders of Mr. Mayor, if there is one maid, wife, or widow, in any quarter of this city, or the liberties thereof, that does not give and take six good, sound kisses, before twelve o'clock this night, she shall stand in the pillory in default thereof;' aye by my oath of office, I'll make it a serious affair with ye all. There is an act of parliament for it—the first of the merry king Charles, and by that act, the mayors of all corporate cities in his Majesty's dominions, may remit the punishment of every stubborn delinquent, upon payment of the ungiven favours to them—that is, to the mayors themselves.

"Will you take a friend's advice, please your worship?" asked Rose.

"Not upon that. I know my duty as mayor of this city; and the law shall be carried into effect, according to my oath of office, without favour or affection, malice or ill-will, unto any girl or girls whatsoever: but let me hear your advice, Rosey."

"Just give commands to the bellman, Sir, not to mention the chance of getting the punishment of the pillory taken off, if your worship wishes to make any thing for yourself out of the matter."

"And why so, Rosey, my posey?"

"Because I'm given to undherstand, that there are few who wouldn't choose any other body's lips as soon as those of his worship, the mayor of this city corporate, and the liberties thereof."

"Hah, you little baggage! seldom have you let me off without a tap on the knuckles; but it isn't ould times with you at present; I'll let you know I am mayor of this city at last; and here, to my face, you have just been guilty of an offence against my office and its dignity, and there's a fine on the spot; I fine you a kiss, good and legal coin current, this moment."

"Mr. Lodge," said Rose, with a deep sigh, "tho' I try, I cannot be as merry as I used to be; my heart is heavy, Sir."

"Ulb-bub-bousy! and that's true; I forgot myself;

but those murdering eyes of yours, Rose, and your red lips, would make King Solomon forget his proverbs. Well, by my good conscience, little girl, 'tis a thousand pities anything should damp your blithe sperits; for a sweeter, and a better, and a more soul-cheering lass isn't under my authority."

"I thank you, Sir, for your good word; and I am come to ask your advice and your assistance in my throuble."

"And, by the rod, my advice and my assistance you must have — provided you don't ask me to, walk overmuch; I'm spancelled ever since last night, Rose."

"Indeed, and sorry I am for it, Sir."

"Between you and me, this is a bad affair of your young, wild-pated brother; but don't be cast down, ducky; what good is it to be mayor of a city, if he hasn't more power than your tag-rag and bobtail; a better ambassador than your purty self couldn't be sent to me. I'll clear your brother, Rose, or there will be wigs on the green."

"Thank you again, Sir. The matter I come on concerns yourself, Sir, as much as it does me or mine. But we must be private, plaise your worship; this place is too open."

"Hah, you rogue! with all my heart; yes, we'll be so private that there will be no mobbing out what we are doing; I knew you had a sneaking regard for me, Rosey; aye, we'll put our heads together; and when heads are quite close, lips, you know—but, confound it! I'm forgetting myself again; I'll keep in all my humour till there's nobody by. Here, you rascal; hollo, there! take me up, and jaunt me into the parlour. Rose, like yourself, I never kiss and tell: easy, you rascals; easy with me, I say!"

Two of his bailiffs, who had been lounging outside the door of the shop, came at his call, to lift him up in his chair, and bear him inward.

"You'll spill his worship," said one of them to the other, jeeringly.

"If you do, you scoundrel, I'll have you in the stocks!" roared the mayor.

"By dad, there's a horse-load in your worship."

"Mind what you're about, you grinning raps! come, Rose, you little rogue."

They carried him off slowly, with his rod over his shoulder, and conveyed him into a little parlour at the rear of the shop. The widow brought his footstool, and adjusted his limbs in the positions which she knew, from long experience, gave them most ease. But, though thus attentive, the widow *na sedhogue* wore a cloudy brow; and while his worship screwed up his mouth and eyed her askance, with a look that told he comprehended her mood, she uttered one or two tolerably significant "umphs!" as she closed the door upon the dignitary and his fair and well-esteemed visitor.

A full hour Rose and the mayor remained in close conference, to the great chagrin of Mrs. Sheehan. Many a peep did the good dame give through the key-hole; many a time did she raise the wing of her cap off her ear, and apply the inquisitive organ to the same orifice, to try and catch the tenor of the conversation going on in her parlour. But her optical scrutiny produced no results calculated to give a pang to her bosom; and not a word distinctly reached her ear.

The observations which she was able to make, however, greatly surprised her. The merry old man seemed to have quite thrown aside his previously inveterate habit of jollily smirking at all comely maidens. Mrs. Sheehan saw his worship knit his brows, and intently fix his eye, now grown cool and keen, upon Rose Brady, who spoke to him in the lowest possible under tone. The widow also remarked, that the young woman's countenance wore, instead of the seducing smiles she had expected to catch upon it, an expression of deep seriousness, while, earnestly bending forward, she seemed to recommend to the first magistrate of her city some very important subject, in which he apparently, as well as herself, was concerned.

At length Rose stood up to take her leave; and now Mrs. Sheehan heard one sentence.

"By the soul of my body, it shall be done, Rose! aye, and to your little heart's content; depend on me; and God be with you, my good girl; God bless you."

The chastened old satyr extended his hand only in a fatherly manner to Rose; and Rose took it cordially, and thanking his worship, dropped her courtesy, and issued into the shop.

To her "kind good bye, Mrs. Sheehan," the widow's answer was scarcely civil. We would not be uncharitable towards the fair dame. Female curiosity alone may have been her sole motive for watching her lodger so closely: and disappointment in a great craving may have solely caused her to behave coldly to Rose Brady. However all that may be, her good-humour was not restored at finding herself baffled, after Rose's departure, in all her efforts to pick information out of the worthy and worshipful mayor of her town; nor could she bear to see him, through the whole day, so completely changed a man as in reality he was. No more jests escaped his lips, and his mind seemed wholly engaged on serious business.

To give every one his due, we will note, that although our mayor was jocose, and, considering his years and the dignity of his station, perhaps a little too free with every pretty maid, wife, or widow, he encountered, yet could he, on necessary occasions, throw all that aside; and then no man saw his way more distinctly before him, or acted with more promptness, steadiness, and resolution.

CHAPTER XXII.

It will be admitted that William Duncan had seemingly good grounds for being wroth against his mistress; yet did his mind work as the minds of many lovers have done before and since, and, we believe, as they are doomed to do, " while the world is a world."

During the night after his hasty separation from Rose, or rather during the remaining darkness till day broke, jealousy, resentment, and wounded pride, kept him in a continued turmoil. And under the influence of these passions she appeared to him faithless, forsworn, unprincipled, unfeeling, and, consequently, a little person to be very heartily detested; and he did, accordingly, he was sure he did, very heartily detest her.

But it was remarkable that, after having come to certainty on this point, he should continue to worry himself about her; that he did not, like a consistent man, leave her to her fate and return into the country, there to attend to his lawful and now neglected business. It is still more striking that but a few minutes had elapsed, when he began to contemplate poor Rose in nearly as amiable a mood as ever. In truth, there is so much positive wretchedness in a jealous breast, that the harassed spirit, weary of hating, and loathing, and most extravagantly depreciating, will unconsciously seek refuge in opposite extremes of sentiment. And so William Duncan, having clearly settled with himself that Rose Brady was all that was abominable, and having nothing to add on that exhausted subject, could do little else than set to work to pick to pieces his own deep conviction.

First—and he jumped up and paced about the room at the thought—it did appear to him exceedingly unaccountable and unnatural, that one who, until the previous night, had been, in the opinion of every creature who knew her, so candid, so frank, so moral, so pure-hearted, should all of a sudden become so deceptive, so treacherous, and so depraved. Had he seen a peach, full grown and fully ripened on its tree, change in a trice into a little old crab apple, William protested to himself he could not be more astounded. And having once started on this train of thought, away he whisked, re-endowing his mistress, from the plentiful stores of his recollections and associations, with every quality, mental and personal, which could make her dear and dangerous to the peace of poor mortal man.

We believe, indeed, that your true lover uses very few neutral tints in his portrait painting of his mistress. Jet black, or else *couleur de rose*, will, we fear, be found to be almost the only colours on his pallet: and it is strange enough, too, that, whether he adopt the one or the other, according as he is jealous or adoring, he never fails in convincing himself that he has produced a very striking likeness. But we must not spin out this subject. William Duncan, after much tossing on his bed, and starting up from it, and stamping about the room, and putting on a number of very unbecoming grimaces, and making oaths and vows of eternal estrangement from Rose Brady, ended, about the noon of the day which followed their quarrel, by setting off to her house.

On his way he arranged in his mind the prayers, the beseechings, the exhortations, and the reasonings, which he would successfully use to get her to place full confidence in him, and to prove herself the paragon which it was necessary for his dignity and happiness she should be. Just as he was about turning up the lane in which she lived, the state of his mind when he had last been there, together with her audacious conduct, suddenly recurred to him, took possesssion of him like a devil, and drove him, like the possessed swine of old, to the river, which was near at hand.

During his race, down came tumbling upon him, even as an old house long propped up might come, all he had suspected, doubted, and feared the night before. Indeed, had he been doing his best to escape being crushed to death, or buried alive under a mortal shower of decayed slates and brickbats, and rotten laths and rafters, he could not have acted a more energetic part. His neighbours thought him suddenly bewitched. Hobbling old men looked back at him aghast, and strove to hurry out of his way, and mothers pulled their children out off his path.

Having gained the river side, up he shot along a zig-zag track, which wound over the side of a green hill above the gentle waters. A convenient spot being found, down he flung himself on the soft sward. For a long time his brow was frowning and most forbidding; the long, long sighs came, however; a soft sadness crept over him; he shed some silly but medicinal tears, and at length condescended to sit up, and look at the fair face of nature before him and around him.

Every object brought Rose to his recollection, and brought her, too, in some bewitching point of view. A little way under him, on the hill, was a fine old thorn tree; for certain reasons he arose, descended to it, and sat under it.

Reclining under this very tree he had first seen Rose Brady. On a subsequent occasion, ere she was yet known to him, he had himself been sitting under it, when she tripped by with some young companions, upon a May morning, as merry and as bright as that morning itself. His eye followed the descending path which he had then seen her take; it rested upon a little level sward by the river's brink, where for a while she and her youthful friends had reposed. William remembered well the little airy step, scarcely, it seemed to him, bruising the tender grass, with which she had danced along; and he called to mind, too, that while her own features mantled with only a sedate mirth, the laughter of her companions had rung high at her jests.

William, indeed, went on to remember and remember. It was under that same thorn tree, then sheeted with white blossoms, that he and Rose had sat upon the happy and gracious day when she listened, not offended, to a tale he had long been anxious to tell her. Oh! at the thought, the delicate perfume of those glorious white blossoms seemed, though it was now a damp and comfortless November morning, to float and float around him! Could he help recollecting the frank modesty of manner, of look, of action, and of word, with which Rose had responded to his ardent declarations?

His mind ran over the whole progress of their acquaintance, till that almost perfected consummation of it. In its earlier stages, how his soul used to glow with admiration of her gentle seriousness, when seriousness was natural or necessary, or bound to her merry tones and words, when there was no good reason why she should not be gay and happy! After a longer intimacy, when, at any time, he would have snatched a little favour—a very little one—with what modest, timid, yet decisive reserve had she checked him! And then, over and over again, he pictured to himself with what subdued sportiveness she had re-assured him, when she found herself understood and respected! Those were blessed days. Blessed days for the thorn tree, and for him. He started up and looked at it —blossomless, leafless, bare, and dripping, it stood; bereft of beauty and of fragrance, a sad, a desolate, and a solitary thing. Perhaps William's mind was not sufficiently poetical to institute a comparison, at full length, between himself and the object of his interest; yet something like a consciousness of a similarity did touch and affect him. And, in conclusion, he retraced his steps soberly to Rose Brady's dwelling.

But Rose was from home. William asked her sister Nancy where she might be found. Now Nancy, although she would not admit, even to herself, that such vain notions ever crossed her mind, yet without resolving it should be the case, she *was* a little spiteful towards Rose, because Rose had so many lovers, and she had not one. And, flowing from this, came a disrelish of those lovers themselves; and hence she could give William Duncan no satisfactory account of Rose's absence. She hoped Rose—" Miss Rose"— might be doing what was right, wherever she was;

but she supposed Rose had her own reasons for keeping her secrets to herself.

As for young Daniel, he, as usual, wagged his head cunningly,—" Rose had been in the *mumps* with him," he whispered, " for telling William on her last night; and to keep him from saying anything else that he knew, she had promised him a new suit of clothes, and a carline hat; and he wasn't the fool to say a word more, and lose the new clothes and the hat for his pains."

It will be conceived that the words of her brother and sister, concerning Rose's puzzling conduct, gave little ease to William Duncan's heart.

"If there was nothing wrong to be hidden," he argued, as he again suddenly quitted the house, " she would not give a bribe to hide it:" and on he walked into and through the town, not knowing exactly where he was going, and again daubing a very black portrait of his mistress for the satisfaction of his own mind.

Happening to raise his head as he industriously tramped onward, the grated windows of the city prison attracted his attention. It occurred to him that Rose might be with her father; if so, she was meritoriously employed. He asked permission to pay a visit to Randal Brady, and was admitted. Before entering, however, the outer door of the jail, an old woman came out of it, and hobbled past him. It was Hesther Bonnetty. Further doubts and fears fell upon him. Why should the old wretch be there? Was it Randal Brady she had come to see? And if so, could father and daughter be in league against his happiness, and even against their own honour?

His suspicions were gathering deep on his brow, as he followed the turnkey to Randal Brady's place of confinement. The old man met him with his bland smile, and his usual sedate cordiality of manner."

"Well now, William, my boy," he said, stretching out both his hands, "I am heartily glad to see you, and I take your visit as a mark of your good wishes to me and mine; but what is the matter with you? *You* don't seem glad to meet *me* afther all; tho' I know, it isn't in your nature to look could on your friends in their misfortune."

"No, Sir, no; do not think that; I never did such a thing in my whole life, and I never can do it to my dying day."

"I tell you, man, I don't suspect you of it; but I see what ails you,—you grieve for us. But, good boy, heaven will justify us in its own good time. A little suffering on this earth is good for us all. We are never betther Christians than when the hand of affliction is on us."

The surmise which had momentarily wronged his old friend in William's esteem, passed away. He looked in Randal Brady's guileless face, and he listened to his melodious voice, and he could not entertain it a moment longer. Moreover, the old man's calmness had a good effect upon William's fiery mood; it cooled and made him somewhat rational. "Is Rose with you, Sir?" he asked, anxiously, after a moment's pause.

"No, I have not seen Rose to-day; nor, indeed, any of my family: and it is inconsiderate, I must say, William, to lave me so long without the consolation of a visit from one or other of them. Can you tell me, William, how is my poor woman?"

"I did not hear to-day, Sir,"—his face darkening.

"Is there any news of my poor foolish boy? Has any one found out where he is hiding?"

"I believe not; but, Sir, I have something very particular to say to you; can we discourse here alone?"

Randal Brady looked steadily and studiously at him.

"There is throuble in your mind, William, my good boy; follow me."

At the time we treat of, little good arrangement, or even humanity, was apparent in the internal economy of the jail of our city. Felons, debtors, all—those guilty of every gradation of crime, and the victims solely of extravagance, or of misfortune, were promiscuously crowded together; so that, to a prisoner who disliked vice, or the words and habits of wicked associates, a temporary confinement was something horrible. Rose Brady was not aware of the extent of the inconvenience, nay, the sufferings experienced by her father. Whenever she had come with his meals, the jailor, out of a manly feeling towards the daughter, and at the old man's urgent request, gave him the use of his own room. But, on the present occasion, the termination of the arched passage running from a large cell occupied by a crowd of prisoners, was the most private spot to which he could conduct his young friend.

"That bad ould woman, Sir, Hesther Mac Farlane," began William.

"What of her, my boy? It is a rason of surprise to me that she has been sent with my breakfast this morning; and at a late hour too, when I was well hungry for it; only that, on the last point, she admitted to me she had loitered on the way."

"She spoke with you, Sir?"

"Of course, William; poor Hesther couldn't help that, for the life of her: and her words would have been a plague to me, if I was not acquainted with the poor crature's manner of tormenting all the world. But, even as it was, her carping tongue was but a poor exchange for the soothing comfort my own little Rose used to bring me at my meals. William," he continued, laying his hand on the young man's shoulder —"the fate of that poor boy throubles my sperit very much: his place of retrate and his proceedings hidden from me; and my poor wife sick, and needing the hand that, whenever she was so before, always supported her head. I declare to you, William, with all *that* in his mind, it is as much as a Christian man can do to bow to the will of God, and not repine when he looks at his prison bars."

"What were Hesther's words to you, Sir?"

"I inquired of her why Rose staid away? and she answered me that my Rose had affairs of her own to mind, that she thought more of than she did of her ould father. I asked again what those affairs were? Hesther said I should know in good time, and to my grief into the bargain. I put no more questions to her, knowing that it was half-mad, spiteful folly; she spoke of my child; but she then informed me, of her own accord, that my wife would never rise from her bed, and that my son Morris would certainly die a shameful death on the gallows-three. This, again, did not throuble me, on account of my knowledge of the gall of her nature. The only thing that gave me wondher was her being sent to me with my breakfast."

William paused, heaved a deep sigh, and his look was sorely agitated.

"William, you had something particular to tell me; by your face, I see beforehand it is not good news; let me hear it, for all that, in the name of God."

"No, Sir; no—I have nothing to—I mane I can't say it to *you*—I will be going, and I'll send Rose to you."

Only at the instant that he was about to unbosom himself to Randal Brady, did William Duncan become conscious that he was on the point of coming forward as Rose's accuser to her father. The tumult of his mind had previously confused its perceptions. Now he suddenly felt that such conduct was paltry and unmanly. It would be despicable to be a tale-bearer; and at the risk, too, of giving anguish to the bosom of a virtuous father, already laden with suffering. Accordingly, he turned away from the old man, and was leaving the prison.

"Stop!" cried Randal Brady, with a catching of the breath, and in the half-shrill tone of sudden alarm. William turned round, and saw that the old man was pale and trembling.

"My wife *is*—" he could not proceed.

"No, indeed, Sir; no, indeed—I see what you mane, but Mrs. Brady is in no danger; tho' I forgot to ask afther her an hour ago at the house, yet I heard no ill news of her there."

"The bailiffs have taken Morris?"

"Not that I heard of, Sir."

"Thank God, twice over; thank God." He sat down on a stone bench: "don't stir yet, William Duncan; I have more words to address to you, and I will be able in a moment."

After recovering breath and self-possession, Randal Brady continued:

"You said, just now, you would send Rose to me to tell me what you yourself couldn't find heart to tell; she also must be well, then; well in health, for the walk from the home to this jail; has your particular news anything relating to Rose in other respects?"

" I—I *will* send Rose to you, Sir—a good day."

" Do not leave me, young man, I desire and command you!" Randal Brady stood up from the bench, eyed William Duncan attentively and seriously, and then spoke to him in the tone of steady authority which occasionally, though rarely, he found it necessary to adopt towards the more immediate members of his own family.

" William Duncan, you began with an unthruth on your lips, but I'm glad to see your conscience doesn't let you go on in it. Before now I have known you pay reverence to the commandment, that warns us against bearing false witness. I see plainly it is no small matter that is on your mind. Answer me, Sir, does what you intended to tell me concern me or my family?"

" There was vexation on me when I came in here, Mr. Brady; it is gone off now; and I b'lieve I was wrong in my thoughts."

" Against what person were you vexed, William Duncan? tell me that plainly."

" Against that ould hag, that ould imp o' Satan, (if she's not his mother,) Hesther Mac Farlane."

" And you'll answer me for what rason. I know by your eye this moment, it is a serious affair that makes you angry with her."

" For the rason, Sir, that I think she intends evil to me, and to you and your family, and to all of us."

" Come, my good boy, this cross questioning is all to no purpose, and will never do between you and me," continued Randal Brady, rather sternly; " I'll spell out for you a part of your vexation. Something has happened between you and Rose, and this foolish old woman has contrived it." William's look told his agitation.

"I perceive I guessed near the mark; and I'll put you further on your way, William. If the misunderstandin' between you and Rose was about some look, or some word, or some pin's point, I should have heard the whole of it from your lips long ago; or, what's more likely, you'd never have thought of calling in Rose Brady's father to settle the quarrel. What you have on your mind, William, is a serious thing; and you must tell me every word of it."

William walked about, biting his lips. The old man regarded him in some anxiety, which increased every moment. To even a less attentive observer of human nature than Randal Brady was, William Duncan's unwillingness to explain must have been proof of the important nature of the matter which he had to communicate.

"I am the father of a family, William," he resumed, in a softened voice, and the longer I am kept in doubt the more I have to fear."

William suddenly turned, and came close to him; "I did not, Sir, as sure as I stand before your face, I did not come in here to be a tale-bearer, or a disturbance-maker; no, Mr. Brady: I came in thinking Rose might be with her father, when I could not find her at home."

"William, that was plain enough to me before you went to the throuble of telling it."

"There is no one but a villain would come to disturb the peace of a family, Mr. Brady."

"Now, my good boy, I think I understand you. You are vexed against Rose, and your vexation betrays you every step you go. First you wanted to accuse her to me; and now you would hould back, because, on second thoughts, it appears a mean thing to you to complain of her to her father. But neither Rose nor myself want to be trated that way. I look on you almost as one of my family, William; at least, I may call you a friend of it: a friend will give warning when there is danger; a disturber will guard his tongue until the mischief happens. Come, let me hear your secret, in God's name."

Besides his antipathy to the sin of tale-bearing, even were Rose incontestibly in error, William had now an additional dread of accusing her. Within the last half hour, in fact, it had occurred to his mind that Rose might be as pure as the snow-drift; and must he, of all others, be her calumniator? he who, of all others, ought to stand up for her against all calumny? But he had unwittingly gone too far; he was awed by the determined tone assumed by Randal Brady; he did not wish, nay, under the piercing eye of the old man, he did not dare to lie; and William Duncan therefore found himself compelled to disclose the proceedings of the previous night. He endeavoured, however, to qualify his story, and, instead of an accusation against his mistress, he put it forward only as matter of wonder.

Randal Brady left no circumstance unquestioned: and when the examination had closed, he fell into a deep reverie.

"William," he said, after a long pause, "we all know that while great throuble is on the mind, a man can't think rightly. When the morning dawns in upon me here, and when I find bad people about me, and when I think of my own home, where I used to be so happy; and of my wife and my childhren wanting a head to guide them, and a hand to keep them; at such times, William—and I said words of the same kind to you this day before—it is only by bowing with submission before the face of heaven, that I can keep my mind at rest. Now I feel the want of my liberty more than ever: though I hope for the grace to bear up, were it even worse with me."

" May the curse that is due to a thraitor fall upon me!" cried William.

" Shame on you, boy; shame on you: bend your knee as soon as you can, and ask forgiveness."

" There is no punishment too bad for me: I came in to bring double grief to you in your prison: no, there is no fate too dark for me!"

" William, hearken to me. You did what was right. Were Rose herself in your place, she would not equivocate to her father. But Rose has not come near me this whole morning, and now a good part of the day; and in her stead she sent that ould woman to me. What is the reason of that? It seems very dark and doubtful to me. Rose is the pride of my age; the child that delights my heart. What Joseph was to Jacob, Rose is to me. For many long years, whenever her father wanted support and comfort, support and comfort he had from her." He stopped, pursuing his train of thought, until, through starting tears, his eyes brightened, and his whole face glowed, as he suddenly added, " No, my girl, no! you could not do what is wrong for a virtuous woman to do. Of that I am as certain as that the life is in me. William, she could not."

" The saints in heaven are not whiter, Sir!" boldly asserted her consistent lover.

"I have no suspicion of her, boy; none whatever. If I had—God help me then indeed! No, no; I am grateful, on the knees of my heart, to the Great Giver of all goods for that child, William; I am proud, very proud of her, at his hand; this moment I am proud of her, not to talk of suspecting her. Rose and you, I know, William, have spoken together about the throubles of our family; has she tould you, as she tould me, that she doesn't think Morris a robber?"

"She has, Sir, and I think the same; I would stake my life upon it."

"Give me your hand. That is one little solace to me. Well, then, William, if the boy is not guilty of stealing from his neighbour, he is the dupe of some plot against him. And it seems now to me, that there is a plot against poor Rose, as well as against her brother; but for what rason, or who the plotters are, I cannot think, or make the slightest guess at. The poor boy and the poor girl never, I am sure, gave cause to any human being to do them harm; nor did I, as well as I can remember."

He paused and sunk into another reverie, from which he started quickly, laying his hand on William's shoulder, and gazing earnestly into his face.

"William, a thing comes into my mind of a sudden. When that ould woman was quitting me to-day, just before you came in, she said some words that I couldn't find a meaning for at the time. I was beginning to pay a little attention to them, but when I saw you, they passed out of my head. Now I turn back to them, and I think I can unravel them. And this was what she tould me, grinning wickedly at me while she said it: 'Randal Brady, the forty years are past an' gone this day, when I took an oath to you, and made a promise to you; an' that oath I will keep, and that promise I will perform.'"

"And do you remember what oath and what promise she meant, Sir?" asked William.

"I do now, William; and I will tell you her meaning. Forty years ago, Hesther and I were young, and a little known to one another, and she wished to get the love from me, but it wasn't in my heart for a woman like her. She spoke plainer to me day afther day, and followed me, and plagued me, aye, and worse than that, disgusted me. I turned to her at last, and tould her she was a light and scandalous young crature; and I bid her mend her heart and her ways, or else she would never win the love of an honest man. My own present wife was then running in my head, and the difference between her and Hesther made me more angry than, perhaps, I had any good right to be, particularly as Hesther was spaking venom against her from morning till night, to my own ears, as well as to other people. Well, I can never forget the rage she flew into, or the language she uttered. But it was not then she took the oath, and made me the promise. It was the first evening that I walked out with my new married wife. Hesther was sitting under the thorn on the hill, with the marks of her disgrace, by some other man, plain upon her; and she caught my skirts, as I passed her by; and she knelt down and swore, that if she were to wait forty years for her opportunity, that day forty years she would be revenged on me and mine. Shortly afther, she went away from this town, and I forgot her, and I forgot her words: but now she forces me to remember them; this day she tould me that **the forty years were passed away, William.**"

" 'Twas a terrible threat, Sir."

" William, mark my words; Hesther M'Farlane was wicked in her youth, and ould age has not mended her. She will keep her oath, if she can. And she is the plotter against Morris; she was the first who put wild-fire into his brain, by telling him of the ghost in the *bosheen;* and she is the plotter against Rose — that's plain from your own story; and she is the plotter against myself; I am here by her means, that I may be kept away from my family, while she is practising on them. My good young boy, you saved Rose last night. But Rose may be enthrapped again, and that's frightful to think of. William, if anything happens to that good child, I have a fear—unless the God above is very good to me—that I will die a most miserable old man. William, William, I never felt that I was a prisoner until now. My children are in danger, and I cannot put my hand beyond those bars to thry and save them. The wolf is on my little flock, and where is the shepherd? Oh my God!" prayed the old man, joining his hands before his breast, " be you a father to my family! protect them for your name's sake!"

" Sir, Sir," said William Duncan, " lay your hand on my head, and give me your blessing; the blessing of heaven will come of it; and if I had the undher-standing, I have the courage to do anything—to face any danger for you and for Rose."

" May God give a blessing, my boy;" the patriarchal hand of Randal Brady rested, at his desire, on the young man's head; " may He give light, and grace, and strength to your mind, for now, indeed, friendship like yours is a threasure."

William was hurrying away.

"Stop, my son; stop a moment. Give me a little time to recollect myself. We are only poor, weak cratures. When the head should be clearest, then it fails us most; what a fool he indeed is, who calls himself a wise man."

William waited silently and respectfully, while the old man bent his eyes on the ground.

"Until Rose informs us why she went to Hesther M'Farlane's vault, and who she met there, it is hard for me to know what directions I am to give you. If I were a free man, I would learn all about last night's doings in the first place. The understanding between you and Rose, William, ought to be enough to make her fully confidential with you; but she was not, and you quarrelled with her, and I do not wonder; nor do I blame you. I can't imagine her rason for being silent. But from me she never kept anything, and she will not now leave me in the dark. There is a part of her conduct which puzzles me very much. Having such serious things to tell me, this morning Rose has staid away from me. 'Tis by some contrivance of that sinful ould woman. Go you to Rose, William. Tell her I wish to see her; tell her I command her to come; tell her that, and she *will* come. William," he continued earnestly, "I do my endeavour to be calm, but it is a great sthruggle for a father. Good bye; I can't see you past this iron dour; I know you will be a thrue and steady friend to me, and to us all; aye, and a cool-headed one; do as I tell you, William: but, till I see you again, do nothing more."

CHAPTER XXIII.

Light was William Duncan's foot as he sped on his errand; and he was soon in Randal Brady's house. But Rose was still from home; and again no one could tell him where to seek her.

Her mother was up, and seated at the fire. As she spoke to him of her family, the poor woman became extravagant in her wailing. And she did not feel quite strong to-day, she said; but on the morrow she was sure to be well enough to go out: and, as certain as the morrow was to come, she would bring her husband home with her.

William asked her what means she intended to use in accomplishing so desirable a result; but she would not communicate the nature of her project, whatever it was; one thing, however, was as sure as that the sun gave light to the world in the day-time; to-morrow, before dinner hour, she would lead Randal Brady to his own house by the arm, through all the streets of the town, from the jail where he now lay a poor prisoner.

William did not very anxiously pursue his inquiries. It struck him that the poor woman might be a little lightheaded, after her illness, and from the pressure of her sorrows. And he was on the rack, during the delivery of her voluble lamentations and her fluent hopes. Alternately agitated with hope or fear, his eyes watched and watched the open door-way; but Rose's form shadowed it not.

Although his suspicions of his mistress were at rest, his mind painted her surrounded by every villanous machination—perhaps already a prey and a victim; and becoming too feverishly impatient to await her arrival, he set out to seek her. With Mrs. Brady he could hold no confidence: he had already done Rose injury enough by accusing her to her father, and he would not now direct towards her the suspicions of her mother. Hurrying through the town, he gained Hesther M·Farlane's place of refuge. Her door was well secured. He listened for a voice or a step within. No sound—not a stir met his ear. He knocked loudly; no one answered him. Indeed he knew that the vault was seldom or never tenanted, except in the night time.

Once more traversing the streets without any settled purpose, his steps almost unconsciously led him back to his mistress's dwelling; and now he found her at home.

She was quietly seated at dinner, with her brother and sister, and some refreshing nutriment lay before her mother, on a chair at the fire, of which Rose was tenderly pressing the querulous invalid to partake.

William started when he saw her sitting so much at her ease on her own floor, at the very moment he had thought her spirited away from it and from him. As Rose recognised her lover, a slight suffusion overspread her face, and her manner shewed a little embarrassment, but almost instantly she regained the natural tint of her cheeks, and with it her usual calmness and self-possession. She held out her hand to her visitor, and her voice was sweetly affectionate as she spoke the words of his welcome. She invited him to sit down, and partake of the more than usually homely repast. He obeyed in silence. William had snatched hastily but one or two morsels that day, and ought to have been hungry, but he was not; and his plate lay untouched before him, while his eyes fixed on Rose's face. She seemed conscious of this, but did not press him to eat. Their glances often met, and the look which spoke to him was the same open, loving one to which he had been used. But her frequent sighs, and, now and then, her low, suppressed moan, did not escape his notice.

He sought the first opportunity to be alone with her.

"Rose, you will never forgive me, and ill do I deserve that you should."

She took his hand. "I have nothing to forgive you, William dear; your little hastiness last night gave me no offence whatever."

"But, Rose, I have done shamefully, disgracefully by you, in another way, since."

"And in what other way, William?" she looked up into his face, in growing alarm.

"I went to see your father."

She started, almost shuddered, and turned pale. Then laying her hand on his shoulder, and still gazing into his face, Rose asked:

"You did not tell what you know to the old man, William, did you?"

"Rose, I told him every word."

She shrank back, clasping her hands, and looking around her fearfully, as if she dreaded that some dangerous listener might have caught her lover's avowal. They stood together, in the little garden attached to the house.

"I am sorry for that, William; more sorry than I can tell you."

"I know I did what you would not forgive, Rose, and I don't expect you ever will."

"I do forgive you freely, freely." Again she stretched out her hand—(did William refuse it?)— "Oh, how unhappy my poor father must be on my account! But William dear, I can easily excuse you. I know the state of mind you were in; and indeed, and in thruth, you would not envy me if you knew what lay before me."

"There is the fear I have, Rose darling: and there is your father's fear also; there is what makes us both thremble for you. My brain was wild last night. I couldn't think like a man that had reason. I had doubts of you,—aye, and terrible doubts. But since your father spoke to me, my mind is quiet, and I say to myself you never could bring grief to your father, and ruin to me."

"I am thankful to you, William, for trusting me, while matters appear black enough against me; and I tell you, and you will find, that Rose Brady will never forget it to you. It can never go out of my mind that, altho' you had cause to think ill of me, you put faith in my thruth and in my honesty."

"But, *ma-colleen*, I have my fears of you, I say again, and so has your father. We both think that there is danger round about you; and he says that ould Hesther Bonnetty is hatching a plot against you, in the same way as, he is now certain, she did against your poor brother Morris."

" Oh, William, let me hear every single thing my father thinks and says."

" He thinks that you ought to be open-hearted with him and with me; because neither he nor I can save you from enemies if we don't know who they are, nor keep danger from you, if you leave us in the dark about it."

" Well, William, for all that, my father and you must not change your good opinion of me, if I hold my tongue for a little while. Everything I do or say is watched or listened to. I am not sure we may not be overheard this moment; and, take my word for it, danger would double and treble itself over my head, and over all our heads, if I told anything more than *you* know of last night's business."

" Then, Rose, I will leave the question between your father and yourself. Your are going with his dinner to him?"

" He has eaten his dinner by this time, I hope."

" Then you have seen him to-day?"

" No, William."

" Not take the ould man his dinner, no more than his breakfast?"

" It was not in my power to do so."

" And who has taken it to him?"

" The same persom who took him his breakfast, William; ould Hesther M'Farlane."

" My God, Rose!" ejaculated her astounded lover, " and could you send her to him a second time this day? this day, of all days in the year? Why there doesn't breathe a crature on the face of the earth, counting the toads and all, that we havn't in this counthry, that your father has such a dread of seeing or spaking with."

" This day, of all days in the year ? What is the meaning of your words, William ? "

He related what Hesther M'Farlane had reminded Randal Brady of that morning, and the opinions entertained by her father on the subject.

" May Heaven guard me," cried Rose; " she is a very, very wicked ould woman."

" And you have let her go again to plague your father in his prison."

" It is a terrible thing for me to be obliged to let her go; but I could not say no to her, when she insisted on it."

" Tell me, Rose, do people spake thruth of that ould limb o' Satan ? is it witchcraft she has put on you ? "

" No, William, not witchcraft; I could laugh at her as far as that goes; no, but she has me and others in her power."

" Well, Rose, I have one thing more to tell you. I bear a message to you from your father."

" And what is it, William ? "

" He lays his commands, his positive commands on you, that you go see him in the jail, and spake with him."

" Hah! that's the worst of all. Alas! one disobedient child is enough in our family, and that one has been punished. Oh! I could have no courage to begin the work that lies before me. I would tremble every step I took, if I was in rebellion against my father, and dared to disobey his commands."

Rose paused in great embarrassment. After some time, she turned an appealing countenance to William **Duncan.**

" William, you must give me a proof of your complete confidence in Rose Brady. The time is come for me to ask you, and for you to do it. You must go back to my father, and get him to retract that command. There is nothing else for it. We are all destroyed if you refuse, and if you cannot succeed with my father. Do this for me, William, and during my life I will bless you, and try to reward you."

The young man looked quite confounded.

" Rose, now you astonish me beyond the powers of my tongue to tell you."

" And, in good thruth, it is natural you should say so: but, William, you must grant me my heart's prayer notwithstanding."

" Rose, Rose, what am I to think? To say nothing of myself, there is your grey-headed father—remember *him;* he is terrified on your account, yet you leave him in his doubt and his misery. Do I hear the thruth from your lips, Rose Brady? You, you will not go see your father, when he lays his commands on you to do it? Are you afraid of his questions, Rose?"

Mr. William Duncan was, as he might himself have expressed it, " beginning again."

" I *am* afraid of his questions, William; but on account of others, more than on my own. Tell me this, William; when you and my father spoke together about me, had *he* any doubts or suspicions of his daughter? But you need not answer. I know—I am quite sure he had not. Examine your own heart now, William, and you will find that your hard thoughts of me are stealing upon you again. William, it would be a poor thing for a father to suspect his child in that way; and it *is* a poor thing for a young man to suspect the young woman he has chosen for his wife. And it would be a wretched, wretched thing, for either of them to be obliged to keep her in the right path by force. Oh, no, no, no! The girl that cannot be good for the love of God, and for the love of the good itself, is not worth the thought of a father or of one human crature. And it is not from anger I say this, William, but I want to show you that if you can't depend thoroughly on me, it would be better to think no more of me; watching me, or suspecting me, could never make me worthy of you."

" Rose," said William, snatching her hand, after he had pressed down his hat tight over his eyes, " Rose, you are in the right, as you always are; and to show you I think so, I *will* try to work what you bid me with your father."

" You will never be sorry for it, William, and I thank you from the heart. Go to him, then, and tell him from me, that I know well the danger I am in; speak to him so close, and in such a whisper, that the walls can't hear you. But tell him that; and tell him, too, that I see through all the wiles of the wicked old woman, Hesther M'Farlane; but that, with help from heaven, I hope to turn away the evil from us all. Plant in his mind that there would be greater danger in going to see him now, or in spaking of what I will fully tell him another day, than there really is in what hangs over us already. And William, when you have whispered all this into his very ear, then go on, in a loud voice, and say I sent you to pray of him, for heaven's sake, to retract the command he has laid upon me. William, I stake my life my father will not say me nay."

" Rose, I will do as you bid me." They parted.

"Say to Rose, from me," was Randal Brady's answer, when the message and the request had been conveyed to him—" Say to my child from me, that I have never suffered as I am now suffering; say to her that my eyes and my mind can never know rest, while she stays away from me, and leaves unexplained to me the danger that darkens her path; but say to her, at the same time, that her father places reliance on her; that he never had a fear for her, but on account of her youth, and because she has only the bodily strength of a young girl; say that I take off my command, and leave her free; that though I tremble for her, I have a great prop in my knowledge of her sense and prudence; that I send her my benediction; and that the moment you quit me, William Duncan, I will go on my knees and offer up a prayer for her, to my Father, and to her Father."

CHAPTER XXIV.

It was almost night when William Duncan left Rose Brady, after having delivered her father's answer to her request. She had expressed a wish for his departure; and she informed him that she had serious occupation for the rest of the evening, which would require her whole and undivided attention. William silently took his leave; and he imagined that he saw an unusual degree of trepidation in her manner, as she bade him farewell till the morrow.

Admitting that her lover placed upon Rose the full reliance which he avowed he did, yet was there some little soreness lurking in his heart, on account of her want of confidence in him. Without endeavouring, however, to analyse his feelings—a thing we profess our incompetence to do when a lover is in question—there was one fact plain—Rose herself had acknowledged that danger hung over her, and William Duncan found it impossible to sit moping at home, under this consciousness. He would set out and be on the watch, some way or other, and chance might afford him an opportunity of rendering her service.

On his vague and wandering mission, he frequently

found himself in view of Rose's dwelling; and more than once he was prompted to raise the latch, just to prove to himself that she was safe at home. But he had enough of reflection left to call to mind that this would look very like as if he were " watching and doubting her" still, and so he resisted the temptation, and retreated from the house stealthily.

Rambling through the streets, William listened to every unusual noise, but nothing occurred to call for his interference, or even for his *surveillance*. Opposite the old crazy mansion, in the profoundest depths of which old Hesther Bonnetty resided, he made a full stop, and formed a sensible resolution. He would pay Hesther a visit, not one of compliment indeed, but in the view of forcing her to confess the nature of her machinations, and of discovering through her, Rose Brady's secret.

Walking rapidly by the river side, he soon cleared Hesther's frontier line of rubbish. Her door was now opened. He descended into the vault, and found the old reprobate sitting on her *boss* over a few embers. At his rapid entrance, she turned her head quickly round, and instantly addressed him.

" What's your business here? What do you want on my flure?" the full force of her venom was thrown into her tones.

" You'll soon know that," answered William fiercely; " and if you don't answer me in the thruth"——

" Hee-ee!" interrupted Hesther, with her jovial squeak, " an' if I don't, how will you help yourself?"

" I—" William Duncan paused at fault. He rummaged his head for an answer to her question, but found none. He could not say to the shrivelled hag that he had power over her life, in case she proved sufficiently unamiable to tell him a bundle of lies, or to tell him nothing at all; he could not even threaten to raise his hand to her.

"Why do you stop so short in your brave speech?" continued Hesther, chuckling; "why don't you swear a big oath that you'll have my blood? *och-hone-a-ree*. It isn't the heart to do id you want; but I defy you; I bid my defiance to you; I spit upon you."

She tried to suit the action to the word, and the young man bounded backward, with the same feeling of avoidance which he would have experienced had the foam of a rabid old cat been flung at him.

"Hee-ee-ee! loocky 'tis for you that it didn't stick to you." She seemed delighted at the vague terror which she was able to excite. "Hee-ee, 'twould be betther for you if biling lead was sprinkled over you."

"Tell me—tell me, you foul *culloch*—and tell me at your peril—why did you bring Rose Brady here last night? who was it that met her here?

With the crook of her crutch Hesther hooked the three-legged stool, drew it close to her own esteemed seat, and then glanced up at her catechist.

"Squat down upon that close by me, an' we'll have the *shannachus** together; you must hear all the how-an'-about-it; sit you down at my side I bid you."

William Duncan loathingly, and not without a strange sensation of terror, drew back from the proffered fellowship.

"*Hannuch thu, murroch thu*—let it alone then: hee-ee! I hard o' the story Randal Brady tould you

---

* Pleasant gossip.

to-day." William started. "Hee-ee; an' he said the thruth o' me; I liked a comely boy by my showldher, ever since I was the haighth o' my critch—he-ee."

William Duncan, as the depraved old sinner writhed her wrinkles at him, moved to leave her den.

"Aye, you're for quitin' me; but what I have to tell you is worth the hearin'."

"Tell it at once, then."

"Tho' you're a bad graft, you're a comely *garçoon*, an' it's a great shame, an' a great schandle for little Rose Brady to be makin' a fool of you."

"What—what do you mean?" gaspingly demanded William."

"The rason you come here is, to make question why I brought Rose Brady to my flure last night?"

"That is my business, and I tould you so before; give me a thrue answer."

"An' who tould *you*, my brave buck, that I brought her? If little Rose Brady didn't come wid her hearty good will, was there strenth in my ould bones to force her? Rosey wanted no pressin'—hee-ee."

"An' what did she come for?"

"What is id that makes the girls come and go the world over? well-lookin' *bouchals* like yourself, isn't id? an' Rose Brady came here to discoorse wid as brave a blade as ever rowled an eye; an' she came wid the good will, I tell you."

"Ould witch, you lie."

"Hee-ee! you won't b'lieve that cosey Rosy, the posey, has e'er a sweetheart but one Billy Duncan? *Och-hone-a-ree!* to-morrow will tell you another story. I know every word that her ould fool of a father, Randal Brady, spoke to you to-day; an' he put it into your head that Rose was a little *votheen** of a saint. But smooth wather runs deep; an' that may be said of the father and the dauther together; they know what to tell and what to hide between them. Did neither of 'em ever inform you, that once upon a time there was a slashin' blade that made sthrong love to Rosey, an' was so hot on id, he thought to dhrag her away by main force? *Och-hone-a-ree!* they never tould you that little story."

William stamped in a fury.

"Hee-ee—aye, you may hit your pump against my flure till you knock fire out of id; but you went to-day to comfort Randal Brady, an' purty comfort you brought him; an' he tould you that I swore an oath to him, and made a promise to him, forty years ago; an' I tell *you* now, that the oath an' the promise are both of 'em fulfilled. When you go to Randal Brady again to comfort him, don't forget to say that the young blade that thought to force his dauther from him, met her here last night; an' tell him, moreover, that she met the same bould fellow this night by her own free askin', where there's nobody to be the wiser o' their meetin'."

"Are you an imp of hell?" shouted William Duncan, nearly deprived of reason.

"A blisther on your foul tongue. But I knew I could tell you news worth the hearin'; and now that it's tould get you over my thrashold. Lave my flure an' lave my house."

She rose up from her boss, and hobbled rapidly across the apartment, threatening the young man with her crutch. A strip of paper fell from her person on

---

* Devotee.

the floor, near the fire; the light of the embers glanced on it. William Duncan thought he knew the handwriting; he snatched it up and read, by the thin ray of Hesther's rush, the following words:—

"I will meet you, at eight o'clock this evening, in the garden at the back of our house.

"Rose Brady."

Everything seemed to swim round before William Duncan's striken vision. He leaned the palm of his left hand for support against the wall; in his right, extended from him, the paper remained. The wicked crow's quick eye soon ascertained the cause of his agitation.

"Fire burn you, sowl an' body," she hideously screamed out; "give that writin' from your hand. Give, give."

William Duncan became aware of her approach. He crumpled the scrap of paper between his fingers, locked them around it, and hastened to escape from the foul place which, considering the character of its proprietor, Morris Brady had not inaptly called a toad-hole. The hag was quick upon William, and ere he had quite cleared her door, he received a blow on the side of his head, from the heavy end of her crutch, which nearly staggered him.

His first impulse, naturally enough, was to chastise his venomous assaulter. But when he turned round and looked at the shrivelled and bent creature, whose skinny arm, nerved for the occasion by the devil she served, had contrived to give him such a blow, he withdrew his raised hand, and ran away from her as from a fiend. Hesther pursued him as well as she was able; but when she had gained her rubbish rampart, she seemed to give up the chase as hopeless, and materials being plentifully at hand, contented herself with pelting him—every throw accompanied by screaming curses—till he was out of sight.

During William Duncan's headlong career through the streets once more towards Rose's residence, the town clock began to strike. He stopped to count the hour. With suspended breath he reckoned each clang. It struck eight—it tolled again; "an hour too late," he cried, rushing onward.

At the end of Randal Brady's house was a little gate, leading into his little kitchen-garden, which extended to the rear of the premises. Upon reaching this, William stopped out of breath. A chilly dislike to find his fears verified crept over him; an unwilled repugnance to face the certainty of his doom, held him back. He tried, however, to man himself, and had just become steeled to brave whatever might be before him, when he hastened to conceal himself from observation. Cautious steps approached the gate. He took off his hat, put it down stealthily by him, bent his person below the height of the pier by which he stood, and advanced his head a little beyond one side of it, so as to enable him, he hoped, to see the persons advancing from the garden. A distant though loud noise, in some other quarter, fell on his ear, and disturbed its power of hearing, and he muttered deep curses within his breast at whoever it might be who had caused it, for just then he had begun to catch voices in conversation.

The noise passed away, and the steps and the voices drew near to him, without his having been able, except at the risk of premature detection, to see who came so close. At length Rose's well-known accents sounded distinctly; and she was speaking with a man. They stopped just at the other-side of the gate, within arm's length of the crouching listener.

"Well, a good night to you, Rose my darling," said the man, " and you see you can do any one thing with me."

" Good night," responded the soft and harmonious voice of William's mistress, " now I may depend on you?"

" As sure as the sky is above us, I will be with you to the moment. Your own fair hands will admit me?"

" With the last stroke of the clock, I will open the door for you myself."

" Good night, then, and give me your parting benediction; won't you, Rose, the Rose of this garden and of every other?"

" Go, go, for gracious sake!" pleaded Rose, after a moment's successful struggling; though William thought the struggle something else, and never dreamt of the victory being claimed by her; " go—it is late, and I cannot stop longer."

William Duncan tried to keep down the choking in his throat. He was barely able to understand that did he clear the gate, and try to secure his detested rival, while he stood at its other side, escape might be probable from the uninclosed garden; and that by staying where he was, he could best insure his fell purpose; for fell it had now become. The gate creaked; no tiger ever watched a prey with an eye of more determined ferocity: it opened—a man in a cloak advanced beyond it, and with a savage, gulphing yell, William sprang at his throat. The assailed person raised his arm, and struck his assaulter; Duncan loosed one hand from his collar, and his answering blow sent them both down together.

"Oh, good Lord have mercy on me! and on us all!" shrieked Rose, hastening to the scene of deadly struggle. The fallen men exerted each their utmost strength for mastery. Rose, without an instant's hesitation, cast herself upon William Duncan, and seized him round the body.

"Free yourself of your cloak, and fly!" she cried to her mysterious acquaintance; "free yourself! quick! quick!"

And at the same instant, William saw his unknown foe jump up, dart away, and disappear, leaving the cloak in his grasp. He also would have started up to pursue, but was impeded by Rose's desperate exertions to keep him down; and, did he dream? or did he really hear Hesther Bonnetty's voice screaming in his ears, as again she struck him with her crutch:—

"Now, now, Billy Duncan, was there thruth in my words?"

"Loose me! loose me!" he shouted to Rose; "loose me, you base young crature! loose me! or by the heavens, I will not spare you, if you hold me back from him!"

"Oh, William, William, it is only for your own sake I try to hold you!"

He tore her grasp asunder; the effort of his great strength sent her staggering aside, and with a faint but piercing shriek, Rose fell prostrate. At the same moment William contrived to dispose of the hag, who had fastened her bony fingers in his hair; and a few bounds sent him out of sight of either.

Rose sat up, and listened to his quickly receding steps. Then, with heavy sighs, she was about to enter the house, when Hesther M'Farlane addressed her.

" You said you'd tell him everything in the garden ? "

" Go your ways, woman : you and I have nothing to say together."

" That's not the thruth from your tongue, Rose Brady; you an' I have a grate dale to say together, now an' to come. Deny me, and defy me, and I'll make you rue it to the day of your death."

" Go, go; I cannot and will not speak with you now ;" and Rose retired into the house, and secured the door.

CHAPTER XXV.

It has been noticed that Mrs. Brady was connected with many wealthy and influential persons of the town in which she resided. Among them, upon occasions of family difficulties or of rejoicing, shew as in the habit of coming forward with her condolence or her counsel, or her congratulation, or her services; and this, although no longer their fellow-believer, upon the principle, as she herself expressed it, that " blood is thicker than water." Neither deaths, nor births, nor christenings, nor weddings, nor illness, could, in Mrs. Brady's opinion, be properly attended to save under her superintendence. And, notwithstanding some little unconscious arrogance in the assumptions of the simple old woman, so really useful and agreeable did she prove to be upon every occasion, that, down to tenth and twelfth cousins, she was much considered and looked up to.

In other matters, too, Mrs. Brady felt herself called on to interfere. One of her female cousins who had a good dowry, happened to light on a very indifferent husband. When the man became outrageous towards his wife, either Mrs. Brady was sent for, or, having heard of the matter, she went to his house unsummoned, and, strange enough, although he was in the habit of inflicting manual chastisement on his spouse, yet did he wince under Mrs. Brady's moral and religious discourse upon the duties of the married state, and bow before her illustrative proverbs, and, for some time, really refrain from violence.

Another of her cousins was a very severe father to his children. One of them was a fine, rosy-cheeked, potatoe-stuffed boy, of a choleric disposition (" kind father for him," remarked Mrs. Brady,) and in their personal contests together, the parent used to tie the little wretch to a great chair, deprive him of his food, and most inhumanly flog him. The mother would send private intelligence of the matter to Mrs Brady: the good woman would issue forth to the rescue; work her way to the room where the urchin was incarcerated; break his shackles; mount him on her back; cover him with her mantle; smuggle him to her own house; and there keep him well fed, but at the same time well lectured on his hereditary faults, until the storm had blown over, and she had gone bail for him, and reconciled him to his father.

Whenever called upon to appear in her capacity of family directress, Mrs. Brady equipped herself in her best attire. She mounted her very stiffest " high caulled cap," quilted most precisely in front; she put on her green silk quilted petticoat, delicately shaded before by her thin sprigged muslin apron; her flowered calico gown, of such solid fabric as would astonish a modern manfacturer, was nicely pinned into three festoons at the tail; her clocked, sky-blue hose were drawn on; ponderous silver-buckles, each half a pound net weight, ornamented her sharp-pointed shoes, at the instep; a crimson cloth-mantle, hooded with silk, trimmed with fur, and fastened with a great silver hook and eye, was finally put on; and thus attired, and assuming, with her other finery, a look of severe sagacity, tempered by a matronly air of patronage, the worthy dame considered herself perfectly qualified to lay down the law to any of her numerous and wide spread kindred.

On the morning following the adventure related in our last chapter, Mrs. Brady surprised her family by sailing forth from her chamber, equipped as we have just sketched her. The parched crispness of the poor woman's lips, the unnatural flush upon her usually pale cheeks, and the heaviness of her eyes, proclaimed, however, her unfitness to go out in any attire. But it was in vain that Rose remonstrated with her on the subject. She had arisen that morning determined to visit her husband, and then set to work to lead him home to his family. She demanded from Rose the old man's breakfast, and immediately sallied forth with it to him.

The meeting between the old couple was as naturally tender as if they had still been unmarried lovers, and as fresh and as primitive as the consciousness of having nothing to hide could make it. Mrs. Brady's ardour might be called, however, a little too strong for her years. She hung upon her husband's neck; she kissed his forehead, his cheeks, his lips; nor could the sight of his snow-white hairs, nor the furrows on his brow, moderate her demonstrations of devout affection.' Nay, even Randal's own greeting of his faithful Betty was scarcely torpid enough for a man upwards of sixty. But we pause to reprehend ourselves for an approach to levity, while describing the simple and touching manifestation of a pure love between the good old couple. Yes, Randal Brady and his wife still loved one another. The sun which had risen on their youth, and made resplendent the meridian of their prime, still shed a mellow radiance on the evening of their days; and the very clouds of misfortune which at present hung over their heads, became beautified in its beam.

To say that Mrs. Brady felt intensely the captivity of her husband, and the uncertainty of the fate of her favourite son, would afford but a feeble idea of the manner in which the natural enthusiasm of her heart regarded the present situation of two people so dear to her. Nor could she control her tongue from giving vent to what she felt: so that, instead of consoling her husband, he found himself called upon to comfort his wailing wife.

The interview between the ancient lovers was protracted in discussing, as far as Randal Brady could get his wife to do so, their family affairs. He discovered that she was ignorant of what had happened to Rose during her illness; and he rejoiced at this, because the poor woman was already more than sufficiently unhappy, without any additional cause for sorrow.

More than three hours passed away, when Mrs. Brady suddenly announced her intention to depart. The old man accompanied her to the iron door, and there begged of her, (for he had noticed all along how feeble and feverish she was,) as she loved him, to retire to bed as soon as she reached home, and to take care of herself a few days longer, till her health should be re-established. Mrs. Brady, for the first time in her life, cunningly avoided making any promise of obedience, but parted rapidly from her anxious husband, praying every blessing on his head.

Randal Brady hastened to the common day-room of the prison, and gazed out at her through the iron bars of the window. He perceived that her step was languid, or, when she strove to quicken it, unsteady. Continuing to watch her, he was greatly surprised and sorely troubled to observe that, instead of facing homeward, she hastened in an opposite direction. He called to her as loudly as he could, but it seemed that his voice did not reach her, for without turning her head, she persevered in her route, and was soon lost to his view.

" May God support her! I fear she will fall down in the streets," he said; and never before, perhaps, had he so bitterly felt the loss of his liberty as at that moment, when he saw his aged wife tottering along, and knew himself unable to offer her a supporting arm. For some time he stood at the window, hoping to see her repass on her way home; but she did not soon return.

At the time Mrs. Brady left the prison, her daughter Rose was again seated with his worship the mayor, in widow Sheehan's little back parlour. Papers were on the table before them; and to these, in succession, Alderman Lodge was affixing his signature. Some one rapidly entered the shop without.
" Mercy to me, Sir!" cried Rose, " my mother's voice in the shop!"

" Ub-bub-bousey! By the life, Rose my ducky, we are caught. My best wig to a chaney orange, but my cousin Betty is come to put the relation on me, to get your father out of prison."

"Oh, Sir, I am certain you have guessed it! And it will be a sore affliction to her to be refused. Oh, the bitterest thought to me, in all I have to go through, is to know that my poor father and mother must suffer by my means!"

"But it can't be helped, Rosey—here, bundle up these,"—his worship pushed the papers to Rose,— "the sign manual is to them all."

"Be kind to my poor mother, Sir, in her great distress, and I will for ever pray for you!"

"And I will, Rosey: but, by the rod, I had just as lief she stayed away for the present: cousin Betty, as we all call her, isn't the woman to be put off with a kiss-hand-and-ta; by my good conscience, I have a hard card to play. Rose, you slut, are you deserting me at my need? Stay where you are, and help me to coin lies to your mother. Hah! well you know I can't run after you; if I could I'd soon arrest you, you bright-eyed baggage!"

During the latter part of this speech, Rose had been opening a little side-door which led into the narrow hall of the house; and before the alderman had concluded, she made her exit through it, just as her mother entered the parlour from the shop, bestowing upon her good-humoured ally before she disappeared, a silent injunction to caution and secrecy.

As may be inferred from previous hints, Mrs. Brady had not put on her best attire this morning, only for the purpose of visiting her husband. In every possible point of view, as far as human agency could effect an object, she had, since her union with Randal Brady, indeed before that event, habitually and invariably reckoned on his all-sufficiency: and she now felt sure, that were he at liberty, he would in a trice, somehow or other, restore peace and happiness to their hitherto delightful home. The worthy woman had not the least idea that her husband was charged with anything save his battery upon the town-sergeant, Jack Withers: this, in her eyes, was not only no legal offence at all, but a very praiseworthy action. She convinced herself that Alderman Lodge, the Mayor, fully shared her ideas on the subject; and it was only necessary to ask him to set Randal Brady free, in the name of cousinship and old friendship, and, as she had promised William Duncan, home she should triumphantly lead Randal, " to his dinner, thro' the thick o' the town."

Nor, indeed, were these conclusions grounded on any great stretch of fancy on Mrs. Brady's part. It was generally presumed, and not without reason, that previous to the arrival of the assize judges, the mayor had the fate of an accused party pretty much at his disposal. In fact, fifty years ago in our good city, " such things were."

In the alderman's reception of Mrs. Brady in the little parlour, embarrassed consciousness tempered the usual bluff cordiality of his manner. Yet, as he listened to her doleful and weeping statement of her bodily and mental sufferings, and of her distress for her good man's imprisonment, and of her fears for her favourite son, the mayor's sympathy was evident and natural. And he fully agreed with her that Randal Brady was the most likely person to ascertain poor Morris's present fate, and shield him from future danger. But when Alderman Lodge found her coming to the point he had anticipated, he grew very fidgetty; and before he could find terms to reply to her request, or rather to her demand, for the immediate liberation of her husband, often did he " hem," and " haw." At length, affecting a close, pursy look, as if to give Mrs. Brady to understand that there was much magisterial wisdom shut up within him, and that, upon this especial occasion, his gold coin of sterling sagacity was to be expended, the " divartin' ould aldherman" tried to deliver himself.

" Cousin Betty," rubbing down the side of his face and his chin, " we will see ; we will see ; we *will* see what *can* be done for you."

" Why, *aroon*, 'tis the asiest thing in the world to see what's to be done for me. Just take up your pen, and write word to the jailor to let my poor man come home to his dinner, arm-in-arm with me."

" I'll think of it, Betty ; and to-morrow, suppose, if you call on me again." He drew out a watch of such dimensions as would burst in tatters a ridiculous modern fob, and he kept his eyes fixed on it that they might avoid those of his cousin. " It is now just half an hour past two o'clock in the day, and, at half an hour past two o'clock in the day to-morrow, if nothing particular happens, I—"

" There's a good ould sayin', cousin Ned," interrupted Mrs. Brady, beginning to lose patience, " ' do to-day, and you may rest to-morrow:' moreover, ' make your hay while the sun shines ;' an' that manes, don't lose time ; for ' time lost can never be regained.' I tell you my heart is set on bringin' Randal home wid me this day ; an 'tis the first time I ever asked one o' *ye* to do *me* a sarvice; but, praised be heaven, ' a friend in time o' need is a friend that's thrue indeed;' an' I'm sure I little thought a fortnight ago, that I'd be comin' here a beggin' this misfortinate day for us all; aye, a beggin' to you, cousin Ned, to let Randal

Brady out o' your jail, that he may be free to stop them from callin' my son Morris a robber; but, 'man proposes an' God disposes,' *aroon;* an' so here I am."

During the latter part of this appeal, Mrs. Brady spoke with difficulty, and the corner of her fine flowered muslin apron was often held to her eyes.

"Betty, it is totally beyond my power and skill to set your husband free till to-morrow."

"'*Nie vaheen, na breerah, na brausha,*'* is a thrue sayin', Ned Lodge; and 'words an' promises won't pay a score;' and 'the empty sack never stood against the wall;' and, 'one penny is worth the promise of a pound.' Cousin Ned, the sorrow's in me, but if I was a mayor to-morrow, an' you were shut up in a jail, where the sunshine doesn't come, an' where God's fresh air doesn't blow, an' where you can't have the wholesome use o' your limbs; an' wid a lock o' sthraw for your bed, an' rogues, an' robbers, an' rapparees, your companions for the night; I wouldn't sleep asy till you'd be a free man, cousin Neddy. You'll have the blessin' of a thankful family to-night, if you let me take Randal Brady home to sit at his own hearth."

"I would, indeed, Betty, if—"

"And in thruth, Ned Lodge, I don't think it was over justice to keep my poor man so long from us. The wound that the bailiff gave me isn't yet haled on my forehead; and Randal only sthruck the man that drew his own wife's blood on the thrashold of her own little bed-room."

The mayor thought he had now good argument to convince his cousin, that there was more difficulty than she imagined in granting her urgent request.

---

* The preacher can't dine on his sermon.

"Ub-bub-bousy, Betty! if nothing stood in the way of getting Randal home again, but the hole he made in Jack Withers' woolly skull, he'd have been in the same house with you, long enough ago; but there's a more serious charge against him, cousin Betty."

His worship did not well know how to interpret the look with which his cousin regarded him. There was more in it than he could fathom; though he hoped it principally meant only surprise.

"And what more have ye to say against him, I'd be glad to larn?" demanded Mrs. Brady.

"I'll tell you, Betty. It is sworn, in black and white, that he is suspected of having assisted his son in the robbery at Barney Roundhead's house; and that he assaulted my sergeant to escape detection."

"Och! tattheration to your wooden head, you rapparee!" Mrs. Brady started up, to continue her address to the mayor; the mayor started up too, clutching his rod—not in his magisterial capacity, however, but for support, as his gouty limbs shook under him.

"An' is it to my face you dare say the like of Randal Brady? Aye; I see you are a mayor, with your long, white stick in your hand; but, let me tell you, that if you were the King of Morroccy, you'd never be as honest a man as my husband: is id the name o' rogue you'd thry to fix upon his grey hairs? would you cry shame, shame, upon our ould age?" her feelings overcame her; she staggered; she sunk upon the chair from which she had arisen; her person swung to one side; her head fell upon her shoulder, and her eyes closed.

His worship violently rang the hand-bell which lay on the table, and the widow Sheehan and a servant came rushing into the parlour together. He then directed wine to be brought, and the touch of the glass upon her lips revived her. The alarmed cousin pressed her to take some of the proffered cordial; but she declined it with a look and motion of disgust: and, exerting a sudden and unnatural energy, a second time started up, and hastened into the street.

But her strength soon failed her; she tottered and was about to fall, when a strong arm kept her from the ground; and—" In the Holy Name, what is the matter with you, Mrs. Brady?" asked a young man, in a tone at once anxious, affectionate, and impetuous.

"That's William Duncan's voice," said the old woman faintly: and William it was, who, with drooping head, had been hurrying along, regardless of everything and every person, until, by chance, his eye caught the startling vision of Rose Brady's mother about to fall in the mire of the public streets.

"And it's the Lord sends you to me, my good boy," continued Mrs. Brady; "I could go no farther without help, William; William Duncan, my son, I think I am dying; I"—

She could not continue. He bore her into a shop, where he procured and administered to her some effective cordial; and now she did not push away the hand which offered the glass, but put her dry lips to it, and kissed it. And she blessed him for his attention; and after a short rest, professed her capability to proceed, alone, on her way.

But once again in the street, Mrs. Brady soon found it would have been impossible to get on without the young man's assistance. So she clung to his arm, leaning heavily upon it, as she tried to move her almost useless limbs.

Her supporter was so alarmed at the condition she was in, that he did not think of making inquiries as to its cause. He concluded she was going home; but to his surprise she turned in another direction.

"Where am I walkin' to?" she said, in answer to a question from him; "I'm goin' to the jail; to Randal, my good boy."

He represented her present unfitness for such a place, and impressed upon her, that even her life might be the forfeit of the attempt to stay away from her home and her bed. But she would go to Randal, and no where else; wherever he was, there was her home; it was no time to stay away from him, when sorrow and shame were his portion; and, at any rate, she believed she *was* dying; and if so, Randal would not like that any one but himself should close her eyes.

CHAPTER XXVI.

RANDAL BRADY received his wife at the iron door, of which mention has before been made. He saw her helpless state; and, with William Duncan's assistance, bore her to the straw on which he had lain since entering the prison. The poor woman was exhausted in mind, as well as in body. She spoke not a word; and her throbbing head would have fallen upon her chest had not her husband's hands supported it. Her brows hung down; her eye-lids half closed over her now sunken eyes; and moanings and shudderings accompanied her heavy respiration. Now and then, she would start and look around her; fix her eyes vaguely on her old partner, and mutter something of her determination to stay by his side to the last, although the world wronged and scorned him; then she seemed to sink back again into unconsciousness; until, by degrees, she became incapable of any exertion; her murmurings growing less and less distinct; her features waxing duller and more stupid, and finally losing all expression, except of that physical suffering, which is almost without the cognizance of the mind.

With the most intense and affectionate solicitude,

Randal watched over his wife's illness, marking its gradually overpowering effects; and it was in a broken voice that he endeavoured to whisper consolation in her ear.

She fell into a feverish dose. He laid her head upon the pillow; he covered her with the bed-clothes, supplied from his own house; and then slowly drew his hand across his moist brow, and remained a moment silent, as if reasoning with his weakness,

When he re-opened his eyes, they were sad, but neither morose nor gloomy. His look rested for a moment on William Duncan, who had been a silent sympathizer in the scene before him, and he then arose, slowly and cautiously, and beckoned the young man to approach.

To his inquiry of William, as to where he had met the old woman, Randal received a satisfactory answer; but he could obtain no information concerning the cause of her sudden and increased illness, and her great and obvious agitation of mind.

"This is a poor place for her to be sthruck down with sickness in," said Randal; "but I know she will not go from me of her own free will; and if we remove her by force, it will be a removal for ever. I should never see her alive again; most likely never see her dead, unless they brought the corpse to me in this jail, to give me a last look at it."

"God forbid that should come to pass, Mr. Brady," said William Duncan, much affected.

"Amen, amen, good boy. And here is a second day I have heard no word from Rose—no, not one word—not one."

"What, sir! has she not come to see you this whole day, no more than the last?"

"Speak lower, William, speak lower;" he pointed

to his sleeping wife. " William, you said those words as if your fears for her were greater than ever; as if you had new and good grounds for your fears on Rose's account; tell me everything you know."

Poor William, while he spoke, was terribly agitated; for his recollections of the previous night crowded upon him. Let us add, while we think of it, that his furious pursuit after the hero of the cloak had proved only very fatiguing.

He did not immediately reply to the old man's last words, and Randal urged him to speak. William, indeed, felt that openness was almost a duty; but he shrank from heaping upon the white head before him the new affliction which his disclosure would produce.

" Mr. Brady, it was not to bring more sorrow on you that I spoke."

" No matther for that, boy; go on; it is very painful to me to look on your throubled face, and be left to guess your mind."

William tried to avoid the sore point.

" I went last night to Hesther M'Farlane's vault, Sir, and I spoke with her there."

" Well? well? don't stop in your speech, good boy; it is not acting well by me."

" I questioned her about Rose; and she tould me to ask of you, Sir, whether or no it ever happened that some one attempted to force Rose away from you: has such a thing come to pass, Mr. Brady?"

" Yes: there was one who did his utmost to lure my child from her home, her innocence, and her God; and who, when he found himself disappointed, thought to take her by force from her father's side, at the very moment she was leaning on her father's arm."

" Well;—and Hesther M'Farlane said it was from that man's hands I saved Rose, when I burst in the door at her cry for help; and Hesther said, moreover, that although Rose escaped for that time, she would be with the same person again, where I could do nothing to save her."

"William, that sinful ould woman has tould you an unthruth to vex you; but there is enough in the threat she made, to give me grief and fears for my child."

"Who was the man that thought to take Rose from your side, Mr. Brady?"

"I was going to tell you, William. Afther Barnaby Roundhead lost his wife, little Patty, his daughther, spent some weeks with her uncle, Alderman Lodge, who is now mayor of the town. Rose Brady used to go to see her there; and undher that roof she met with the hardened young bravo, Joe Wilson; whose mother, and Mr. Roundhead's wife, were both sisthers of the mayor, so that Joe Wilson was Mr. Lodge's nephew, as Patty was his niece. The poor foolish scapegrace followed Rose home one night from the alderman's, and wished to come into my house; but Rose begged me to shut my dour against him, and I did her bidding: and she would not go out again to enjoy herself with her little cousin, till I took her myself to Alderman Lodge's, left her at the thrashold, and promised to call for her at an early hour of the night.

"I kept my word; and Rose and I were making our way home thro' the *bosheen*, when Wilson stopt us. He was alone. Because I am an ould grey-headed man, he thought I could not check his youthful arm. But I had to keep my child from him; and my cudgel was in my hand, and I struck him to the ground: and Rose and I got home, safe and sound, together.

" Now, William Duncan, I will tell you what happened further, and you will say there was something wonderful in it. The very next morning, his mangled corpse was found in the *bosheen*, about fifty yards from the spot where he had met Rose and me the night before."

" That's wonderful indeed, Mr. Brady."

" There he was, stiff and could; every feature of his face so disfigured, that his clothes, and some papers in his pockets, were the only guides to tell who he was. But there his dead body lay, for all that. And now, William, you see that ould Hesther lied, when she tould you that the man who tried to force Rose from my side, could be the same who met her in the vault the night before the last. Oh, William! if that man was, in thruth, in the land of the living this day, then, indeed, woe to Rose, and woe to me! Never did he know what it was to have pity on the innocent; never did he rule a passion. Oh, he would break twenty hearts sooner than give up one single bad purpose!"

" Mr. Brady, there is wisdom with your years. If you can give me the most distant notion of the man who met Rose in the vault, he shall not hide long from me."

" Thinking of that very thing, William, banished the sleep from my sthraw all last night. But, tho' I put the question over and over, I could not make answer to myself. However, one point is quite clear, I believe; and Rose herself was right upon it, the first of any of us. Some one is playing the part of Joe Wilson's ghost; and that some one, whoever he is, led my poor boy Morris into mischief, and, with Hesther M'Farlane's help, decoyed Rose to the vault.

And, moreover, I have come to the certainty that Rose ventured to that wicked den, in the hope of doing her brother some good; nothing else could draw her out of her own house late at night; but I know she would go thro' fire and water for Morris."

"And if Rose met the man who led her brother into danger, Mr. Brady, and now knows who he is, she ought to discover on him," said William Duncan, rather bitterly.

"William, believe her father's word; it is not with her own good-will that Rose keeps the mystery of that night shut up in her own bosom. The man she met has her in his power; of that I am sure; and she is afraid to tell his secret; tho' I cannot, as yet, clearly make out why."

"He must have her in his power, beyond doubt," assented William Duncan; his face again blackening under a recollection of the garden scene, and of what followed.

"And William, tho' she still stays away from me, I have not yet the slightest iota of a doubt of Rose Brady; I mean, of her honesty; a doubt of her freedom from danger is another thing. No: Rose keeps herself at home from her father, thro' fear of the consequences to us all of breaking thro' a command not to come to me; and she thinks she is acting for the right. But, my good boy, I will not any longer leave Rose depending on herself, great as is her share of good sense, and foresight, and fortitude—yes, great, above what commonly falls to a young girl's lot. You must bring her to me, William, and the advice of age will help the arm of youth to protect her. Tell her, my son, that her sick mother wants her help: and if Rose will not come at my command, and for her mother's sake, then heaven help me; for then I shall have the worst—aye, the very worst to fear."

William Duncan was soon on his way to the suburb where the Bradys lived.

The old man returned to his place, at his wife's bedside. Noisy and disagreeable conversation, and other riots, were usual among his fellow-prisoners. He besought them to respect her sorrows and her illness, and they did so; all speaking in whispers, and one or two, who were ironed, controlling the clank of their fetters.

Randal Brady noted the spasms which occasionally passed across the invalid's face; felt the heavy throbbing of her temples; and listened to the wretched moanings which broke through her feverish slumber. As the door of his dungeon now and then grated on its hinges, thither was directed a glance of deep anxiety and expectation; but hour after hour wore away, and neither his daughter nor his messenger appeared.

At dinner time, his little basket of provisions was handed to him; he eagerly inquired who had brought it to the prison; and learned that it was one of his neighbours.

The shades of night stole round him; he was still alone at his wife's pallet. Full night came on, and his soul darkened with the darkness. Oh, cold, cold was the pang at the doting, but now doubting heart of the virtuous father!

"Randal Brady," whispered some one close to him, in the thick gloom of the dungeon.

He started; but immediately answered, "I hear you, whoever you are: what have you to say to me?"

"I overheard most of the words you spoke to-day to the young man who was here with you."

"Well? that's nothing to boast of; I never undherstood it was called a good or a manly thing to be a listener on the private words of others; what is your name?"

"No matter about that. But tho' you need not know my name, I will tell you a little of who and what I am. You are conversing with a friend of Joe Wilson."

"And that again is not much to make me think the better of you. A friend of Joe Wilson's; and a prisoner, I suppose, in this place, along with me?"

"Yes: but listen. You told the young man to-day that you were sure my friend Joey was not in the land of the living."

"I did: and I am sure he is not."

"You mistake, then."

"Pho," said Randal, "you want to torment my mind, out of spite and wickedness against me. I saw the corpse in the *bosheen;* I followed it to the grave, as a forgiving Christian man ought to do; and I saw it buried outside the wall of St. John's Abbey."

"You saw the corpse; did you know it to be dashing Joey's *by the face?*"

"No, but ——"

The invisible speaker interrupted Randal with a loud scoffing laugh; and then added—his whisper assuming an expression worthy of an honourable member of "the hell-fire club"——

"Your little daughter Rosey guesses by this time whether the ghost that stole Morris Brady into Barney, the miser's house, *is* a ghost, or good sound flesh and blood."

Randal Brady darted forward in the direction from which the voice came, intending to grasp the speaker, but he encountered no one. The next instant another scoffing laugh sounded from a remote part of the dungeon.

The old man had instantly seen the great advantage likely to redound to Morris, as well as to Rose, if he could secure and identify the wantonly malignant person who addressed him. Having failed in his attempt, Randal Brady stood motionless, stricken with horror, and, for a moment, almost despair. If Joe Wilson's friend spoke what was true, gone, gone for ever, were the old father's hopes and joys in this life. " The glory had departed from his house."

His attention was aroused by the sudden entrance of the jailor with a lantern. It was the man's nightly visit to the common dungeon, to peer at the rivets on the felons' fetters, and to pass the light over their scowling features, as well indeed as over those of every other prisoner, for the purpose of identifying and assuring himself of the presence of each. Randal Brady reclined over his still unconscious wife, and gently took her burning hand. The jailor advanced to him. At first the old man drooped his head as the lantern was held to his face, but he almost immediately raised it again, at the thought that he was no malefactor, and did not merit to be treated as one.

" Mr. Brady," said the man, " it goes to my heart to tell you, that your poor wife's presence here is against prison rules; she must be removed to her own home."

" Oh, my God! I hope not," replied Randal; " it is a poor boon to crave, but I ask you, in the name of charity, to leave her with me; if she is sent out into the night air without help, or care, or love around her, never will her eyes open on the morning's light."

"How can I disobey my orders, Mr. Brady? my bread depends upon my place; how can I?"

"For the love of God let her rest on this sthraw, at laste till you are going to shut up the prison for the night. I expect a young friend here before that time; if he comes he will assist her; if he does not, why then I have only to resign her into the hands of her Maker."

The jailor, assenting to this prayer, withdrew, and the dungeon was again in utter darkness. And again, while listening to the feverish beating of his wife's heart, great horror fell upon the old man's mind. When not absorbed in almost the lethargy of his emotions, his ear measured every sound without, anticipating the entrance of Rose and William, or even of William alone, the young man's aid being now doubly desirable.

He was endeavouring to reduce his thoughts to some order, and his breast to some tranquillity and fortitude, when his wife, shrieking fearfully, sat up in the bed, and shook with ague-violence. He spoke to her such words of comfort as he could.

"Is this Randal's hand in mine?" she asked, with some difficulty.

"Yes, Betty, it is Randal who is at your side."

"'Tis very dark here—what place are we in, Randal *a-graw*?—hah! that's his voice I hear again!—I was beginnin' to have some hopes it was a dhrame—but there is his own voice;—and you and I are concealin' ourselves in some dark place, from the people's eyes—but 'tis no use, Randal—all the world knows that he is our son—and we may as well come abroad, along with the rest of the neighbours, and see him die."

"Don't speak so, my poor Betty: let us hope and pray for the best."

"If it was a thing we could hear his words— whisht! listen!"

And if Randal's ear deceived him not, he did catch Morris's accents, mingling with those of other people, in the passage without. Doubt soon fled. The door of the dungeon suddenly opened; men appeared at it, with lights; and Morris Brady, heavily bolted and hand-cuffed, was thrust in.

"There they are!" cried the jailor indignantly to the young man, as he pointed towards Randal and his wife; "your aged, and your good father and mother, —look at them!"

The lad stared at them almost stupidly. Without moving a step, he suddenly dropt on his knees, and extended his manacled hands. Supplication—miserable supplication for pardon was in his look, and on his haggard and bewildered features; but though his white lips moved, no word escaped him.

"They let him come to crave your last benediction, Randal," said the old woman, feebly and wildly, yet solemnly; "an' 'tis very good of them: and, Randal, *a-vourneen*, you won't let him depart out o' this life unblessed; he is a sinner—a poor sinner; but he is our son—your son, as well as my son: so, lay the father's hand on his head, and pray to God to bless him, for the last time."

"Come here to me, Morris," said the old man; "stand up, and come here to me."

Suddenly, Morris found words—low, hoarse, heart-changed words.

"No, Sir, no; I will not stand up—but I will obey you, and come to you:" and, clasping his hands, he moved on his knees towards his father, and remained still, a short distance before him. " Father, father!" he continued, " do not lay your curse upon me! Hear one word from my mouth! Until this night fell—until Hesther M'Farlane opened the door of the place where she had hid me—I did not know that the world called me a robber, or that my father was in jail thro' the fault of his son!"

" It was Hesther that set him for the bailiffs," said the jailor.

" When she gave me lave to quit the dark hole where she had locked me in, then, father, she tould me what I had brought on you; an' she said too, that, thro' my doings, my sisther Rose must hide her head from the world. Oh! may a curse from heaven fall—"

" Silence!" cried Randal Brady, loudly and sternly; " silence, wicked boy! Do you dare, to your father's face, and on your knees, to pray a curse from heaven upon a single human creature?"

The old man paused a moment. When he spoke again, his voice was gentle, and a little broken.

" Morris, my son, they tell me that I am to see you condemned, before the world, for stealing your neighbour's property; and I have the great fear on me that I am the father of a disgraced daughter. I have little hope that your mother will live many days; it may come to pass that, during the remainder of my life, I shall be a woe-sthricken ould man—companionless, childless—or worse than childless; but I must not let all that make me forget my duty as a Christian: and so, Morris,"—putting his hand on the young man's lowly-bent head—" I lift up my voice, and I lift up my soul to heaven, and I say, may God vouchsafe to bless you still. If you are innocent, may He guide and help us to clear you, before the eyes of men; if you are guilty, may He give you the grace of a true repentance, and pardon you, and show you mercy in another world; and I say, too, for myself, no matter what happens, the Will of God be done—blessed be His name, for ever, and for ever!"

Randal's fellow-prisoners were grouped around him. Many of them were evil men, who had not prayed for years, nor uttered the Most Holy Name, save to profane it, yet all listened in deep silence; none scoffed at his pious, his unaffectedly pious resignation, under a heavy load of calamity; and when he had ended, more than one voice cried "Amen" to his prayer and to his ejaculation, and more than one eye yielded him a tear.

CHAPTER XXVII.

JAMES BROWN (how we do like having come to the proper place to recur to his honest, simple name!) James Brown, the shop-servant of Mister Barnaby Roundhead, had been recommended to the little old miser by a friend, upon whose observation of character he could place great reliance. It was with much unwillingness he admitted a stranger into his establishment; but he found that his own physical strength began to extend little farther than the effort necessary for gripping and hoarding, and that, under his watchful eye, a youthful assistant, to serve customers all day long, became indispensably necessary for the continued success of his business.

Barnaby's most trust-worthy friend stated, that such another as *the* James Brown, could hardly be found, high or low, for love or money; for he had proved beyond a question, James Brown's scrupulous and primitive honesty. He had placed, for a number of years, the most unlimited confidence in a certain person in his employment; and it was altogether owing to James Brown's upright vigilance that a discovery had been made, even while James Brown (pleasant it is to repeat his worthy name!) was but the lowest errand boy in his shop, which demonstrated how very slight were in reality the grounds upon which the head clerk of the concern was trusted by the proprietor. In fact, by the boy's advice, his master put a certain sum of marked gold and silver in a certain drawer, to which no one but the now suspected person had access; and in a little time part of the money disappeared, and was detected in the thief's possession. The head clerk suffered for his crime the law's extreme punishment, professing (it was strange to observe) his innocence to the last. He had previously been offered a merciful commutation of his sentence, provided he would only acknowledge his guilt, and promise to refund, from time to time, the property proved to have been stolen, together with more considerable sums which disappeared in the most unaccountable manner. The wretched man, however, rejected everything that resembled a compromise, and died silent and impenitent.

Along with this recommendation to Mr. Barnaby Roundhead, came another, praising James Brown's virtue in the particulars of abstemiousness, industry, and the talent of saving and taking care of whatever money fell honestly to his own lot; and Barnaby, at once agreeing that thriftiness and honesty ever go together, and that it is only spendthrifts who can rob or embezzle the property of a good and a kind master, heartily engaged the lad, at almost a nominal salary too; so modest of his own deservings, amongst his other shining qualities, was the peerless James Brown. We add still a new temptation in, or rather on, the person of James, calculated to overcome the little old fellow's scruples to take an assistant into his shop. Barney glanced from his own habiliments (such as we have previously sketched them,) to those of James, and his soul owned a sympathy of tastes between itself and that of the candidate for his favour. For, from his twelfth to his nineteenth year, poor James had worn the same suit of clothes; and his patched coat, refusing to stretch with the growth of its wearer, now yielded him sleeves no farther down than the elbows; while, upon the same principle of non-accommodation, the little small-clothes of the growing boy ascended almost half-way up the thigh of the adolescent; assuming moreover, in some degree, the appearance of the slashed Spanish inexpressibles, from the circumstance of the frequent oblong rents being mended with patches of another colour, curiously stitched between the gaping edges.

James Brown was fresh-coloured and well-featured; and had he but held himself erect, and looked knowingly, as other lads did, Ailleen Lahon declared he would have been a " very clane crature of a boy." Ailleen had it in her power to be useful and obliging to her meek, almost cringing fellow servant. The quantity of food allowed for their joint sustenance was very scanty, and its quality the cheapest and the worst. But her kind young mistress enabled her to fare better than Mr. Barnaby Roundhead knew anything about; and the good-natured girl liberally shared her secret store of good things with the grateful James Brown. For her goodness to him, as he called it, the youth showed much feeling; and Ailleen found that he could flatter— no, we must not say flatter, but recognise, admit, and laud, her many perfections, personal and moral, in a soft and insinuating way, and with a piquant sincerity and innocence of manner, the more gratifying to her that it differed so widely from the empointed, rollocking gallantry addressed to her almost every day of her life, during her perambulations through the streets, by forty others of the deceiving sex. In fact, Ailleen began to feel some tender inclinations towards the quiet modest lad ; and perhaps this was on the natural principle that the conferring favours, when the giver's heart is good, creates a feeling of soft attachment to the acceptor of them. At all events, if Ailleen's growing preference had not so originated, it was considerably increased by her constant habit of re-toasting scraps of toast and re-buttering them, and of pouring out cups of " the second-hand tay," and broiling limbs of chickens, and so forth, and then placing them at the tender mercies of James Brown.

But a little incident set Ailleen into a kind of puzzle about the well-fed lover—at least for a time. It happened that, on a Sunday evening, Ailleen had stolen off to a pattern, just to shake her fat sides with one dance, leaving, as she thought, James Brown at home. Great, however, was her surprise, to behold either James Brown, or else " his livin' moral," standing among the genteelest portion of the company of the rustic Almack's, at the very extremity of a long booth. Metamorphosed, indeed, James seemed—if James it was. He wore a modish suit of clothes, drank deeply, laughed, joked, and sang a merry, hearty song, for the amusement of a coquettish young lady at his side; nay, while poor Ailleen gaped with her mouth wide open, up he jumped, led out his partner, and danced a jig to perfection. His stoop was gone ; and he more than realized even her own former idea of " a clane crature of a boy."

Ailleen endeavoured to approach him; but the booth was crowded to suffocation, and she could make no way. Their eyes met, and she nodded to him; but he took no more notice than if he had never, never shared her hidden feasts. She called to him by name; he did not turn his head. She shouted to him—it was all one. In a wrathful fit, she waddled homeward, determined to be in the house before him, that she might demonstrate the truth of her intended accusations, by opening the door to his knock, and throwing in his face his palpable absence from home at an unpermitted hour. But to her increased astonishment, it was James Brown who opened the door to *her* knock, upon her arrival at home. And now he was the old James Brown she had always known. His scanty jacket and knee-breeks were on; his stoop also; and his face looked as simple and as innocent, and his words and manner were as quiet and as stupid as ever.

Though greatly staggered, Ailleen coldly asked him how he had liked the pattern, and his trumpery partner at it, that evening?

James Brown had not been to any such place; he had gone out only to church that day; and he requested Ailleen to inform him what people did at a pattern, for he had never seen one in his whole life.

Bother! hadn't Ailleen "two well seein' eyes in her face?"

Aye, and two of the prettiest that James Brown had seen since the world's sun first shone upon him.

In fact, it was all nonsense to accuse him of having been out at a merry-making, without his own clothes, and his own stoop, and—for shame!—dancing with a young girl. But James saw how it was. He had heard before now that there was one Jerry Donelly, who lived somewhere or other, and who bore a great likeness to him, James Brown; so much so, that he, James, (poor boy!) was often accused of wild, foolish, improper " goings-on," committed by Jerry, and which *he* could be no more guilty of than he could of going that moment and robbing his good master. And the tender-hearted Ailleen was convinced, and she sincerely pitied poor James for thus undeservedly suffering in reputation for the irregularities of another person.

Some time after, however, Ailleen was beset by a new mystification about her friend. Unseen by them, she detected James in an interview with Hesther Bonnetty; and though, to be sure, he had his old clothes on, he forgot from time to time, while they conversed in a low voice energetically together, his habitual stoop, and again looked uncommonly like one Jerry Donelly.

Ailleen now began to be interested on another point. It seemed to her very extraordinary that James and Hesther should converse together in such a business-like kind of way. Watching closely, she saw the hag give her poor Jim a letter. This was still more suspicious; and, saying nothing of her little *penchant*, which, after all, might be only a slight excoriation on the mere surface of her heart, a sexual and laudable propensity set her to use every means of discovering the contents of that mysterious epistle.

In order to avoid all possibility of James guessing her purpose, Ailleen changed in no respect towards him; her laugh, her joke, and her scraps of good cheer, were, as usual, cordially—that is, seemingly so—at his service. Day after day, however, she diligently rummaged his sleeping apartment; and finally, by dint of honest perseverance, Ailleen secured the important letter.

Forgetting, in the eagerness of her curiosity, that, according to herself, "she knew no more about the readin' an' the writin' than a blind cow does of a holiday," Ailleen gazed wistfully at the paper, wrong side uppermost, but gazed in vain; and with a testy and impatient sigh was forced to admit to herself that, without the aid of a literary interpreter, she stood as far as ever from a solution of the mystery which sadly disturbed her peace of mind. Whom should she select for this office? Her mistress was too ill to be applied to. Rose Brady occurred to her mind; and upon Rose's known prudence and sagacity, as well as upon her learned fame, Ailleen determined to throw herself.

Accordingly, when Rose came to visit Patty after her second interview with the mayor, as glanced at in a recent chapter, Ailleen handed her the letter, and begged to be enlightened as to its contents.

The moment Rose cast her eye on the writing, she started as if she had been electrified; and then she eagerly read it through; and when she had done, cast her eyes upwards, and murmured some words, as if in pious gratitude to heaven.

But she seemed not at all eager to read the document aloud for Ailleen's edification; and as the latter had attentively noted the wonderful effects its silent perusal produced on Rose herself, this omission greatly tantalized the poor girl.

"An' am n't I to get no light on the head o' my own letther, that I thieved so cleverly wid my own hands?" demanded Ailleen.

Without replying, Rose cautiously shut the kitchen door; and then whispering Ailleen, implored her to make no farther present inquiries on the subject; assuring her that the epistle contained no love secret—that it did unfold, however, one of vital importance to Ailleen's mistress, to Rose herself, and to all connected with either; and that the future welfare and happiness of those alluded to depended upon Rose being the sole depository, for a time, of the matter of the epistle; while, in fact, Ailleen's own personal safety, nay, life, would be at stake, should she confess to another human being that she had purloined the paper, or what she had done with it. At length, by adroit arguments, and eager persuasion, even to the extent of shedding tears, Rose so wrought on the susceptible Ailleen, that the girl suddenly flung herself on her knees, and voluntarily made a solemn vow of secresy to heaven.

Rose then succeeded in persuading her that she had taken an oath of as awfully-binding a nature, as if it had been sworn in a court of justice; and concluding by giving hopes of relief to Ailleen in a very short time, perhaps to-morrow, she put the letter in her bosom, pinned her handkerchief in numerous folds over it, and went up stairs to converse with her cousin. Their interview is due, and shall be given to the reader.

For the present, however, we pause to condole with Ailleen. How she did ponder, and guess, and sigh, for the far off morrow! Never, during her whole previous life, had she shown so saturnine a humour as during the remainder of that day. Rose's estimate of the overwhelming importance of the stolen document heated her former curiosity into a feverish, abiding, all-engrossing idea. She felt a kind of choking sensation at the root of her tongue, which, we believe, had become really swollen by her incessant efforts to keep down her secret, each time (and that was every two minutes) that her heart sent it up for publication to the world.

Before Rose, who staid a long time above stairs with Patty, prepared to return home, we fear that all poor Ailleen's virtuous resolutions began to yield to her great and devouring yearnings to be delivered of her mental burden. So Rose Brady herself seemed to think, when, with flushed cheeks and watery eyes, the poor girl appeared before her mistress, and urgently petitioned to be allowed to make a visit of only half an hour to her cousin and gossip, Honor Morrissy; for before Patty could reply, Rose whispered her, and then Patty firmly refused Ailleen's request —and, moreover, imposed upon the poor girl her positive commands not to leave the house that day and night, on any pretence whatsoever, nor even to receive a visitor of any kind in her kitchen.

The day wore heavily away. It was eleven o'clock at night. Ailleen's mistress had been led by Rose Brady to Alderman Lodge's house, and was to stay there until next day. Ailleen sat by her kitchen fire, musing and pondering: her truckle bed lying waiting for her patiently in the next apartment. Half an hour previously her master had locked her in, and she had heard him take the same affectionate care of James Brown immediately after; and then the shooting of the lock of his own chamber door struck on her ear. The house was perfectly still, and Ailleen had uninterrupted scope for her reveries.

Oh, that some one human being, no great matter whom, was seated before her, or beside her! Ailleen's soul almost sickened to speak out—to "wreak her thought upon expression." Her favourite and smooth-coated cat was fast asleep at her feet. Suddenly she pounced upon the animal; snatched it up to her bosom, and formed a resolution to pour forth her confidence into its ear.

Notwithstanding its residence in Barnaby Roundhead's house, we have called this creature smooth-coated; and, thanks to Ailleen Lahon for her charitable attentions, we are entitled to apply the epithet. Mr. Roundhead would allow nothing but mice for its support; but as provisions were scanty on the premises, mice were in proportion scarce; so that but for Ailleen's gentle care, the cat must needs have been a skeleton.

Ailleen smoothed down her pet's back, and thus addressed it:

"*Musha*, then, pusheen-cat, my darlint, did id ever come to your knowledge what happened to myself this blessed day, of all days in the year, *a-lanna?*"

"Pusheen-cat" mewed softly in reply, and looked up into her benefactor's face.

"It's 'no, in throth, Ailleen my *cuishla*,' you're sayin' to myself," continued Ailleen.

There was another assenting mew.

"Well, then, *a-lanna ma-chree*, listen to me, an' I'll spake it over to you."

The cat now gave a very soft mew, stretched out its paw, widely extended its claws, and first glancing upward, by way of agreement to Ailleen's proposition, (so, at least, Ailleen was pleased to interpret its language,) set up a continuous contented purr, or, as its mistress styled the sound, a "*cooramuck croonaun*," and then half-closing its eyes, seemed pleasedly attentive to the tale it was about to hear.

Ailleen went on.

"Pusheen, my own darlint cat, I b'lieve that cats an' dogs, an' all other sorts o' people, as well as themselfs, 'ill have no dispute on the head o' saying that them boys is given to roguery in all kinds an' sizes. Bad sorrow may come over me, if I'm not thinkin' o' doin' penance on myself, by not goin' near one o' them, from this night out! But, of all the boys that ever come in my sight, Jim Brown, you bear the bell. Aye, in throth; even puttin' young Fennelly himself to the fore. You know, my darlint pusheen, that I never can put my feet over the thrashold, that *he* doesn't make me pay turnpike, as he calls it; an' I'll tell you what's more, he takes turnpike on every road; no matther what sthreet I turn my face into, up he comes, axin' turnpike, turnpike— aye, an' takin' id too, whether a body is willin' or not to pay him; an' more betoken, over again, my jewel, he thinks no more of id, in the face o' the noon day, than if it was pitch dark night.

"Well, pusheen-cat my *lanna*, Jimmy Brown bates young Fennelly out an' out, not in that way, but in regard o' bein' a curiosity of a boy; an' by this tail o' yours, that I hould in my hand, pusheen-cat, I'm given to thinkin' that it war'nt a boy o' the name o' Jerry Donelly I seen at the patthern last Sunday three weeks, but Jimmy Brown's own four bones.

"Well, again; what would you have of it, my duck-o'-dimonds? as sure as you're here, at your aise in my lap, I seen that ould weazle of a woman, Hesther Bonnetty, whisperin' and *culloguin* wid my *bouchaleen*, Masther Jim; 'an,' says I, houlding discourse wid myself, 'I'll come to the bottom o' that *cuggerin* match, or I have no sense or rason; an' upon that, pusheen my *lanna*, I went peepin' an' sarchin, an' sure enough, I found out the letther, an' laid a good hoult of id; an' my darlint"—

At this period of her narrative, while her tongue was full gleeishly discharging the humour that had caused it to swell at the roots, and while her listener seemed to enjoy her long story with the utmost relish, a key suddenly and sharply turned in the lock of the kitchen-door; the door as suddenly opened, and James Brown stood before the astonished Ailleen.

CHAPTER XXVIII.

But, excepting that his stoop had again disappeared, it was neither the James Brown of the dancing booth, gay, smiling, and rollicking; nor the James Brown she used to patronise, grave, cringing, and grateful for the stolen treats in her pantry: it was neither of these characters that Ailleen, in great consternation, now contemplated. No; the James Brown who so abruptly and unaccountably invaded the midnight privacy of her kitchen, stood erect and stern; his brow lowered over a fierce eye; and his teeth were set, and his hands were clenched, as he regarded her.

Ailleen thoroughly felt the fearful change in the man before her, and shrank from it. Her conscience told her that James Brown had missed his letter. Ailleen's smile told her smothered apprehension, and belied the show of careless welcome she fain would assume.

James Brown walked straight to her, and she started, and involuntarily cried out as he seized her by the arm. She had wished to accost him first, but now felt it out of her power to do so in an unconcerned, natural manner.

"Give me that letter," said the intruder, in a voice that barely passed beyond his teeth; but to Ailleen's ear it sounded deep and hollow in his throat.

"Ah, then," said Ailleen, at last trying to rally, as she smiled coaxingly upon him; "Ah then, Jemmy Brown, my darlint boy, sure I heard the masther lockin' you in, as he does every night, an' sure he locked myself in too; an' how did you manage to work your way to me, I wondher?"

"Did you hear what I said to you?"

"Faix, an' I did, my posey of a fellow; you axed mysef was there anything on the shelf: wouldn't a nice *croobeen*,* or a morsel of a snowy-white *sedague*,† be nate atin'?"

We do not know whether Ailleen's miserable affectation of pleasantry would have appeared most painful or ludicrous to an observer.

"I asked no such thing, and you know I did not;" and the lad's brow fell deeper and deeper, as his eyes glared into those of his *quondam* mistress and benefactress.

"Well then, *a-cuishla*, you're the height o' good nature; an' I b'lieve you axed me how the world was usin' me these bad times, or somethin' that-a-way?"

"I asked you to give me that paper."

"Paper, paper, my duck o' dimonds? Bad manners to the bit o' paper anywhere about the poor kitchen, barrin'—"

"The paper you stole out o' my room."

"Stole? *I* stale? an' isn't it a skandle for you, now, James Brown—"

---

* Pig's Foot. † Cake.

"Confound you! Will you keep me here all night? Give it me, I say."

"You're hurtin' my poor arum, Jem *a-cuishla*"— and the tears started in poor Ailleen's eyes.

"Speak lower! not a word above your breath, or I will choke you. Give what I ask, and give it quick— quick."

"I seen no sich thing as a paper o' that sort, from that day to this, as I'am a sinner"

"You lie! You took the paper out of my room. Give it back, I warn you."

He shook her violently, and glared still more fiercely upon her.

"Och, sowl o' marcies! don't squeeze me so wicked —sure I had no harm in id, my darlint, when I just picked id up from undher the sweepin' brush you know."

"I have no time to lose. Hurry, I tell you."

"Was id herself that tould you about id, Jem Brown *a-chorra*?"

"Herself? who? What do you mean?"

"Herself? did ever sich a word come from my poor lips?"

"Tell me whom you spoke of. Tell me without another equivocation."

"Well, then—only you cumflusther a body so— Rose Brady, my darlint."

"Rose Brady!" he repeated, jumping back from the trembling culprit; "and you have shewn that paper to Rose Brady?"

"*Och, ma-vrone!* what's goin' to happen to me I wondher!"

"Answer me, you jade. Have you put that paper into Rose Brady's hands?"

"Only to read it for me, *a lanna-ma-chree!*"

"Where is it at present?"

"I b'lieve—I'm amost sure—faix, I could well nigh take my oath——" Ailleen pretended to search her pockets.

"Has she it now? answer to that!"

"Och, yes—Rose Brady has it."

The young ruffian glared a moment at Ailleen in silence, pale first, and then blackening with rage and with the consciousness of detection—of open, certain detection.

"By the Eternal!" he then burst forth, springing to a table, and snatching up a large kitchen knife; "By the Eternal! I will pay you for your peeping!"

Ailleen made a desperate bound half across the apartment, gained her closet door, dashed it to, locked and bolted it. The infuriate bravo smote at her, as she darted in, and sank his knife in the pannel. He drew back, and threw himself violently against the door. Then came, loud and shrill, Ailleen's long pent-up shriek, as she anticipated the bursting in of the frail barrier between her, and the murderous-looking James Brown. But soon the quavering and lamenting voice of old Barnaby Roundhead came to her relief, descending the stairs; and Brown, muttering that no time was to be lost, took from his pocket a number of keys, and selecting one, left the kitchen, opened the outer door of the house, and was quickly in the street.

With a hurried step he pursued his way till he had gained Hesther M'Farlane's cellar. This witch-like raiser and ruler of all the storms of human passion that are recorded in our history, was on her usual seat before the fire. Her face exhibited a more than usual contortion of its wrinkles towards a smile, and she muttered something to herself in gleeish retrospection.

"Is Joe Wilson in the house?" demanded Brown eagerly, as he descended into the den.

"Hee-he!" responded Hesther; "Joey is gone to a weddin', an' Joey is to be the bridegroom."

"This is no time for game-making—no time, I tell you."

"An' who is game-making, Jemmy? I tell you Joe Wilson is gone to be a married man."

"Grandmother, he must be found this moment, wherever he is."

"Let him alone, good boy—let him alone, I bid you. He is doing my work for me, Jemmy. 'Tis twenty years since you saw the light, and twenty years before that again, I was your mother's mother; an' about that time, I made a promise to one Randal Brady, that, in forty years, I'd pay him a little debt I owed him. An' 'tis ped to-night. His wife is lyin' on a lock o' sthraw in the stone cage, and he at her side; an' their pet bird, Masther Morris, is makin' music for them in some corner o' the same place, with the iron ornaments on his hands an' his ankles; an', in the to-morrow mornin's light, little Rosey Brady will hang down her head, an' cry the salt tear o' shame. Can ye riddle me that, Jemmy?—hee-he!"

"I have riddles enough before me without it. I say Wilson must be seen."

"I'll riddle id for you, lad. Joe Wilson is gone to be married to Rose Brady; nothing else would satisfy little Rose the *votheen;* but Joe Wilson can't be married to her, because why? He has two wives already, an' both o' them stout an' hearty this holy an' blessed hour."

"Married to Rose Brady! are you certain-sure of that, granny?"

"Is the critch in my hand? or am I spakin' to you, Jemmy? Afther she slipt thro' his fingers here t'other night, he swore an oath he wouldn't quit the town till he was revenged on her, an' all belongin' to her. Sich a disappointment never happened to Joey afore; an' he made shift to tell Rose, that if she didn't behave more civil and dacent to him, he'd get the brother she loved lodged in the jail, an' brought to a high dance upon nothing afore long. And Rose Brady gave me a writin' for Joe Wilson, an' she met him by her own free will last night in her father's garden, an' there they settled matthers between them; an' he tould me, that she swore to him that if he'd marry her she'd marry him, an' then he'd be the brother-in-law of her brother, an', by coorse, the brother's friend; an' she'd have a grand husband to herself into the bargain: but two wifes aforehand is enough for any one, in all conscience — even for Joey himself, honest boy — hee-ee-ee!"

James Brown paused awhile in deep reflection, before he replied to these tidings.

"From what you say, and from something I know, grandmother, either of two things have come to pass by this time. Either Rose Brady is playing us all — Joe Wilson, and you, and I — and has the upper hand of us all; and Joe Wilson is in the jail, where we must follow him if we do not take care. Or — and this is the most likely thing — Rose Brady and Joe Wilson understand each other, and are in a plot to free Morris and to ruin us."

"*Hannuch thu, murroch thu;* may fire burn them both afore that comes to pass! But what makes you say so, Jemmy?"

"Rose Brady knows all our plans. You brought

me a letter from Joe Wilson a short time ago, and she has that letter fast in her hands, granny dear."

"What! what! what!" screamed Hesther; "tell me the words o' that letter; Joe Wilson never read it for me!"

"Yes; I *will* tell you what was in it, and then you can judge if I was right or wrong in what I said just now. You brought it to me the day of the night when we were to raise the money from Barnaby Roundhead; and the plan we were to go by was laid down in that letther."

We will condense honest James's narrative. He truly stated that the measures to be taken—and afterwards in reality taken—upon the night of the robbery, were minutely proposed by Joe Wilson in the document in question; and they were as follows:—

James Brown, when he supposed all at rest in the house, was to arise from his bed, let himself out of his room with the key he had long ago provided for that purpose, and which he had so often used before, when he wished to spend his nights abroad; open the street door with another key suited to it, leave it slightly ajar for the entrance of Wilson and Morris Brady, in the relative characters of ghost and scoundrel, and dupe and goose; and unlock and leave ajar, also, the door of the room into which poor Morris was to be introduced, and therein light a mysterious-looking candle, near the loose board under which, as the plotters well knew, old Barnaby was in the habit of hiding various sorts of valueless trumpery. The pretended "true will and testament, duly witnessed, of Joseph Wilson," had previously been adjusted in its proper place; and this inscription on the otherwise blank paper, Wilson had chosen as one most likely to continue Morris in the delusion under which he laboured, of being the useful and laudable earthly agent of the troubled spirit of the very troublesome man who had borne the name.

The letter continued to instruct James Brown, that when he, James, should become aware of the presence, in the house, of Wilson and his follower, he was to go to the door of the old miser's sleeping-chamber, and, in a feigned voice, alarm him, and then finally retreat to his own room, lock himself in, undress, and affect profound sleep, so as to be found in a seemingly perfect state of unconsciousness, when brought by his master as an ally against the thieves. Thus, and with some reason, Wilson concluded he had, by dint of patient study, hatched a plot, upon the successful result of which two grand points of his present ambition must easily follow:—first, the appropriation of a good portion, if not all, of old Barnaby's gold; second, the destruction of Rose Brady, in the absence of her watchful and courageous old father, whose cudgel, by the way, the bravo had never been able to digest; as also in the absence of Morris, whose spirit chided his, and who, not long previously, had given him a sound threshing in the public streets, for scandalous words spoken of his, Morris's family, and particularly of his beloved sister Rose. The feature of this excellent plot over which its author chuckled most, was that which contrived his own certain escape from suspicion of robbery, by delivering over to justice a member of an unoffending family whom he cordially detested—aye, detested, without the exception even of Rose herself, who was as much the object of his hate as of his love.

A single doubt clouded the writer's mind. James

Brown knew but of one strong-hold to which little Barnaby was in the habit of removing, from the shop, his gold and silver: and query first, was this his only depôt; and, second, how was it to be entered? for the key which controlled it James had never beheld, and therefore never could have got imitated, as he had done in the case of other very necessary ones. It was supposed, however, that this precious piece of wrought iron might be found in the old man's chamber; and Wilson argued, that when Barnaby should arise to summon James Brown, after James Brown had summoned him, it was very probable he would, in his fright and hurry, leave his own door open; and then, while James and he were deeply engaged with Morris Brady, Wilson might carefully search for the object of his wishes. The disappearance of a certain quantity (though by no means the quantity which the robbers had expected to find), of Barney's hidden treasures, proved the wisdom and foresight, in this instance, of the ex-president of " The hell-fire club."

"What do you think now, grandmother?" asked James Brown, when he had ceased speaking.

"Think! I think as you think, Jemmy lad; as you thought when you spoke first, I mane. Rose Brady will turn the tables on Joey, clever as he is, and on yourself, and on myself—may a blisterin' shower o' curses fall on her! Jemmy, we must make quick work of id, or all's over wid us. Jemmy, you and I won't wait for Joe Wilson. You can open the box up-stairs? eh, Jemmy?"

"I was thinking of that," said Brown, brightening up a little.

"Well, then, hurry, lad! hurry!"

They understood each other perfectly. Hesther

provided a lantern. The matting at the head of Hesther's couch was raised; and they entered the small door behind it; then ascended some stone steps, into a mouldering hall; then the oaken stairs of the old mansion; then they passed through many ruinous and completely unfurnished apartments, and finally stopped in one in which there were a bed, a few chairs, thick blinds, as well as shutters to the windows, a table bearing the remnants of good cheer, and a merry fire blazing away on the hearth.

From beneath the bed, they drew forth an iron-clasped box, and James Brown produced his key. The lid was raised—and they interchanged looks of withering rage as they heaped frightful curses and imprecations upon the name of Joe Wilson. The box was empty. Every shilling of the ill-got treasure which they had thought to appropriate exclusively to themselves, had already been removed beyond their reach, by their now detested partner in crime.

And then came the full conviction that, at Rose Brady's instance, Joe Wilson had plotted to deliver them up to the law, beyond the gripe of which he had himself already fled; that, by some subtle management, which they could not fathom, Rose Brady would escape from Wilson with unblemished reputation, and Morris be freed from jail; while they were left to suffer for a daring robbery; and suffer, too, without a share of the booty acquired by it.

CHAPTER XXIX.

We now perform our promise of presenting to the reader the omitted interview between Rose Brady and Patty Roundhead, and which is the last to be noticed as having occurred between them.

With Joe Wilson's important letter to James Brown well secured in her bosom, Rose ascended from Ailleen's kitchen to Patty's room. The timid, abashed, and humbled girl half rose from her chair to receive her cousin, half checked the warm show of welcome which her nature and her gratitude urged her to bestow on her dearest, indeed her only friend; a sudden self-accusing blush dyed her face and neck; and then the blood as rapidly retreated to her heart, and she became intensely, deadly pale.

Rose's smile, as she approached, had no merriment in it; but it was cordial, compassionate, and loving; and as she extended both her hands, to receive those of her cousin, her voice made gentle and soothing music.

"I am with you again, as I tould you yesterday I would be, my own *graw*, my poor Patty."

"Ah, I had my fears, Rose, all last night, and all this morning."

"Fears of me, Patty? of my love for you? or of

my not keeping my word to you? in good deed, *alanna*, if you knew how I spent the time since was here last, you would not say that."

"May God bless you, Rose."

"I think I have done you some good, Patty dear, since I saw you last."

Poor Patty answered her friend with a look of almost wild interest and curiosity.

"But," continued Rose, "I have a few little questions to put to you, before I can say all I am come to say, Patty *graw*.

Patty cast down her conscious eyes; they were full of melancholy self-reproach; she joined the palms of her trembling hands, bent her head, and answered with heart-stricken humility:

"I will confess to you, as sincerely and as penitently as if I were before the throne and the face of my Great Judge."

Rose understood the state of her feelings; she took the joined hands between her own, pressed them softly, and spoke soothingly.

"Have no dread of me, my poor Patty; one word to hurt you I never said, to my knowledge, and I am not going to say such a word now. But the questions I have to ask, I cannot help asking; and it may happen that some of them will give you a little pain; and if so, you won't blame my heart, I'm sure you won't, *ma-vourneen ma-chree.*

"We have said enough before now, Patty, of *that man;* but when I look at you, can I help thinking how very bad a man he is, if he never did anything sinful, but what he has done by you? Oh, Patty, my own darling! hard, and black, and cruel must be that heart, and devilish must be that nature which could throw the blight of shame upon a young crature so gentle, so good, and so innocent as yourself! But, Patty, though before you gave me your secret, I would not for worlds have seen you Joe Wilson's wife; yet, as I now know you to be his victim, I have come to one certain opinion. There would be no means of giving you pace in this life, except by making Joe Wilson your lawful husband—that is—were Joe Wilson now alive, and willing to marry you."

" We shall soon be united," murmured Patty, " and without the aid of an earthly priest."

" No, indeed, my pet; if united at all, it must be by an earthly hand."

Patty again glanced up, as if something like a sickly gleam of hope had shot into her darkened and desolate heart. Then came the recollection that all hope was past for her, and she burst into wretched tears.

" You have no rason to cry this time, at laste, Patty," resumed Rose; " I said to you yesterday, that I knew the obligation that was upon me, to do for you as your poor mother would; and were your mother on this earth at present, never would she rest till you were Joe Wilson's wife—if—as I tould you before—*he*, too, were at this side of the grave."

" And what's the use of saying this now, Rose, when Wilson"——

" Let me go on, *a-lanna*, in my own way. Here is one o' my questions for you. If Joe Wilson *was* alive, would you willingly become his lawful, wedded wife ?"

" Rose, I will bear your reproaches, if any you have to make to me, meekly and penitently, as I ought to do; no murmur of discontent shall escape me; but do not, do not, dearest Rose, describe the summer day to the poor wretch who is condemned for life to the solitude of a dark, dark dungeon !"

"Have more hope, Patty *a-lanna*, and look to prospects, if not very bright, at the laste brighter than those your poor heart is now fixed upon."

"Rose! Rose!" gasped Patty, "surely there is a something in the tone of your soft, kind voice—that—I know not why—but"—she was unable to proceed.

"Make answer to my question, *graw bawn!*" suddenly kissing Patty, while her own tears started.

"I will. Would I be Wilson's wife? That is what you want to know?"

"Yes, my *graw*, that is my question."

"Oh, Rose dearest, why do you put it? Oh why? but no matter. I will answer you sincerely;" her voice sunk, and she drooped her head; "Rose, I cannot help loving him—and—Rose, did Wilson not sleep in a bloody grave, I would—be—his—wife."

"And supposing, Patty, that you were asked to marry him this very night, should you have the strength, and the courage, and *would* you become Joe Wilson's wife this very night?"

"My God, my God, Rose! you are all along supposing a thing that can never be; oh why, I ask you again, and I beseech you tell me, why question me thus?"

"I will answer you fully when you make full answers to *me*."

"And that little smile, Rose!—oh, heavens! what can be its meaning?" Patty shivered in every nerve. "Again!—Almighty Father! you smile at me again!"

"Do what I want you to do, Patty—answer me."

"Rose, I remember to have once seen a beautiful picture of Hope. The fascinating form by which the blessed comforter was personified, stood in the interior of a damp dungeon, at its iron door; a worn-out captive, who had been chained to the floor so long—so long that his ear had forgotten human sounds, lay crippled in a corner of the den; and yet Hope still stood at the threshold of the door, and smiled upon him! Rose, the smile was such as you now wear!"

" And, for all that, you are talking on, and not answering me, Patty dear."

" Oh, Rose, very often since the horrible event, I have had most unaccountable thoughts! Without reasoning myself into the idea—for surely I did not reason on the subject—I have been conscious of a belief that so frightful a misfortune could not have happened; and I have raised up my head in the strong hope that the object of my love, of my adoration! stood before me; and then some minutes would elapse before a certainty of my loneliness and my desolation returned fully upon me; and my mind has often been thus, and—but my head is wandering now, I believe."

" Think of yourself, Patty; I am still waiting patiently for your answer."

" I fear I forget what you exactly wished me to reply to."

" Well, *my graw*, I can ask you once again; and now pay attention to me. If required to become the lawful wife of Joe Wilson this very night, would you consent?"

" Hah—yes—that brings back the vague and foolish thought which had begun to strive within me—and, once again, you smile!"

" Strange things have often come to pass, Patty," said Rose, with meaning.

" How? what? what strange things? Oh, for God's love, Rose! for God's love!"—She grasped her friend by the arm and fastened her large glittering eyes on hers, in the continued appeal for speedy explanation, which she could not articulate.

"Why, Patty, people have sometimes been supposed, to be dead, and——"

"And they were not! were not! Is that what you were going to say!" interrupted Patty, in a paroxysm of such agitation as we cannot attempt to describe. Rose, cautious as she had been, began to blame herself for precipitancy.

"Patty *a-cuishla ma chree*, don't be frightened; depend on your own Rose——"

"Is—he—alive?" again interrupted Patty, in a slow, low, wiry whisper, which, however, syllabled the three words which she uttered with peculiar and extraordinary distinctness.

Rose's answer came, and quick upon it what Rose had anticipated, and which therefore she was prepared to meet. She immediately and assiduously used all the means necessary to restore the flitted senses of her cousin, and was soon successful.

For some time after her recovery from her swoon, poor Patty's mind wandered. She whispered to Rose that she had been dreaming, and detailed the happy but vain delusion of her slumbering thoughts. Her friend continued to smile upon her, however, and so brought back, by degrees, a faint sense of reality to the bosom of the half-bewildered and miserable girl; and then, in her gentlest accents, inspired her at last with confidence and certainty.

"There can be *no* doubt," continued Rose, after they had interchanged some farther words; "I have seen him, face to face, discoursed with him, face to face; and, more than that, heard from his own lips how it was that he has been supposed to be dead and buried; and, Patty dear, a terrible story it is."

"Let me hear it, notwithstanding—oh, let me hear every word!" pleaded Patty.

"I will, then; and the first thing that will surprise you, is to hear me say that I, Rose Brady, had something to do in it."

"I am astonished, indeed. What do you mean?"

"My *lanna*, when I saw your mind so sorely throubled afther it was reported he was dead, I didn't care giving you a proof of what a man he was, in a case that related to my own self. But here's the story, now.

"You know that Joe Wilson and I often met in your company at Alderman Lodge's; but you do not know, and your innocent heart would not let you guess, that, at that very time, when you seemed, as you thought, all the world to him, he was trying, every moment he could spake in private with me, to destroy me, as he has destroyed you. Now, Patty, don't start, nor interrupt me—'tis the thruth—and let me go on. One night he followed me home, insulted me on the way, and my poor father shut our door against him. But, another night—mark me, and mark me well— the very night he was thought to have been murthered, Joe Wilson met my father and me in the *bosheen*, and attempted to drag me from my father's arm. My father left him senseless on the ground, and we got safe home. So much I know, of my own knowledge. The rest I am going to say himself tould me. He recovered in a few minutes. He whistled for his companions, who were lurking at hand. He set them on our track, bidding them take a short cut, to get between us and home, at a bend of the *bosheen*. We had walked too fast for them. They came up with another man, and a single man, on the spot where they thought to find us. In the darkness of the night—for very dark it was—and in their blind and drunken fury to revenge an offence against their head and chief, Joe Wilson, they believed that poor man was my father, and they murthered him!

"When his life was taken they saw their error, came back to Joe Wilson, and informed him of it. Their victim turned out to be a young man of the suburbs, of respectable family, and of Joe Wilson's height, and resembling him in figure and in limbs. And now listen to me, Patty, and believe my words. Partly to avoid suspicion of the cruel murther, he says (as he had enough to bear on that head before-hand); partly to escape his duns, and partly for the frolic, it came into Joe Wilson's mind to make it appear that it was he who had been killed; and, in furtherance of this plan, he and his companions returned to the body in the *bosheen* with a lantern, in the dead hour of the night, when every honest man and woman were in their beds, dressed it in the suit of clothes Joe Wilson was known to have worn that day; put letters addressed to him into pockets of the clothes; and, for their last work— oh, how can I tell it to you, Patty dear!—in order to hinder his features from betraying them, they so mangled the dead man's face that the mother who bore him could not have known her son."

This recital seemed, to Rose's observant eye, to make a deeper impression, connected with the depravity of Wilson's character, upon Patty, than had any facts or remonstrances previously brought forward by her anxious friend. Rose saw the dying creature shudder, coldly and slightly to outward observation, but intensely in her mind, heart, and spirit.

"It is a strange fate and doom that I must love him still," murmured Patty, after a gravely thoughtful pause, which followed the first expression of her feelings: "but I suppose it is the will of God."

"It is, Patty," whispered Rose, blushing to the top of her forehead; and as soon as her words were spoken, an answering suffusion spread over Patty's face. "It is—may be it is—(as far as regards your conduct this night, at laste,) for the sake of another unborn human creature."

Patty looked as if her cousin had hit upon her own deeply-revolved thought. After another reflective moment, she asked, "The man really murdered must have been missed—how was his absence from his family accounted for? Had Joe Wilson anything to do in that?"

"He had, Patty dear; and it was in my mind to tell you what he said to me on that point also. He and his friends easily made up a story that the young man had been seen, the morning after his murther, at a sea-port town, talking to the captain of a ship; and so his family b'lieve that he has run away from them to seek his fortune as a sailor, tho' for what reason they cannot well undherstand. I call to mind myself, as all our neighbours do, his sudden disappearance, and the rumour that pretended to account for it."

The friends were for some time silent. They then renewed their conversation; and we re-commence the report with Patty's question—"This very night, say you, Rose?"

"This very night, *a-lanna*; if you can have heart to say yes to another question I am going to put to you. Do you consent to part from Joe Wilson as soon as you are his wife?"

"To part? and why are we to part?"

"Still, and ever, Patty, remember it is a mother's voice, thro' Rose Brady's lips, that spakes to you. You must part from him, my *graw*, because soul and body would both be periled, did you continue to live with him under the direction of his single and uncontrolled will. These may seem uncharitable words, and improper words, between you and the man who is to be your husband in a few hours, please God. But feeling for your eternal as well as for your earthly welfare, I am convinced I should not be warranted in bringing together a creature like you, and a man like him, except for one purpose; and that one purpose gained, my conscience tells me I ought to save you from him. If indeed Joe Wilson could remain in his native place—"

" If he could remain in his native place !"

" Yes, Patty dear, these are my words. If he could remain in his native place, the eyes of your friends would be upon him and you; and we might manage, with God's help, to keep you (living undher one roof with him), from the effects of his bad opinions, bad counsel, bad example, and tyrannous commands: but spaking, 1 say again, as your mother, I cannot consent, in heaven's sight, to let you share his wandering banishment, alone and unsupported at his side—I must save my child from ruin, here and hereafter, and I am called on to do so. In fact, Patty, tho it is a blunt word to say, Joe Wilson and you never can be husband and wife, unless you consent to part from him as soon as the marriage ceremony shall be over. I have to choose between two evils for you; and great and terrible as would be my sorrow to see you an unwedded mother, still greater and still more terrible would be the agony of the thought of your becoming the poor, passive, corrupted, ruined slave of an evil, evil man; or of your being deserted by him—Oh, my

God! perhaps *sold* by him, in some distant corner of this bad world!"

" Rose," asked Patty, now grown more thoughtful and composed than her friend had lately seen her, " why *must* he banish himself from his native place?"

" Because—to say nothing of his debts—his crimes, *a-lanna*, have become too many and too well-known, to allow his friends to screen him any longer from the law, and the law's punishment."

" Does *he* consent," resumed Patty, after a most painful struggle, " does Wilson himself consent to the measure you propose?"

" He does," answered her friend, expressively; and she bent her eye on Patty, to note the effect of the answer; and that effect was such as Rose had wished for, and, indeed, anticipated.

" Rose, dearest Rose, your exertions for me have been surprising, and their success still more so; are you at liberty to gratify me by an account of your proceedings since yesterday? I need not say I am most anxious to become acquainted with them."

" You shall hear the whole thruth from my lips, Patty, dear; and when I have done, I am in hopes you will be able to see Wilson's character still more clearly, and that then you will not hesitate to give me the promise I ask and expect from you. And now listen to me well, for I have a good deal to tell you.

" When you whispered your secret to me, I knew your desthroyer was not dead."

" You knew it then, Rose?"

" I did, Patty; and reason good I had to know it. The very night before, Wilson, with the help of an old mother of mischief, decoyed me out of my own house, and thought to work ruin to myself; now you start, and you look doubtful, Patty, but you have heard a thruth. And I heard from himself, at that same time, and he was not ashamed to say it—nay, he laughed while he said it, that he brought my poor brother into this house, in order to fix the name of robber on him; and I could undherstand from him, too, that one of his reasons for doing this, was that he might put the question to me, would I save the brother I doted on from a robber's death, by consenting to my own shame?"

"Oh, my God, my God!" groaned Patty, covering her eyes with her hands, and shuddering.

"But the good heaven defend me! he little knew Rose Brady; he little knew that she would die the same death herself, sooner than live in sin. Well, Patty, before I came to you yesterday, I was humbly offering up my prayers that I might be enabled to free Morris Brady of the charge made against him, and fix it on the guilty. I could not go to my father to advise with him, because Wilson had threatened that if I did so, poor Morris should be sent to jail that moment; and I knew there was seeming proof against the boy, enough to make him look guilty to the world. Nor was it in my power to open my mind to William Duncan, who, as you know, has a right to hear everything concerning me, because the same threat was held out to me, if I did so. And I recollected that, suppose I tould my story, who would give it credit? Every one believed Wilson to be in his grave; and I know he would, and successfully could, hide from all pursuit: and I thought, too, that even if a few should listen to my words, Wilson's friends were too powerful for me.

"And so, Patty, I was in this way, without a guide

but God, when you tould me what had happened to you. Till that moment, I had been praying, as I said, for light and advice from above, to enable me to get Morris out of Wilson's hands, and then send the true robber to jail instead of him. But when you whispered in my ear, Patty, oh, Patty *ma-vourneen*, the marrow in my bones grew could! See how I stood. If I succeeded in clearing my brother, and delivering up Wilson to justice, for the one thing could not be done without the other, I must leave my own poor Patty to the world's scorn, to a broken heart, and to an early grave. Oh, indeed, indeed, I was to be pitied that moment!

"It was from my lips you learned the first word you ever spoke, Patty, and from that hour to this, the more you grew up, the more my love for you grew also; and, Patty, there was my promise to your dying mother! Oh, Patty, when I fell on my knees yesterday, the prayers that mounted to heaven came from a bursting heart!

"But I believe they were not entirely disregarded. Here is what came into my head to do, and what I did. After leaving you I went to your uncle, the mayor of the town, and, without a word of disguise or a moment's hesitation, I tould him what you tould me——"

"Oh, Rose, Rose!"

"There was no second thing to be done, Patty. I knew your uncle loved you as if you were his own child, and that he would see justice done to you—the fullest justice, at laste, that can now be done to you. And I pointed out to him the only path left open to us, and he promised to take it with me, and to assist me; and then we came to decide upon our steps.

"Next, Patty, I resolved to do what nothing but what

the welfare, the lives, of a brother and a sister could make me think of,—for as sure as Morris is a brother to me, you are a sister to me, Patty: and I shook from head to foot before I could determine on it. But I *did* determine; and I *did* meet Joe Wilson undher the darkness of the night. He thought he was coming to a shameless crature, consenting to her own disgrace. God forgive him his bad thought!

" I do not know how it happened; heaven must have befriended me; but the man did not insult me. I took care, however, that the first words out of my lips gave him a notion of the business that he and I had to settle together. And this was the business, Patty. I knew the person I had to deal with. I knew that his wealth was gone. I knew that his debts were many. I knew that his cravings after expense in every foolish and wicked way were as great as ever. I knew that the sum he had plundered from your father was little, very little, compared with what he had expected and wanted. And I guessed —may I be forgiven the want of Christian charity if I wronged him!—I guessed he would sell himself, body and soul, to ——; that, in fact, he would do anything for money. And, Patty, I had in my possession one thousand pounds belonging to you—your dying mother's bequest to me for your use; and I believed I could not do better with it on your account, than I was going to do; and your uncle, Aldherman Lodge, let me offer him another thousand pounds; and I ensured to Joe Wilson two thousand pounds, if he would quickly make you his wife: and he did not refuse my offer.

" But I made two other bargains with him at the same time. The two thousand pounds are to be put in an attorney's hands until ye are man and wife; and

I have his written promise that he will not force you to go with him into his banishment, or, if he does, that he is to forfeit the money; and he is to write for it from another country to this country; and then, and not till then, the attorney is to send it to him. And having once left you among us, Patty, even tho' he may want to break thro' all his engagements, and come back to tear you away from us, he cannot, for he will be afraid of the law to come back; and so we are sure of him in that respect.

"And I have another writing under his hand, and witnessed, like the one I have just spoke of, by his uncle, the mayor. I have his declaration in black and white, that my poor brother is innocent, and that it was he himself, Joe Wilson, who took away your father's money, Patty dear."

"What rashness! what daring! to give you that paper, Rose!" said Patty.

"Joe Wilson thinks nothing rash and nothing daring," replied Rose; "and instead of making any objection to my demand, he seemed greatly pleased, and even amused at the thought of granting it. And, at noon-day to-morrow, he tould me he would walk abroad, and publish Morris Brady's innocence with his own lips, and tell the story of his frightening so many "meal-men and grocers," as he calls the honest people of the town, in his part of the ghost, and so bring glory to himself from his comrades; and that for one day he would defy his uncle, and sthrike down any bailiff that dares come near him. And it will be rare sport, he says, to see the whole world wondering at his re-appearance among the living, and praising him for his cleverness. And when he has shown every one of us that he does not at all fear us, or care one farthing about the worst that can be done to him, for a day at least, then he will kick the dust off his feet at the gate of our town, and go off somewhere or other —not a straw does Joe Wilson care where—to earn his good two thousand pounds."

" I am very glad then, Rose—oh, glad at my heart, that your poor brother is proved to be innocent."

" Yes, Patty, my mind is quite at ease about my dear Morris. And even if Wilson had not given me that paper, Providence threw another in my way since last night, which proves the poor boy to be what I always thought him—thanks be to God, for ever!"

" Then you are all a happy family once again," continued Patty with a mournful sigh, " and your brother and father are at home by this time, dearest Rose."

" No, Patty; and, except your sorrows, that's the only thing that rests on my mind, to be a cloud over it. I will tell you. It was indeed in my power to get my father, at least, out of the jail this day, but your uncle would not consent to it. Knowing Randal Brady to be a strictly conscientious and just man, he feared that, upon his liberation, when the whole truth should be told to him, he would not consent to screen Wilson from justice, and that our scheme for your advantage might therefore be frustrated; and my own mind told me there was reason in what your uncle said; and so most unwillingly did I give my consent that the ould man should stay where he is till after your marriage. God grant my good father may easily forgive me! And now, Patty, nothing more have I to tell you; and you are now the person to decide your own fate, according to the answer you are prepared to return to the last question I put to you."

"Rose, give me your hand in mine. I am going to tell you, truly and nakedly, the present state of my thoughts and heart. After all you have said, and fully relying on your truth, my sense of what is right tells me I ought to detest such a man as Joe Wilson. But, Rose, I place my hand here, under my bosom—and how can I? Nay, Rose, more than that; in the thought that the father of my little unborn one is not dead, and in the prospect of once more seeing him— and oh, above all! of calling him my husband—I am happy, Rose, aye, happy, in comparison with the life I have sometime been living. Do not wonder at me, nor blame me, my dearest friend, for telling you the truth. Consider, rather, what a blessed change of circumstances is before me, and then you will call my feelings natural. Oh, Rose! I once read, in my childish years, of a man who had been cast into a charnel-house, bound hand and foot, to breathe through his living lungs the air of that loathsome place, and to listen, in deep darkness, to the small noises made by the worms moving on the dead bodies around him, and to feel them—paugh!—to feel them crawling over his face—and lips—! And, Rose, of late I have been in the habit of likening myself to that man: though nominally living, I was the companion of the dead and gone, and my sensations were as if I had been in a rotting tomb. And you will not censure me, dear Rose, if I now feel happiness at my escape from a state of such great horror and despair. As to the promise you demand of me, this I say: if, after our marriage, Joe Wilson commands me to accompany him—no matter where— out of his native place and mine, branded as he is, hunted down as you say he is, guilty as he is, inconstant as he is, and as he may be—with him will I go, patiently, obediently, and devotedly, (ah, I believe more than that!) over the wide world. My own very weakness and sin, which brought upon me what I have suffered, would of itself require such a sacrifice, if sacrifice it be, to make evident to God my wish for an atonement. You say he may degrade me; prayers to heaven, and, if nothing else, a recollection of you, Rose, will save me from that. Or, you say, he may ill-treat me: let him. Let him raise up his hand, if indeed it is in his nature, and strike me dead; I shall have earned even that punishment, aye, and from his hand too. So much I say, in case he should lay his commands on me, as I have supposed. But—"

"But, my *lanna*," interrupted Rose," if, on the contrary, he lays his commands on you to stay here with me, while he tries his fortune in the world, you will obey him all the same? won't you, Patty?"

"If it is his own wish to abandon me," answered the poor girl, weeping, "surely, surely I will not, against his will, ask to be the companion of his wanderings."

"You do promise me, then?"

"I do, Rose, always supposing our immediate separation to be his wish."

"I ask nothing more of you, Patty. And now may God be with you, my own *cuishla*. I must leave you for a while. I promised him last night, that when the clock should strike a certain hour this evening, I would open the door of his uncle's lodgings for him, with my own hand. So I must go to prepare for keeping my word. When I am sure he is ready to meet you, I will come back here for you, with a chair; and I will be your guard to your uncle's door."

They kissed and parted.

CHAPTER XXX.

Rose was punctual in her appointment with her cousin. On re-entering the unhappy girl's apartment, she started at her appearance. Patty had taken much pains at her toilet. Her dress was uniformly white; her hair was parted once over her forehead, and fell down her neck in natural ringlets; the deep blue veins were more than ever distinct, through the lily whiteness of her skin; her eyes were glassily sparkling; on her usually pale cheeks were two abrupt red spots, and her lips were white and frozen.

As Rose approached her, she attempted to move, but tottered. Rose felt her hand; it was cold and damp, and it trembled. She took her in her arms, and for a while endeavoured, by every soothing topic and expression, to make her tranquil and confident. Patty was at length able to descend to her chair, leaning on her friend's arm.

They entered the hall door of the widow Sheehan's house. Patty rested her back against the wall. "You are sure he is above stairs?" she asked with difficulty.

"He is, my *graw-bawn*, above with his uncle, the uncle to both of you, and the uncle that loves you as well and as tenderly as a father ever loved a child. You are able to take my arm again now?"

"Only a few moments of rest, and I shall be stronger. I am a weakly thing, and this sudden change from misery to happiness has sadly shaken me. Oh, there is a heavy sickness here, Rose!" laying her hand upon her heart—"and objects seem to swim round me so. I will sit down a moment, and then I know I shall be better."

She sat on the last step of the stairs, supported by her cousin. After a short pause, she spoke again.

"Rose, it is to me unaccountable, yet I cannot put the thought from me: I did not, as you know, sink down so very much when I had not a hope in life before me, and now, when my heart should be joyous, it is very, oh! very heavy! A presentiment of greater misfortune than I have yet met, has come upon me, and it is therefore I shake and shiver."

"My darling Patty, do not give way to mere fancies. There is nothing to fear that I can see—in good truth, nothing."

"Well, Rose, I am foolish, and I am childish, and that does not become me. But I think I can go up now."

They reached the door of the room they had to enter. Patty stopped suddenly, and glancing expressively at Rose, held up her finger. Wilson was speaking within, in loud and mirthful accents. Rose opened the door. Having crossed the threshold, Patty staggered back a little, looked vaguely around her, and then drew her hand across her eyes, as if to rub away some film which impeded their vision. Wilson had been striding up and down the apartment, and was at its remote end when Patty and her friend came in.

Turning round, he fixed his eyes for a moment on his poor victim, and then quickly approached her in a joyous manner.

"Ah! Patty, my own girl! here I am, just arrived, booted and spurred, from Kingdom-come, to be your bridegroom: could any man give a better proof of his constancy!"

The sound of his voice made her start, and spread a blush of pleasure over her face; she smiled faintly and almost ghastlily. Her eyes met his as he advanced; she seemed quite to forget that others were present; she stretched out her arms, he opened his to receive her; tears burst from her heated eyes, and she moaned and sobbed on his bosom.

The emaciation of her person, the gentle and clinging character of her loveliness, and her artless and undisguised show of intense affection, seemed to move even Joe Wilson's nature; for his voice softened, and no accents could be more musical than his when he next addressed her.

"Patty, my bride! lift up your dimpled face—dry your tears and be merry! My charming girl, I am all impatience to become your happy husband!"

She did look up; he kissed her; she glanced timidly around, restored in some degree to self-possession. She gently freed herself from his arms; Rose was at her side in an instant.

"My uncle," whispered Patty, casting down her eyes. Rose led her to his chair. Humbly and penitently she murmured something to him without daring to look up. He spoke gently to her; she fell on her knees, snatched his hand, and fervently kissed it. He drew her to him and embraced her, endeavouring to assume some of his usual jocularity of manner; but he failed in shaping his features to a smile; his eyes swam in tears, and no sound of mirth escaped him.

Rose strove to raise her poor friend, but Patty being quite unable to assist herself, was unsuccessful in her attempt. She glanced round for aid. Wilson had been looking on with something like an expression of compassion in his eyes; at Rose's signal he assumed his customary recklessness of manner and bearing, hastened across the room, and bore Patty to a seat. Then he took her hand, whispered softly in her ear, and she gradually became somewhat composed.

"Come, Mr. Parson, buckle, buckle!" cried Wilson a few moments after, as, resigning his charge to her bridesmaid, he flourished about the room; "I remember, Sir, when you married the widow Walters, who was such a cursed scold, to old Dobbin, who used to keep his money-bags so tightly buckled up, it was said that you drew buckle and tongue close enough that night,—ha! ha!"

In contrast with poor Patty's trembling and shrinking consciousness, this heartless levity of Wilson was utterly disgusting; and ere the clergyman began the marriage ceremony, he sternly reproved him for his unbecoming demeanour. Supported by Rose, Patty advanced into the middle of the room, and the minister began to proceed in his office.

A door in the farther end of the apartment opened, and the widow *na sedogue*, the landlady of the house, stalked in, wearing a dark brow and a flushed countenance.

"I have a sthrong notion, Misther Mayor," she said, confronting his gouty worship, "that I ought to be taken into considheration, when matthers of this nature are to be gone thro' undher my own roof."

"All family business, mistress—all family business," sputtered Alderman Lodge.

"And maybe I have more to do in this same family business, as you call it, than people may suppose," continued Mrs. Sheehan; "and if people had just come to me for advice, maybe I could have saved them a good deal of trouble."

"As how, mistress? as how?"

"Why just hindered them from goin' into preparations for a mock marriage, may it please your worship."

The mayor and the clergyman, in utter astonishment, questioned her together.

"Pray, Sir," turning to the latter, "can a man who has a living wife be married to another lady? that's a plain question surely."

"What are you saying, woman?" demanded the good alderman; "what are you saying?"

"Don't call me 'woman,' Misther Lodge: I'd have you to know that my name is Misthress Sheehan. Look at that, Sir," she added coolly, handing a paper to the clergyman; "that, I believe, is the certificate of the marriage of one Joseph Wilson with a sisther o' mine. Come out here to the fore, Kitty, and let no little Miss think to put on your rightful name."

A young woman of considerable beauty and prepossessing carriage entered the apartment.

"Look at that man, Kitty," resumed Mrs. Sheehan, "what is he to you?"

"He is my husband," answered Kitty, modestly.

"Is the certificate good and true, Sir?" asked Mr Sheehan, again turning to the minister.

"Perfectly good and true," he answered; "an

what have you to say to this, unfortunate and wicked young man?"

"That I decline the honour of being Mrs. Sheehan's brother-in-law," answered Wilson, laughing.

"In the teeth of this certificate?"

"Aye, by George! One good turn deserves another, Mrs. Sheehan. I like to pay a debt, unless it be in money. And now I tell you, that if my marriage with Kitty Fulton hinders me from swearing allegiance to my little cousin here, my marriage with another woman, long before I ever had the good luck to fix my eyes on pretty Kitty, hinders me in the same way from being, as I said, your brother-in-law, widow *nasedogue*."

The clergyman indignantly reproached him; the old alderman stormed and swore at him; the voices of Mrs. Sheehan and (once more) Kitty Fulton rose high and shrill. He laughingly gave battle to them all. Suddenly it struck him that neither Patty nor Rose Brady addressed a word to him; but at this moment Rose's voice reached his ear from a corner of the room, in a curdling lowness of accent.

"Come here, Wilson," she said.

He turned to her. Patty sat on her lap, her arms hanging, her feet stretched out, her eyes half closed, and her head drooping helplessly over Rose's shoulder.

"Look at her," continued Rose.

"Dead?" he whispered.

"Yes, villain, dead! Villain, murderer, and robber, dead!" here Rose's voice shook the house, and her eyes flashed a pious indignation, such as never had lit them up before or after; "yes—wretch, monster, incarnate devil, dead! And now prepare for me! For now, by the heavens from which her

her young spirit looks down to hear me! and by my love for her, and by her love for me! now will I hang you as high as the gallows-tree can hold you! Oh, my own Patty," she continued, first hiding her head in the bosom of the corpse, and then rapidly kissing its eyes and lips; "oh, my poor *graw bawn!* Oh, my little *lanna!* my early friend! my heart's sister! my child, bequeathed to me by your dying mother! And have I lived to see the day that I kiss you, and kiss you, and that you can give no return to my kiss!" and Rose's tremendous burst and volume of voice sank piteously low, and her tears fell in showers.

Wilson looked an instant at the poor wreck before him. A dark cloud gathered on his brow; he snatched up his hat, and fled from the house.

CHAPTER XXXI.

We left Hesther Bonnetty and her grandson, James Brown, foaming with rage against Wilson, in his hiding retreat in the old house. While yet in the climax of their fury, Wilson burst into the apartment from his uncle's lodgings. His heart at that moment resembled the heart of a famishing hyena of the desert, rather than that of a man; and the workings of his face well imaged its black and savage emotions.

"What do ye here?" he asked; "how have ye escaped to plague and curse me still?"

"Hee—ee!" squeaked Hesther, "how did we escape? Is that the question you put to us?"

"I told you how it was, grandmother," said Brown, in a tone of dogged sulkiness.

"Aye; and I see you were in the right, lad; I see id now; an' so, Joey, you set us for the hangman, did you? did you?" she hobbled close to Wilson, and grinned up into his face.

"What else could I do with the pair of ye?" in his turn asked Wilson—a sound of fiendish scoffing preceding his words: "did ye really think to share the little my own cleverness took out of old Barney's clutches? or did ye dare to think that such wretches as ye are were to be my companions for ever? aye, or to have me in your power for ever? I tell ye plainly, I believed ye were in the stone cage an hour ago. Begone now, both of you. I am in no humour for your company."

With her bony fingers Hesther portioned out about half an inch of her crutch at its end, and holding it to him, said, "Not the length of that, Joey!"

"Take her away," continued Wilson to Brown; "off with her and you."

"By the book, I stir not, until—"

"Until what?" interrupted Wilson, walking slowly up to Brown, with an expression which left little doubt of his determination to enforce his command.

Brown recoiled a step or two. Wilson repeated his question.

"I say I will not stir until you give us good reason why *that* is empty." He placed open, before Wilson, the box before spoken of.

Wilson kicked it out of his way.

"What! ye came here, into my private room, thinking to plunder me, did ye? Ha, ha! and the nest ye found; but the birds! the little yellow-hammers! ha, ha!"

"It was by my means the money was got, and my share I *must* have," growled Brown.

"*Must!* you skulking thief! is that your word?"

"Aye! must, must, must! that's the word into your very teeth, rapparee Wilson!" screamed Hesther, striking the box with her crutch.

"Thief?" cried Brown; "it was you made me a thief; and you made me worse than that—you made me help to shed blood! you made me too bad for the gallows! and does the devil now refuse to his servant the devil's wages?"

"His reverence never met an apter scholar, Jemmy, than you were. But let me have no more of this. I warn you to leave me alone, and to take that mother and grandmother of Satan's imps with you."

"Hand me the money I ask; it may be better for us all; 'twill end disputes," persevered Brown.

"Money! not a stiver. Quit, quit! I gave you to understand before, that I am in no humour to be trifled with."

"Nor am I either," replied Brown, "and *I* give *you* to understand that, *now*."

"*Will* you go?" demanded Wilson, in a savage under growl.

"No," was Brown's concise answer, while Hesther screamed forth torrents of abuse. Nor did Brown quail under the devouring glance of his old preceptor's eye. Steadily and unwincingly he gave it back, with an expression which seemed watching the depths of its meaning.

A moment Wilson paused inactive, astonished at the change in the character and bearing of one whom he had previously regarded solely in the light of his passive and cringing tool. Then he again advanced on Brown, deliberately saying, "No, to me, you cur?"

Hesther flung herself between them.

"The curse from my tongue, that was never known to fail; the curse that withers the heart and blisters the body—that curse fall upon you if you harm the garçoon!" she cried.

"Don't stop him, granny," said Brown; "let the wilful man have his way."

A peculiar significance in her grandson's voice

struck on Hesther's ear. She peered up studiously into his eyes; obtained one assuring glance from them, and then muttering, "aye, chappy, you may be in the right;" drew aside, and leaning her chin on her crutch, watched the result of the approaching contest.

"Out of my sight, saucy whelp!" exclaimed Wilson, suddenly bursting into a furious roar of voice, when he had come within striking distance of Brown.

His arm was raised, and his powerful hand knit for a crushing blow. Suddenly and expertly Brown jumped back, his eyes, which till now had been but coolly malignant, sparkling with ferocious brilliancy.

"All or none," he cried, in a voice that equalled Wilson's own; "a full purse or an empty pocket, by the Eternal!" and before he had quite done speaking, Ailleen Lahon's kitchen knife was buried to the haft in his antagonist's bosom.

Wilson staggered forward, grappled with his murderer, and both fell. Brown plucked back his weapon as they struggled together, with the intention of repeating his blow, and the life-torrent from Wilson's breast flowed over him. His hand was again descending; Wilson caught it: the thought of revenge before he died lit up hideously his failing eyes, and spasmed his frothing mouth. A horrible struggle ensued. Had Wilson not been enfeebled by loss of blood, it must soon have ended to his advantage. But, at present, Brown was well nigh a match for him. Each tugged at the knife, as they rolled over and over on the floor, their labouring breasts and flashing eyes often almost in contact. Nor was Hesther now an inactive spectator. Hobbling around them, she raised her crutch in both hands, and, as successive blows descended on Wilson's head, squeaked, "I'll help you, Jemmy! I'll help you!"

Feeling vaguely the effects of her crutch, Wilson struck her aside with his disengaged arm; the next instant he was master of the knife; and the next, in a last, desperate effort, he sprang upon his knees, and sheathed it in the very heart of James Brown!

A few minutes after, Morris Brady, William Duncan, and three of the mayor's bailiffs, entered the apartment, and found them both dead: the corpse of Wilson lying cross-ways over that of his old pupil.

Hesther was recovering from the stunning effects of the blow dealt to her by her lodger, as she used to call him. Contemptible as really was the amount of her bodily strength, her resistance to the efforts of the bailiffs to convey her to prison was surprising.

"Leave her to me," cried Morris Brady suddenly, after he had for some time contemplated her at a distance, rolling his half-bewitched eyes, and setting his teeth at her.

And having spoken, he ran to his late landlady, and his first good deed was to wrest her crutch out of her wretched hands, and break it in pieces. Next, he took her by the shoulders and shook her violently, as a short-tempered nurse treats a sturdy urchin of three or four years. Then he slapt her with his open hand on the cheeks and back; turned her round and shook her again; pulled her ears; and in fact, by a ceaseless and most energetic round of such petty annoyances, succeeded in exhausting her muscular activity, so that at last the formidable Hesther lay tolerably quiet, squatted on the floor before him. But Morris did not long leave her time for repose, or for summoning back her offensive prowess. To the surprise of all present, and to the merriment of some, his last act was to hoist her on his shoulders, and gallop off with her through the town to the jail door.

Although surrounded by many fellow-prisoners in the common room which we have before described, the miserable old woman found means to strangle herself during the night.

Before the time at which this story commenced, it had been agreed that Rose Brady should be married to William Duncan in the course of a few weeks. After Patty Roundhead's death, Rose postponed her nuptials for a year and a day, and during that time mourned a beloved sister.

With Rose for his wife, William Duncan gradually advanced in the world's esteem, and became, comparatively speaking, a wealthy man,—being able, long before they arrived at the years of womanhood, to lay by attractive portions for his two daughters; and his three sons he brought up respectably, and settled independently.

His wife gave him a blessing in his children; and we would invite the reader to imagine his smile of happy approval as he looked on at Rose and her little ones—while yet they were but infants—preparing early in the night for bed-time. The boys and girls knelt around her, their little hands joined, and their little red lips lisping the prayers she had taught them, or answering to the simple yet sublime catechism to which she had trained their tender minds and hearts.

We now contentedly follow a good old custom of story-tellers—namely, that of giving some account of the different persons of our tale, who may be supposed to have interested the good-natured reader.

Randal Brady and his wife both lived to a very advanced age. The old man died first, and the parting between the ancient couple was tearless; for Randal fully felt the Christian's hope and consolation, and Betty was sure she should soon follow him. They passed away in fact within a few weeks of one another.

While Randal lay upon his calm death-bed, the house was often filled with people who came to crave his last blessing; and mothers brought their little children, and placed them kneeling within his reach, that he might lay his worn hand upon their heads, pray to God to bless them, and tell them to be good.

The very night of his daughter's interment, little Barnaby Roundhead disappeared, and many days elapsed before it was known what had become of him. At length he was found in a secret cellar of his house, on his hands and knees, quite dead. He had breathed his last in the act of hiding the flowered silk purse, containing the thousand guineas intrusted to Rose for his daughter, and which Rose had handed to him after the poor girl's death. In this hitherto undreamt-of place, a heap of treasure was discovered; and thus the mystery why Joe Wilson and Brown secured so little in the original hiding-hole above stairs, became satisfactorily solved.

Morris Brady, jumping into matrimony, as well as into everything else, married young, and was never able to do much more afterwards than "to keep the wolf from the door." Though not quite so energetic in his pursuit of ghosts as when we first meet him, he retained to his last hour his taste for the adventurous, the singular, and the uncommon, and never was steady enough to pursue perseveringly the drudgery of life.

Daniel, his brother, became a great favourite with the fair sex. He played the fiddle for many of them in turn, and gratified his selfishness with their smiles, but prided himself upon being cautious, " and not follying poor Morris's example." Notwithstanding all his cannyness, however, he found one certain daughter of Eve too clever for him; and even this " second Daniel " made a match which he lived to repent.

Nancy Brady grew into a most devout old maid, sour and disagreeable enough, yet regarded as a saint by those who looked only at the outside; and in the odour of her virgin sanctity she died.

Ailleen Lahon's escape from honest James Brown had the effect of rendering her very cautious of any serious engagement with the rougher and more doubledealing sex. For a whole year, notwithstanding, her cap was pulled away ten times a day at least, in ten different skirmishes; and as Ailleen settled it after each encounter, she would call " them boys the plague of her life." Ailleen set her cap, however, to some purpose, " in the long run." Alderman Lodge quitted the house of her of the cakes for another residence, and the winsome widow's air-castles dissolved in the atmosphere like the smoke from her own oven. Ailleen became his housekeeper; and so jocular, so tender-hearted, and, at last, so necessary to his comforts did he find her, that when she told him how her gossip, Martin Morissy, had given her to understand that the world was saying mighty scandalous things concerning him, and how, in fact, she must leave her place to keep her good name, the ex-mayor offered Ailleen his gouty hand—which hand she took so abruptly, and shook so heartily, that her "divartin' ould aldherman" roared out with pain.

THE END.

VOLUME II.

WILL APPEAR ON THE FIRST OF FEBRUARY,

CONTAINING

SCHINDERHANNES,

THE ROBBER OF THE RHINE.

BY

LEITCH RITCHIE,
Author of "Heath's Picturesque Annual;" " Turner's Annual Tour;"
"Tales and Confessions;" " Romance of French History;" &c.

The List of Titles in the Garland Series

MARIA EDGEWORTH

1. Castle Rackrent *(1800)*
2. An Essay on Irish Bulls *(1802)*
3. Ennui *(1809)*
4. The Absentee *(1812)*
5. Ormond *(1817)*

SYDNEY OWENSON, LADY MORGAN

6. The Wild Irish Girl *(1806)*
7. O'Donnel. A National Tale *(1814)*
8. Florence Macarthy: an Irish Tale *(1818)*
9. The O'Briens and the O'Flahertys *(1817)*
10. Dramatic Sketches from Real Life *(1833)*

CHARLES ROBERT MATURIN

11. The Wild Irish Boy *(1808)*
12. The Milesian Chief *(1812)*
13. Women; or, Pour et Contre: A Tale *(1818)*

Eyre Evans Crowe

14. To-day in Ireland *(1825)*
15. Yesterday in Ireland *(1829)*

John Banim and Michael Banim

16. Tales, by the O'Hara Family *(1825)*
17. The Boyne Water, A Tale, by the O'Hara Family *(1826)*
18. Tales, by the O'Hara Family. Second Series *(1826)*
19. The Croppy. A Tale of 1798 *(1828)*
20. The Anglo-Irish of the Nineteenth Century *(1828)*
21. The Denounced *(1830)*
22. The Ghost-Hunter and his Family *(1833)*
23. The Mayor of Wind-Gap *and* Canvassing *(1835)*
24. The Bit O'Writin' and Other Tales *(1838)*
25. Patrick Joseph Murray, The Life of John Banim, the Irish Novelist *(1857)*

Gerald Griffin

26. Holland-Tide; or, Munster Popular Tales *(1827)*
27. Tales of the Munster Festivals *(1827)*
28. The Collegians *(1829)*

29. The Rivals *and* Tracy's Ambition *(1829)*

30. Tales of My Neighbourhood *(1835)*

31. Talis Qualis; or Tales of the Jury Room *(1842)*

32. DANIEL GRIFFIN, The Life of Gerald Griffin by his Brother, revised edition *(n.d.)*

WILLIAM CARLETON

33. Father Butler. The Lough Dearg Pilgrim *(1829)*

34. Traits and Stories of the Irish Peasantry *(1830)*

35. Traits and Stories of the Irish Peasantry, Second Series *(1833)*

36. Tales of Ireland *(1834)*

37. Fardorougha, the Miser; or, the Convicts of Lisnamona *(1839)*

38. The Fawn of Spring-Vale, The Clarionet, and Other Tales *(1841)*

39. Tales and Sketches Illustrating the Character of the Irish Peasantry *(1845)*

40. Valentine M'Clutchy, The Irish Agent; or, Chronicles of the Castle Cumber Property *(1847)*

41. The Black Prophet: a Tale of the Irish Famine *(1847)*

42. The Emigrants of Ahadarra: A Tale of Irish Life *(1848)*

43. The Tithe Proctor: being a Tale of the Tithe Rebellion in Ireland *(1849)*

44. The Life of William Carleton: Being His Autobiography and Letters; and an Account of his Life and Writings from the Point at which the Autobiography Breaks Off by David O'Donoghue *(1896)*

HARRIET MARTINEAU

45. Ireland *(1832)*

ANNA MARIA HALL

46. Sketches of Irish Character *(1829)*

47. Lights and Shadows of Irish Life *(1838)*

48. The Whiteboy. A Story of Ireland in 1822 *(1845)*

49. Stories of the Irish Peasantry *(1851)*

WILLIAM HAMILTON MAXWELL

50. O'Hara; or 1798 *(1825)*

51. The Fortunes of Hector O'Halloran and his man, Mark Anthony O'Toole *(1843)*

52. Erin-Go-Bragh; or Irish Life Pictures *(1859)*

ANTHONY TROLLOPE

53. The Macdermots of Ballycloran *(1847)*
54. The Kellys and the O'Kellys *(1848)*
55. Castle Richmond *(1860)*
56. An Eye for an Eye *(1879)*
57. The Land-Leaguers *(1883)*

JOSEPH SHERIDAN LE FANU

58. The Purcell Papers with a Memoir by Alfred Perceval Graves *(1880)*
59. The Cock and Anchor: Being a Chronicle of Old Dublin City *(1845)*
60. The House by the Church-Yard *(1863)*

WILLIAM ALLINGHAM

61. Lawrence Bloomfield in Ireland. A Modern Poem *(1864)*

CHARLOTTE RIDDELL (MRS. J.H. RIDDELL)

62. Maxwell Drewitt *(1865)*
63. The Nun's Curse *(1888)*

T. Mason Jones

64. Old Trinity. A Story of Real Life *(1867)*

Annie Keary

65. Castle Daly. The Story of an Irish Home Thirty Years Ago *(1875)*

May Laffan Hartley

66. Hogan, M. P. *(1876)*
67. Flitters, Tatters, and the Counsellor and Other Sketches *(1879)*

Charles Joseph Kickham

68. Knocknagow: or, the Cabins of Tipperary *(1879)*

Margaret M. Brew

69. The Burtons of Dunroe *(1880)*
70. Chronicles of Castle Cloyne. Pictures of Munster Life *(1885)*

EMILY LAWLESS

71. Hurrish. A Study *(1886)*
72. With Essex in Ireland *(1890)*
73. Grania. The Story of an Island *(1892)*
74. Maelcho. A Sixteenth-Century Narrative *(1894)*
75. Traits and Confidences *(1898)*

WILLIAM O'BRIEN

76. When We Were Boys *(1890)*

ANONYMOUS

77. Priests and People: A No-Rent Romance *(1891)*

LIBRARY OF DAVIDSON COLLEGE

Books on regular loan may be checked out for **two weeks**. Books must be presented at the Circulation Desk in order to be renewed.

A fine is charged after date due.

Special books are subject to special regulations at the discretion of the library staff.